Prelude

Every Life is a Prelude to the Next

Cheryl A. Malakoff & Robert A. Clampett

ISBN: 978-1-61296-497-3

PUBLISHED BY BLACK ROSE WRITING

www.blackrosewriting.com

Printed in the United States of America

Suggested retail price $19.95

Prelude is printed in Adobe Caslon Pro

P.Y., your infinite love found me, again.

and to

Julie Lynn Valentine

who graduated with honors.

Prelude

Every Life is a Prelude to the Next

How Fascinating

How
Fascinating the idea of death
Can be.
Too bad though.
It just isn't
True.

Excerpt from The Gift

Poems By Hafiz, The Great Sufi Master

Translations By Daniel Ladinsky

CHAPTER ONE

And the day came when the risk to remain in a tight bud was more painful than the risk it took to bloom.
-Anais Nin

She couldn't have seen it coming.

Windblown, the maple leaf flew free, twisted, tumbled across the campus quad, landing smack onto her forehead, plastering it like a blood-red second skin.

Startled, Carol Klein, newest member of the university's psychology faculty with a freshly minted Ph.D. peeled off the leafskin with a laugh; thoughtfully admiring its beauty and structure, thinking, "You know, you're not so different from us; starting life as a tiny bud, growing ribs and veins, until you curl up and fall, ready to enrich the planet. And like us, probably never knowing what seeds we've planted for future generations. Nature, the ultimate recycler; we should be so useful."

Clutching the leaf in her hand, she walked briskly across the sun-kissed quad, sparkling with the aura of a new academic year. She loved the sight of students scurrying to classes; an age-old scene repeated each fall. The crisp scent of autumn filled the air, triggering a visceral memory of her own days as a student, not that long ago. Drinking in the scene sighing, "Winter's around the corner and this will all be just a memory."

Her offices on the second floor in Watson Hall, an ancient brick building with a chiseled limestone edifice, was home to the university's Department of Psychology. She had entered these doors a thousand times as a graduate student, but now, having traded in her student backpack for her doctor's white lab coat, she recognized, that although the change was small, the difference was great.

Climbing the well-trod stairs that lead to her office, she walked in the footsteps of her predecessors. Opening the creaky walnut door that was part of the original architecture, she was greeted by the receptionist, a bright cheery graduate student only a few years younger than herself.

"Morning Elaine," Carol said, "brisky out, eh?"

Eyes gleaming, Elaine looked up from her desk.

"Sure is. I can see it in your cheeks," she nodded, lifting a file folder, and handed it to Carol. "Your first appointment; in about half-an-hour. No messages. There's a fresh pot in the lounge if you'd like."

"Thanks. Maybe later."

Carol turned, walked through the door into her consulting room, her name imprinted in black lettering with gold trim — Carol Klein Ph.D., Department of Behavioral Medicine.

Once inside, she donned her white lab coat touching the pearl necklace tucked inside her blouse. She'd need them for later. But for right now, it's all business. There were no more training wheels.

Mid-morning was her favorite time of day, the east-facing windows receiving the morning sun; light and shadows bathing her consulting room in a warm glow. She'd decorated the room in robin egg blue chintz, set off by an antique light green Persian rug with an eye towards calming the patients. Her work station: an English wing chair and the matching couch, highlighted by a framed reproduction of Van Gogh's Starry Night behind her desk.

Carol settled into her Queen Anne wing chair with the blue file folder labeled: Susan Alden with the day's date-stamp: September 18, 2000. *"Susan Alden. Age 42. Married. No children. Lifelong chronic RIGHT HIP involvement. The orthopedic team is most concerned about continued damage to her weight-bearing surfaces that may be the source of her pain. Our primary goal is to renew her stability, elimination of pain, and improve her range of motion. Additionally, we're running tests on*

8

possible femoral head necrosis, prolepses of lumbar inter-vertebral discs, osteoarthritis, and osteoporosis. Non-remitting pain, unresponsive to traditional treatment including high dosages of pharmaceutical pain medications. Tensor unit also had no abating effect on pain. Next treatment recommendation is surgical replacement of her right hip. However, given the patient's age and the surgical ramifications, this recommendation is cautioned at this time."

Recalling what she knew of human hips as, "Biomechanical work horses, carrying the weight of our mass in symmetry and balance, the physics of motion, thrusting us forward. Without our hips, we'd be like sticks in the mud. The metaphysics, on the other hand, a different story: hips deal with feelings around our desire to control what happens to us. Our bodies swim in an ocean of emotions, always talking, giving us messages, signals of strain and pain. Sometimes we listen, often we don't. And that stress can lead up to ninety-five percent of our illnesses," she stated with an air of authority born from education, yet devoid of real clinical experience.

She read the yellow Post-it on top of the blue folder:

"Doctor Klein, a colleague recommended you as a specialist in clinical hypnosis for pain management. As you can see by my notes, traditional procedures have provided no relief. Please see what you can accomplish with Ms. Alden. Best to you, David Yarnell. M.D."

She closed the file knowing full well that there were many missing pieces in this picture of Susan Alden. Doctor Yarnell's report only included his best diagnostic suspicions. She glanced at her watch, knowing before she looked—10 AM on the dot. Rising from the chair, she opened her door and walked out to the waiting room seeing a slender woman seated chatting with Elaine.

"Elaine, bless her heart," Carol smiled, "she could make a door talk."

Carol reached down, extending her hand to her new patient, "A pleasure to meet you," while taking in one gulp the whole of Susan Alden. She looked old for 42 and very fragile, like a tower built of wooden blocks not stacked quite correctly. The soft fleshy part of both hands were calloused, likely caused by her having to apply tremendous force on the aluminum walker folded at her side, her weight pressing down on her palms as she hunched over to support her battered body.

Susan's teeth clench as she pushed herself up from the chair, deep lines etched around her mouth as she pulled herself to standing, a task likely repeated many times a day.

Carol's warm smile exuded confidence and trust, an integral practice in meeting new clients. Synchronizing, like a tuning fork, Carol tried conveying her own strength to Susan, thinking; "Psychology's one part science, one part intuition, one part hope."

Susan slowly shuffled into the consulting room, so focused on moving each step that it wasn't until she was in the middle of the room that she looked around for guidance as to where to sit, speaking solely with her eyes. Carol thinking, "What must it be like to live in a body that tortures your mind and hurts that much?"

She motioned towards the couch; noting the relief in Susan's eyes to getting her feet up and taking pressure off her right hip. Susan placed two down-filled pillows as orthopedic supports around her right hip and under her right knee, a pain relief-seeking routine obviously well-practiced.

Carol sat down in the chair facing her new patient. Speaking in her most supportive voice, "Doctor Yarnell has sent me your file and I can only imagine how you must feel that no one's come up with the solution to your condition."

Susan exhaled and nodded in agreement.

Carol beamed a reassuring smile, "Have you undergone hypnosis before?"

"No," Susan uttered, "I haven't. And I'm not so sure of it."

"Well good," Carol reassured. "Then it's a new beginning, a fresh start."

Carol bent forward and began her Lecture Number One.

"Clinical hypnosis has been accepted by the American Medical Association for over fifty years. It's an incredibly powerful tool that can tap into your unconscious mind. Think of it as a window into how your body and your mind are connected."

Leaning back, Carol continued, "We only use about ten percent of our conscious minds. The other ninety percent is our unconscious, the storehouse of everything else. Did you know that our minds are the largest pharmaceutical house on the planet? We posses the inner wisdom that knows exactly what we need and what to do to heal ourselves. Our job is to get out of its way."

Susan's eyes widened as she tried to absorb the barrage of information.

Sensing her plight, Carol paused, switching streams. "Susan, have you ever been driving along, just cruising as usual, then somehow, you miss your exit?"

Susan uttered a barely audible, "Yes."

"That's like being in a subtle trance. We often put ourselves in a light hypnotic state. We do it all the time. It's like a little bit of a rest, rejuvenation break from the endless chatter that goes on inside our heads."

Susan nodded, smiling at having understood something.

"Actually, hypnosis is a natural state of mind. It's simply what happens when we increase our concentration on a particular thought. It's a kind of light sleep in which you're able to access your subconscious intelligence."

Carol paused, letting that thought soak in before venturing to the next phase, lowering her voice into a soothing lilt, "Susan, today, I'm going to take you into a light alpha state. It's the frequency we use to access meditation or like when you're daydreaming."

"Your subconscious is similar to a computer; one you can program with specific information. Believe it or not, this part of your brain holds seventy trillion memory traces, the complete record of your experiences. And our goal today is to tap into this storehouse and bring information into your conscious awareness that can help reveal the source of your current condition. Then, hopefully, we can eliminate it."

"Now, before we get started—anything you'd like to share with me that maybe Doctor Yarnell hasn't included?"

Susan's glazed eyes darted around the room. Carol could tell that she was running through the files of her mind, scanning what to share and what not to. She understood. It's difficult to fully trust someone you've just met a few minutes ago. In fact, it may be almost impossible.

Trust is something that develops over time and usually has to be tested.

"No," Susan sighed, "not right now; nothing I can think of."

Carol did an internal check of her own readiness. Pen in hand, notepad open, double-cassette tape recorder ready, one tape to record the session, the other to provide tranquil background music. All the equipment a doctor could need.

"Okay," she grinned, "here we go," turning to push PLAY on the recorder, the room suddenly filled with soothing music. "Now, Susan, I'd like you to look at the picture behind my desk. That's Van Gogh's Starry Night. Just quietly look into it, pick out a set of stars and let yourself be drawn into that night sky. Drift with the music; let it take you where it may. Feel like you're floating on a soft fluffy cloud on a warm summer's day. That's it. Just float."

Susan's eyes honed in on the painting, her eye lids, fluttering, closer together, getting heavier in wave-like motions until they rested, closed.

"Good," Carol whispered, "keep focusing on the night sky behind your closed lids. Let the music soften all the inner noise. Whatever was concerning you when you came into the room today—just let it float away like a soft spring breeze. Let the music relax you even further. Now, a nice deep, breath. Low, slow, full deep breaths into your lower belly. Good. The more you let go, the more supported you'll feel. You're doing great Susan. Just notice how the music unwinds your whole body. Now, letting go still more. Drift even deeper into the couch, feeling how completely the pillows support you. Allow yourself to let go completely, you're feeling lighter and lighter. Good."

Carol watched in silence for several seconds assessing the session thus far.

"Now, just listen to my voice. I'm going to count down, from five to one. When I get to one, you'll be more relaxed than you've been in a long, long time. Let your subconscious open its wisdom to you."

Carol took her own advice and drew in a deep breath. She felt her own spine flattening into the back of her Queen Anne chair, soon relaxing more fully into herself as well. This was very familiar territory. Her confidence grew when she could reach this point, doing that which she was most familiar. In her training, she'd been here many times. This territory was well mapped—here she knew exactly what to do—hypnosis for pain relief, psycho-neurology, releasing the mind's powerful healing effect on the body.

Hypnosis was like a beautiful symphony with a beginning, a middle, and an end. As the conductor Carol, had memorized all the notes. And Susan Alden, eyes fully closed and breathing deeply, was going to be a prototypical client, a willing participant, one precisely for whom these procedures were developed.

Carol glanced at her watch, "Right on schedule."

CHAPTER TWO

The greatest use of life is to spend it on something that will outlast it.
-William James

It was a command, "Look into their eyes."

George Mansbridge III stood tall, pointing to a mounted painting of a crowd assailing four young women whose faces were frozen in horror.

"Feel the fear in those eyes, the terror in their hearts."

He faced a joint session of the Massachusetts House and Senate, one hundred sixty in all, called to exonerate the few remaining victims of the 1693 Salem witch trials.

His voice echoed throughout the Chamber as the assembled squirmed in discomfort, wincing at the sight of mounted oil paintings depicting scenes from the Salem horrors.

He walked the floor fronting the paintings slowly, allowing the silence to intensify the impact, news cameras in the aisles following his moves. He sensed feelings of disgust, shame and guilt from the onlookers, as if they themselves somehow had been at fault.

Dressed in a perfectly-tailored navy blue Southwick suit, he'd added a powdered wig for the occasion. Well-known by his audience, he was a member of the state House and the latest in a long line of a powerful political family. His father had been a state senator for four terms, while his Uncle Nicholas served first in Congress and then as a member of the Cabinet during the Carter Administration in the 1970s. Now, at age thirty-one with ruddy good looks, it was George

Mansbridge III's turn to fly, having recently announced his candidacy for the United States House of Representatives.

He leaned forward, shoulders squared, his baritone voice rising with every sentence.

"Ladies and Gentlemen, what we do today will provide long overdue aid and comfort to the poor souls so unjustly charged and punished. Punished by those who went before us in the colonial days of Essex, Suffolk and Middlesex counties of our own Commonwealth. In Boston, Salem Village, Salem Town, Ipswich, Andover and Charleston. Twenty-six innocents, convicted, set afire, hanged, crushed to death under heavy stones, some imprisoned until death."

He trumpeted, "One hundred fifty citizens, men and women, all cited as witches or wizards, were tried and convicted, with fourteen young women and twelve young men, executed, their lives snuffed-out, in the name of, what, the Colony? Or was it simply marching to the drumbeat of false beliefs in order to maintain a superstition?"

Turning again, he took several steps, stopping before a cameraman. He reared his head back, lifting his baritone voice. He spotted two men standing far up in the back row of the balcony, his father and uncle, nearly out of sight, hidden in the shadows.

George straightened, making him appear somehow taller, more imposing. His head turned, eyes searching the audience before continuing, now in a cadence of measured words. "They were not choked by the hanging rope. They were not crushed by the granite stone," his words soaring through the hall, rising to the balcony above.

"No," raising his right arm, "not by rope!" Then raising his left arm, "Not by stone!"

He brought both hands together over his head, for an instant. "They were strangled by the beliefs of their age. Crushed by the intolerant. The fearful. The ignorance of their times."

He lowered his arms, dropped his head as if looking at the floor, his wig slipping forward covering his eyes and nose. Quickly, he slid the wig back in place, muttering just loud enough for some to hear, "No wonder we gave these up!"

Polite laughter and mild applause filled the chamber, followed by a wave of mumbles.

George walked to stand between the two largest oil paintings, spaced just far enough apart for his presence to fill the void between.

In lowered voice, he declared, "While most of these victims have been exonerated, eight souls still remain to have their names cleared. That is our purpose here today; to finally give exoneration to them all. Do it for them. Do it for us."

He paused, looked left, pivoted, than glanced right, before arriving directly into the focal point of the audience, "Today, together, let us be the ones to correct yesterday's wrong, with what we know today is right."

His voice rising to new heights, "Representatives of the Commonwealth, Senators of the people, you have the power, and the opportunity, to make an impact of historic proportions. Your vote today for exoneration will erase the ugly stain of ignorance, the stench of injustice, and the horror of unspeakable punishment from a history that is ours and ours alone. Please join your colleagues, in both the House and the Senate, to place your vote for exoneration."

Once again opening his arms wide, his head arched forward, gaze fixed on the center of this auspicious audience, he passionately advanced, "Today, join me in this vote. A vote, to make a difference."

A lone male voice rang out from the assemblage, "Hear, hear," followed by a buzz throughout the room, the echoes reverberated for several seconds.

George lowered his arms, winding-up for his grand finale, eyes set directly into lens of a TV camera, smiling, "Thank you, one and all. God Bless this Commonwealth. And God Bless America."

Applause erupted like a tidal wave undulating off the mahogany walls of the old state house building. George bowed grandly, one hand holding his wig firmly in place, much to the crowd's delight as the sound of a gavel pounding called for decorum.

"Order!" the voice of the Speaker rang out. "Order. We shall recess until two o'clock, at which time the vote on exoneration will occur. We thank you, Representative Mansbridge, for your leadership on such an overdue cause."

George nodded deferentially to the Speaker, then glanced up at the balcony. Empty. The roar of the audience went silent in his ears, the

16

vacuum in the balcony having deafened him.

He snapped back to attention as several people walked up to congratulate his performance. Handshakes and pats on the back abounded as he removed the powered wig, setting it on the arm of the adjacent easel.

"Good show, old man," said an elderly Senator. "For such a noble cause, it's nice how you got your slogan in there," stated another. George grinned, nodding in amusement. "Don't think we didn't notice," smiled an assemblywoman, hand extended, "good luck."

To his left, a young woman called out, "ABC Boston. May we have a minute?"

George's antenna went up as he motioned to her in response. He excused himself from the small crowd starting to break up before him. Running his hands over his recently trimmed hair, he walked to where she and a man with a shouldered camera stood waiting.

"Alicia Rhodes, ABC Boston," she announced, extending her hand to George. A camera light suddenly brightened them both. She clenched a hand-held microphone, signaling to the cameraman, then turning back to face George, with a thought-provoking piercing look in her eyes.

"Representative Mansbridge." She began, "Just how important was it to exonerate these final victims of the Salem trials."

George put on his most somber politician-running-for-office face. "Alicia, anytime we can do something that brings justice to the people of Massachusetts, living or dead, it's important," he answered. "It's taken far too long for this injustice to be made right."

"Does today have anything to do with your campaign for Congress?" she asked brashly.

George smiled at her, "Let's just let the people decide whether my taking this stand and providing the leadership to exonerate the final innocents makes a difference or not." He paused, adding, "I believe anytime we can do something to right a wrong, to overcome an ignorance, to move past faulty beliefs, well, let's just say I'm pleased to play my part."

Alicia nodded, "Well, Congratulations Representative. Thanks for your time." She turned full-face to the camera, "Alicia Rhodes, from the State House, ABC, Boston."

Standing alone, leaning against the back wall of the chamber, a thin man in an ill-fitting suit, arms folded nonchalantly, caught George's eye. The man nodded at George, who frowned slightly, then nodded in return. He walked slowly to the back of the chamber, stopping before him. George glanced to see who remained in the chamber, then in a near whisper, "Okay, Harrison, over there, conference room B."

Before long, he and Harrison stood behind tightly closed doors in the mahogany and leather darkness of conference room B for an impromptu meeting.

George looked inquisitively at his Uncle's longtime aide and strategic gofer.

"Looks like they ate it up," Harrison said.

"Yeah," George III responded. "Shootin' fish in a barrel."

"Saw your Dad and Nick showed up, sorta." Harrison smirked, "Enter stage balcony, who'da guessed it? No one runnin' the firm?"

"Knock it off," George spouted at the verbal jab, "whacha' got?"

"Good stuff," Harrison's lips curling into a sly grin. "Up to seven commissioners now along with two union bosses, all bought and paid for. The right guys too."

George's eyes squinted tying to get his world in focus, "Can you, no, guess not, eh?"

"Names?" Harrison countered, "You know better. No way, José."

"But they're cool?" George asked, feeling the tainted words under his skin.

"As ice," Harrison softening the blow. "No way anyone will know nothing. Not to worry, pretty boy. Keepin' your profile clean as a whistle. You're our go-to-guy."

"Okay," George said accepting the benefits, "let's leave it at that."

"Pleasure doin' biz with you, future Mister Congressman," Harrison voiced. "The media's still be out there. You go now. I'll stay here, then slip out in a few. After things calm down. We'll be in touch." The two men shook hands concluding their tacit agreement. George walked out into the House floor, relieved to be in cleaner air.

"Mister Mansbridge. Over here, please. Channel Seven News," calls out the perky young reporter, standing near a man with a handheld camera.

George smiled broadly, adjusted his tie and walked towards the waiting interviewer.

CHAPTER THREE

Experience is not what happens to a man, it is what a man does with what happens to him.
-Aldous Huxley

Carol was pleased.

Susan was a great subject. She had taken to hypnosis easily, going under in less than seven minutes; breathing rhythmic, face relaxed and feet slowly turning outward, as her leg muscle tension eased.

Carol had instructed Susan to drift into her own inner awareness. Then, to go deeper still, searching for "the part of yourself that holds the key to releasing your pain."

Something on Susan's face caught Carol's eye, "Why were her closed eyelids flickering?" she wondered. Then, with a sudden jerk, Susan's shoulders twitched as if startled, her right arm grasped her hip. Grimacing, her mouth opened as she took one deep breath, then, suddenly screamed as if in extreme agony, "AEEIIEEAHHAAEEE," her eyes filling with tears; her body elevating above the couch for just an instant, then falling onto her side, twisting in order to grasp her right hip with both hands.

Carol jumped to her feet, notepad and pen flying to the floor. A cold sweat coated her forehead, ice coursing down her spine. Susan screamed again "EEEEEEEEAHHII," an eerie, tortured cry; her body twisting over, contorting into a pretzel-like bend as the last howls drooled from her mouth, like the bloodcurdling scream of a wounded animal.

"Susan!" Carol blurted, "Listen to me. Please! You're okay; you're safe here. Whatever's happening, you're only witnessing it, like a movie. Susan!"

"My God," breathing hard, she realized, "I've got to get her out of this!"

She forced herself to speak calmly, "Susan! Listen to me! You're in complete control here. Whatever's happening, you're just watching it. It can't hurt you."

Horrified, Carol heard the voice screaming in her head, "No harm, no harm, no harm. *Primum non nocere*, first, no harm!" Her heart raced, pounding the beat into her ears, the voices arguing, "Bring her out of the trance now! No. Go even deeper! Don't lose this chance! No! Just end it, get help. Call 911?"

Carol squeezed her eyes shut, "I bring her out too quickly, nothing gets resolved. If I keep her in this trance too long—I don't know what." She was well aware of the downsides; from post-traumatic stress to possible irreparable harm as a catatonic psychotic break."

Going on pure instinct, she trusted her choice.

Delivered in carefully measured tones, "Susan, pay attention only to me. Now, take a deep breath, we're going deeper; 3–2–1. Tell me every detail, what's happening, what are you seeing?"

Susan slowly rolled onto her back, stretching her legs out on the couch. She crossed both arms over her bosom, a smile forming on her face as her eyes remained closed.

The incongruence of the blood-curdling scream and now this soft smile was extremely disturbing. Carol noticed something different, a qualitative shift even more puzzling about Susan, "Is it my imagination, or does she look, younger?"

The dominant voice inside Carol's head commanded, "Let Susan take the lead."

"Susan," she urged, "the movie? Tell me what you see...."

All at once, in the voice of young girl, Susan began singing, "*Oh where have you been Billy boy, Billy boy? Oh-oh where have you been charming Billy? I have been to see my wife, she's the apple of my life. She's a young thing and cannot leave her mother.*"

Carol's mind raced wildly; yet she forced her voice to remain calm and gently prodding, "Susan? What're you seeing?"

Susan, back in her own voice stated with detachment, "*A little girl, maybe twelve or thirteen, sitting on a wooden bench. It's a covered wagon. Only, it's me. I, I'm right there, on that bench, singing.*"

"What else?" begged Carol, "What else do you see?"

"*Well,*" Susan continued, "*a long line of wagons, both in front and behind me. We're on a real rocky trail. Going up a slope, pretty steep, heading into the mountains.*"

"Where?" Carol urgently probed. "Where are you?"

"*Don't know exactly,*" Susan reverting to the child-voice, "*except Pa says we're headin' west to Oregon, someplace like that.... I think he said somethin' about goin' into Wyoming, into the Laramie range.*"

"Susan, this is important. Can you tell me when this is happening to you, what year?"

"*It's July, 1838 I think,*" she stated matter-of-factly, "*don't know what day it is though.*"

Carol's thoughts were spinning, "Was this some kind of reactive psychosis or a delusional episode? Was Susan's pain so unbearable that she's losing her mind?"

Grasping at straws while trying to find solid ground in this shifting landscape, she push forward, "What else? What are you wearing?"

"*Oh, my blue calico dress, with white polka dots. Ma' made it for me, just before she died, back on the farm.*"

Carol began sweating with worry. Had she gone too deep? Should she keep going? It was like being inside a kaleidoscope with every turn changing the picture.

Susan continued in the child's voice, "*I'm all by myself in the wagon, holding the reins. That's Billy and Brutus up there, the oxen pullin us.*" She beamed a bright smile, "*Kitty, she's here, on my lap. She likes it when I sing.*"

Susan's right-hand was making little wavelike motions in the air, as if she were petting a kitten. Her face softened, she looked remarkably calm.

"*Then, oh, loud thunder! Scared kitty. She jumped off my lap, back into the wagon. I, I reached for her, but then, a really loud crack noise. But it wasn't thunder; it was a wagon wheel snapping into a rut, or something.*"

Next thing I knew, I'm flying off the bench, out of the wagon, into the air. Oh!"

Susan's breath-rate increased, her child voice rose, nearly staccato. Tears started forming at the corners of her closed eyes.

"Ow!" she hollered, *"The rocks hurt, hard, just off the trail. Oh No! The wagon, it's tipping! Towards me! Gotta' get outa' the way! Gotta, can't move! Here it … OOF, it's on me! My hip! Ow. My legs! My, Oh God in heaven!"*

Torrents of hot tears began flowing down Susan's cheeks.

"Oh, it hurts. I'm scared. But, huh; I don't hurt no more!"

Susan's eyes flashed wide open. *"I see Pa and my brother, Jeremiah, they're both running to see me. Pa's crying. Jeremiah, oh no, he's throwing up, I think. It's really raining hard. Then kitty's here, licking my face. Pa and Jeremiah, they're trying to pull me out, to lift the wagon. But they can't do it. Pa's grabbin 'my shoulders, he's pulling, hard. But I'm trapped under the axle. I tried telling Pa that I don't hurt no more, but he don't hear me."*

Susan's breath became short and rapid. Her eyes remained open.

"It's still on me—and in me. But, I can't feel it. I don't feel nothin!"

Susan's eyes widened, her pupils rose up to the top of her eye sockets, as if looking up to the sky, her voice faltering, falling slowly into a whisper, *"Now they're pulling back, standing up, looking down at me I see their faces, they're crying. Now Pa's on his knees. Then, then, I'm floating. I can see the whole scene from, well, just above them. Just above the wagon, with me half under it. Even though, I, I could … Oh, no!"*

Susan's breath sputtered, panting, out of breath, her face tensed, her teeth ground together.

Carol commanded with raw instinct taking over, "Susan! Let it go! You must let it go. Now!"

Carol cleared her very dry throat and firmly directed Susan out of the abyss, "Listen to me, only to me. When you hear the clap of my hands, you will wake up. You will remember nothing of this event. Nothing. Then, you will let it go, forever!" In a command, she mustered her most authoritative voice, "When you hear my hands clap, let it go!"

Carol clapped, sharp and loud, "Now!"

Susan's body relaxed as she slowly began to stretch, full-bodied like a cat. She blinked, her eyes fully opened, wiping her wet cheeks with her fingers and turned her head, looking around the room, eyes stopping at Carol who sat with a look of alarm on her face.

"Susan," Carol exhaled in relief, "it's over."

Susan's forehead furled, "Is, uh, anything wrong?"

"No, no," Carol reassured her, "but, how are…. how do you feel?"

"Great!" Susan chirped. "Just, well, great. Wow, I feel tired and at the same time, well, refreshed. How odd. This happen with hypnosis often?"

Overwhelmed by what she just witnessed, Carol nodded while hiding the trembling inside. "Keep it together!" The right words, which more often than not, effortlessly flowed out, just wouldn't come. Her mouth felt stuffed with cotton balls. At this moment, there wasn't a cogent thought that she could pull together. "What could she say? Holy- holy cow! Where do we go from here?"

To Carol's amazement, Susan effortlessly rolled her hips off the couch, placed her feet squarely on the floor, a Cheshire cat-like smile on her face.

Still mystified, Carol managed to utter an encouragement, "You did great for a first session. Really. Great. I'd like you to make another appointment with Elaine on your way out." Well aware of her complete ineptitude, "How lame was that?" And yet knowing that was the very best her tattered nervous system could muster.

Susan stood with ease and stared directly into Carol's eyes, saying, "I don't know what you did, but this is the best I've felt in a long time. I can't thank you enough."

With that, Susan turned and began walking towards the door.

"Susan," Carol pointed, "your walker?"

"Oh. Sorry. Thanks." Susan chimed, grasping the familiar but folded-up piece of equipment. Without unfolding it, she walked to the door carrying it with one hand, leaning it upon her right hip. She walked out saying over her shoulder, "See you next week Doctor. And thanks again."

As the consulting room door closed, the doorway to Carol's whirling mind opened wide.

She paced absently, running her fingers over the familiar objects in the room, desperate to confirm a tangible reality. "God in heaven!" she muttered pleadingly, throwing herself into her chair, shoulders trembling, questioning the validity of her senses, "what was that?"

She sat up, feeling a shudder course through her body. She threw back her head, fingers tightening into fists, crying out, "What have I done?"

CHAPTER FOUR

It is a rough road that leads to the heights of greatness.
-Seneca

A sharp gust of autumnal wind blew across the steps of the Statehouse as two imposing men pushed through the exit doors, stopping only to wrap their raincoats tight against the wind-blown rain. Protection from the elements securely fastened, they walked down the well-worn marble steps of the State House, striding nearly in cadence as if in a changing of the guard ceremony.

Shoulders back, eyes looking down, both men walked stiffly, not unlike the marble columns rising behind them. George Mansbridge, Jr. and his older brother Nicholas, a former Congressman and Cabinet officer in the Carter administration, navigated the downward trail of steps that resembled an enormous frozen river cascading to the sidewalk below. The men flowed down the staircase with a well-practiced gait.

Over the years, they had done this many times.

Below, parked alongside the walkways, media vans loomed in shapes not unlike moon-based land rovers, satellite dishes and antennas raised on high.

"Looks like it's time to rein him in Nick," declared George, Jr. with an air of finality.

Nicholas, without turning his head, agreed, "We've just got to put an end to these sideshows, George. Gotta' stay on message. Do as he's told, for God's sakes! We've a lot riding on this. Especially now, what with Global and all." He shook his head in disgust, "Gotta' keep his eye on the ball."

George looked at his older brother as the two men stepped onto the sidewalk. He had aged considerably; the years in the White House had taken their toll. "Don't underestimate him Nicholas, he knows what he's doing. Besides, I had Harrison brief him just as soon as the media circus ended."

Nicholas turned, spat on the sidewalk saying, "Sure. That'll work. If he can get Georgie-boy away from the news cameras for a minute."

The younger brother laughed. "You should talk, Mister Secretary of bullshit, long as there's limelight."

Nicholas harrumphed, "Polls show this bachelor thing's hurting us. Hard for people to take him seriously."

"What'd you suggest?" George smirked.

"Well, isn't he pretty involved with that doctor at the university, the Klein girl?" Nicholas asked. "Couldn't we get him to move that along?"

George turned his head, squinted at his older brother. "Could be," he said grimacing, leaving nothing to chance, "not sure. Klein? Could be Jewish. Might be a problem."

"Nah," Nick barked. "We can camouflage that. I'll talk to the kid about it soon; get him to announce an engagement. Doesn't have to go any further than that."

George's gaze dropped, "Guess not," he mulled over, now looking at his Berluti shoes on the pavement. "Guess not."

They walked to a waiting limousine. A uniformed man slid out from behind the steering wheel to open the back seat door for the two. A sudden squall of cold rain started to pelt the windows just as they entered the confines of their warm vehicle.

Ominous black clouds pushed towards them from the south.

"Looks like more rain," Nicholas stated.

"Ever the obvious, old boy," chuckled George, Jr., "ever the obvious."

CHAPTER FIVE

To find yourself. Think for yourself.
-Socrates

Carol sat motionless behind the steering wheel of her blue 1998 Volvo sedan.

"She walked out under her own power?" she said aloud. "That scream, that child-voice and the whole covered wagon thing?" The only thing she was sure of was that this was a work in progress.

She'd recognized that things are rarely what they appear to be; knowing each patient speaks in their own private code. Her job was to unearth the Rosetta stone capable of cracking their secret ciphers.

She turned the ignition key, shifted the car into drive firmly, needing something familiar with a known cause and effect.

Losing herself in the pleasure of doing something habitual. She flipped on the radio, retreating into the comfort of memorable tunes from the eighties.

As she left the wooded acreage of the University, rain began coming down, so light she couldn't hear it but could only see the remnants streaking the windshield.

Distracted by her wandering thoughts, she drove onto the highway, as if the car knew precisely where to go. She was at last ready to put aside the day's events, leaving her role as doctor in the rear view mirror thinking only of the evening ahead simply as a woman in love, "something about as non-scientific as you can get."

Steering with her left hand, she loosened the French twist atop her head, shaking her tresses, which fell into place around her shoulders. She freed the top two buttons of her silk blouse, pulling out the pearl necklace that had nested on her bosom all day. She caressed the pearls for a brief moment. They had been her mother's favorite. Smiling, Carol feeling these pearls was like being embraced by her mother's love. "I may've been raised by Grammy, but I'll always be my mother's daughter."

From the radio came the lyrics, "*The Things You Do for Love.*" Laughing aloud, "Oh yea, the things I do for love!" She began humming slowly recalling a moment, one she would never forget. She was five, maybe six, sitting on her mother's bed, watching her brush her lustrous dark hair with a tortoise shell-handled hairbrush. Carol had been chatting non-stop, telling her mother all the things she wanted to be when she grew up, "How about a nurse, that would be good, or maybe a teacher, though bein' an astronaut would be more fun, and ...."

Her mother slowly lowered the hairbrush, turned fully around and in a knowing voice stated, "Carol, just remember this—life is one disappointment after another." She turned back to the mirror and continued brushing, Carol was speechless as she attempted to ponder her mother's message, "One disappointment after another?"

She had since come to believe disappointments simply meant she was pointing in the wrong direction. "Isn't that why I studied psychology; to learn a science that gave meaning to the world created by our minds and to trust only the quantifiable; what I can see, feel, touch?"

Approaching her destination, she reached into her leather satchel on the passenger seat, pulling out the black silk evening purse. She snapped open the rhinestone clasp and pulled out two pearl earrings, clipping them onto each earlobe to complete the picture. She reached back into the satchel lifting a black satin evening shawl like a trick from Houdini. Flipping it around her shoulders, finally feeling better than she had all day.

Slowing the car, she pulled into a driveway leading to the Commonwealth Club, coming to a stop under a portico set aside for valet parking. Instantly, a familiar face appeared through the driver's side window, Nigel in his valet uniform, a short red jacket, and black tuxedoed pants. He opened Carol's door, his grin a crescent moon.

"Evening, Doctor," Nigel warmly greeted her with, arm outstretched in a well-practiced gesture.

"Evening, Nigel, could you?" She handed him a pair of black satin high heels. Grinning he carefully set them close together on the curb. Slipping off her practical pumps, Carol swung her legs outward, slipping her feet snugly into the waiting sexy heels, her evening transition complete.

Nigel leaned back, applauded, "Eight second shoe switch," he whistled, "a new record."

He extended his hand to help Carol rise to her feet, steadying herself onto the heels.

The transformation from Doctor Klein to Carol the lover was complete.

He grinned it, "Funny, our uniforms define us at work then, after hours, we change back into our real selves."

Carol nodded, "You're so right," pausing, "on more levels than you know."

"Well, have a good evening, doctor; or is it Miss Klein?"

"Right now, lets hope it's just Carol," conducting a quick inventory of herself from head to toe: everything in place. then moved past him through the double front doors of the Commonwealth Club, a portal between two worlds.

Carol walked to the freestanding desk of the maitre'd, Godfrey.

"Good evening Doctor Klein," Godfrey said. "Your Mister Mansbridge is waiting; follow please." He took the lead, escorting Carol to the far end of the elegant and dimly lit dining room.

From across the room Carol easily picked out George's profile. She could recognize the back of his head in any crowd. How many nights had she lain awake, watching him sleep; the silhouette of his head etched into memory. She could easily trace his outline on the canvas of her pillowcase with the brushes of her fingertips.

"You beat me here, darling," Carol smiled it as Godfrey pulled out a chair for her as George stood, smiling back.

"Thank you, Godfrey," she said, speaking over her shoulder.

"Bon appetit," he responded, walking away leaving the couple to connect.

"Only by a few minutes," he said. "I've just ordered."

"So I see," Carol grinned, eyeing the martini before him.

George shrugged off her comment, "Rack of lamb tonight with a nice Bordeaux."

She gazed at him warmly, feeling relaxed for the first time since this morning's incident. Scanning his eyes as if they were readouts on a computer screen, she saw beneath his confident exterior a hidden need for reassurance, a call for loving support. She knew instinctively something was troubling him.

Carol reached across the table and clasped her hand over his, "How'd it go today?"

His body language read like a mystery, a smile contradicted by a shrug of his shoulders.

She tried using another tack, "It went well?"

George shifted in is chair, leaned back, raised his head as if announcing it, "Well enough, exoneration passed unanimously. I got a standing ovation. Media was all over it."

"Good," Carol smiled it. "I'm proud of you. It was a noble thing to do."

George nodded, smiled.

"You wore the wig?"

His smile evaporated.

Carol read this one loud and clear; nothing incongruent here.

"Yeah, it slipped once. Gave them a good laugh. But all in all, a good day."

"Well then, congratulations," wondering what blanks needed to be filled in.

He lifted the stemmed martini glass, sipped it, looking into Carol's eyes, "You look terrific tonight, as always, that is," chuckling at his near faux pas.

She grinned, letting the silence bring more conversation out of him.

His eyes left Carol's.

"Father was there. With Nick," he said, in a low monotone.

The picture was coming into focus. Before she could offer soothing words, Rodney and Henry, two of George's former colleagues from Harvard appeared at their table.

"Good show today, Georgie Boy!" bellowed Rodney, fingers holding a tumbler of some amber-colored liquid.

George acknowledged both men with one perfunctory nod.

"Loved the powered wig," scoffed Henry, tugging on his own styled hair.

George laughed, "Had to get into character guys."

Henry barked a taunting laugh.

George winced at Henry, "Besides, it passed. That's bottom line."

"Too bad you weren't around back then to defend those poor souls, eh?" Cajoled Henry.

George stared at Henry, "C'mon you guys, justice, better late than never." He chuckled out loud, glancing down as if enjoying an inside joke to which only he was privileged.

Flinching at the hollowness of this juvenile male bonding, Carol shifted in her chair.

Henry snickered, "Nice how you got your slogan in there."

Rodney, as Henry's Tonto, blurted, "Yeah, Georgie. Got to make a difference."

Both men laughed, a little too loudly. Carol noticed nearby diners turning their way, scowls on their faces.

The Sommelier arrived at the table, adorned in his black tuxedo, white linen towel over one arm carrying a wine bottle, the Bordeaux George had ordered.

"Thanks gentlemen," George said dismissively, "do have a good night."

Henry and Rodney nodded towards George, then to Carol.

"Night, you two," Henry throwing in his last two cents.

Carol forced a fake smile.

Snickering, they turned away, whispering together like secret conspirators.

George shook his head, looked at Carol as the Sommelier opened the wine.

"Some fan club." he said, "Glad they have such a good time at my expense."

"Don't listen to them," she countered, "What you did was important. I'm proud of you."

His shoulders dropped noticeably, "I'd like to think so."

"Your father? What'd he think?" Carol asked, stepping through the land mines that potentially lay ahead.

"Don't know. He left before the close," George concealing the raw nerve as he reached for his martini glass, a higher priority, took a long sip, draining the glass, then smiled shyly at Carol.

This was apparently the source of his distress. She leaned back in her chair, eyeing George cautiously, testing, sticking her toe in, "You know dear, today I had a big day too."

CHAPTER SIX

Man cannot discover new oceans until he has the courage to lose sight of the shore.
-Christopher Columbus

It was a short drive from the Commonwealth Club to George's waterfront condominium overlooking Boston's historic harbor, one he could navigate in his sleep. So, why this feeling of anxiety?

He wondered, "Was it adrenaline lingering from my State House act, or just 'cause Dad didn't stick around? Or is it the dirty work I'm doing with Harrison?" It gnawed at him, the incongruity of aiding criminal polluters while being called a hero for righting a wrong. "Some hero," he echoed.

He slowed the Mercedes to a stop at a red light; he took the opportunity to unbutton his collar. Things were already too tight around his neck. He longed to be more comfortable in his own skin. The sidewalks were empty. Finally, the traffic light switched. The green light shone. He started forward a bit too fast, tires slipping on the wet pavement. It took the car a moment to regain forward traction on the road.

"Then, there's the campaign," How he dreaded what lay ahead: the meetings, the promises, the deal making, the lies. "Make a difference," he muttered. "Sure."

Looking into his future and weighing the consequences he foresaw, he squinted hard trying to erase these taunting thoughts. Leaning back against the car's headrest, he inhaled deeply, seeking respite from these haunting implications. Things just didn't feel right.

"Was it that I was so short with Carol tonight? Or today's Statehouse dramatics?" Pausing, he cleared his throat. "Rod and Hank certainly didn't help. Then, there was that last martini." He felt a flush of wet heat infuse his face.

"What was that she said?" The thought struck him like a two by four. "Something about her day?" he tried to remember. "Better call her when I get home," he reasoned.

Suddenly, a deer, a mature doe, standing on a downtown Boston street corner in the rain, ears up, nose shining wetness in a streetlight glow, eyes honed in on George. He blinked, squeezed his eyelids hard; opening them within a second. Sure, there were wiper streaks distorting images through his windshield, but he'd seen it through his side window as well. Hadn't he? A deer, here, in the middle of Boston?

He slowed the car, looking into the side mirror viewing the corner now behind him. Nothing. He considered turning and driving around the next block, returning to the intersection from a different angle.

"No," he said aloud, convinced whatever he'd seen was a figment of his imagination.

He took a forced, sobering breath, blowing out, "Quite the day, quite the day."

Once inside the security of his high-rise penthouse condominium, George saw the blinking light of his telephone answering machine in the darkness—a message. "Friggin' media," he said under his breath, switching on a lamp. He stared at the nagging light, pulsating incessantly as if it was the most important thing in the world.

He turned away from the machine, walking instead over to the teakwood sideboard holding a number of bottles, all shapes and colors. Opening one side of the cabinet's doors, he looked over the collection, finally reaching in and grasping an unopened bottle of single-malt Scotch. From another shelf he opened the door of a bar refrigerator and pulled out an ice tray, extracted two ice cubes, clinking them into a waiting crystal tumbler. Twisting open the bottle, he covered the cubes with Scotch, stopping just as the ice was beginning to rise from the bottom of the etched glass.

"There," he said to himself, swirling the elixir around the tumbler.

He took a sip, a short one, followed by longer one, then set the glass down on the tray.

He turned to the red flashing machine, reading it's only visible information: one message. He pushed the Play button, plopped down in an overstuffed leather chair and listened to the raised telephonic voice of his father.

"My God, George," it said in a tone of rebuke, "what was that? You think that fiasco, that clown act in the Statehouse helped? A powdered wig? Where did that harebrained idea come from? What the hell you thinking?" The voice made an inaudible sputtering sound. "You're not a court jester! You're a Mansbridge! And for God's sake, start acting like one!" clearing his throat, a sound of disgust. "Okay. Now get this straight. Nick's got some campaign guys coming to the office Thursday morning. First thing. I expect you to be there on time. Don't even think about being late." A loud click, end of message.

George stared at the machine, head drooping from the weight of his father's voice. He sighed, reached for his tumbler, took yet another long sip, emptying the liquid amid the clink of the ice cubes.

He stretched, slowly rose from the chair, tumbler clenched tightly in hand. He walked back to the cabinet, poured yet another heavy load of fragrant Scotch over the now somewhat diffused cubes, filling the vessel to the brim. He turned, and walked to the glass doors at the far wall of the condo. Sliding them open, he stepped out into the damp night, onto a terrace overlooking Boston Harbor. A light rain added a somber mood.

The tall ships were in port, at least some of them. He stared at these symbols of nobility for some time, thinking about the men who once sailed the world in the narrow but sleek confines of these stately creations; men who stood tall and firm; men who conquered the challenges of the sea, the world. Men who would never back down, partly because they had little choice but to face each and every challenge as it came to them, their currency nothing less than bravery and daring.

George took a long sip of his drink, toasting his acknowledgement to the tall ship men of the ages, his gesture sailing into the night. His eyes rose to the sky. The moon was vivid, shining its brightness intermittently between the cover of dark moving clouds. He looked down, turned, walked back inside, and sliding the glass doors closed behind him.

He turned to face the far wall, where atop a mantle over the marble fireplace stood a framed portrait photograph, taken three years ago when he was made a partner in the prestigious Mansbridge, Perkins and High legal firm. He is seated before the standing president of the firm, his father George Mansbridge Junior, whose palm rests upon the seated George's shoulder. Both men dressed in tailored business suits, unsmiling and serious.

George stared at the portrait.

"When?" he said, his voice rising, "when is it ever going to be enough?"

He plopped down hard in the overstuffed leather chair, Scotch splashing from the tumbler onto his hand. He set the almost half empty glass down on the tabletop.

He buried his face in both hands. "Why?" he muttered aloud, "why?"

He leaned back into the cushions, thinking; "Wasn't there something else, something I was going to do?" He closed his eyes as the muted haze of Scotch captured him. "A deer." he thought, smiling. "How about that?"

He fell into a dreamless sleep, blissfully oblivious to the world and everyone in it.

CHAPTER SEVEN

Great spirits have always encountered violent opposition from mediocre minds.
-Albert Einstein

The mid-morning sun streamed through the broad lead-paned windows. A shaft of brightness crossed the room illuminating an engraved nameplate: Isobel M. Freeman Ph.D., Dean, Behavioral Science, atop an oversized walnut desk. Carol sat, silently, in a hard-backed visitor's chair, leaning forward on one side of the dean's desk in the appropriately sterile office of the department's head honcho.

Sitting behind the desk was Doctor Freeman, a woman in her early fifties, today sporting a tailored red wool business suit with brass buttons. It was styled to complement her strong frame. A translucent smoky Topaz ring, the same honey-brown as the Dean's skin, shone in the glare of the sunbeam; the tones so well-matched one might think the only difference between this jewel and the long slender finger it encircled was internal temperature. Small diamonds surrounded the gemstone, sentinel-like, as if protecting the prismatic crown.

The chasm between her and the dean was an assumed slanted playing field. Atop Isobel Freeman's desk lie the open file labeled Susan Alden. Carol tried to appear calm and confident in her white lab coat, pen in hand, notepad on her lap. Inside, she was anxious to the point of dread, fearing the dean's rejection of her own explanation of this, the most unsettling case she had ever encountered.

The only sound in the room was the continuous whirl of the tape recorder's motor rewinding between them. Then, slowing, followed by a sudden, disturbing loud Click, as if announcing the raising of the curtain to the first act of a drama. The play was set in motion.

Isobel's poised finger pressed the Play button, topaz hand hovering over the recorder for several seconds, like a sentry ready to pounce at a moment's notice.

Carol's voice, speaking slowly and warmly reassuring, is heard administering the steps of putting her patient into a hypnotic trance. Doctor Freeman's finger descended, fast-forwarding the tape for several seconds skipping this predictable opening.

She pressed Stop, then, Play.

Carol's voice, sounding desperate, "Where? Where are you?"

The child-voice, *"Don't know exactly, 'cept Pa says we're headin' west to Oregon, someplace like that.... I think he said somethin' about goin' into Wyoming, into the Laramie range."*

"Susan, this is important. Can you tell me when this is?"

"July, 1838 don't know what day though."

Isobel frowned, reached once more for the set of buttons, Fast Forward, Stop. Play.

"Ow! I'm, on the rocks, hard, just off the trail. Then, then, Oh No! The wagon, it's tipping! Towards me! Gotta' get outa' the way! Gotta' but I can't move! I couldn't move. And, OOF, it's on me! My hip! Ow. My legs! My, Oh God in heaven!"

"Oh, it hurts. I'm so scared. Then, I don't hurt no more, not at all."

Isobel sighed heavily, hit the Stop button firmly. Click, the sound reverberated throughout the room.

"That's enough," Isobel declared. She picked up the folder, quickly browsing through the file, turning pages a bit too rapidly, as if some clue, some hidden information might pop out and reveal itself.

"Don't you want to hear the rest?" Carol pleaded.

"No," Isobel replied sharply. "What I need to know should be in this report. No need for theatrics."

Perplexed by the reaction, Carol sputtered, "Is, is that what you think, theatrics?" She hushed, instinctively silent while the Dean, brow furrowed, turned back the pages of the folder to the beginning. Without looking up Isobel restated, "Forty-two, married, no children."

She paused for what seemed like an eternity, until, "Long-term condition. Usual medical protocols failed to relieve pain."

The stifling quiet continued. Dead silence like the prismatic crystal in her ring, the vitreous luster would not reveal its specific gravity. Isobel continued turning pages without taking her eyes off the file, "No head trauma. No history of delusional behavior. No hypochondria. No drug abuse."

Carol felt Isobel was talking to herself, rather than engaging in the problem-solving discussion she had hoped for. Isobel lifted her right hand to her lips, tapping her polished fingernails repeatedly, pondering the implications of what she'd exposed. She closed the file, folded her hands on top of it, uttering a statement of fact. "Facing hip replacement surgery."

At last on *terra firma*, Carol nodded in the affirmative.

Isobel gently shook her head side to side, looked up, eyes boring in on Carol's, "You say her pain was relieved. You're certain?"

"Doctor, she practically danced out the door. She folded up her walker and carried it out! I've never seen anything like it."

Reluctantly, Isobel nodded her head in acknowledgment of Carol's clinical account. However, the deep furl in her brow clearly communicated how incredulous this therapeutic disclosure seemed.

"I've spoken to her orthopedic specialist twice since," Carol pounced, pressing what she saw as her advantage, "her pain seems nearly gone. She's gaining greater functionality."

Isobel continued nodding her head, lowered her eyes to the opaque folder before her.

Sensing an opening, Carol scooted forward to the edge of the chair, "What'd you make of her voice?" she approached cautiously, "the young girl's voice? And the wagon train?"

Slowly, deliberately, Isobel looked back up, riveting her stare at Carol.

"A dream," she said firmly, "something she read. Or saw on television. This is an obvious case of suppressed memory. Possibly some form of cryptomnesia."

Carol caught her breath as Isobel paused. "Those are the explanations you should be looking for."

Carol's head was swirling. She leaned back in the chair to regroup, reeling with soundless internal cries. "No, no, no, I know what I saw. That's why I brought you the tape. Please, help me understand!"

Isobel waited for a reply. The silence felt like a suspended sword over Carol's head.

Finally, she blurted it out, "Yet it's as if she was there. An experience she'd had in a previous...."

Instantly, Isobel interrupted. "No!" she pounced. "We do not go there!"

Carol shuttered at the fierce rebuke, eyes widening.

"But, you heard her," she pleaded. "Doctor Freeman, you've got to hear the entire tape, the whole session. Being thrown out of the wagon onto the rocks, Susan experienced it! And then to awake with her pain resolved? There's got to be something else.. Or..."

"There is! And you should be looking for it. Go back and retrace your differential diagnosis, but only in the realm of clinical protocols. You must stick to our accepted medical standards."

Carol caught her breath, regained her composure attempting to project a modicum of professional decorum in this otherwise mismatched relationship.

"Doctor Freeman, I've heard the tape a dozen times. I *saw* what happened, with my own eyes. I know that whatever caused the pain in her hip, it was ended by her reliving the accident while under hypnosis, almost immediately."

She stared pleadingly into Isobel's eyes, "Please Doctor Freeman, couldn't the pain in her hip have been lodged there from a trauma? And by experiencing it again, resolved this problem buried in her psyche? Maybe correcting something so traumatic that happened, trapped from the past, embedded in her cellular memory?"

Isobel's agitation was becoming more visible. "No. Don't even think about it," her body language as terse as her reply.

"What else could it be?" Carol objected.

"That's what I'm instructing you to find out," Isobel bellowed in a raised voice, "within accepted medical standards."

At an impasse, both doctors sat silently reassessing their positions. Gradually, the air settled quietly between them. Isobel's face softened, she smiled warmly at Carol with a more conciliatory tone.

"Look, Carol, I respect you. I want to see you succeed at this University. You're a good therapist. But please don't jeopardize your career by going down the wrong road. You've a future here, don't put your career at risk."

She paused, leaned forward and spoke the words in a near whisper, "I know this, trying to practice medicine outside the lines does not work."

Her face tightened, "I've seen it. It happened to one of our most gifted staff doctors, a colleague, one who I deeply respected; until he started dabbling into the past lives of his patients."

Carol's throat tightened, she gulped.

"He saw some of the same things you're referring to, sudden, unexplained healings following deep hypnotic regressions. He was told to stop. When he refused, his defiance cost him his University professorship and professional clinical standing. A very high price to pay for curiosity."

Carol's eyes widened, eager for more, "On staff, here?"

Isobel turned her head and fixed her eyes beyond Carol, as if looking into the annals of her own history. Her demeanor changed, softened with apparent sadness, "Yes, Phonyong Lee. He was a brilliant doctor. But, he wouldn't listen to reason. Got carried away. Way away. Just, too bad."

Isobel stood, scooped up Alden's file in one fluid motion, handed it to Carol, "Forget this nonsense, find an answer that's within standard medical protocols and write it up. Your conclusions in this file are not acceptable. I've a funding committee meeting in less than an hour. Now, you're excused."

The cues were unmistakable. Carol rose from her chair and instinctively reached for the tape recorder. Isobel clasped her hand on Carol's arm, "I'll keep this."

Carol let her hand drop to her side, knowing it was the end of their meeting. Turning, she walked to the door, feeling both dissatisfied and rebuked.

Isobel called after her, "On your way out, tell Randall I need to see him immediately."

Carol nodded, walked out, stepped to the desk of Dean Freeman's administrative assistant, Randall, who was an enigma to many in the department. Young, gangly, a splash of human gaiety, he was a sharp contradiction to everything else within the somberness of Isobel's well-appointed department. Randall seemed thoroughly out of place in the pristine setting of the university.

"She said she wants to see you. Now."

He leapt up with exuberance, nearly bumping Carol. "You got it, Doc," with a smile of sarcasm, walked quickly into Doctor Freeman's office.

"Monitor Klein's e-mails from here on out," the Dean directed her subordinate.

Randall grinned it, "You got it, Doc."

Isobel dismissed Randall expediently, "That's all."

Randall pivoted on his heels, rubbed his hands together and sniggered to himself as he walked back to his desk.

CHAPTER EIGHT

Faith is the bird that feels the light when the dawn is still dark.
-Sri Rabindranath Tagore

Despondent, Carol walked down the shadowy corridor of Watson Hall to her office.

She sat down, heavily, before her computer, feeling hung out to dry. She stared into space not really knowing where to go next. Heaving a sigh, she absent-mindedly began opening her e-mail file. Several messages immediately appeared. She glanced at them for a brief moment, then began the process of scrolling down, deleting the waste-of-time e-mails, one by one.

The last message caught her eye, *Yarnellmd@Mercy re: Susan Alden.* She highlighted the line and clicked it open.

"Impressive work with Susan Alden. I'll be forwarding files on three more patients seeking similar results. Let me know when you can schedule them." David Yarnell, M.D.

Carol was knocked back in her chair by the weight of the message. The strain of today had put her close to her tipping point. Now this.

She felt trapped, cornered, without recourse. Her only retort was to push herself back from the computer. She began to walk slowly in an elliptical path. Her eyes scrutinizing the pattern on her rug as if looking for the trailhead, thinking, "There's got to be a solution, an explanation, but what? Does Isobel have an ax to grind, her own private *bete noire?*"

She was not ready to throw in the towel. She stopped, looked over her shoulder at the monitor screen, feeling the pull from one end of this tug-of-war.

She walked to the window, seeking solace. It was dusk. The sun had set and there was a pinkish-orange hue remaining on the horizon, a watercolor background beyond the silhouettes of deciduous trees in transition. A few leaves remained, holding on tenaciously as if to defy their inevitable fate. Others, the leaf leaders, had relinquished their posts and had gone on to become fertilizer for next year's assemblage of foliage as a matter of course.

Pivoting on the ball of her right foot in a spontaneous pirouette to gain some forward momentum, she squared off facing the computer screen again. The one-eyed Oz might have the elusive explanation, a unified field theory embracing the elusive art of human consciousness and the science of medicine.

The weight of this monkey on her back added to a desperation welling up inside her gut. She felt fractured like a broken mirror, unable to accurately reflect the picture she saw. She only wanted to clarify this conundrum. She loathed this feeling of split loyalties, between trusting her intuitive truth on one side and the age-old institution of proven science that had guided her this far on the other.

What could she count on? Who should she believe? What was the real truth?

Staring back at the computer, she reached for the mouse, hesitated, her hand frozen in midair. This was now one of those decisive moments; one in which you either stay sitting on the curb watching life—or you move into the uncharted territory of action.

She looked straight into the face of the computer, "In order to see the invisible, I've got to go for the impossible."

She had to find the truth, to make sense of Susan's experience. In the back of her mind, she saw a small light through her bundled nerves. Determined not be at the mercy of Isobel Freeman's limitations, she leaped into the deep end; moved her cursor, clicked on the search box, typing in, the name: Phonyong Lee M.D.

"There it's done; once something becomes visible it can no longer be denied."

Instantaneously, the website appeared, a navigation bar at the top of the home page. She clicked on 'About the Doctor'.

Phonyong Lee, M.D., Ph.D. -- medical degree, New York University, 1973; doctorate in psychology, Yale University, 1983; behavioral psychologist, Tufts University; behavioral research, Jakarta Institute (Indonesia); Medical Fellow, London Psychiatric Society; Director of Research, Santa Barbara Institute of Consciousness; Founder and Editor, Journal of Science Frontier, Boston, Massachusetts.

She crossed the abyss, the bridge between science, new and old; one absolutely known and agreed upon, the other—a horse of a different color. She scrolled across the navigation bar, clicked on 'Research Papers'.

She felt her body warming, "Could it be?" she thought, "was there an understandable explanation of what I saw with Susan?" Her apprehensions feeling temporarily assuaged just by finding somebody out there who is prepared to look beyond Doctor Freeman's standard medical protocols; someone who might help her comprehend this inexplicable episode.

She scrolled down the long list of titles. She had no idea that research like this even existed.

- *Diagnosing, and Treating Antisocial Behavior Through Past Life Hypnosis.*
- *Hysterical Blindness: Three Case Histories of Unresolved Past Life Trauma.*
- *Beyond Fear: Relinquishing the Ties of Our Past.*
- *The Future of Psychotherapy: Optimizing Interdisciplinary Therapies--Including Past Life Regressions.*
- *Eliminating Pain Neuropathy by Removing Past Life Memories.*
- *Substance Abuse: the Etiology, Pathology, and the Roots in Reincarnation.*
- *Personality Theory: A New Perspective of East-West Philosophy on Reincarnation.*
- *Ethical Considerations For Mental Health Professionals Regarding Past Life Accounts of Regression Through*

Hypnosis.
- *Understanding Previous Existences and Their Positive Influences on Your Life Today.*

She was racing through these articles as fast as her eyes would move across the computer screen.

The references at the end of the articles seemed even more enticing than the research papers. Page after page read like an anthology of collected western philosophy, eastern spirituality, quantum physics and modern psychology.

Filled to capacity, she was overloaded. This was way too much additional input on top of today's turmoil. She'd have to come back to this another time and cut it down into more digestible bite-size pieces.

But the glaring question couldn't be dismissed as easily as book-marking this website: "Why was this immense body of information completely absent from my training?"

She was at a turning point. Maybe like Christopher Columbus claiming the New World, again, one thousand years after it had been first discovered by the Norseman. "Is each generation required to rediscover the evidence of previously known facts? Does the wheel need to be reinvented in every age?"

She wanted to study the entire website, but this was not the right time. She had a more urgent and immediate need. She went back to the navigation bar and pressed the contact button. Immediately, Phonyong Lee's address appeared:

http//www.jsf followed by the e-mail address: *Leemd@jsf.com.*

Hitching her fate to someone else's wagon, her fingers hit the keys.

To: Leemd @ jsf.com.
Subject: I've had an incident.

CHAPTER NINE

You must be the change you wish to see in the world.
-Mahatma Gandhi

Even with the buzz of the crowd, the music seemed a bit too loud.

Stepping outside the jam-packed hall festooned with red, white and blue campaign banners, television reporter Alicia Rhodes had to speak loudly into her microphone to be heard.

"The mood here in the Colonnade ballroom is festive," she reported, "as George Mansbridge the third officially opens this, his campaign for Congress before a gathering of what appears to be some three hundred or more supporters. If elected, he will become the fifth Mansbridge to represent this district in the nation's capitol. Former Congressman and Secretary Nicholas Mansbridge is about to take the podium to fire up this noisy and appreciative band of supporters. For now, the crowd is content to tap their toes while the band plays, as I'm sure you can hear, the campaign theme song, 'What a difference a day makes.' Live from downtown Boston, Alicia Rhodes, Boston ABC News."

Men and women of all ages, from children to octogenarians, filled the ballroom, sitting at tables, standing in clusters, chatting, some swaying to the music as waiters wended their way between tables and through the crowd, attempting to deliver hors d'oeurves and keep the drinks flowing.

On stage, draped with one large banner, *"Mansbridge—Make A Difference,"* behind, the small band ended their number with a crescendo flourish, giving rise to scattered applause.

Two tables had been set up closest to the stage, one for the Mansbridge women, including George's mother Althea, his aunt Rosalyn, cousins and nieces, all cloistered together as if in a nunnery. As the family's matriarch, Althea was holding court. Despite the proceedings going on before her, she was intent on telling anyone who was listening details of a major kitchen remodel she was planning. Her husband, who was standing behind her was focused on seeing who was seated where and with whom in the ballroom, and was not listening. However, the aunts and cousins were utterly engaged in the slightest details of cabinet color, assorted appliances and features that were part of the matron's master plan, including the state-of-the-art wine cellar.

The adjoining table, was reserved for George's father, the VIP guests, and other clients including local political bigwigs, men in blue suits leaning their heads close together, some chuckling as if sharing a joke. An empty chair was yet to be filled.

Off to the left, at the fray of the crowd, seated at a table with young supporters, many of college age, Carol Klein watched the proceedings with the keen eye of a social observer; her head shaking in awe and wonder at her boyfriend's political right of passage, the initiation party of the Mansbridge men.

"Am I alone on this island?" Carol sighed to herself, wondering what life might be like were she seated at the table of Mansbridge women, with whom she had yet to be invited.

Backstage, George was deep in conversation with his Uncle Nicholas. "We've got you a bought-crowd out there," Nicholas spoke commandingly, "so things should go well. Got some of the big guns in the house too, so do your best. I know you will. Just play the regular 'Joe' role, be humble, thank everyone you can think of. For everything."

He gave George's shoulder an attaboy pat, "Now, before I go out there, there's one more thing I want you to think about. You and that Klein gal, you're pretty smoochy, right?"

George winced, "Yes, you could say so."

"Good," Nicholas said, "that'll make it easier. Here's what we all want you to do. Get her an engagement ring. Whether or not you really mean it. Just do it."

"You're not serious," George flinched.

"Dead serious," pausing to let it soak in. "Look kid, long as you're single, people'll think your an irascible playboy and it will leave you open to speculation. It will cost you votes. People want a family man. Got it," an order from his Uncle Spin.

Backed into a corner at sword-point, George stared at him in dead silence.

"Okay, we'll go into this in more detail later. You won't really have to do anything. I've already got Harrison taking care of details. Now, watch me go warm 'em up."

Nicholas stood up, smiled down at the shell-shocked George.

"Knock 'em dead, kid," Nicholas ordered, knowing the sky's the limit, having been there himself. "Break a leg."

With that, he turned and walked towards the closed side curtain behind the band, which was ending a number right on cue, the crowd politely applauding for the musicians.

The cheers grew louder as the smiling Nicholas Mansbridge walked out from the curtain to a flag-draped podium on center stage, accompanied by a brief fanfare from the band. As the notes faded, Nicholas raises a hand signaling silence, still beaming ear to ear.

"Alright, sports fans," he boomed, "quiet down. Please. Your attention please."

The crowd grew quiet, slowly.

"As you know," broadcasting it, "I am Nicholas Mansbridge," before he could finish applause and cheers erupted. "Nick, Nick, Nick," followed by appreciative ovations and the buzz of chatter. Several people left their seats, crowding up to the stage, some, drinks still in hand.

Nicholas loved every second of the crowd's adulation. He missed being in the political spotlight, wishing he could once again throw his hat into the ring, but he knew this old battleship had long since been decommissioned.

His voice boomed, "Many of you know me as your former Congressman, or as the Secretary of Interior in the administration of our great president, Jimmy Carter."

Another round of cheers erupted.

"Thank you, thank you all. But tonight, my role here is to help kickoff this important campaign to elect a very good man to serve you in the House of Representatives of the United States of America, my nephew and colleague, George Mansbridge the third."

Another cheer, this one louder than the others; a chant began, as if orchestrated, "Mansbridge, Mansbridge, Mansbridge."

George listened passively to the roaring crowd, "Had he heard Nick right? Really? Guess it can't hurt, probably inevitable. I do love the girl. But, what's Harrison have to do with it? Jeez. Can't deal with it now. Back to you, Unk." He focused on Nick's performance on stage.

"Let's hear it," Nicholas hollers over the crowd. "Wanna' make a difference?"

"Difference. Make A Difference," the crowd shouts back in waves of sound, then breaks into one loud, long cheer.

"Fire 'em up Nick," he thought, "nothing like an opening act before the main show." George had been through this routine many times, even from childhood. He had learned all the tricks, all the edges. "Keep 'em laughing or keep 'em scared. And be certain you build a wall between you and them. Convince the poor saps they can't do without you. And be certain to tell them you're the key to making a difference. Whatever the hell that means!"

Glancing out through a fold in the backstage curtain, George caught a glimpse of his father sitting up close with some Global honchos. He frowned, turned, seeking familiar faces, finding many. "Looks loaded alright, can't miss."

"Ladies and Gentlemen," Nicholas boomed it, "it's time to put your hands together for the next Mansbridge to serve as your voice in Congress, following his great-grandfather, grandfather, yours truly and his old man, George the Second." He paused as laughter built, then subsided, "Tonight, it is my privilege, to give you, as the next Congressman from Boston, Massachusetts, the best of the breed, my own flesh and blood, George Mansbridge the Third."

Spotlights raced across the ballroom, bathing the stage in red, white and blue as the curtains part, revealing George, standing stiffly, head lifted high, a big smile on his face, arms raised in the air forming a giant 'V'. He puffs out his chest, turns his body left, then right, beaming as the crowd erupts in applause and cheers. He lowers his arms, bows his head slightly and walks to the podium where he reaches his arm out to shake the hand of Nicholas, who leans in and hugs him tightly.

Speaking low into Nicholas's ear, George hissed, "Nice job, Unk, thanks for the warm up."

"Go get 'em." Nicholas said firmly as he squeezed George's arm as though passing the torch, "Don't screw it up."

Cheers and applause are nearly drowned out by the band which begins playing the tune of "People" as a female singer with a too-nasal voice started singing a set of re-written lyrics, singing, "*Mansbridge, we who vote for Mansbridge, are the luckiest people, in the world.*"

George III released Nicholas, who turned to the audience, waved his right arm high in the air, walked off the stage to the applause of this cherry-picked crowd.

George beamed at the assemblage, turned to Nicholas stepping down from the stage, "How 'bout that man? Secretary Nicholas Mansbridge, my dear uncle."

The cheers increased.

"Thank you, thank you for being here. Each and every one of you," nodding in appreciation to the turned-on crowd.

"So" he said in an amused voice, "you wanna' keep this Mansbridge thing going?" The crowd roared in approval. "Well then, let's see what we can do, together, to make a difference."

Carol's back stiffened, sitting up even straighter, straining to see Nicholas Mansbridge joining the table with George's father and the bulky men in blue suits and one slight man in an off-brown sport coat. They all shake hands, grinning at each other, like the cat that just ate the canary.

George III pulled out his note cards, waited for the noise to lessen, then began, "Fellow Bostonians; fellow Americans, I am humbled ..."

CHAPTER TEN

The hardest thing to learn in life is which bridge to cross and which to burn.
-David Russell

"Damn!" Carol huffed, kicking her shoes off, one by one and tossing her bag onto the antique marble Bombay chest by the front door. This was not her usual entrance into her 1920's Beacon Hill brownstone apartment. Tonight she did not feel the comforting sense of warmth and balance that the high ceilings and Turkish tapestry carpets usually afforded.

Tonight was different, she felt agitated and put upon. The evening events made her loath the social spotlight and the unremitting pressure of George's burgeoning political career. The sides of her mouth ached from the jaw stretching forced smiles. "As if I'm not under enough pressure already! Now I'm supposed to put up with his dog and pony show too?"

Even though her black silk sheath and white St. John's sweater had formed the perfect evening ensemble, her inner voice told her she'd become little more than a prop in George's campaign circus. She began to strip away what felt like contaminated clothes, leaving a trail of garments resembling the strewn bones of a recent massacre.

"I will not be the sprinkles on his icing! And if I hear 'make a difference' one more time, I'll scream! As if he's the only one to make a difference? Must I give up who I am, just to be loved by you, George?"

In her head, she knew this wasn't where she wanted to go, but her heart had a different agenda. Knowing power struggles could kill a relationship, she didn't want to make this a push-pull contest.

Brushing her resentful thoughts aside, "Okay, what's the real truth here?" Her inner voice replied, "You're cranky and tired." A genuine half-smile emerged.

She recalled her Grandmother's trick. Even before grade school, whenever she was upset, her Grandmother would chant, "Carol, my dear, when things around you don't feel good—stop, stand very, very still and hold onto your heart with both hands. Hold it tight. Until everything is alright." Carol knew it was true then and even truer today. More relaxed, her instincts called for solace in a warm bath.

Carol turned the antiquated bathroom faucets of her claw footed tub on full force and poured in a generous handful of lavender bath salts. Submerging herself into the foaming liquid, she slipped deep into its luxurious warmth allowing herself to slip, far away from this long day, drifting in wonderment, "How does this work? Is it the negative ions in the water? Or is it just the placebo effect? Who cares, really? This is Heaven." At last coming down from her psychological ledge, she stepped out of the tub and wrapped herself in the softness of an oversized Egyptian cotton towel.

Snuggled in a thick fleece robe, she walked into the kitchen for a cup of soothing chamomile tea. Finally, she was glad to be home by herself, knowing George, his father and Nick would be up all night reviewing reaction to the announcement and awaiting media coverage. The stats would be in before dawn.

Waiting for the water to boil, she set the laptop up on the kitchen table and opened to the current e-mails. Five new messages flashed in succession, one catching her eye; D.Yarnell.MD@Mercer. She hesitated only a moment, highlight, clicked.

Doctor Klein, I recently met with Susan Alden again and am pleased to share my report on her functional improvement with you in the first attachment. The other two attachments are the additional cases I would like you to review and schedule at your earliest possible convenience. Thank you. D.Y., M.D.

She closed her eyes, allowing everything to go blank not unlike like rebooting a computer, "No. Think. What are the ramifications? Say 'yes' to Yarnell, I violate Isobel's order? Yet, by scheduling his patients, and if it works like it did with Susan, I might get more ammunition, more results to convince Freeman."

Her thoughts swirled with splintered possibilities. The burden of proof was hers; was this just a wild goose chase, or window of opportunity? She didn't like being out on the skinny branches.

As the teakettle whistled, her thoughts evaporated. Absentmindedly, she opened the cupboard door, and reached for the tea canister, when the blue box of pasta caught her eye. She stared at the flat boards of lifeless lasagna noodles through the small cellophane window. But on the left side of the box, was a colorful photo of a sumptuous lasagna, dripping with melted mozzarella, chunks of tomatoes, shredded basil, grated Parmesan sprinkles. Lifting the carton from the shelf, she turned it over. There it was: directions on how to transform the lifeless pasta into an epicurean masterpiece.

"That's it; follow the directions," she mouthed, "follow the recipe." The sudden 'ahha' moment extinguished her doubts. She would see Yarnell's patients. She would research Phonyong Lee's works. She would temporarily suspend Isobel's warnings to leave it alone.

Yet, she knew one other dilemma was not so easily resolved, as she thought of George. "Of course," she reflected, "it always came back to him. Despite whatever her head spoke, her heart had the louder voice. George was the wild card in her life's equation. His solitary vote counted over all others."

In affairs of the heart, self-analysis can be a bitter pill to swallow. She was well aware of the one last itch that was not yet fully satisfied. Like the irksome grain of sand in an oyster that becomes the prized pearl, her irritation, even though she was ashamed to admit to herself, was to be more than Doctor Klein.

She longed to be Mrs. George Mansbridge III. Then her struggles would be over, wouldn't they?

PRELUDE

CHAPTER ELEVEN

It is our choices…that show what we truly are, far more than our abilities.
-J.K. Rowling

The day was glorious, breaking like an impressionist's painting in the most vivid palette of fall colors, one of those peak New England days they touted in tourism brochures.

Although it was Saturday, she still felt like she was playing hooky. If she weren't going here, she'd be on her way to the Cambridge flea market, her favorite excursion that often would turn into an adventure of treasure hunting.

But today, she was headed in the opposite direction.

The doubts she harbored a few days ago had given way to a new feeling of determination. Her decision to resolve this academic question that had captured her curiosity in a most compelling way. She could hardly stop thinking about the possibilities. At the very least, it would make today a totally non-habitual experience.

Carol knew the biggest mistakes of life were always made when she didn't follow her intuition. She wasn't going to repeat that mistake again, if she could help it.

Driving down the road of this well-kept neighborhood, she drank in the grandeur of this cultivated community. These big older homes with manicured lawns and great oaks on the outskirts of the University's hub probably had decades of stories to tell. She felt her own deep longing to be settled in such a home; to have her own place in the world.

Carol's trusty Volvo slowed as it pulled alongside the curb scanning the numbers on the houses. There it was, #196. Her destination. From the outside, it was indistinguishable from the other well-kept houses on the street.

Taking a moment to gather herself, she glanced in the mirror, checking herself out, just like before meeting George at his club. Common sense told her this was going to be quite different, this wasn't George she was meeting. A voice within whispered, "It's not too late, just leave now; no harm, no foul." She knew she could leave, just drive away and go back to living life in peace. Peace with Isobel, George, her students, and herself. No ripples in the current of her well-planned life.

But the louder counterpoint was more enticing. Knowing that she was about to cross a threshold from which there might be no return. She wanted answers, today. "Get on with it already," she spoke it, "finis, kaput, the end," this, the goal. "Indecision brings no reward."

The mere fact of being here, parked in front of #196, was the choice, even as her inner voices completed their final arguments. The verdict: 'go forward, damn the consequences'. As she opened the car door, a burst of cold fall air sent a chill to her bones.

Grabbing her briefcase, she shut the car door, walked up the sidewalk, past a manicured lawn, a laurel hedge, a couple of soaring sunflowers, towering lavetera, bowing down in vivid bloom. Facing the ornately carved wooden front door.

She pressed the doorbell, Asian bells chimed in melodic succession, like a Pavlovian response, echoing back to her for what felt like an eternity. Moments after the chimes silenced, the door opened, slowly.

There, standing in the doorway, with no shoes, was a slight Asian man in his 50s, Phonyong Lee, M.D., Ph.D., his face an enigmatic smile with piercing black eyes. He bowed his head slightly, looked at her, grinned it, "I've been waiting a thousand years."

She recoiled, trying to interpret what she had just heard, "A thousand years?"

He stepped back to open the space for Carol to enter, keeping his eyes on her. They remained fixed as if he were scanning her like a rheostat assessing every pixel. Her comfort zone stretched, she was used to being the gazer, not the gazee. His stare made her feel uncomfortable and she was grateful for the distraction of the small bench just inside the door inviting visitors to leave their shoes behind. She broke the eye contact, while bending forward to step out of her shoes.

"Come, this is the way," he said, pointing toward a door at the end of a long corridor.

For the first time she looked around, into a long hallway that appeared to stretch the length of the house. Doctor Lee turned, walked down the passage. She followed, painfully aware that she had yet to say a word. The hallway served as an art gallery, featuring an ornate mirror and dozens of wall-mounted ceremonial masks from varying cultures, each illuminated by an overhead track light. She slowed, admiring the play of shadow and light that no doubt defined their significance. Taking it all in, she wondered where they were from, how old they were, and how they gained their status.

The doctor disappeared through a doorway to the right. She followed and emerged from the subdued hallway lighting into a bright, sunlit room that obviously served as an office. Slanted window blinds modulated the intensity of the daylight casting parallel shadows across the room.

To get her bearings, she quickly surveyed the room with her eyes. Standing as a sentry at the inside entrance was a large brass doe. The back wall was lined with floor to ceiling bookshelves filled with a mosaic of magazines, a vast array of books of all shapes, sizes and colors, and other artifacts which spoke of travels around the world.

To the right was a wooden display table that held a life-like model of the human brain and two statues of Buddha; one laughing with the characteristic large Buddha belly and one contemplative, slender with head slightly bowed and hands palm up at the juncture between hip and thigh. She knew that the Buddha's belly is not large from overindulgence but because he is so filled with enlightenment.

In front of the table was a carved rosewood raised platform bench with two very thick red Chinese silk embroidered pillows. From the corner of her eye she picked up a sudden movement near the ceiling. To her surprise, a bright green speckled gecko darted across the wall and came to rest near the ceiling effortlessly clinging to the wall.

Without a word, Lee motioned to a maroon velvet chair, welcoming Carol to sit. Realizing she was still clinging to her briefcase like a security blanket, she looked for a place to set it down securely and decided to put it on the floor next to the leg of her chair. Its not as though her briefcase held the answers she came here for anyway.

Before sitting down, she slipped the coat off her shoulders. Without hesitation, Lee extended his hand and completed the task. The coat bridged the space between them. He folded her coat over his left arm. It was the unexpected fluidity that Carol noticed first.

He ran his right hand over the cloth of her coat, his fingers slid along the texture of the hand-stitched outer seams. "Peruvian." he said in a whisper to himself.

Startled, Carol murmured hesitantly, "I'm not sure. Farmers market in Westport, street vendor. Think she said Columbian."

Lee nodded knowingly, "Handcrafted. Someone true."

She watched him place her coat with tender care over the back of his desk chair. Once again, he pointed deliberately to the upholstered maroon chair, she quickly sat down, voice cracking, "Doctor Lee, I'm so pleased ..."

"Pay most attention to the nouns," he interrupted, "only nouns are true. Question all the rest."

Disarmed by the interruption, she couldn't help but wonder where on earth that came from. Since walking through the front door, she felt like she was foreigner in a foreign land. Was Isobel right? Was Lee really in his own private Idaho? She'd come here to get answers, not to be mired down by riddles.

She reached for her briefcase intent on reviewing the case of Susan Alden. Her mission was to get the information needed to understand what happened in that session, Susan's unexplained improvement of symptoms, and to clear up this mess with Isobel Freeman.

"No," Lee's eyes tracking her every move, "we won't be needing that."

Midair, Carol released her grip on the briefcase handle. Without describing Susan Alden's case, she had no reason to be here. Not knowing the next move, she looked at Lee expectantly waiting for his cue.

Doctor Lee lowered himself onto the rosewood bench and settled into the red silk pillows cross-legged. He folded his hands together in what appeared to be meditation pose as he closed his eyes for several moments, rhythmically breathing from his lower abdomen.

Unconsciously, Carol could feel her breath start to track with his, perceptively slowing her mind, a momentary welcome relief. While she didn't know what to expect next, she did know that from a place of quiet calm she could navigate with greater clarity.

His eyes opened, his piercing glare hitting the bulls eye. "You have witnessed a bleed-through from the past, one which resolves a pain remaining in this life, embedded, from before."

"Yes, that's true," she started to explain. "You see, my patient, Susan, ..."

Lee cut her off with a hand signal to stop speaking. "Now you know," he paused, eyes boring into hers. "You must explore this power of the past that lies within the present. There is more, much more, something of extreme importance awaits in your future."

She flinched at his declaration. This was not what she wanted to hear. She tried to regain some control, find footing in her training, "I, I've been told not to go forward in this work. It's not an accepted protocol, and...."

"Your precious protocols? They will be obsolete in your lifetime."

Every muscle in her body tensed, the bottom of her world was falling out!

She sat speechless as he stared at her, adding nothing for a long period of silence before smirking, "Your western science of psychology? Barely two hundred years old! Not even a wrinkle in time."

Lee arched his back slightly, raised his index finger to his right temple. "Your patient's pain was embedded within her subconscious, to be healed only by revisiting her earlier existence, clearing a blocked energy path, one left over from her previous incarnation."

Carol didn't know which was fluttering more, her blinking eyes or her pounding heart. She was being given an explanation for the unexplainable, but it flew in the face of everything she had been taught.

He lowered his right hand from his temple and went on to explain with an open handed gesture, "For thousands of years mankind, on every continent, in every culture, has accepted soul migration from one existence to another as a universal truth. Until your western religions banished this reality, to use fear of death as a tool to control, to gain power through perpetrating ignorance." His cadence was like a drum beat counting the rhythm; only his instrument was words. They required periodic pauses to fully burrow in.

"I, I'm being told it's nonsense."

"Would such nonsense be believed by Einstein, Edison, Gandhi, Carl Jung?"

"No, but ..."

He interrupted, "Mark Twain. Tolstoy. Dostoevsky. Schweitzer. Ben Franklin, Henry Ford, General George Patton? All were believers in the reality of human reincarnation."

Carol began opening her mouth to put together an intelligent response, when Lee raised his hand, the universal sign language silencing her unexpressed outcry.

"If science understood the laws of the universe, there would be no need for research. In truth, science has only been able to discover that which already exists, that which is already there. Scientists do not create. They do not invent. They only uncover and verify what has been placed before them."

He made a sweeping gesture pointing high up, over the far wall bookcases, his pointer finger directed toward the gecko effortlessly cleaving to the wall, "Today's science? It's just now catching up with what our little friend here learned centuries ago."

Her eyes riveted on the speckled gecko, grasping the magnitude of the small reptile's capabilities for the first time.

"The molecules of his feet mesh with the molecules of the wall. He interacts with the universe in ways we only wish we could."

Mesmerized, she could only nod.

Lee pushed himself up off the rosewood platform and came to standing.

Carol noticed how fit Doctor Lee was as he rose, moving in one fluid motion. For a man his age there were no adjustments of joints or muscles. She guessed she likely practiced yoga or Tai Chi.

In what seemed to be one long glide, he walked to his bookshelves and with methodical deliberation pulled several issues of the *Journal of Science Frontiers* from the self, handing them to her. "These are the histories that will show you why I left University to pursue the truth. Here you will find an entry point of embodied knowledge, well-developed, tested, accessing the body's profound knowing. Retrieving the elusive memories. Ultimately, a transference of energy, nothing more, nothing less, only steps to realizations." He smiled, "And a road to truth."

Here it is. The answers she came here for. She had homework to do.

Deep inside she knew no one could serve as judge and jury of this evidence other than herself. The scales for weighing the facts; what she had observed with her patient Susan Alden and what was being offered her as an explanation. She was about to step onto a bridge between two worlds. She extended her hands, and took the Journals from Lee.

Lee nodded in response to his own inner timing, turned and walked out of his study. Apparently, this was the signal that their meeting had concluded. She felt like a bystander watching someone else's script play out. It was hard enough following his dialogue, no less getting a grasp on who he was. Maybe Isobel was absolutely correct; he'd gone off the deep end.

She started to rise. Lee reappeared in the doorway, announcing, "You will return two weeks from this time, Thursday afternoon. No commitment is of greater importance. You must have first-hand experience, nothing else will do."

He walked away adding, "You may find your way out. Good day."

Looking down at the journals in her hands, she felt exposed and unsettled. They were only invitations to continue their dialogue. She had come here today for answers, not more mysteries. There were no pieces of this puzzle she could put her arms around yet. She wanted to see the whole picture, now. "*Quid pro quo*, Doctor Lee!"

And, what of his invitation? Two weeks from today? That's it. That's when she'd insist on getting to the root causes of Susan Alden's case. Any other agenda items are off the table and were of no interest.

Let's just dispel Isobel's concerns and get back on track.

She was sure she had heard him say something about … "experiencing?"

She turned from the maroon velvet chair, taking one last sweeping view of the room. Everything seemed as it was when she arrived, except the gecko, now moving across the parallel lines of light and shadow cast across the room coming to rest by the window. Without a sound, it had moved stealthily onto new territory.

Reclaiming her coat from the back of Lee's desk chair, she wrapped herself in its comforting familiarity as she walked directly down into the long entry hallway on her way to the front door. The only sound that could be heard was her stocking feet gliding over the bamboo wooden floors, quiet as a mouse.

She sidled into the hallway, slowly indulging her fascination, studying each of the ceremonial masks that were displayed down this long gallery-like wall. Her curiosity was piqued and it would get no satisfaction other than a visceral appreciation. One by one she considered each mask; "who, where, what, why?"

More questions, always questions.

Reaching the end of the display, unexpectedly since she hadn't seen it when she entered the house, was an ornate, oval mirror, spotlighted by overhead track lights.

She stared into her own face blinded by the truth of the revelation; *vuitus est index animi,* the eye is the mirror of the soul. So, she thought what's behind this, my own mask?

CHAPTER TWELVE

Life can only be understood backward, but must be lived forwards.
-Soren Kierkegaard

They called these their Getaway Sundays.

Once a month, weather permitting, Carol and George planned a road trip together to escape the grit and glare of their professional lives. This being likely the last sunny Sunday of autumn, George decided on a special treat, something not even Carol had yet the clearance to participate in: a drive upstate in his most cherished 1953 vintage Morgan Plus 4 Roadster, a classic automobile he called Maggie.

Yes, he'd named it. And quite the beauty she was. Brilliant yellow in color with black leather upholstery, Maggie featured the Morgan's trademark leather strap, crossing the bonnet from one side to the other, along with sculpted, elbow-high doors. Powered by a Triumph TR-2 engine, the '53 was the first Morgan so endowed and the first to feature a chromed upper grille with headlamps integrated into the fenders. A true classic, Maggie is one of only nineteen Morgans built that year. To George's left-brained thinking, submitting Maggie to the indignities of the road made him feel guilty.

Yet, on a day like this, with winter and months of no-road trips on the horizon—this was the best of the best. To find a twisty road on a beautiful day in a classic Morgan with the top down, well, he wouldn't soon forget it.

Wrapped snugly in a thick cable-knitted fisherman's sweater and brown corduroy sport coat, he steered Maggie along a two-lane road into the wilds of New Hampshire, having opted off Highway 93 in favor of a variety of country roads. Their destination was Hillsborough in the center of the state, or so George had promised, where a surprise awaited Carol, who sat enjoying the scenery bundled in a thick navy pea coat, a plaid scarf tightly covering her windblown hair. As the brilliant colors of the deciduous autumn foliage sped by.

"Wheels made of solid steel," George boasted, a combination of authority and pride. "And sliding pillar independent front suspension. You notice the windshield folds down? Of course, a bit chilly today, for that," chucking.

"Really, sliding suspension," she chirped. "That's good," trying to sound engaged or at least, somewhat interested.

George laughed, turned his head to grin at her, "Of course it's good. It's Maggie!"

She leaned in, kissed him on the cheek, pleased to see him this happy.

As Maggie rounded a curve, a small doe, head down munching undergrowth, came into view ahead. The deer looked up, locking eyes with George for a millisecond, her head turning as she followed the flight of the curious yellow beast that roared.

Leaving Dustin Tavern Road, they turned towards the town square of Weare, New Hampshire, population 8,000 and home of the 1772 Pine Tree riot. George slowed Maggie, turning into a parking slot in front of the Old Brick Antique Shop.

He took a deep breath of fresh air smelling the scent of burning leaves off in the distance, turned to Carol, smiling. "C'mon," he cheered. "Let's see what they've got."

Hopping out of Maggie, they both stretched their legs and walked through the front door of the shop. Once inside, they are surrounded by tall shelves of memorabilia from eras long past. They walk together down the closest aisle, shelves covered with metal goblets, ceramic statuary, hundred-year-old hardware items.

A clerk appeared from behind the counter, a young woman in her early twenties, with spiked magenta-dyed hair, sporting hoop earrings and a metal ring piercing her eyebrow, yet dressed in an1800s-style calico dress.

"Hey," she called out, "anything I can help?"

"Just looking for now," George answered, walking towards an aisle full of old flintlocks and revolution era single shot pistols. "Got some good stuff here."

Carol scanned an aisle featuring shelves of pottery. She lifted an ornately hand-painted vase, about six inches tall and surrounded by dainty ceramic rose-shaped filigree. She turned it slowly in her hand.

"By someone true," she whispered to herself.

"What's that?" George asked from the next aisle.

"Oh, nothing," Carol replied. "It's just ..."

She set the vase back on the shelf, walked into George's aisle. He looked up, turned to face her, his shoulder nudging a display case like the bull in a china shop.

"Oops," he huffed, reaching to steady the case.

"You know," she said, "sometimes you see something you've never seen before, but when you see it, you feel like you have?"

"Sure," George absently answered. "Deja Vu?"

"How does that happen?" Carol asked. "How does it work?"

"Right on," called out the clerk, "we get that a lot. That 'Honey, I know I've seen this before,' thing."

"Yeah," Carol supposed. "You wonder why? How?"

"Don't ask me," George answered, hefting a long-barreled flintlock pistol with an ivory handle, raising it with both hands, leveled it to peer down the barrel's gun sight, "You're the shrink."

"Looks like you've done that before," smiled the clerk.

George grinned back at her, handed her the pistol, "I'll take it."

"Well, to be honest, I gotta' tell you, it won't fire. Mechanism's disabled. It looks good, but it's just for show."

"Perfect," George remarked, "me too. I'm a lawyer." They all laughed.

George and Carol walked out of the store toting the bagged flintlock, which he placed carefully into the back of Maggie under her black vinyl tonneau cover. While waiting for George, Carol reached down and picked up a reddened maple leaf, twirling it in her fingers. "So many questions," she sighed, dropping the leaf in wonder.

Gathering herself she slid into Maggie.

"I miss something?" George asked.

"No, nothing, just, it's that client I told you about. The one who screamed, then saw herself as a young girl on a wagon train."

"Yeah?"

"Something erased a pain she'd had most of her life. And I've found hundreds of cases like hers, unexplained. Patients cured of long-standing ailments through deep hypnotic regressions. Into what may well be their past lives."

George swung himself into the car behind the wheel.

"Nonsense," looking straight ahead. "Don't let it worry your pretty head. Besides, we've got someplace we're supposed to be. You'll see."

He started the powerful TR-2 engine, roaring it a coupla of times for effect.

"Nice car," the clerk shouted from the porch, having watched them step into Maggie.

George waved back to her, "Now there's a girl with her head on straight."

They arrived at Grimes Field off Henneker Street by 3:00 PM. George parked Maggie out of sight in a pre-arranged garage. They walked across a path heading into the offices of Hillsborough Balloon Park.

"Ah, Mister Mansbridge and the lady," greeted the receptionist behind a counter. "Everything's arranged. Your Mister Harrison's taken care of it all. You're good to go anytime. Carl's your pilot today and you should have at least a good hour of flight time."

"George," Carol cooed, "what's this?"

"We're going up, up and away, my dear," he grinned. "You wanted to see autumn, you'll see autumn like you've never seen it before." He grabbed Carol, hugged her close. "Trust me," he jibed, "you'll love it." He kissed her check, turned to the receptionist, "We're ready."

Carl was a man in his 60's with a grizzled look that spoke volumes. He helped both Carol and George into the wicker-covered basket of a large, multi-colored hot air balloon that was being inflated noisily by a propane burner, the roar nearly deafening.

"We'll be taking off soon's Ralph and Claude clear them tethers for us," Carl hollered. "You folks been balloonin' before?"

"Nope," George winked at Carol, "this is something special for both of us."

"Case you'd like to know," Carl shouted, "these here modern balloons are made from about a thousand yards of ripstop nylon or polyester, this 'uns all nylon. She's sewn together with miles of seams. This here basket you're in's woven wicker. Floors light plywood. Use 'em both 'cause they're light, strong, and flexible. Gonna be noisy for awhile. But with these light winds we'll be floatin' in the gloamin' in no time." Carl looked up at the flaming burner as two teenage boys approached.

"Ready to shove off," he shouted to the boys, each one grabbing a tether line. Carl turned-up the flame, its roar drowning out all other noise. The basket lifted with a slight jolt. Carl nodded to the boys below. George beamed at the excitement of his surprise adventure for Carol as heat from the flame warmed the basket. The two boys below released the tethers once a balanced attitude had been reached. The balloon began quaking, then lifted.

Up they rose, passing branches, than treetops, into the New England sky. The sun was far into the West but still well above the horizon. Carol was weirdly disoriented as she clutched the basket's wicker railing, eyes focused on the patchwork dotted landscape below, getting smaller every moment.

"You mighta' noticed," Carl shouted, "there's no steering wheel," grinning at the expression on Carol's face. "Only way to change direction is by ascending or descending into a wind goin' the direction you want."

George looked up into the bowels of the heated balloon, then down at the receding earth beneath them. "See," Carl continued, "air moves in different directions at different altitudes. So we's shiftin' directions by goin' higher, or lower, till we gets what we want. Never know where you're goin' till you be gettin' there. That's part of the charm. Balloon's gonna' go wherever the winds take it."

He reached up, turning down the burner, eliminating the roar of the now flickering flame.

"Here we go," he hollered, still a bit too loudly.

"This one time," Carl continued in his rambling voice, "after I'd left my home in Tennessee, it was back in the 1960s. I was hired to help open an amusement park in L.A. They had me dress up in an Uncle Sam suit, striped hat, white beard and all, then take off in a seventy-five footer with a red white and blue balloon."

Carl now had the full attention of both George and Carol.

"So's this band's playin' *America The Beautiful* as I fire her up and lift off above the park waving my top hat, expecting the offshore winds to blow me down the coast a ways. Well, didn't happen that way. Damn Santa Ana winds blew me out over the Pacific halfways to Catalina Island."

Carl chuckled to himself, then went on, "So then the wind just flat out stopped, a dead zone, and here I'm stuck just sittin' there, waitin' for some breeze to blow me back to shore. And since it was an event, the L.A. news folk are followin' my flight and reportin' it on radio, TV, the works."

Carl turned his head, coughed, continued.

"So's finally, after a coupla' hours just sittin', I get lucky and finagle my way back to shore with a slight onshore breeze, 'cept the only place I can come down is in a restricted Naval Weapons Station in Seal Beach. Lookin' down I see three sailors, rifles pointed at me. One of 'em flippin through a manual, lookin' to see what your s'posed to do when Uncle Sam comes at you in a red white and blue balloon."

They broke out in laughter. "That really happen?" George winced.

"Yup! Goes to show ya'," Carl laughed, "them damn rules and regulations can't keep up with everything." Carol shivered, goosebumps signaling her recognition of such a pervasive truth in his words.

Carl reached over to the burner, turned it off; the sudden silence a surprise to both.

"There's, no wind?" Carol asked. "I thought it'd be windy."

"Nope," said Carl. "Can't feel it cause you're movin' with it. Wouldn't know you was movin' f'you couldn't see the ground."

"Well, I'll be," Carol relaxed.

Turning, she grabbed George by the lapel of his coat, kissed him with unembarrassed passion, leaning back into his arms, "You never cease to amaze me."

Carl turned his back to them, busying himself with this or that.

George wrapped his arms around Carol, held her close, the beat of his heart danced to it's own inner tune. "Well, I certainly hope so," George whispered into Carol's ear. "Because I've one more surprise for you darling. One I've been waiting for, for a long time. Especially now, in this setting, away from the rest of the world."

With that, George released Carol and dropped dramatically to one knee. He reached into a pocket of his sport coat, pulling out a little blue box with the white ribbon, the signature of a purchase from Tiffany's.

Carol stumbled backwards slightly, mouth agape as George snapped open the box, revealing a beautiful diamond engagement ring, the facets catching the last of the day's light sparkled brilliantly.

"Carol Klein, love of my life, will you marry me?" George's voice boomed it.

Carol sputtered. Suddenly, she was mute. Tears filled her eyes, a joyful smile lit up her face. She didn't need to be in a balloon to be floating on air.

"Looks to me like you've caught one," giggled Carl, peering over his shoulder at the scene.

"Oh, George," Carol blurted. "Yes, yes. A million times, Yes!"

"Congratulations." Carl added. "Harrison's got champagne chilled for ya' we get down."

George rose, gathering Carol in his arms. They kissed with a tender passion, holding each other in a tight embrace. They didn't even hear the roar of the burner as it fired up again.

CHAPTER THIRTEEN

We must be willing to get rid of the life we've planned, so as to have the life that is waiting for us.
-Joseph Campbell

Carol was grateful for Wednesday nights. It was George's night to play tennis at the club with his father. She could always count on Wednesdays to catch up on lecture preparation, grading papers or just decompressing. She snuggled on her bed in her favorite flannel pajamas. "If George could see me now he would laugh at such a contrasting costume: plaid pajamas, serious reading glasses; hair in a ponytail right out of the 50's."

Officially engaged for a week, Carol had added the idea of being George's fiancée into her everyday life. She'd begun to see herself in the role of Mrs. George Mansbridge III.

She had so much to plan, the wedding and of course, the honeymoon and the house—his, hers, maybe?

The ring of the telephone popped her daydream. She set down Doctor Lee's Journal, stared at the phone, the reverie of concentration broken, the ringing insistent. One... Two... Three... She heard the familiar click of her answering machine, filling in as her surrogate, then, "Darling? You home? Pick up," the voice of her beloved.

She reached for the phone, hand hovering, then—she dropped the idea. She simply was not in the mood to shift gears to go from flannel pajamas to George's world of white linen and wool tweed. That time was coming soon enough. For now she would just listen.

"Honey? We have an appointment with our PR people, both of us, tomorrow afternoon. Hope you can make it, they want to measure you for wardrobe. You'll look like a million bucks. Love you." Abruptly, he hung up.

She scoffed at the request, This was not what she'd bargained for. She wanted a leave of absence from jumping through these campaign hoops. "Measure me, for a wardrobe? College professors don't wear wardrobes. Look at me now," she chuckled.

She settled back into the pillows against the headboard, looking at the side of her bed that George slept on. Lifting her left hand, grinning at the sight of her engagement ring, admiring the perfection of the taper-cut stones, "George, are you the rough diamond I've been waiting to discover in the rock; is this like Michelangelo's carving his *Pieta*, removing the excess marble only to reveal a statute of pure perfection?"

Free-associating, "And why is it diamonds? Nature makes no such distinctions. coal or diamond, to nature it's all just carbon atoms, arranged this way or that. So, where did the consensus come from making carbon atoms in diamonds more precious than those of coal?"

She smiled, recalling a plum from her undergraduate years, "The word 'fact' comes from the Latin 'factotum', which translates, 'to make it up'."

"Perfect, maybe we're all just making everything up; what suits us is a 'fact; what doesn't fit we dismiss. Maybe we don't see things as they are, only as we want them to be. So, does George see me as I am, or as he wants me to be?" Quickly, wiping that thought off her mental blackboard.

Giddy with the free-fall of these thoughts, she turned to the balancing act of making George happy while pursuing her own career. She hadn't invested all these years becoming a doctor to let it slide away. No way. Along with loving George, her goal was to passionately pursue her career.

Smiling at the thought of their picture-perfect marriage, "Such a pair, congressman George Mansbridge the third and his lovely bride, Doctor Carol Klein-Mansbridge, a leading-edge clinical psychologist." She paused, "Of course, we haven't addressed the hyphen issue yet, but surely, he'd be reasonable."

Smiling at her foolishness, she turned back to the copy of Lee's Journals that were spread out over her patchwork quilt like large playing cards The contrast of these journals reminded her of the evolution of early medical research. In Hippocrates's time illnesses were believed to be caused by bad humors; to be treated by bleeding bad air out of patients, hopefully before the practice killed them. Not until six centuries later during the Renaissance did the invention of the microscope along with the practice of surgical dissection inspire a major a shift in medical understanding.

And today's changes move faster. Especially with all the technological innovations which have radically changed our lives over the past 30 years; computers from room-sized to laptops. In ten years, what by then? What will we believe to be true? Can our understanding keep pace with advancements? Shouldn't our facts be constantly upgraded, like software?

Scanning the covers of Lee's Journals spread before her, "If these studies show that the body reflects the mind, shouldn't medicine look to the mind first? Are these case histories pointing towards a better answer? If Lee is right, that the source of all health crises originate in one's past, even though consciously forgotten—isn't that the first place to look?"

She recalled the words of the balloon pilot, what's his name? *"Goes to show ya', rules and regulations can't keep up with everything."*

She turned to a new page in her notebook and wrote, "Could past life regression be the future of a new medicine?" She underlined the question twice, leaned back and laughed, "Well, sure would change my intake interviews!"

She re-opened the Journal to a marked page, drinking in every word, *"that the breakdown has roots in the body as the result of a prior event. Everything has a context; all events have a sequential logic. Nothing comes from a void; there is no misfortune without a cause. Today's approach to treating symptoms is no more effective than cutting the grass; the lawn will continue to grow. Only when we look deep inside the past for the answer, only then do we pull the weeds out at their roots, eliminating the true core of the problem."*

Case after case portrayed convincing examples of recoveries following hypnotic regression into patient's past lives. Each history led to better, more comprehensive diagnoses while dissipating debilitating chronic problems before they became more serious or even catastrophic.

Closing Lee's journal, she snuggled back into the feather pillows, reminiscing about George's campaign to right the wrongs of the Salem witch trials. Now, we all agree that those ignorant beliefs were flat-out wrong. Couldn't it be the same with our current protocols? Isn't this the same dispute that I'm having with Isobel?"

It was getting late, "Well," she sighed, scooping the pile of journals and papers off her quilt, "later." She was ready, all geared up to discuss these issues with Doctor Lee tomorrow, colleague to colleague.

She switched off the bed lamp, settled back into the deep over-sized, down-filled pillow. Drifting off to sleep, she questioned, "Wonder what's the difference between an innovator and a heretic? The eyes of the beholder, like with the diamond and the coal, or? Hmm. How's that go? If you want to know if a peach is juicy, bite into it."

"Juicy. A peach. A bite. Mmm." She fell into a dreamy sleep with balloons, wedding gowns, towering white-tiered cakes and cherubs dancing around her.

CHAPTER FOURTEEN

This above all: to your own self, be true.
-William Shakespeare

She hadn't agonized long over the choice to be made: follow through with Doctor Lee or spend the afternoon with George's PR people. The last thing on earth she'd wanted to do was disappoint her fiancée, but—there was a stronger pull from Lee's comment, "You have no greater commitment?"

So here she was, standing at the front door of Doctor Phonyong Lee's home, having told George that she had an important professional meeting she "just couldn't get out of." He had little choice other than to accept her little white lie.

Still, she felt torn. If she could just share her dilemma with George; but not yet, the timing's not right. She pushed the button, heard the solemnity of the Asian chimes doorbell.

Doctor Lee appeared, greeted her at the door with a deep, arcane bow.

"Sorry I'm late. Thursdays are so..." Carol stammered.

"Not true, you are precisely on time." He rose, hushing her with a finger to his lips, turned, walked down the mask-laden hallway. She followed, noting the empty stares of each mask she passed by, a chill coursing through her bones.

She entered his office, eyes drawn to the gecko, now clinging to the opposite wall from where it had been during her last meeting here. Lee already was seated cross-legged atop the rosewood platform bench, the picture of serenity. He motioned Carol to a couch across from him.

He cocked his head, peering at her. "Your energy field is different; an added layer of vitality."

"Well," she blushed, "I became engaged to be married a few days ago," unconsciously raising her hand adorned with an engagement ring.

He nodded, face showing no emotion, "A qualified peer?"

"Yes, you might say. He's an attorney, George Mansbridge, the third. You may have heard of ..."

"Ah," his face lit up, "an ambitious attorney with an appetite for politics. Yes, of course I have. His family is well known."

He paused for a long moment, asked, "What was his full name given at birth?"

She winced, You mean on his birth certificate; George Emerson Mansbridge. Emerson's his mother's name going back to the..."

Before she could finish, "The central mystery of human evolution, and the date of his birth?"

"October 1, 1968, why?" She had no idea where this was going, or why.

"These are the things that matter, as...," he drifted into some inner realm, fingers moving in the air as if on an abacus calculating a complex equation, "there are consequences to this development. While we do not know fate, what we can know is destiny. There is much yet to be done."

She got the words but her mind flooded with confusion. She had no idea what George's name and birthday had to do with this meeting. She began to feel she'd made a big mistake coming here today.

Trying to salvage her cause, she decided to ignore his mysterious line of conversation. She'd come prepared to conduct this meeting on a footing stronger than the last time, armed with questions demonstrating that she'd read his case histories. She wanted to show her mettle.

She quickly took the lead, "So Doctor, from your journals I have a few questions, what part of our free will plays into..."

If Carol was more attentive to his queues and less immersed in her agenda, she'd have seen that although Lee's eyes were on her, he was paying not the least bit of attention to her content.

Having uncovered this new evidence on George, Lee concentrated on the structure of Carol's face; noting her oval shaped features, chevron cheekbones and pale complexion— a picture-perfect model of the Chinese element's 'metal face'. He had learned Chinese face reading at the knee of his great aunt. Back to the time of Confucius, in the sixth century BC, Chinese doctors understood that the face represents our inner energies and fortune, revealing knowledge of one's true personality traits. He had spent much time studying the classic Treatise of the Bamboo Chronicles and the Golden Scissors. The lessons show that the face reflects our emotional profile while mapping our past history, our present condition and predicts future fortunes, "reflecting that which we've earned."

Oblivious, Carol hummed along to her own drum, "... Your hypothesis of why your patient's had such rapid improvements, when you. ...."

Intrigued by her features, he concluded, "Yes, she is the one tapped for this assignment."

The cogs in the wheel of time were now aligning. He admired her stubbornness, determination, strong will and achievements against many odds. He respected her work ethic. It was a pleasure watching her impassioned enthusiasm. The next few moments would unveil what they both had been waiting for, however, at this moment, only Lee possessed this insight, well aware that both parties must consent. He smiled, "Yes, she will pass the test."

Still sailing through her notes, she was unaware of the workings of Lee's mind, as she continued to elucidate her insights, "Of course, your evidence appears anecdotal. However, like physical DNA the meeting of our emotional and ..."

Lee knew that time is our most valuable commodity and that while the young are very rich, we all must spend it wisely. He'd waited this long for her path to cross his. He could wait patiently while she droned on, oblivious to why she was really here.

Ignorant of the impending deadline, Carol ended her barrage, "Doctor, having analyzed what you've seen, do you believe we might be able to contact our departed loved ones?"

What came next was the last thing that she expected.

He spoke as if continuing a conversation that had begun some time ago, totally ignoring her presentation, announcing, "Doctor, your legacy will be to show the healing power of repairing past traumas."

She shuddered at this sudden turn of events as if the rug had been pulled out from under her. She was freefalling, totally incapable of processing what she'd just heard.

Then, the brickbat, "Today we begin our search for decisive moments from your own previous lifetimes."

Did she hear that right? "No" was her fragile defense, "this is not what I signed up for, I came for answers. Not, what?"

She bolted from the couch. "Doctor, I am not one of your research subjects, No! I'm not here to be a patient, I'm a doctor, just like you!"

In a mock reproach, he nodded politely, listening to her protests. He understood her, in ways she had yet to understand herself. Like an iron fist in a velvet glove, Lee motioned her to sit, disarming her, "One question, Doctor, do you ever have the feeling that you've lived before?" Without waiting for her reply, "You know your days on this earth are numbered; the hourglass sand is running. You don't know when you will be called to leave or return. Think about it Doctor; you are what you were!"

Folding her arms across her chest and determined not to acquiesce, she refused to engage with him. She was clearly over her depth. Trepidation permeated her every pore.

He motioned her to lie back onto the couch, all but dismissing her resistant protests.

"But, that's not what, I …"

Without warning, he leaned, whispered into her right ear, "Your only assignment is to follow your rightful dream."

The words triggered a code that unlocked her core. Astonished, emotion flooded her being, "Follow my dream. Those are my Grammy's very words!"

She saw no other choice. It was time to surrender.

Lee raised his hand, a finger pointing skyward, eyes burning into hers. She blinked, feeling thoroughly disarmed. It was hard to put into words, but Lee's calm presence exuded a quality of confidence that filled the entire room with peace and harmony. Applying his gentle gaze, he penetrated her armor, barricades breached. She laid down her arms. Up until this moment she'd never considered exploring such a domain about herself, thinking, "It's one thing to write a prescription for a patient, it's another taking the medicine yourself."

It was incredulous to her that she would ever be searching past lifetimes of her own.

She drew in a deep breath, feeling as if the air in this room were impregnated with powers of its own.

She knew what to expect. This was terrain she'd often explored with her own patients, but now here she was traversing the landscape for herself. She settled deep into the couch with a newfound sense of tenuous comfort. On her own, she took in deep breaths, eyes slowly closed as she drifted inward, deep inside, curling up into that familiar cove of self-awareness, hearing only what sounded like an echo, the distant voice of Phonyong Lee, "I implore you, part the curtain of illusion that separates time now, from time past."

Having fallen into the dimension between the in-breath and the out-breath, she reached her destination, a dominion beyond current experience, fresh, ripened with profound familiarity.

She drifted into a slightly altered state of consciousness, a light trance with a fleeting thought that she'd remember decades from now. But, for now that's all it remained, a fleeting thought, erased as she felt herself drifting into a realm familiar.

The origin of psychology comes from Greek word Psukhe, defined as the study of the soul and the journey of the spirit. Her book of life open to a page she had once viewed long before.

In utero, auditory senses develop well before those of our visual acuity.

Perhaps that was why the first thing she became aware of was the music.

CHAPTER FIFTEEN

Life is the soul's nursery–its training place for destinies of eternity.
-William Makepeace Thackeray

At first, she heard only the piano—rich chords underpinning a melody.
Her awareness sharpened as a scene began to take focus as if out of a fog.
There it was: sheet music, open and propped atop a baby grand piano.
Clefs with musical notes peppering the horizontal scales filling the sheet, a
title centered on top:

Prelude
Words and Music by
Iris Middelton Paulson
©1941

Now, the hands of a woman playing came into view; fingers moving
lightly, easily over the field of black and white keys. The woman, perhaps in
her late forties, wearing a neck-high dress with short sleeves at the piano,
was playing, rocking side-to-side, head lolling, eyes closed shut.
Filling an alcove, the piano stands framed by a set of double French
windows looking over a cityscape, tall buildings beyond a peek-a-boo view
of a large park. A summer sun glowed into what likely is a west-facing
room. Tucked behind the piano bench, a large davenport in a mohair velvet
chocolate brown, close to a French secretary's desk. Across the room a portrait
came into focus: a man and woman seated behind two young boys.
Carol saw this as an upscale townhouse, furnished in fabrics of rich

brocades, brown and gold before floor-to-ceiling drapes with delicate fleur-de-lis white-on-white patterns, a dark brown parquet floor, covered partially by an intricately patterned Turkish rug.

For a moment, Carol floated with the melody, the piece sounding somehow familiar to her, like a visit from an old friend. Rising, the music flooded the room. She began humming the tune, surprised that she knew the melody.

Suddenly, the woman stiffened, fingers frozen on a chord. She pitched forward; forearms landing hard on the keys, a crashing sound of discordant notes.

Out of nowhere, two young men scrambled into the room, racing to the woman's side. As she gripped the sides of the piano, her face pressed against the keys.

"Ma!" shouted the taller of the two. Both men grab her arms, slowly lifting her from the bench, a grimace of pain twisting her face.

"My God!" said the shorter man, helping move her to the large davenport where she lie breathing in short bursts, chest heaving, panic in her eyes as he lifted her outstretched hand, fingers pressed into her wrist.

"Ma!" Screamed the taller man, "can you hear me? It's Will. Ethan and I heard the crash, and ..."

The woman's eyes opened, like curtains parting, eyes darting at the men leaning over her.

"It's okay Ma. You'll be okay!" Ethan blurted in a high pitched voice.

He grasped her shoulders, lifting her head slightly while Will placed a pillow behind her neck. He turned to the younger man, "Ethan. Go tell the doorman! I'll call an ambulance. Hurry!"

Ethan leapt to his feet, raced out of the room.

Will hollered after him, "Take the stairs!"

The woman's face turned to the left as she closed her eyes shut again, a long exhale puffed out from her lungs. Will took hold of her hand, pulled it tightly to his cheek.

"You'll be alright Ma," he cried fighting back tears. "Hold on. I'm calling for help."

The woman's eyes follow him as he scrambled to the secretary desk, picked up the telephone, frantically dialing, "Hello, Yes. We need an ambulance!" speaking rapidly, "Immediately. Yes! Two-five-seven, Park Avenue, fourth

81

floor. The doorman knows. It's my mother, Iris Paulson, what? Don't know. Maybe a stroke or something. Forty-eight. Yes, not very responsive. Yes, yes. Me? William Paulson. Her son. Look, just hurry!"

The woman named Iris Paulson closed her eyes, and with the remaining strength in her right hand grasped a gold heart-shaped locket hanging from a twisted gold necklace clutching it tightly.

Ethan reappeared in the room, eyes darting between his mother and Will, "How is she?"

"Don't know," William blurted, eyes glistened with fear, "Ma? You hear me? MA!"

Abruptly, the sound of a loud CLAP shifted Carol's attention; the scene fogging over, fading into nothingness, replaced by the sound of Doctor Lee's voice.

"You will remember every detail. When I count down now from three to one, you will be fully awake, alert and rested. You will remember everything you witnessed, every detail, everything; 3—2—1." Carol became aware that her body was lying on Lee's couch, eyes opening, scanning the room, coming to rest, locking in on Lee's stare.

"You did well," smiled Lee, poised with a notepad, "tell me."

Carol's eyes were blinking as if trying to come into focus. She pressed her head into the pillow trying to find some reference point. "I, a woman. Iris, something." She murmured stumbling through her mind's cloud. "Iris Middelton Paulson. I saw the name on sheet music ... then, she collapsed."

Lee looked up from his notepad, "Yes, where often we meet, a point of mortal crisis."

"Pre, Prelude," Carol stuttered, "I saw the title, of the song. Prelude."

She bent her arms, interlaced her fingers feeling as if she'd been swept away by a roaring river. She placed her hands under her head. Her impulsive posturing surprised her, recognizing the vulnerable circumstances into which she was treading.

"Then," she went on, "these two men..."

"Prelude?" Lee interrupted, "you say the title, Prelude?"

Carol nodded "yes" never taking her eyes off Lee, a smile brightening his face.

"It has been written, each existence is but a prelude, one that leads to the next. Then adding on to another, then yet another, as every soul is a complex melody on a journey of transformation. Until, at last, it is complete."

Unlacing her hands, she propped up on an elbow, furled her brow as she attempted to find the right vocabulary, then echoing Doctor Lee's words…"A prelude, that each one, I mean, our lives are just part of a journey? One after another?"

"Yes," he stated, "one after another. And this woman, named Iris, she knew."

A puzzled look crossed Carol's face.

"You will learn soon enough," he grinned. "This moment with Iris, it was no mistake. There is always a reason. Now you have been made aware. No longer can you ignore this truth. More will follow. But for now, tell no one of this experience. It is too early."

They looked at other in silence until Carol nodded in agreement.

Lee rose gracefully, stood, placing the palms of his hands together, bowed his head in respect, underscoring their implicit pact of secrecy.

"Please remember, there is more here than is visible. Your Iris will let you know."

He straightened, turned, and stealthily walked out his office door. She heard from the hallway in the wake of Doctor Lee's footsteps, "Worth the wait, well worth the wait."

CHAPTER SIXTEEN

Life shrinks or expands in proportion to one's courage.
-Anais Nin

She had to tell someone.

She desperately needed George. She craved his understanding of what she'd gotten caught up in, despite her promise to tell no one. "But George isn't just someone, he's *the* one," she mused; further justifying her action.

George had agreed to meet her at Emmett's on Beacon, his favorite downtown pub, for a mid-afternoon beverage. She saw him from across the room as he sailed through the door in his tan London Fog trench coat. Anxiety filled her; she had no idea how to explain her plight, let alone make it understandable to her fiancé.

George spotted Carol at an oaken table against the back wall, as far from the bar as you could get. She saw him wink at a female bartender as he walked by. Reaching her table, he pulled out a chair, leaned, lips pursed for a hello peck, then plopped down, heavily.

"Splendid idea," he grinned. "Told my secretary I had an appointment with Mister Adams. Think she's onto me?" laughing at his own joke.

Carol's sugarcoated smile belied the task at hand, a story, improbable, but true. She held her gaze on the bottle of Adams Ale sitting before her, alongside her half-empty schooner.

"Same for you?" asked a waitress in Emmett's shamrock-green apron who suddenly appeared, smiling down at George.

"Yes, please," he answered, eyes darting to Carol, "another?"

Carol shook her head, "No thanks."

"Missed you at the photo session," baiting his remark. "Still gotta' get you measured, for wardrobe you know. Can you get to it soon?"

Carol nodded, guilt coloring her face. "George," she sheepishly uttered, "I have a confession to make."

"Well," he chuckled with playful sparks, "perhaps we can plea bargain. Let's hear it."

"When I missed the meeting Thursday I wasn't at a professional meeting," she admitted demurely, eyes looking into her glass. "Well, not really, it was more like an appointment."

George's brow furled, his grin fading.

"No, George," she smiled, placing a hand over his on the tabletop, "nothing like that. But it's something I want you to know."

The waitress returned with a frosty bottle of Samuel Adams Ale and an equally chilled schooner, placing both before him. "Maybe I'll have that next one after all," Carol conceded, "next time you're coming this way, might as well bring him one too."

"You make it sound like I'll need it," George groaned.

Carol shifted in her seat, pulled her hand back and leaned in on her elbows.

"What I'm about to tell can't go anywhere else," she blurted out, "at least not now. In fact, I shouldn't be telling you. It's just—I love you! I'm not to tell anyone, but ..."

"What the hell you talking about?"

Carol leaned back, "Okay, remember that patient I told you about? The one who seemed to return to a past life? As a young girl in a covered wagon in the eighteen-fifties?"

George's eyes rolled, "Not that again."

"And," she pushed, "re-living some event from the distant past, then she practically skipped out, carrying her walker? And now her doctor says she's nearly recovered!"

George blinked, turned to fill his schooner. He paused, taking a long sip, a practiced timeout ritual learned from years of litigating, his way of pressing the refresh button on his nervous system: Stop. Regroup. Charge forward.

"What's any of this got to do with your missing our PR session?"

"That's the thing," she pleaded, "I've met this researcher, a medical doctor, with a Ph.D. in psychology. He's been studying, cataloging past life regression cases for years. Hundreds of them."

"And," peering into her eyes for answers he'd understand.

No longer able to beat around the bush, she launched headlong into her confession, "That's who I met with Thursday. I'm sorry!" Her face turned crimson, she was on the verge of tears. She looked up at George, pleading with her eyes, thinking, "How can I make him know how hard this is for me?"

Her voice quavering, "He said I had no choice; that I had to be there, that nothing's more important than ...," flashing back to her session with Doctor Lee, her voice broke off, she fought to hold back the flood of emotions. She had to be taken seriously, not just as some wimpy woman.

"Jeez, Carol, calm down," sympathetically taking her hand in his. "Get hold of yourself."

Carol squeezed his hand a little too tightly.

"That's not it," she blurted out, "there's more."

"Shoot," pulling his hand back, grasped his schooner.

"Here you go," said the waitress, two fresh Sammies on her tray. Looking at Carol, she knew better than to linger.

Carol composed herself, took a slight sip from her schooner fearing how volatile this confession could get. "Okay, this doctor, his name is Lee, Phonyong Lee, he used to be at the university. But his work in past life therapies got him fired. So, that's all he's been doing for years now. As a full time researcher."

"You already said that," George's voice tinged with impatience.

"Sorry," summoning her remaining strength. "See, I've been reading many of his case studies, his research papers." She paused, gasping for another breath. "I think he's onto something."

"You do?" George speculated, "Past life research? Like reincarnation?"

Eyes watering, "Yes. Yes, I really do."

George huffed, leaned heavily back in his chair.

"There's more," she cried, thinking, "here it comes, the big-ticket

86

item."

Trying to speak as softly and calmly as possible, "On Thursday, Doctor Lee, he put me under. Hypnotically. He wanted to show me; to experience it for myself, go back into a past life. One of my own."

"Holy shit," George spewed too loudly. "You didn't."

"Just, let me tell you! I saw an event from a past life. I felt it. It could be mine!"

"And who might that have been Carol, Cleopatra?"

"C'mon George! Please! Listen. I really, really need you to understand."

He turned stoic, saying nothing.

"I saw a woman, an older woman, playing the piano in what looked like a Park Avenue apartment. Yes, that's it. It was Park Avenue because I heard them mention the address."

"Them?" George questioned.

"Wait. You'll see. As she's playing the piano, she collapses, a stroke or something, falls onto the keys, and two young men, her children I think, come running in to help her. They call for an ambulance, that's when I heard the address. And, and well, that's it."

"That's it?"

"That's when Doctor Lee brought me out of it. He said there's a message there. That something profound is happening that it was not by accident. And that I'm a part of it." Her mind raced, exhausted at banging her head against George's brick wall.

George leaned forward to grasp his ale, downed half the schooner.

Carol knocked her knuckles on the table, "George, believe me. It was as real as this table. I saw her playing. I saw the sheet music. Something I've never heard, called Prelude, but then again, I knew it. I knew the tune, without knowing it."

"OhmiGod," George sighed.

"What I'm telling you is, I went back to a past life, one of mine," she blurted.

She paused, looking for a reaction other than the one she was seeing as he gaped at her in shocked silence, the logic eluding him completely.

"I know it sounds strange, but it happened," in a staccato outburst, her eyes moist with tears, "I can't refute it. Not now, not after this. I know for certain they exist, past lives. And we can reach them. I reached one myself. Don't you see? How can I ignore that? Just because Isobel told me to stop?"

George's ears perked up, "Your department head? What'd she say?"

"She told me to come up with solutions other than past lives, that they're not on the approved list of acceptable standard protocols."

"You mean, she told you to forget this past life nonsense?"

Carol nodded, cheeks flushing red.

"Maybe that's what you should do then," he reasoned, "stop."

Carol's face tightened in anguish, "But what if I find that by accessing past lives, I can help heal patients, like in Alden's case? Don't you see? I've seen what it can do."

He leaned forward, reached, took her hand in his.

"You know," he said tenderly, "if she told you that, that's what you should do. You've got your future, our future, to think about."

Carol pulled her hand out of George's grasp.

"You don't believe me!"

"I don't know what to believe. All I know is, in law, what's true, is who wins."

He lifted his schooner, finished off the ale, set down the empty vessel, looked at Carol.

His voice was soft, but his eyes were firm, "Sweetheart, it's best you just give it up."

CHAPTER SEVENTEEN

Our destination is never a place, but rather a new way of looking at things.
-Henry Miller

Ground fog drifted in wisps across the empty campus, wrapping Watson Hall in its embrace.

She adored the early Sunday morning silence, freedom to think in the softness of the quiet surroundings, alone in her office, journal in hand, Carol's thoughts spilled out about how the concealed truths of our lives shape our experiences.

Except that today she faced a turf war; on one side—that which she knew, on the other—that which she needed to know: pitting the known of medical science against the unknown depths of the mysteries of human consciousness.

She began rocking in her chair, too hard, back and forth, fuming, "Must everyone tell me what to do? Isobel, Lee, George. GEORGE? *SWEETHEART MY ASS!* I can't begin to describe how ticked off I am at you right now. Don't you see how serious I am? You get anything I said yesterday?" She cupped both hands over her face. "And Isobel? What's she so afraid of?"

"Doctor Lee's probably right—what we know of human consciousness hasn't gone far enough. Why do some become a Mozart, others an Attila the Hun?"

Questions racked her brain. Rising, she began pacing back and forth. "If Lee's right—that unresolved issues from past lives are the root causes shaping who we are; influencing who we could become, then, Bam! Its a whole new ball game!"

Her training had stressed that there is no better proof of a scientific hypothesis than direct experience. Anything less is mere speculation. Her meeting with Lee had been just that, personal and tangible. And Susan Alden's episode, and her rapid recovery was also just as transparent.

How could she possibly begin to explain these experiences from everything she had been previously taught?

Scanning her inner files on behavioral medicine, the branch of science bridging the body-mind connection; where psychology and physiology intersect. Somewhere, there must be a brain-heart-soul link, a place where we seamlessly interconnect with the universe. The mystery of mysteries: how does this work?

Before running too far ahead, she planted her feet firmly back on the ground. Diagnostically, the litmus test of clinical regression is that the person actually *feels* the scene, all the tastes, smells, every sensation—the experience is as if fully being there. It's the difference between reading about swimming and actually jumping into the deep end of the pool. This form of personal knowledge cannot be imagined.

The implications of recalling our past lives to create a better future felt both daunting and compelling. She began to scroll through the seemingly unlimited applications of regression therapy. "What if the people we know are actually an extension of relationships that were left incomplete from another time? Are we just continuing what we didn't finish, last time? Holy cow! Would that ever change our understanding of the entanglements in our family dynamics! Or explain the contentious challenges in marital therapy; continuing the relationship we didn't fulfilled with the same players—again and again? Or....," she trailed off into the most irrational thought of her life, "And how does this redefine 'until death do us part'?"

She treaded lightly on the repercussions to her career by promoting treatments grown from the seeds embedded in another time.

"Well, either it's real or it's not! The only way to test this hypothesis is through scientific analysis," she mumbled.

Staring down the deluge of uncertainties, she gave voice to her qualms, "How can I continue current treatments when I know there may be a better way?" The sobering thought seized her breath, "Am I willing to risk my career to find out? Do what you've been trained in; prevention, diagnosis, treatment. Catalog the observations, then consult with Doctor Lee." She had to admit, as incredulous as it was, she trusted him. She'd read enough of his papers to know that he was onto something. And she had to know more about it.

"What are my choices?" her tenuous resolve questioned. "Feign ignorance? Pretend I hadn't opened this door? Conform to current protocols, accepting the limitations of incomplete science masquerading as adequate treatments when I know there is a yet another way?"

Carol rose from the chair, walked back to the window, seeing her own reflection mirroring at her against the background of heavy mist, and like a whisper from eternity she declared aloud; "Okay Doctor, you're either in or you're out, there is no second way."

She turned to her laptop computer. The machine hummed into life. She clicked on the e-mail that was highlighted Susan Alden—David Yarnell M.D., moving the cursor to the reply box, clicked it open.

Carol's fingers glided over the keyboard. What was previously a blank screen was rapidly filled with the words: *Doctor Yarnell, I've received your referrals. I can begin therapy with your patients in two week's time. C. Klein, Ph.D.*, moving the cursor to Send, clicked it, saying, "One down," began typing anew.

> *Doctor Lee: Though I may be out of my league, I am committed to exploring your implications of reincarnation for myself. My knowledge on this subject is limited. My tools for making this connection are inadequate. I'll need your help in order to understand. When can we meet again? Carol Klein, Ph.D.*

Either through ignorance or sheer innocence, the tide had turned. Carol closed her eyes, pressed Send, saying, "Game's on!"

PRELUDE

She had one more e-mail to write, one which never would be sent.

It was the source of her greatest conflict. Carol wanted to e-mail George and share with him her decision to see Doctor Lee again. But she couldn't. And wouldn't. That risk likely had no reward. Misleading him was wrong. But being disingenuous to herself was even worse.

Outside, the fog had lifted.

CHAPTER EIGHTEEN

Security is mostly superstition. It does not exist in nature, nor do the children of men as a whole experience it. Avoiding danger is no safer in the long run that out right exposure–life is either a daring adventure, or nothing.
-Helen Keller

Carol awoke slowly the next morning, feeling vaguely uneasy.

"This must be what a butterfly feels like, wings folded back, about to be tested as it emerges from the shelter of the cocoon." She knew there'd be no going back to caterpiller-dom, not now, not ever.

Enlivened by her new sense of resolve, she stepped into the bright autumn morning, striding off to teach her Advanced Personality class of graduate students. She'd become quite fond of this small class, as it gave her an opportunity to really get to know her students and mentor them through their internships.

Walking through the quad, she mulled over her new determination, feeling the weight of yet another transition, first George—and now, this?

Knowing she was about to dive into the deep end, swimming in a new, pristine sea of discovery, ready to challenge the very authority she'd always relied on. Surprisingly, she felt completely refreshed, more alive than ever. "After all, life can't be lived by proxy, either you're on the field as a player or in the stands watching."

Basking in this new identity, she entered the classroom, chirping a bright, "Good morning, doctors," as her students eagerly took their places around an oval conference table.

PRELUDE

Perhaps overly inspired, Carol inexplicably stepped onto an invisible soapbox.

"Okay students today, doctors tomorrow," she grinned it. "This morning, I have something different to offer, rather than recap where we left off last week. Today, I want us to look at the history of flawed science and its consequences upon medical treatment."

Her statement captured their attention; it was not like Doctor Klein to deviate from the syllabus. She waited as the students settled into their chairs, their full attention on her.

"All set?" she began, "good. Our focus will be on incidences in which mistaken beliefs and faulty science led to errors in treatment, that too often ended in fatal results. Not for the purpose of criticism and judgment, not at all. We know medical mistakes can be made by well-meaning people, doctors who followed the Hippocratic oath. But rather, let's examine the blunders made due to accepting beliefs in flawed science, causing medical procedures that led to no benefit for the patient or worse, a catastrophic outcome. Over the centuries, too many doctors have been blinded by the ignorance of their times and clinging stubbornly to beliefs that were dead wrong."

She let the last two words sink into their minds.

"Always remember, doctors, that in spite of our highest ideals; medicine and science are merely man-made constructs, subject to our limitations as human beings. This is not to point fingers or find fault, but rather to learn from the misconceptions in order to advance to the next level of medical knowledge. Doctors, this is your utmost duty: to find the prevailing errors in today's science that will go to heal your future patients."

The thought flashed in her mind, "Where're these words coming from?"

She cleared her throat, "One only has to look back to the once-acceptable treatment of bloodletting, a belief that led to George Washington's death, for an example of a mistaken belief of their times. And it lasted for decades; until the practice was finally discredited by an advancing medical community."

Her students nodded, glancing among themselves as she continued.

94

"Unfortunately, the list of blunders goes on; such wrong-headed treatments as the practice of injecting mercury as a cure for syphilis. Or in the early days of mental illness treatments, which included a protocol of injecting patients with insulin, inducing a comatose state. Bad as that seems today, this practice later paved the way for ice-pick lobotomies, a dangerous, sometimes deadly treatment. Both therapies rendered the patient docile and quietly manageable, that is, before they died. Do no harm? Hardly in play, when you look back at it today."

Several students looked at each other, showing signs of uneasiness at the topic.

Her voice rising, "It's barely one hundred fifty years since Doctor Ignaz Philipp Semmelweis contradicted the medical wisdom of the day. It was a time when doctors believed diseases of all sorts were caused by a wide variety of sources, few of which had any relation to the illness themselves. What he observed was a direct correlation between women dying of childbed fever while in the same hospitals where autopsies were being performed. What he deduced while monumental, though most unpopular in that days' medical circles."

She smiled, "Why? Because he claimed that the deadly fevers were being transferred to their patients by the doctors themselves. You see, first the doctor's were performing their autopsies and then going directly to examining obstetric patients."

A few students nodded in acknowledgement of these archival facts.

"So," she beamed back at the attentive stares, "what was Semmelweis's radical innovation, his answer to solve this fatal problem?"

She waited, no student raised a hand.

"Semmelweis's simply recommended that before conducting internal examinations, doctors should scrub. That's all, just wash up. Once scrubbing became routine, the number of childbed fever deaths dropped radically. His conclusions were empirically validated."

Watching her student's reaction, a general murmur throughout the room, she spoke up, passion in her voice, "So, how did the establishment react to the good doctor's scientific discovery? He was ridiculed, rejected and dismissed from his hospital. He was committed to an asylum where he died. Why? Because having to take the trouble to scrub was antithetical to the medical procedures of the day!"

She paused, letting the point sink in.

"Shortly after his death, Semmelweis's call for cleanliness by scrubbing was vindicated by one of his students, Louis Pasteur, who discovered the source of the bacterium responsible for childbed fever was indeed transferred following procedures during autopsies. Obviously, his mentor had been right all along."

She dropped her head as in a show of respect, then raised it in challenge.

"Were those doctors of that age indifferent, irresponsible? No! Of course not—they just couldn't, or wouldn't, let go of their established ways of doing things. *Res ipse loquitu,* it speaks for itself. They just couldn't let go of their beliefs, and the consensual definition of their known reality."

She paused, caught her breath.

"Why am I telling you this today? You students, future doctors, all of you; you must be willing to stand up to those who stubbornly hold onto past precepts rather than accept advances in procedure. You must join the struggle to find new solutions, new protocols if necessary, to do justice to your generation. Just as Semmelweis did for his."

Pivoting, she turned her back to the graduate students and wrote on the chalkboard in large bold print, *"Verbum Sapienta."* She turned, looked back at the Latin term, spoke the translation, "Word to the wise. It will soon be your turn to leave your mark. Stand on the shoulders of the courageous pioneers who dared to tell the truth."

She peered into the eyes of her students, "Even today, medical errors, idiopathic causes, are responsible for more deaths than car accidents, AIDS, and other diseases combined! More than one hundred thousand people still die every year in our modern hospitals from infections received in these institutions and the same number die from surgical mistakes as well."

She paused, trusting the sheer numbers to soak in. "Time is an equal opportunity employer. We all have the same twenty-four/seven each day. What will you do with your time? We know science can't discover or invent more time. It's impossible to save it for the future. And not even a king's ransom can buy it. And yet we all want more.

Life is all about time and how we use it. Think how much time you've already wasted. How are you planning to invest your future? Particularly, because you don't know how much you have left. Maybe it seems like you've all the time in the world but don't waste a moment of it. Life goes by way too fast."

With a grand sweeping gesture towards the large classroom windows she said, "Just look at those falling leaves. Only a few months ago they were green, dancing freely in the sunshine, dreaming of the future, a future they ultimately knew nothing about. And now their time is at an end, at least in this form."

Having struck a raw nerve in the collective consciousness of her students, their restless squirming ignited a quick inner review of their own timelines.

"I'd like to leave you with this thought before we go on with the rest of our curriculum today, you can change the past with the present. And maybe, someday we will use the mind as a time machine to...."

BRRRRRRING. A cell phone ring tone blared.

All eyes turned toward the piercing sound, as student Dennis O'Reilly fumbled with his phone, quickly turned it off, mumbling an apology.

Carol took this alarm bell as a wake-up call for herself and changed gears.

"Okay. Now, let's pick up where we left off last week," she said. "Let's explore the effects on shaping one's tendencies through Aversion Theory, Temperament Models and Neural Memory Synapses."

She gestured towards a male student seated at the opposite end of the conference table, "Doctor Barnett, would you begin by sharing your report please?"

Thomas Barnett pushed his chair back, stood, he adjusted his notes, cleared his throat, "Theoretical Advances in the Behavioral Diagnosis and Management of ..."

Carol could barely keep her attention on Barnett's oral report. She kept drifting back into the errors of medicine's history. She felt like she was straddling historical dilemmas in current time. At this moment all she could do was lean forward into the prevailing wind to see where destiny would direct her.

She knew instinctively that when she got back to her office there would be an e-mail waiting from Doctor Lee. She needed to unveil the 'yet to be explored potential' she felt in her bones, wondering, "How can I feel so strongly about something I know so little about?"

It was no longer a matter of if she would go forward; it was only a matter of when. Her intuition told her it would be soon, very soon. What she didn't know was that her 'intuitive-soon' was coming before she could've guessed.

The class continued with no one noticing she wasn't really there.

CHAPTER NINETEEN

The greater the contrast, the greater the potential. Great energy only comes from a correspondingly great tension between opposites.
-C. G. Jung

It was well past midnight.

The heavy mist off the harbor coated the windshield like a woven linen blanket. Nicholas Mansbridge turned the windshield wipers on reluctantly. Not only did it smear the dirt, but they reminded him of the syncopated metronome that sat on the piano and ticked away his youth.

"Damn waste," pushing the past out of his head.

Pressing the Bluetooth button on the car's console, he bellowed at the lighted dashboard; "Call Harrison." The familiar female computer voice immediately replied, "Did you say, call Harrison?"

Annoyed at being dictated to by technology but having no recourse, Nick spat out, "Yes, Dammit!"

Across town, the jarring ring of his cell phone snapped Harrison from a dead sleep. Like all foot soldiers, he knew the first law of duty is sleep when you can. War does not keep convenient hours.

Caller ID announced in bold letters the sleep-intruder's name.

"Nick?" Harrison hastily answered, knowing full well his job was 24/7, on call. He was the elephant sweeper, cleaning up the messes after the parade. It suited him well. If he weren't doing Nick's bidding on this side of the law, then…we'll he'd be a mercenary by any other name for any other side. Either paid very well. He was looking forward to an end-of year annual bonus; his eyes on a new Silver 911 Porsche sports car, just under six figures. So—a few midnight runs a year, easy money.

"Harrison, that Klein woman, I want her vetted, well vetted; to her third grade report card. Go back as far as you can. And her family, too. Don't want any surprises, got it?"

"Yes, sir." Harrison well understood the chain of command. He'd hunker down into the trenches tonight and with any luck, he'd have the preliminary report on Nick's desk by the first light of day. It wouldn't be the first time he'd arrive at the office door at the same time the Wall Street Journal was being dropped off. Yes, he was Nick's delivery boy, but the pay was worth it.

The phone line went silent. Nick was never one for formalities.

It would be a long night. Harrison stomped into the kitchen and pounded the strong dark Turkish coffee grinds into his espresso maker. The aromatic steam wafted up from the espresso machine. The dark chocolate colored coffee grounds melting under pressure dripped into the awaiting demitasse cup. The aroma itself had a caffeine charge that alerted his brain cells to 'come to attention'.

In the old days, when they first got started, he'd hit the road in the middle of the night to do his vetting. But tonight the internet, what a marvel for his line of work—more dirt, less time.

"Let's see what your hiding, Georgie's girl," he chuckled with anticipation.

CHAPTER TWENTY

What lies behind us and what lies before us are tiny matters compared to what lies within us.
-Ralph Waldo Emerson

The slant of the blinds muted the sunlight's intensity into the room.

Carol stretched out on Doctor Lee's couch under a small hand-woven woolen lap blanket covering her from toes to torso, like a corpse. The warmth was welcome on this, a chilly fall afternoon.

Carol knew this was to be her first big test, a requirement to graduate to the next level. She wasn't fully prepared for this moment, but knowing that taking the test sooner was better than later.

She wanted this chapter behind her, to find out once and for all whether to say 'yea' or 'nay'. Her inner conflict came to an end at the drone of Lee's voice: "Life is one great dream from which we all will awaken. Carol, see yourself stepping onto an escalator, going down. Feel the gentle gliding movement down, down, as you relax, deep, now deeper. You are moving ever-so-slowly. Relaxed, so relaxed. You are nearly there. Sights are coming into view, in sharp focus as you move close, ever so close to your goal. You're coming to the bottom now. Take your first step into it, now ..."

At first, Carol saw a man's face slowly come into focus. He is seated at a table at an outdoor café on a sunny afternoon. Then, a young woman arrives, stopping at the table.

"Mister Eastman?" the woman asked, extending her hand, "I'm Iris Middelton."

"And, I might add, right on time," he greeted.

Carol recognized this Iris as a younger version of the older Iris she had seen during her last such encounter. This time she was in her early 20's, wearing a green tweed skirt and a stylish open necked pale yellow blouse that draped beneath a short double-breasted wool jacket.

Eastman motioned her to sit. Iris pulled out the metal chair across from him. On the table Carol saw demitasse cups and a stack of magazines, 'The Masses' dated May, 1916.

Carol's attention riveted on the scene, as if she was watching a movie, frame by frame.

Iris nervously blurted out, "Mister Eastman? I..."

"Max," he corrected, looked her up and down, a sly smirk on his face, "Sherwood Anderson says you've the right stuff. Known him long?"

"Yes. I mean, no. He knew my father and,..." Iris replied a little too quickly, then tailed off.

Leaning back, elongating the moment, he seemed to enjoy her awkwardness, "Before we published him, he worked in advertising. You know that?"

Iris shook her head, "No."

"He hated advertising. That's what I liked about him," laughing at his insight. "Fear not dear lady, your work is impressive. I like what I've seen of your writings. I believe we think alike; unless I'm wrong, and I seldom am, you'll fit in quite nicely."

She nodded. He smiled, reached for his wallet, pulled out a five-dollar bill and plucked it down on top of the magazines that were stacked on the table. "Let's go meet your new mates."

Just as abruptly, sliding back his chair, Eastman stood. Iris looked up, alarmed as he pivoted on his heels, motioned her to follow, then, in long strides, began to walk away.

She jumped up, rapidly walked to catch up to until they were walking shoulder to shoulder.

Carol began to notice familiar landmarks as Iris and Max walked through Greenwich Village. The landmarks were unmistakable: right behind her was Washington Square Park. Remarkably, Carol could hold her awareness of the landmarks and her attention on the storyline at the same time.

Iris asked, "Mr. Eastman? You forgot your..."

He interrupted, "Max, and I always leave copies for the proletariats. It's good for them."

Iris looked up at him nodded, a relaxed grin brightening her face.

Eastman continued with a blaring prideful grin, "You'll be joining the best damn team of writers in America, the ones who actually run The Masses. We writers do as we please. We bow to no one. Not our advertisers. Not even our readers. We print what's too true for the moneymaking press of this belligerent nationalistic country."

Iris's glanced away in astonishment, having no idea how to reply.

Eastman stopped abruptly before a brownstone, stepping up onto the landing of the entrance. With a sweeping motion, he motioned to the door. "Welcome to the infamous salon of Mabel Dodge, the second home of The Masses."

From the building's alcove, Eastman ushered Iris into a lavishly decorated parlor room, a loft overhead and an upright piano on the back wall. They stood in the back, unnoticed for the moment. Carol could see in addition to Max and Iris, two men and four women sat around a dining table with teacups, wineglasses and notepads randomly placed before them. One of the seated men, in is late 20s, handsome features topped with a shock of wavy black hair, was speaking as he leaned toward a trim woman who appeared to be in her late thirties.

Carol recognized both, recalling photos from the annals of history: radical writer Jack Reed and feminist Margaret Sanger.

"You still at war with us, Margaret?" Reed asked.

Margaret Sanger smiled at Reed, "Jack, we women, we control birth. We have the power to remake the world. You and your diplomats? You form leagues of nations and have spats like the one I just left in Europe."

Reed grinned at her, "Yes, this Austrian-Serbian conflict? It's as if Hoboken declared war on Coney Island."

The entire group laughed.

Reed continued, "Just watch. All the capitalists will be drawn in. The Germans want the profit. English, French? They both want it all too."

A man turned towards Reed, "This is their war Jack, not ours."

"Mister Sinclair, you would think so, but don't bet on it, Upton old man."

PRELUDE

"Won't Wilson keep us out of it?" asked a young woman.

"Miss Eastman," Reed said, "Crystal, since when did you or your brother start listening to the pronouncements of the politicians?"

From across the room Max Eastman answered a little too loudly, "Lies! All lies!"

The whole group at this point turned and looked back at Eastman, "I don't believe Wilson and neither does my sister. We know all they ever need to start a war is a steady supply of lies."

Max grabbed hold of Iris's elbow and guided her to the center of the room.

"Max. Your friend?" asked Crystal.

Eastman replied, "My colleagues. Our newest contributor, Iris Middelton, a Chicago-bred crusader for truth, justice and the righting of wrongs."

Iris hesitantly nodded towards each of the people around the table making eye contact with each as she scanned their faces.

Max Eastman simultaneously gestured toward each one of his friends one by one introducing them with his characteristic flair, "Our hostess, Mabel Dodge."

Max paused, "Emma Goldman, champion of the oppressed and in some circles, public enemy number one."

Grinning broadly he quickened the tempo, "Over there, the infamous commie-loving Jack Reed, one time amigo of Poncho Villa, currently the enemy of the Kaiser."

Laughter broke out around the table while Max pivoted ninety degrees and gestured towards the remaining men and two women seated at the table. "That well known muckraker Upton Sinclair. My dear sister and co-author, Crystal and, of course, just back from exile in England, our own sexual freedom crusader, Margaret Sanger."

They all greeted Iris with polite nods as if not quite sure what she was doing there.

Max Eastman continued to dominate the conversation, "Chicago, a cornucopia of talent. Where we found Sandberg. Dreiser, Anderson. Please, welcome to The Masses, Iris Middelton."

Led by Reed, the group applauded politely.

"Welcome, Chicago," Reed said. "As a native from the hinterlands myself,

it's good to have you aboard."

This brought a great smile to Iris's face.

"WHACK," a loud clap of hands shocked Carol back into the current time and space.

Her eyes immediately snapped open. She was a well trained subject and very responsive to Lee's instructions.

"Deep breath," he urged.

Carol's breath came easily and deeply. She stared resolutely at Lee, then finally spoke, "A writer. Iris wrote for a paper, The Masses, in New York. She, she was a crusader of sorts."

Phonyong Lee nodded knowingly, "Something solid, something to follow. It's nearly time to cross the bridge."

He abruptly walked out of the room.

She knew better than to lag behind his lead. She lifted herself off the couch and followed him into the room across the hall. She found him already on his computer typing in the search field: *The Masses,* scanning for the name *Iris Middelton.* By the time Carol could put two and two together, the laser printer beside the computer was verifying Iris's identity and her connection to the magazine. Engrossed in the avalanche of these mounting facts, she hadn't noticed that Lee had left the room.

She stood alone, trying to decide what all this meant.

Then it hit her, "Bridge? What bridge?"

CHAPTER TWENTY ONE

Shoot for the moon. Even if you miss it you will land among the stars.
-Lester Louis Brown

Had she done it?

Little did she know that she'd already crossed the bridge. On the other side was pure chaos.

Her ordered life was about to be fractured, like Yin and Yang, the irreconcilable opposites that complement each other: male and female, shadow and light, life and death. "You can't know one without the other," she reflected.

Only a few days had past since her discovery of Iris's existence as a writer for *The Masses* when she arrived for another session with Doctor Lee. She knew, down deep, an irrefutable link had been formed between Iris and herself. But, what? She was determined to find out.

As Lee appeared in the doorway, nodded knowingly before she could say anything, "Yes," he stated, eyes glistening, "I agree, you must visit your Iris again."

Once in his office, he lifted a finger to his lips, "But first, we must agree on two points: one—say nothing of this to anyone. It is too early. Two—now that you have embodied this ability, you must agree to explore it, for itself and for the good of your patients."

Carol's brow furrowed, knowing she'd already broken one of the two agreements, blurted, "Doctor, forgive me, but, I have told someone, my George; about our first session, about Iris. I had too."

Interrupting her, "Do we know what is good? Bad? Everything is constantly changing. Fortune can turn to misfortune, bad can become good." Nodding, he smiled broadly, "Nothing happens by chance, there is a reason. There are no mistakes. Our lives unfold as they should. Now that the secrecy is broken, it shall become of immense value."

Carol looked back at him, dumbfounded.

"Really, I'm sorry," she whispered, "it's just ..."

"Don't be," he interrupted, "we will learn the reason in due time."

Embarrassed, she turned away from him, walked to the window and peered out through the slats in the blinds. Had she blown it and lost his respect? "And what did he mean, 'in due time'?"

Knowing now there was no turning back; she had to go through with it. She had a responsibility, a duty to pursue this goal to the end. "Besides," she justified, "if as Lee's research shows regressions can reach into past lives eliminating negative habits, phobias and traumas, well, I've got to find out."

Lifting her head, she stared into Lee's eyes, "What would you like me to do?"

Lee smiled reassuringly, sensing her disappointment in breaking the promise and her desire to continue, "What we have always done, doctor, we shall visit Miss Iris, together."

"Yes, Doctor," Carol yielded, "let's."

Lee resumed his characteristic cross-legged lotus pose on his platform pillows, motioning from this perch for her to lie down on the couch. He had a look of equanimity on his chiseled Asian face, like the statue of the Buddha that was on the table behind him; a bearing that was ageless, timeless and infinite.

"This session, we go deeper, to the root. Take a very deep breath, fill your lungs to capacity and hold this breath until I instruct you to let it go." Lee paused, continued, "deeper, hold, now, let it go. Again breathe in, deeper, deeper still, hold, keep holding. Let it go. One more time, feel the ebb and flow as the veils part. There is no one place to arrive, it will find you."

Lee leaned over Carol's prone body and with two fingers gently tapped the center of her forehead three times, she instantly shifted into a deep trance.

Lee continued, "Three..., two..., one..., what is happening now?"

Carol began again as if watching frame by frame a motion picture from an ancient archive.

She saw Iris, who appears as a young adult woman, crouching, an arm covering her face, sobbing breathlessly, "Stop it! Herb. Please don't!"

"Didn't I tell you to stop, didn't I?" screamed a man, red-faced, seemingly out of control. In exasperation, he reaches, slaps Iris's arm away from her face. Iris recoils from the blow, falling heavily onto a carpeted floor, strewn with scattered folders, pamphlets and sheets of paper.

The man screamed at her, "This trash, in my home? Why can't you just listen?"

The picture from Carol's inner eye focused, continuing in slow motion. She noticed a ring on Iris's finger that matched one on the man's hand that had slapped her.

He stormed away to a filing cabinet on a far wall, yanked it open, grabbing handfuls of folders, tossing them into the air as if they were confetti; cascading to the floor, some tumbling onto Iris's languid torso, coiled and quaking on the carpet. Cowering in fright, she scoots across the carpet to cleave at the edge of a nearby couch.

Gasping between sobs of fear, Iris cried out, "Herb, you've no right. That's my work!"

Herbert spitting in a rage bellowed, "Socialist crap! Not in this house!"

Iris scooped a handful of folders, pulled them tightly to her chest and scrambled to her feet. Herbert lunged, grabbed her right shoulder, spinning her around, folders flying back onto the carpet. Like a rag doll, Iris slumped against the wall. She slipped down, inch by inch, in a torrent of tears.

In one last fit of frenzied temper Herbert kicked the pile of folders at Iris's feet, emphasizing his disgust, then angrily marched away.

Tears rolled down Carol's cheeks feeling the empathetic resonance with Iris being so misunderstood and abandoned.

With wet eyes still closed, Carol heard Lee's voice, "Now, we go even deeper. Deeper still. It is time to ask, to learn, what it is she wants you to know." Carol shifted perception following his command. Her awareness dissolved into a totally different scene, the townhouse that she'd seen in her first regression session.

Iris appears much older, in her late 60s, in night clothes with a short quilted pink bed jacket over her slender shoulders, lying in a walnut sleigh bed under a fully puffed-up satin down quilt, a gold heart shaped locket hanging around her neck that was softly nestled atop her pink gown.

She is holding a well-worn letter in her thin and bluish hands, the skin on her fingers appeared as paper-thin sheets of onionskin. Now, she held it out at arms length, as if putting it on display, like sharing it with someone or ..."

Carol's focus now was only on the letter, hand-written in clear cursive on printed letterhead paper. The moniker on the letter read:

Joseph Arthur Middelton, CPA
1122 Allied Commerce Building
Chicago, Illinois

Iris half-read and half-recited from memory this very old letter;

My dearest daughter, I must make this brief. The indictments will be coming down, I fear for my life, and for your welfare. I have placed valuable secure bonds in your name in a Canadian bank. Only you may access them. Use the numbers inscribed inside your locket. They will open the safe deposit box at the main office at the Bank of Montreal. This, my gift to you, is to further your work and heal my shame. You make me so proud. Dad

Iris fighting back cascading tears, clutched the letter to her bosom, weakly whispered, "Thank you, father. Thank you."

She set the letter down on the satin comforter, reached for the gold locket, held it up, caressingly, turning it over and over again in her aged hands as if warming it up between her palms filling her heart with bygone warmth.

Through tear-filled eyes, she slowly opened the locket. Inside, photos of two young boys, one on each half. And below their pictures are inscribed numbers under each of the photos: 5– 29–19 on the right and under the left picture is 7–8– 20.

"Oh, boys. My dear boys." She cried tiredly.

A thunderous clap from Lee marked the end of this frame on the reel of Carol's movie.

Carol's eyes slowly opened. Her breathing was ragged. Blinking she looked at Lee with questions in her eyes. Too much had already fallen through the cracks, she wanted to know how this movie ended.

"Now you know." Lee smiled. "You have been called to complete what Miss Iris could not. You now know what it is you must do."

CHAPTER TWENTY TWO

The life not examined is not worth living.
-Plato

The handsome young African-American's face momentarily was distorted, reflecting his inner torment as he cried out, *"Oh, no! Not that! Not ...."* his baritone voice bellowed, suddenly switching to French, in a slightly higher octave, *" Marie Sainte, la Mere de Dieu!"*

Carol Klein watched carefully as Jonas Tomlinson, David Yarnell's latest referral, twisted on her couch. The double tape hummed as it recorded yet another session of hypnotic regression; seeking to erase what seemed to be repressed memories imprinted in his cervical vertebrae; a condition possibly causing his case of life-long neck pain.

She continued to direct Jonas coaxing the frozen emotions of his past, "Deeper! Deeper. Your body knows how to heal itself. Push! Find it, now!"

Jonas stopped writhing, emitted a long drawn-out exhale. His body stretched, unwinding as if a rubber band pulled to maximum tautness. All at once, the room was shaken by his scream: *"Vous avez votre guillotine Je na'i aucane crainte de la MORT!"*

Carol recoiled. Blinking, she saw his body slowly begin to unwind, his face softening; a small smile. Taking her own deep breath, she offered, "Jonas, when you hear the clap of my hands, you will awaken; with no memory of what has taken place; absolutely none!"

Carol's clapped firmly and loudly, her eyes riveted on him. She wanted to memorize Jonas's every move. As a case study, every nuance and subtlety that was not being picked up by the audio was important. She didn't know why yet, but she knew someday it might be of immense value.

Jonas slowly opened his eyes; reached his hand to the back of his neck instinctively.

Carol could not see what he was feeling. But his beaming smile that followed said it all.

"Wow," he said, simply, "wow!"

Without further analysis, Carol nodded, "That's good, Jonas. That's very good."

CHAPTER TWENTY THREE

Your time is limited, don't waste it living someone else's life. Don't be trapped by dogma, which is living the results of other people's thinking. Don't let the noise of other's opinions drown your own inner voice. And most important, have the courage to follow your heart and intuition, they somehow already know what you truly want to become. Everything else is secondary.
-Steven Jobs

Carol stood before her class of graduate students, all in their white lab coats after having returned from their clinical internships at the University Hospital.

Carol was on a roll, "Take particular note of the powerful treatment possibilities in the complex field of quantum biology—the dynamic field of messenger molecules. Here in the study of Epigenetics the data points to the impact our thoughts and feelings have on which sets of genes get tuned on or off. Our beliefs are transformed into our biology. The only question is relative to our thoughts that........"

Mid-sentence her classroom door opened and Randall, Doctor Freeman's administrative assistant, in his flamboyantly out-of-place Hawaiian shirt popped his head in through the doorway and said, "Freeman wants to see you. Right now."

Annoyed by this interruption, she reluctantly nodded to Randall in acknowledgment.

Folding her lecture notes, she directed her students, "Okay, for now, let's focus on the functions of neural connections. I'll be right back."

Carol walked briskly to her department head's office wondering what could be so damn important to interrupt her lecture time.

Carol knocked on Doctor Freeman's door, entered, stood before Isobel at her desk.

Isobel looked up and motioned to Carol to sit in the chair facing her.

"Doctor Klein. I wish we weren't having this conversation."

Carol blinked, a look of confusion on her face.

"I thought we understood each other." Isobel droned. "Didn't I specifically ask you to stop therapies outside our standard protocols? Didn't I tell you to stay with our medical standards?"

Dumbfounded, Carol nodded, "Yes."

"I've seen your e-mails to Doctor Yarnell. And your communiqués with Lee."

Carol's gasp propelled her backwards.

"My e-mails? You what? My mail? You can't do that."

"You've been in contact with Phonyong Lee. After I warned you!"

"Yes. I have, but, my e-mails?" she gasped again.

The air between them couldn't have been thicker if it had been solid.

"Isobel, I'm sorry. I'm a doctor. If I find something that helps my clients, I've a moral responsibility to pursue it! For them!"

"I'm not going to debate with you, Doctor Klein," countered Dean Freeman.

Carol was beside herself, her two worlds colliding.

"What about the Alden case? Chronic hip pain. Gone!" Asserted Carol, "If I found a key that, somehow, unlocks a significant healing, then..."

Carol leaned forward and placed her hands on Doctor Freeman's desk continuing her retort when the Dean raised her hand in the universal code of: "Silence!"

"Do you realize how close you are to committing actionable malpractice?"

Stunned at this accusation, Carol caught herself holding the arms of the chair.

"What?" Carol tried to blurt out, "it's just that, there's so much we don't know. Do you deny what happened with Susan? Don't you think there's something there?"

"If anything had gone wrong," Isobel challenged.

"Nothing went wrong! It went right!" Carol pled.

Isobel pursed her lips as if in restraint, softened her tone of voice, "Look Carol, I know we haven't found all the answers, but I cannot let you shift the playing field. And I'm not going to debate with you. Do you have any idea how close you could have put us into a malpractice suit?"

Carol was visibly shocked. She put her right hand into her left palm to keep both from shaking.

"How can I make this any clearer to you, Carol? Unless you stop this, I have no choice but to suspend you from practicing therapies at this university."

Carol's eyes squeezed shut, trying to shake off this nightmare, her voice now choking up with tears, "Dean Freeman, please, I cannot deny what I saw," placing her clenched hands together as if in prayer.

Isobel leaned forward, tried to soften the tension, "Look at it this way, Carol. I'm just looking out for you, for your own good. Do as I say. Just stick to our medical standards." She paused, looked imploringly at Carol, "That's it. We're done here."

"But Doctor Freeman! I ..."

Isobel shot up from behind her desk.

Carol blinked, forestalling tears, slowly rose from her chair.

"No more." Isobel ordered, eyes averted, looking down at her desk.

Carol turned, walked awkwardly to the office door, opened it, feeling as a *persona non grata*, unwelcome in her own department.

She spoke tersely over her shoulder, "Thank you, Doctor, for looking out for me."

Closing Doctor Freeman's door, her mind running wild remembered Schopenhauer's observation, which until now, she had never fully appreciated; "*all truth passes through three stages. First, ridiculed. Second, violently opposed. Third, it is accepted as being self-evident.*"

Apparently, she was in phase two. She walked out, closing the door behind her.

CHAPTER TWENTY FOUR

Live a life as a monument to your soul.
-Ayn Rand

If walking the plank has a modern day analogy, the walk back to her classroom felt like it—taking her last gulp of air before plunging into the sea.

Pulling open the classroom door, she refocused on the scene before her: students in their lab coats, some sitting, others standing, a small group huddled around the brain CT scans on the light board; conversations blurring into a cacophony of sounds, drowning out the roar in her head.

She closed the classroom door firmly. A sudden wave of awareness surged through the room. Students turned to face her; many with quizzical looks on their faces; the room paused in silence, followed by the muffle of movement, and then, like a flock of birds, in unison, each settling into their seats around the conference table.

All eyes were riveted on their teacher. The tension in the air pitched like a violin string, ready to snap. Silence filled every crevice of the room as Carol walked to the blackboard, picked up a stick of chalk and in large letters wrote the words reverberating in her mind:

FRONTIERS OF SCIENCE

Turning, she faced her class straight-on, eyes blazing, "Close your books."

Fighting back the moisture behind her eyes, she walked to the end of the conference table, looked down both rows of students, "You. You wish to be doctors?"

She reached, lifted the nearest textbook from the table, raised it shoulder high, "So be it! Be a good one. But never forget, there are issues, greater than anything in your textbooks—issues beyond anatomy, chemistry, neurology, psychology." She dropped the book, slamming it on the table with a thunderous bang, startling the now wide-eyed students.

"Today's new therapies? Not in any of my textbooks, not even a few years ago. Does that make these new advances any less true back then? Just because they weren't yet accepted by the medical establishment? Just because they didn't fit the conventional understanding of the times."

Voice breaking up, she barked it, "Doctors, the study of life is science—the science of discovery, is life! We have yet, to uncover Nature's great mysteries!"

She cleared her throat, "For every mystery, there are many possible answers. We need to learn to look deeper. If there's more than one answer, shouldn't we explore them all? As scientists, shouldn't we look beyond the accepted, the obvious?"

In raised voice she invoked, "In the words of a wise man, 'the beliefs of one age become the absurdities of the next. And the foolishness of yesterday becomes the wisdom of tomorrow.' There are truths yet to be uncovered, new realities to be revealed."

Her eyes widened as she scanned her students, one by one, pausing for a moment wanting to ground this runaway train, "Yes, think about it. You do realize the crisis we face in medicine today. Costs escalating at staggering rates, yet without measurable improvements. Is medicine healing more problems or just managing new symptoms? We spend the most money on healthcare than any other nation, but do we have the healthiest population? No, not by a long shot! What is the best medicine, or the most effective therapies? People are looking for answers. The landscape of medicine is changing—one-third of Americans are seeking alternative therapies. Why? Because standard medicine's not providing adequate results! What's that tell you, doctors?"

She turned abruptly, walked to the blackboard. Picking up the chalk, she underscored the words, FRONTIERS OF SCIENCE. Turning back, she forced a smile, "Doctors, if we want different results, we need to be begin to think outside the box of our current understanding!

"An example? When Copernicus observed that the sun was at the center of our galaxy, not the Earth, his theory ran afoul of the politically powerful church of the times. And for supporting this theory his colleague, Bruno, was burnt at the stake; and Galileo was imprisoned. But that didn't, that couldn't, change the fact that yes, the sun is the center of our galaxy."

"Historically, our country's pharmaceutical monopolies are suppressing alternative cures. Management of disease with drugs is big business! Don't be surprised if, in your lifetime, today's pharmaceuticals will be seen like blood letting was two hundred years ago."

A few students shifted uncomfortably in their chairs at the intensity of her rant.

"Today, medical science's cutting edge is Epigenetics, the frontier where genetics are modified by the subjective states of our minds. Memories aren't just stored in the brain, but in the trillions of body cells. They are capable of modifying our DNA. One researcher has described epigenetics as life's Etch-A-Sketch, saying: 'Shake it hard enough, you can wipe out a family's surge.'

"Irrefutably, current research shows these cellular memories, activated by our feelings, memories, thoughts—are major contributors capable of causing health problems. These findings show that the ability to choose which genes get switched on and off, through our memories, is the most exciting advancement in medicine over the last six centuries!"

Carol noticed looks of disbelief on more than a few faces.

"Yes, Doctors. The research supports that. We can change gene function, our physiology, by changing our thoughts. The most important thing you can do as Doctors is address the underlying emotional issues and the unresolved traumas as causes of illness in your patients.

"Doctors, please, look to the facts. Let the theories you uncover be secondary to the facts of discovery. Too many people are suffering needlessly."

Striding around the conference table, she fixed her gaze on the eyes of her students. "You," pointing her finger at each student, one-by-one. "You are the pioneers on the frontier of science. You will choose between what has been, and what will be. With the power of truth as your guide, you will steer healing into the uncharted waters of this twenty-first century. Sail forward, never backwards. Don't let anyone stop you. Especially your own self imposed obstacles."

Having circumnavigated the table. She positioned herself at the front of her class, throwing down an invisible gauntlet, "Now, here's my challenge to each of you. What will you do when you come face to face with circumstances you can't explain?"

She placed her hands atop the shoulders of the first student to her right, Thomas Barnett, "Tell me, what will you do when you uncover a successful result you can't explain?" The bemused student shrugged his shoulders, hoping it was a rhetorical question.

Carol tightened her grip on his shoulders, "Doctor Barnett, what will you do when you face clinical situations that contradict medical beliefs you have learned?" He squirmed under his teacher's grasp, beginning to answer, but Carol had already turned her attention to the student on his right, Joyce Brulé.

"Doctor Brulé, should you find alternative medical practices more effective than the existing protocols, what would you do?" Brulé glanced at Barnett, seeing no help there, shifted her gaze down at her hands, saying nothing.

Carol pointed to the doctor sitting directly across from Brulé, Dennis O'Reilly. "Doctor O'Reilly, what will you if you uncover abilities within your patient's subconscious that you've never seen before?"

She sensed that she was losing her students. She may have gone too far over the edge and had better state her case or lose all credibility in front of them. Stiffening her back, she lowered her eyes mustering all the strength to steel her convictions, " Doctors, how will you address symptoms revealed within your patient's psyche, embedded perhaps, from a previous life?"

"From, what?" stammered O'Reilly.

Carol's eyes were now glazed over with moisture, her bravado wearing thin. This was the most unacceptable state of presence in front of her class she could ever imagine. "What is expected of us as scientists? What should any of us do as researchers?" stammered Carol.

O'Reilly stuttered, his voice a confused plea, "Did I hear that right? A past life?"

CHAPTER TWENTY FIVE

Our greatest glory is not in never falling, but in rising every time we fall.
-Confucius

Carol sat stiffly, very much alone.

She stared out the dirt-crusted window from her hard cushioned seat on the train, scenery streaking by, frame by frame, as if she was watching a movie, complete with a soundtrack—clanking rims against steel rails. She looked out the window, her reflection looking back at her, blankly. "Was she really doing this?"

Yet, here she was, riding the train to New York City, on a mission to confirm or deny the reality of her own regression into the life of Iris Middelton Paulson. If she could only verify what she'd experienced, or find it false—then, and only then, could she move on.

Rolling through her mind was her last class session. She knew she had gone too far. Straddling the fence between her regret for influencing them in her bias and being true to herself—the *nosce te ipum*,' know thyself, your whole self,' seeking to prove something she could not deny. That door had been opened and she'd walked through.

As the landscape transitioned with each approaching mile, she watched as the postcard landmarks announced the approach to the city, daring not to think how implausible, how impulsive this trip really was. Where was she headed: the future, the past? She fiddled with the notebook in her lap; thoughts of this mission burrowing into her psyche, pondering, "What choice do I have? None, but to put this hypothesis to the test."

She had been trained to examine the psychological forces that are so much a part of the human struggle: the obstacles in our way, the challenges we face, the unsatisfied needs.

She was willing to at least go this distance from Boston to New York City to seek verification and to examine whether the themes in her life, much as the life of Iris, were reenactments from past imprints. There were so many parallels between Iris's life and hers. "Lee," she mouthed, "he was so insistent I make this trip. Why me? Isn't this task better suited for the sages, or the insane? Both of whom see what isn't there!"

She shook that awful thought from her mind, saying under her breath, "Okay, I'm here and I'm committed this far. It could come to an end right here, and then I will go home and sweep this episode under the rug, as only an asterisk in my autobiography."

Yet, she knew that this gate had been unlocked and would not easily be closed. "No," she admitted, "this won't be so easy. Does anyone know the cost of the choices they make, until the payment is due?" she sighed. Lost in thought, she failed to notice that the train had begun to slow its pace.

Whatever lie ahead, she was almost there.

CHAPTER TWENTY SIX

Be realistic: Plan for a miracle.
-Bhagwan Shee Rajneesh

The train heaved to a halt—Grand Central Station.

Carol stepped off the train, headed for an escalator to ride, shoulder-to-shoulder amid a horde of fellow travelers, up into the rotunda, jostled by the maelstrom of people moving in all directions around her, a swirl of humanity in wave-like undulations, a kaleidoscope of colors.

The chaos theory came to mind; that a seemingly minor event, like the flap of a butterfly's wings, can result in far reaching outcomes, a ripple-effect setting into motion a chain of immense reactions. Was she that butterfly?

She knew that coming to this place, taking this one impossible opportunity to confirm her incredulous belief had to be witnessed in person: nothing less than a first-person, direct experience would satisfy these curiosities—both personal and scientific.

Nagging 'what if—and then' questions hammered her mind. "What if Iris's offspring were alive, then they'd be well into their 80s. What if they are alive, then could one or both of them still be living at Iris's address? What if they are still alive and I find them, then, will they even agree to talk to me? Could I make them believe I'm a writer? What if I find … it's all true? Or not? Then, what?"

She maneuvered over to a row of phone booths, stopping momentarily, assessing which cubicle would forever be marked in her mind as 'crossing the line.' She chose the one that was dead center.

She lifted a tattered Manhattan phone book from beneath the small ledge under the phone; opened the section of the white pages marked 'residences'. She turned the pages deftly stopping at the alphabetized heading on the left-hand side on top of each page, stopping suddenly at 'Pastinni—Paumsa'.

Her fingers flew on autopilot scanning down as the names evaporated above her fingers; coming at last to an eye-popping dead halt: Paulson ... 257 Park Ave.

She bit her lower lip, ripped open her purse with an awkward urgency, fumbled for a pen lodged at the bottom and in unsteady nerves, jotted the address in her notebook. Although she knew the address by heart from the information she had received in her regression, she had to write it down to verify and double-check its reality. Glancing again at the phonebook, she verified that which she already knew was correct.

The moment of truth had arrived. She'd been practicing her lines on the train ride down. Her cover story was complete with means, method, and motivation; a sleuthing worthy of Sherlock Holmes.

Taking one last deep breath, she picked up the receiver, nestling it between her ear and shoulder as she inserted her phone card, punching in every number with surgical-like precision. The ring she heard sent a wave of shock through her spine: step one, a valid phone number, the rings continued: time stood still. She never before noticed how long the phone signals take between electronic pulses. Then ... a voice: "Hello?"

Carol's heart nearly leapt out of her chest.

She squeezed her eyes shut, blotting out all other input. The moment felt like a monumental hurdle. Forcing herself through this imaginary barrier, she exhaled and said, "Yes, hello. Is, is this—the Paulson residence?"

The elderly male voice, clearing his throat, "Yes?"

Carol blurted out a little too quickly, "Sorry. I mean, could you have been related to the late Iris Paulson?"

Time stopped. The longest pause in Carol's recollection. She could feel the pressure of the handset wedged between her head and shoulder, grabbed it with her free hand. She felt immobilized—waiting, then …

"Yes, that I am. Why do you...?"

"My, my name is Carol Klein. I'm a writer, doing a book, on the staff of The Masses, which includes Iris Paulson." Carol stammered with her lamely rehearsed probe, "You were related?"

"She was my mother."

Carol felt like she was walking on eggshells when she said, "Would you be—Will? Ethan?"

"Ethan reservation in his voice. Why? What is it you want?" Rushing forward without any caution Carol said, "Hi Ethan, yes, you see, I'd like to make an appointment, come meet with you. To talk about your mother. For the book. It would be a big help."

"When? When do you want to do this?"

"Well," Carol replied, "I'm in from Boston for a convention. Could it, could we make it sometime today?"

"I don't know. What is it you want?"

"Just some background on your mother, and her writings." Carol said with a sense of authority that camouflaged everything she was feeling.

"Okay. Let me check. Hold on."

All Carol could hear were muted mumbles as Ethan continued to speak to the other invisible person. Back on the line, Ethan said, "Today's not so good. Tomorrow? After two?"

Carol's pulse was racing out of control, sweat on her upper lip and palms. But, she never missed a beat, "Wonderful, just after two, I'll be there," speaking as casually as she could.

Ethan politely followed up the invitation, "You know where we are?"

Nonchalantly, Carol replied, "I have the address. 257 Park?"

Carol mouthing the words: "apartment four—oh—two. Like a Zen koan," she thought, "if a tree falls and there's no one to hear it, is there a sound? If no one were to witness my revelations, are they real?" But nobody was there to witness this moment other than the oblivious humanity that was chaotically surging around the rotunda.

For the last time today Ethan replied to Carol, "Fourth floor apartment, four—oh—two. I'll tell the doorman we have an appointment."

"Thank you, I'll be there. Thank you."

Quivering from head to toe, Carol hung up the phone, exhaled for what seemed like an eternity. She needed to empty, freeing her inner space knowing soon enough it would be filled to the brim.

Closing the phone book, a quote written in magic marker on the back cover caught her eye: *"The future of all depends on the few who suspend the belief of the moment."*

"Okay Miss Doubting Thomas," she said to herself, "have a little faith. Let's see what's next." Placing her notebook and pen back into her purse, she exited the phone booth with a burst of energy. She wanted to savor this moment feeling a sense of unexpected euphoria, "Depends on who's suspending the belief of the moment," the thought snapped short, drifting away before it blinded her.

With that, she stepped through the doors onto the teeming streets of New York City.

CHAPTER TWENTY SEVEN

What the caterpillar calls the end of the world, the master calls a butterfly.
-Richard Bach

The dawning of the day couldn't come soon enough.

Carol awoke in an overpriced room of a Central Park hotel, steam radiators hissing, garbage trucks roaring amid the cacophony of New York City—squeaking brakes, revving motors, clanging cans, ear-piercing sirens.

As the sun arose, Carol tossed one last time, sighing. She'd barely slept a wink all night.

Tossing and turning, she'd wrestled with the specter of her own moral dilemma. It was one thing to turn her own life upside down, but by what right did she have to drag others in—her fiancé? Isobel? Her students?

And now, was she really going to purposefully deceive two old men she had never met?

"What am I doing!" she pummeled herself, "I could still walk away; take the next train back; simply resume where I left off. Yet, walking away makes a mockery of what I believe in, to say noting of what I'm trying to instill in my students. It would just turn the pursuit of scientific truths into meaningless platitudes."

There was no blueprint on how to proceed, other than to continue forward. The only solace in this whole mess was her ace in the hole; an imaginary exit card, carried in her mental back pocket, knowing she could execute it at any time. Maybe.

Groaning, she stretched her legs, sliding them before her as she left the bed, yawning as she walked into the tiled, antiquated bathroom. That the mirror was speckled and fuzzy she considered a blessing at that moment, splashing cold water onto her face, eyes blinking, then, widening.

It was time. She stepped into the yellowing tub and turned on the shower, nearly scalding herself. "So, is this the way the day's gonna' be?" she resigned, turning the hot water down.

It was but a short cab ride from her hotel. Trying not to look like a tourist, she wore her "I'm here for business uniform," a navy blue suit, briefcase in hand.

The yellow cab pulled up in front of 257 Park Avenue, a stately upscale apartment building of the type that is New York's signature, a forest green arched canopy spanning the front doors to the curb. The gold letters on the awning read: ParcVue Arms.

Carol paid the driver, stepped out onto the curb and was greeted immediately by a middle-aged doorman in a black, high-collared uniform with double-breasted brass buttons and gold braided epilates on each shoulder.

Without hesitation she announced, "Carol Klein. The Paulson's are expecting me."

The doorman smiled and opened the polished brass-framed glass doors. Carol stepped onto a royal blue carpeted foyer that was flanked on two opposing walls with heavily carved gold-framed mirrors born of an era of high society. There were two large Chinese blue vases filled with fresh white and red gladiolas adorning the side tables strategically placed beneath mirrors which optically enlarged the bouquets of flowers so they appeared quite grand in size—a formidable introduction to storied ParcVue Arms.

She walked directly towards the brightly polished brass elevator doors, pressing the UP arrow button, gazed towards the ceiling, wondering what awaits three floors above.

A full minute passed before the elevator arrived. Slowly, the door opened. Carol stepped inside the rectangular confines of a smaller-than-most elevator. Pressing the number four button, she watched the door hesitate, then, oh-so-slowly, close.

Her ride started with a mild jolt, followed by a long, slow incline. Looking around the elevator, an odd thought filled her mind: "Are these walls ones I've seen from a past life, and what's my current life—a future past life?" She forced a laugh trying to cut through her nervous tension.

A mild claustrophobia took hold, the elevator motor humming, unidentifiable creaking and groans as it rose, ever so slowly, up. Her eyes focused on the control panel's floor buttons, inching upward—Mezzanine, a long pause.

Up, up ... TWO—a long pause—THREE.

Slowed, then slowing further, the vessel edged to a halt...FOUR.

She had arrived.

She blinked at the door, feeling the confining walls closing in on her. The door remained closed. "My fate," she breathed, "alone in the nether-land of an ancient elevator, stuck?"

One last, short jolt, the elevator door creaked itself open.

She stepped out onto the carpeted, well-lit hallway of the fourth floor, noticing security cameras conspicuously adhered to the ceiling. With only four doors off this central entry foyer, she stopped at the door, numbered four—oh—two.

She gathered herself, took a deep breath, lifted her hand.

Her hand poised to knock, the glistening diamond encircling her engagement finger caught her eye, grimacing, "Forgive me George, I must."

She knocked, tapping the door three, then four times. Silence.

Soft footsteps signaled an approach, the brass knob turned, the door gradually opened.

There stood an elderly man, smiling, shorter than Carol by inches, sporting a well-worn smoking jacket over a plaid shirt. He stared at her in silence. Carol's mind blanked.

She sputtered, "Mister Paulson? I'm Carol Klein. We spoke yesterday," raising her right hand. He reached, shook her hand, softly.

"Ethan. Please do come in. May I call you Carol?"

Carol silently repeated, "Please, do come in," questioning what she was coming into.

Regardless how prepared she thought she was for this moment, nothing had equipped her for seeing the physical manifestation of what she had experienced in her hypnotic trance. The stark reality was—"yes, this is the place I have seen." Calling it *déjà vu* would be a gross misrepresentation: this was beyond surreal—it was real!

She walked into the three-dimensional living tapestry of a scene she had seen only as a diorama, scanning every detail of the living room: it was exactly as she had seen it in her regression. Only the colors had faded, furniture aged over time.

Somehow, it had retained its once-lavish décor: the same fleur-de-lis drapes, Steinway baby grand piano, the chocolate brown sofa, now with a beautiful Tiffany-like floor lamp standing at one end.

Drenched in the vivid details she was now experiencing for a second time, Carol's mind swirled, eyes drawn to a brown-toned photo of a woman with two teenage boys against a far wall—a shot taken at least 65 years ago. A second framed photo was of Iris and her husband, both in their mid-sixties.

Carol noticed immediately the resemblance of the teenage boy in the framed picture with the gray-haired elderly man she just met as Ethan. But, nothing prepared her to compare the picture of Iris. "She? Me?" Carol gasped, her jaw dropping as Ethan turned to face her, motioning her to a chair facing the couch.

Relieved, she sat immediately, before a coffee table, upon which an ornate heirloom silver music box and two photo albums were waiting.

"Please." Said Ethan, "We've pulled these out for you. It was fun for us, looking at these. Mother was quite a character." Looking at Carol intently, Ethan continued, "Uh, some tea? Or maybe..."

She replied nervously, "No. I mean, yes. Tea. Thank you. Yes."

He then shifted interest away from Carol and called into another room, "Miss Klein's here. Bring tea. And don't forget the lemon this time."

The familiarity in which Ethan snapped these orders, Carol could only assume; either it was a spouse or a sibling. She wouldn't have long to wait to find out. She heard an elderly man's voice reply, "Hold your horses. Be there in a minute."

Ethan seated himself across from Carol on the couch. "Don't let Will bother you. Sometimes he's like this. You know cranky old men?"

CHAPTER TWENTY EIGHT

The only way to discover the limits of the possible is to go beyond them, to the impossible.
-Arthur C. Clarke

Carol shyly looked down, fumbling for her notebook and pen in her briefcase, trying to look professional in the part she was playing— a difficult task with every fiber of her being on fire.

She nearly jumped at the sound as an elderly man appeared, pushing a wrought-iron teacart from a bygone age. Atop the teacart was a tray that held a silver teapot accompanied by three sets of matching delicate white Limoge tea cups with matching saucers along side a beautiful serving plate in which lemon wedges were fanned in a pin wheel.

He stopped before her, lifted the tray and set it down on the coffee table before he looked up sighing, "There," extending his hand, "I'm Will."

Instinctively she blurted, "Will. Yes. Glad to meet you, I mean, thank you."

She grasped Will's hand and shook it as her heart began to liquefy at the flesh and blood warmth of his hand in hers, thinking, "This is no dream. I'm not in a trance. It's real!"

She had to shift gears fast or risk losing the few threads holding her together, quickly focusing on the tea tray. Something solid.

Will happily replied, "Oh no. Thank you! We're glad to have the company."

Ethan nodded in agreement.

Will lifted the silver teapot and poured the aromatic hot beverage that smelled of cloves and oranges for the three of them. But, before handing the china tea cup to Carol, Will flamboyantly opened an ivory linen napkin and placed it on to her lap. "A remnant of our Mother's insistence," he beamed.

A part of her couldn't help but enjoy the attention bestowed upon her by these two gentlemen. Their hospitality buoyed her confidence, making it much easier to play her role in this charade.

Will continued, "It's nice to know someone else remembers our mother, besides us."

She forced a grin, nodded, somewhat uncomfortably.

"I was just telling Miss Klein here what a character mom was," Ethan boasted.

"A real spitfire, our radical mom," chuckled Will.

Carol interjected, "Spitfire?"

Both men simultaneously nodded and smiled, a shared gesture between the brothers.

"No doubt. Isn't that what you're looking for?" asked Ethan.

Will turned his body sideways to face Ethan, "Have we forgotten our manners?"

Looking back at Carol, "What he means is, how can we help?"

She winced at their willingness to enable her scheme. She quickly flipped open her note pad, burying a rising sense of disgust at her own deceit. She motioned towards the two photo albums on the coffee table. "Well, may we start with these?" Carol reached into her purse and pulled out her reading glasses placing them in the most dignified manner on her face.

Will leaned in, picked up the first black leather album, opening it to page one. He lovingly offered it to Carol as if it were a sacred object. Carol met him halfway across the distance between them and took the open album in both her hands: taped, faded newspaper clippings and photographs of Iris—her timeline frozen pictorially.

"Besides her music," interjected Will, "she was an early voice for women's rights."

"I know, she wrote for The Masses. I've seen her byline, quite the strong voice."

"Too strong for Dad," Ethan chimed. "He said her writing nearly cost him his career. That's why she had to write under her maiden name, and then aliases at the end."

"Really?" she asked, "aliases?" She was totally unaware of this development.

"Yeah," Will beamed, "her favorite was Susan Donim. Get it? Sue, Donym?" Both men laughed at this insiders joke.

"She said nobody ever caught on," Ethan giggled, "not even once."

Will blurted, "She said she got to like being someone else for a change; that she could easily get used to it."

Carol stifled an internal gulp.

"The Masses," Ethan added, "that was the reason she had to hide her identity after awhile. It was a branded pretty radical back in the twenties. Some even called it communist."

"Nonsense. It was just ahead of its time," Carol replied, jotting a note in her pad; surprised at the boldness of her statement.

"Yep," said Will, "that's exactly what mom said, word for word."

She smiled warmly, "You don't say? Interesting," eyes back down to her note pad, her mind spinning from Will's comment.

Nervously looking up, she began turning pages from the album before her, a distraction to mask her inner turmoil with an outward calm.

She began speed reading, absorbing the material like a sponge, page after page of headlines calling for an end to child labor, opposing the entry into the war; support for a woman's right to choose, column after column by-lined by Iris Middelton, John Reed, Sinclair Lewis, Max Eastman, Floyd Dell, Margaret Sanger.

Ethan interrupted her concentration, saying, "Seemed like father was always mad at her. He was in the diplomatic corps, and here she was, hanging around with The Masses crowd that was criticizing the very government he worked for, radicals like Jack Reed, Lloyd Eastman, Emma Goldman, Margaret Sanger."

"Goldman. Dad despised Emma Goldman," Will added, leaning back into the couch, grimacing in some discomfort. "He called her a full-fledged traitor."

"Had the statement triggered a painful memory for Will?" she silently asked herself, "Or maybe just arthritis or something else?"

Ethan interrupted, "Goldman was a total anarchist. Mom's working with her certainly didn't help dad's career."

Carol absorbed the album pages as quickly as she could, her eyes glued to each page, trying to assimilate as much as she could. However, she felt as if she were eating three Thanksgiving dinners back to back. There was way too much to digest all of this in one sitting.

"That's why mom turned to music," Will added, his back pressing against the couch. "Dad made her leave the magazine and quit writing. So, she composed music instead."

"Same thing," Ethan tagged on, "the messages in her songs were just like her writing for the magazine. Dad never did figure it out."

"Yeah," smiled Will, "he never did quite get it."

Ethan finished his brother's thought, adding, "He couldn't grasp that her focus was all about peace, happiness, finding harmony in the whole of life. She believed everyone in the world was somehow connected. That everything was joined and continuous, a journey without end."

His words hit a nerve, knocking Carol back off center. Something inside her reverberated, wavelike, throughout her system.

"Continuous. What, do you think she meant by that?"

Ethan and Will shot knowing glances at each other.

"Mom believed in reincarnation," Ethan boldly replied.

Hearing those words aloud from someone other than Doctor Lee had a searing effect. They echoed in her mind like reverberating timpani drums.

Will grinned it, "She said she'd come back to visit us." Both men laughed. "Or at least keep a close eye on us," Ethan added, wistfully; followed by a pause in the conversation. Then, as if a chorus on cue, they all reached for their tea cups; Carol's cheeks reddening at that thought.

"She was dead serious about it though," Ethan chimed in, setting his cup back in its saucer, "she wrote about it. Said someday, people would finally understand."

Ethan uttered a deflated sigh, "She always hoped she could prove it; that somehow, we'll all come back in another life, for another chance."

"Another chance?" stammered Carol, hoping her interview voice would mask her roiling emotions.

"You know, to get people to listen, to embrace this real truth, what she believed," Will said, lifting the tea pot. Nodding to Carol, he refilled her cup, then Ethan's, then his own.

Carol continued jotting in her notebook, trying desperately to retain as much as her memory could. "Another chance," she uttered offhandedly, "she really said that?"

"All the time," Will grinned. "More so in her later years. I think she knew the end was near. Her health was failing. We all knew it."

Carol shook her head side to side as she turned the pages in her notebook and continued to take down as much detailed information as quickly as possible. She didn't want to lose one shred of evidence.

"What about her relationship with her father, Joseph? Weren't they quite close?"

"Grandpa Joe?" Will leaned back into the couch, apparently more comfortable this time.

"He was in cahoots with some crooks," answered Ethan. "Got put away, sent up for stuff today they'd call cooking the books."

"He worked for some strong-arm Chicago thugs," Will chirped, "as their accountant."

Carol could barely hold herself back from probing too deeply, "But, wasn't he ... really close to your mother?"

Both men locked eyes, a brotherly communication warily acknowledging a heretofore little discussed family dynamic; slowly turning back to their inquisitor.

His head shaking, Ethan snickered, "Yes, Very close. He probably went overboard, writing her, promising things. See, it seems he felt he'd done wrong by her. That he'd let her down. So, he was always trying to make it up to her."

"And he never did like dad that much," added Will.

"Grandpa!" Ethan grinned, "Here's his daughter, with all these causes. And he's in jail. He died in prison, penniless. Some accountant!"

Now skating on paper-thin ice, she shifted in the chair not quite sure how far to go. Tentatively, she reached for the brass ring, "Didn't he...?" She stumbled hoping to snag the elusive key that remained unspoken, "he was penniless? He left nothing for her?"

Both men shook their heads, silent.

Taking a breath, regaining her composure, she motioned towards an unopened album on the coffee table. "And—that one?" she ventured.

Ethan grinned, "That's mom's music book. All her songs."

Will placed his right hand over his chest, patting it up and down in a rhythmic heart-felt manner saying, "She wrote wonderful music. Nothing popular, mostly for herself."

She nodded politely, recognizing a sense of impatience burrowing in; a call to rip off her mask and simply come clean, screaming, "I want all the details now!"

She wished she could do it the right way; conduct a full-blown intake interview as if Ethan and Will were her new clients. This cat and mouse conversation was more than frustrating. How long could she keep it up?

Wishing she could tell them everything she knew, what she'd experienced in her regression into their mother's life; to tell them who she really was—but, of course, she wouldn't dare! "Patience girl, patience, all in good time," she silently surrendered. Reminding herself, "There's much more at stake here than my needs."

In desperation to get back on track, Carol pointed to a closed silver music box, the only remaining artifact on the coffee table, timidly uttered, "And, in there?"

Ethan bent forward, carefully opened the lid of the delicate-looking container.

From her angle, it was difficult for her to see anything other than the stacks of letters that were piled high in the box. The letters were tied with a blue satin ribbon with frayed aging edges.

Impulsively, she scooted forward in her chair with no regard for staying in character and began to remove the top layer of letters out of the antique silver music box. Under the aging letters, was revealed at the bottom of the container, a cluster of jewelry.

136

There it was, amongst the others: the heart-shaped, gold locket.

She dug the fingernails of her right hand into a fist as a means to divert the feelings of lightheadedness into a more centralized focus of a painful distraction. The pain helped her ground the reality of being here, in the revelation of this moment and not to get ahead of herself. Modestly, she pointed to the locket, "That's lovely. May I?"

Ethan volunteered, "It was mom's favorite."

With surprising dexterity, he pulled out the gold locket without entangling it with the surrounding jewelry. With agility using only his right hand, Ethan opened the heart-shaped locket and handed it to Carol.

The nanoseconds between Ethan opening the locket and Carol taking it from his outstretched hand felt like she was reaching back in time—through the fabric of space—and recalling something once remembered that have been lost and now was found. How could she ever describe this moment of revelation? It was beyond all the words she had at her disposal.

"Something once forgotten and now remembered, is this Iris's locket or mine?" Carol couldn't believe she was even entertaining this inner conversation. She had no reference points for this pattern of thinking.

If she had heard these words in her office during an intake interview, she would have considered a very serious diagnosis, maybe even delusions of grandeur. And yet, right here, Carol never felt more sane, more in tune or more alive in her entire life.

She held the locket cupped in both her open palms. She just stared at it for what seemed like the longest stretch of time. There they were, the small photos of the two boys, one on each side of the locket, and the numbers, just as Carol had seen them before below each of the pictures: 5-29-19 on the left and 7-8-20 on the right.

Carol felt like she was dancing on the razors edge. This was way more than she bargained for. "Be careful what you ask for, you might actually get it," was the voice in her head.

Her heart raced. How she wanted to call Doctor Lee right now; to reach out to George, But she couldn't. She felt like she was gasping at air like a drowning man, with nothing to hold onto. Nothing had prepared her for this bleed-through of realities.

Ethan broke the spell, "That's me and Will. I was eleven, Will was nine."

She ever-so-gently closed the locket, handling it like a fragile flower, blossoming after a long, dormant winter. She looked up, eyes moist, handed it back to Ethan. The glue that normally kept her together had evaporated. The moisture in her eyes began to trickle down her cheekbones.

"You okay, Miss, Klein is it?" Will asked.

"Yes, thank you," she shuddered, I'll be all right. It's just, I find this very emotional, your mother's struggles. Guess I can relate."

Both men smiled in sympathy, moved that she was so affected by this discussion of their mother and her life.

"Yes, it was a gift from Grandpa Joe to her just before he went to prison," Ethan said, carefully placing the locket back inside the open music box, softly closing the lid.

Carol watched the locket disappear from sight, looked away, dipping into her reserve glue bucket. She picked up her pen and began jotting notes in her journal, confirming these artifacts, photos, and dates of birth. She would need this validation to authenticate the significance of today.

She was afraid if she didn't write it down, right now, she would intellectualize this day as a psychological fugue, a temporary break with reality; or worse, a crack in her own psychic egg.

When she looked up she saw that both men had broad beaming smiles on their faces.

"They were close, weren't they." She said to them in reverence to what she already knew.

Ethan burst into a giddy light laughter, "Like two peas in a pod."

"Her music?" she asked, "Prelude? One of hers?"

"Yes, you know it?" Will asked, "one of her favorites. She said some day it would make an impact of sorts, or something like that."

Ethan tilted his head and asked, "Would you like to hear it? We have a recording."

It felt like there was a stone in Carol's throat, but in spite of it, she managed to say, "Yes. That would be....I'd like that."

This was totally way over the top of Carol's capacity to hold. She wished she'd had a larger emotional container to hold all this added content. She was in the overflow tank of her emotional universe.

Ethan pushed himself up off the couch, walked over to a vintage wooden Victrola in the corner of the room. Carol had not noticed it either in her time with Doctor Lee or when she had scanned the living room earlier this afternoon.

Ethan opened the cabinet and pulled out a 78 RPM vinyl record that was encapsulated in a yellowing paper sleeve with a window to the black-and-white label at the center of this LP.

Ethan pulled the record from its previously secure dust jacket and placed it on the short metal spindle. He placed the manual stylus on the vinyl recording.

A low hum of static began to fill the cavernous living room, then a cascade of musical notes flowed. Each stanza of the music was followed by a series of chords that melded into a crescendo of rich harmonies, each building on the previous melody. Carol recognized it as the music indelibly imprinted in her memory from her regression. Both men were immersed in the music and were impervious to the invisible signs of Carol's dilemma: How could she ever explain to them that, "she knew things she'd never experienced... before, yet again?"

She felt overwhelmed by the flood of facts, the verification of data and the personal infusion of re-experiencing this information. Although she was a much better actress than she thought, her emotions were like a run away train; there were no brakes to stop it.

"Ah." said Ethan, joy in his voice, "haven't heard this in years."

Carol's eyes moistened, she did everything in her power to hold back tears, remaining cordial and appropriate— despite the insanity of this experience.

All three of them sat in silence as Iris Middelton Paulson played Prelude from the grooves that had been etched into a vinyl disk decades before. The piece played on impeccably. The composition was emotionally riveting and evocative as a musical voice of an impassioned woman whose verbal communication had been stifled, but whose creativity continued to be channeled as a means to express its message, enduringly through time.

Iris was with them through her music.

When the composition was complete and the music silenced, she commented in a surprisingly steady voice, "She was good wasn't she?"

Of course, that's not really what she wanted to say. She wanted to scream at the top of her lungs. The flood of feelings was overpowering; the colliding of worlds within and without. But she knew she must keep on pretending. So, in lieu of stepping out of her writer's character, she reached for her teacup, nervously sipping from it as a diversion from her real feelings while adding a distraction for the men to focus on.

In that instant, it felt like there was a momentary electrical-like connection, a circuit of consciousness that was linked between them. Something completed.

Will looked up at Ethan who was still standing by the record player, who looked over at Carol who in turn, made eye contact with Will; like electrons moving at the speed of light around the electrical circuit only faster—moving at the speed of love.

Ethan removed the vinyl record and slipped it back into its yellowed jacket, saying with a teary-eyed smile, "Yes. She was. I'm glad you enjoyed her."

"Now then," he added, "tell us about this book you're writing."

CHAPTER TWENTY NINE

The roots of education are bitter, but the fruit is sweet.
-Aristotle

It took a long time for them to break through the clouds.

George craned his neck to look at the lake below as the helicopter turned on its side for a better view. Through squinted eyes, he saw the root of the problem, a tongue of discoloration at the water's edge, a sure sign of industrial pollution as seen through the rain from above.

"Thar' she blows," Harrison pointed out, a grin on his face as the pilot righted the copter, the sound of the rotors drowning out George's response.

Turning his head, the pilot nodded to the elderly man seated next to him, then began rapidly dropping altitude, heading for a landing strip in a meadow at the lake's edge. Within minutes the bird had landed, engines off and rotors slowly spinning as the men slipped out onto the wet ground, one at a time.

Hunkering down against the weather, three men began walking, heads down, towards the lakeshore, the pilot remaining behind as the sound of rotors finally came to a halt. They stopped close to the edge of the lakeshore, looking out at the tainted waters of the otherwise misty but pristine view of the New Hampshire wilderness in autumn.

George was the first to speak, "Chester, How long you known this?"

"Not long, maybe a month," said the 72-year old Chester Monson, President and CEO of Sterling Chemical, a Global Industries subsidiary. "Maybe a bit longer," his overcoat billowing in the wind, momentarily revealing his tailored blue pin-striped suit noticeably wrinkled by the seatbelt.

"See?" said Chester. "From here, you can't tell a thing. You can only see it from the air."

Lips tightening, George nodded his head, saying nothing.

"Looks okay to me," said Harrison, "how 'bout you, Georgie?"

George shook his head, blinked. "I'll be dammed, up there it looked awful, but from here...," his voice trailed off. "How many know?"

"Not many," Chester replied, "maybe four, five at the plant, now you. And Blankenship."

"Blankenship?" Harrison blurted it, surprised to hear something he hadn't already known.

"The pilot," Chester answered, nodding back towards the grounded chopper, the man still seated, awaiting the return of his passengers.

"How 'bout Harrison here?" George questioned.

"I've known for quite some time," Harrison interjected, "that's why I've been wanting to get you up here for the past three months."

"Three months?" George spun around, looking at Chester, "I thought you said ..."

"Could be," Chester stammered, "told you. I wasn't sure."

A gust sprayed moisture on them, rain swirling with sprinkles of tiny snowflakes. They all turned their backs to the breeze.

George scowled at Chester's answer visibly disturbed at this update, speaking firmly, "What've you done about it?"

Before Chester could respond, Harrison jumped in, "Look George, it's just a little wastewater, maybe some of it a bit caustic, but Chester here, he's has taken the right precautions to keep from being detected."

"Like what?" George questioned, internally running through the legal implications.

Chester jumped in, "We've been diluting the wastes with fire hoses before discharging anything untreated into our local sewers, and some of it just ends up here in the lake. And I've personally instructed our employees to say, if asked, that 'yes,' we are in fact treating all of our wastewater."

"I thought you said only four or five at the plant knew." George repeated.

"They don't all know it," Chester defended, "just told them what to say, didn't tell them why."

"Holy shit," George bellowed, "you don't think they can figure it out?"

He backed up a few feet, looked out over the waters as the snowfall increased, saying "Where's it come from, this wastewater?"

"Comes from cleaning out our tanks," Chester answered under duress. "Something we've gotta' do, regardless of these new fangled environmental laws. *Geez*, if we tried complying with all of them we'd take a huge hit on the bottom line. And from Global's standpoint, you know we don't want that."

"Anyone onto you yet?" George asked.

"No one important," Chester under pressure answered, "a coupla' nosy reporters is all. But, so far we've got them diverted, you know, smoke and mirrors."

"Holy crap!" George scoffed. "You can't be breaking federal and local laws. You buying off reporters? You're just asking for deep shit."

"That's why I wanted you to get together with Chet here, see the situation for yourself," Harrison interjected. "Look out there," pointing to the sparkling lake waters, "can't see a thing, just the beauty of a lakeside paradise."

"Until they test it chemically," George barked, "and you can bet your ass they will."

Turning to Chester, George stammered, "You'd better do your best to find a way to treat this crap properly and legally or there's nothing else we can do. You can't keep paying off regulators, reporters, politicians, forever. Someone's gonna' break and talk. Then, it's state fines, fed fines! And the iron bar hotel! What the fuck, Chester!"

Turning on his heel, George walked back towards the helicopter, "Let's get outa' here before someone sees us."

"Or we get snowed in," Harrison offered light humor, trying to take the edge off.

Chester sneered at the comment as the snow began to fall in earnest.

CHAPTER THIRTY

You are here to enable the Divine purpose of the Universe to unfold. That's
how important you are.
-Eckhart Tolle

Overnight, the first snowfall of the season blanketed the streets of Boston. Not enough to tie up traffic, just enough to hint at the magic of the upcoming holidays.

George, claiming he was up to his shoe tops in alligators, had agreed to meet her late that afternoon at their favorite pub, reluctantly, she thought.

"I've gotta' make it short," he insisted on the phone.

"It's important," Carol urged. "One drink?" Knowing full well he wouldn't refuse her.

When George arrived, the bar was filled with shoppers and others who managed to skip out of the office early, "A growing trend," he thought to himself. He spotted Carol, standing near the bar.

"It's too noisy here," she said as George approached. "I can't even get the bartender's attention." She suggested they just go for a walk in the snow, that she had something too important to tell him with all the distractions around.

George agreed, pleased this would shorten their meeting. Bundling up in overcoats, they both stepped out onto the sidewalk, wide snowflakes floating down from above, decorating foliage without sticking yet on the cement. Heads down, they walked away from the direction of the windswept snow.

Without regard for the chill, Carol spilled her whole heart out to George telling him of her visit to the Paulson's in New York City.

"It was all there," she spewed, as they trudged along. "The same room, the same locket, even that song, the one I saw her playing. She wrote it, I found out. George. It's all there, just like I saw it."

"Whoa," he stopped in his tracks, "what're you talking about?"

"My regression," her trembling voice rising, "the one I told you about. I've seen it. It's real. Every detail."

"Hold on. Where're you going with this?"

Carol tugged her cap a bit lower on her forehead, blurted out, fully loaded with the facts, "Don't you see? What I saw was, is—real, the whole thing's true. Real as, as this snow."

George stared back at her with bemusement, saying nothing.

"George," she spoke ever more rapidly, "if I find the safe deposit box in Iris's name, and am able to open it with the code her father left her, that clinches it!"

"Clinches what?"

"That reincarnation is real," she screeched with exuberance. "That regressive therapies into past lives could be acceptable, because our past lives are a part of us. Today."

Carol turned, looked directly at him, grasped his overcoat's lapels, blurted out, "Look. Since my episode with Susan, I've used past life regression to resolve the underlying conflicts in four more of my patients. And it's worked. Every time!"

She paused, scanning his face, searching for his reaction.

"Four?" his voice quavering.

Carol shook her head, saying, "Don't you see how important this is?"

George glared back at her in silence.

Tears began welling in Carol's eyes, in a last ditch attempt, "You with me on this?" she pleaded.

George averted his eyes, saying, "That depends on where you're going."

Her eyes brightened at what she thought might be a glimmer of acquiescence, "To Montreal," she shouted it. "We open the safety deposit box with the code, and we know for sure."

George stepped back, removing her hands from his coat lapels. He shook his head, "Look dear, you can't just walk into a bank and open someone else's safety deposit box."

Lowering her hands, she took out the only remaining ace, gloating, "I've got the six digit code to open it. Isn't that enough?"

"I thought you said only what's her name could open it?" he quizzed.

"Then I guess that's who I'll have to be."

Turning, they began walking together in silence, backs to the blowing snowflakes.

Carol cocked her head, peered into the wind at George, "You still don't get it, do you?"

Wanting this conversation to be over as soon as possible, he dismissively sighed, "Guess not."

Carol stopped in her tracks. George continued on a few steps before stopping, turned, looked back at her.

"Okay," she spewed, "Iris Paulson was the only person on the planet who knew where the safety deposit box was, and what the code numbers were. And now I know, me!"

She paused letting the image soak in, then rolled out the coup de gras, "If I can find that safety deposit box, open it, and find that it holds what I think it does, what the letter says it does, then you've got to believe me that I, Carol Klein, your fiancé, was in a past life, Iris Middelton Paulson."

Stunned at her proposal, George stared back at her in dead silence.

"Don't you see?" she pleaded, "how else would I know?"

George lowered his head, trying to hide his utter disbelief in this farfetched tale and who in the world is this woman he's with? All he could do was look away from her.

"George," she cried, "wouldn't that show that, past lives, reincarnation, is in fact, real?"

Growing irritation mounted as, he looked back at her almost like a stranger, saying in a pacifying voice, "Now Carol. Let's slow down here. There's lots to … "

Cutting him off, she interrupted, "The least you could do is help."

"What on earth could I do," his impatience now more visible

throwing his arms up helplessly.

"There's lots you could do," she insisted, "look up the record of Iris's father, a Joseph Middelton who died in an Illinois prison sometime in the nineteen-forties, you could research Iris herself, get her records."

She took a long calculated pause navigating this delicate negotiation, then throwing down the gauntlet making her final request, "And you could go with me to Montreal. You could get us into the bank. You're a lawyer. You're supposed to know how to do these things," defiantly shaking her head, snow flying off her cap.

Sensing his irreconcilable conflict, she began tearing up, her voice trembling, "You could try to understand just how ...," her voice trailing off.

George lowered his shoulders, trying to adjust the burden he now carried.

"You don't understand," she appealed.

George lifted both arms, threw them out in exasperation, still silent.

"You really don't," she repeated in a deflated sigh, the wind having gone out of her sails. Then with one last gust of strength blurted, "Think what you want. I'm going to Montreal!" Carol turned, walked away, heading directly into the blowing snow.

Stunned, George hollered after her, "Carol, c'mon. I need you. The campaign. I ..."

His face drooped as she disappeared into the growing whiteness.

"What the hell am I saying?" he moaned aloud.

The snow began sticking to his eyebrows and the sidewalk.

CHAPTER THIRTY ONE

What you seek, is seeking you.
-Rumi

Carol sat at her desk, alone.

Three days had drifted by since she'd heard from George.

She felt badly about her impulsive retreat in the snow. In her heart, she knew she was off base. It was unfair to expect George to share her belief in the importance of her findings. It wasn't his monkey, it was her's alone. If she wanted to validate that Iris's gift from her father was in a Montreal bank, then she'd have do it single-handedly.

She felt like a tightrope walker at the half way point, there was no advantage to turn back. Although exhausted by this pursuit, Doctor Lee's insistence on the importance of her mission kept her focused on the quest, knowing full well that her career and possibly her relationship were in jeopardy.

"This is a mad chase. I simply want to return to the normalcy of my old life." But the persistent idea haunted her relentlessly; "What if Iris's father's gift is there, right before my eyes, in my hands, confirming what I experienced of her life is true?"

She began a swaying motion in her chair, unknowingly in time with the music of Prelude in her head. Her mind wandering all over the map, retracing Iris's steps and plotting her own trail to Montreal.

The loud buzz of her intercom jolted her back to reality. Elaine's voice stopped the merry-go-round in her head, "George, line one." Carol slowly reached for the phone, hand hanging in the air a moment, lifted it, "Yes?"

"Carol," his voice at once excited and protective, "I'm sorry I haven't called you since, well, you know, but I've great news to tell you."

Carol hesitated, "And, that might be?"

"Please, don't be angry with me. I've found what you wanted. I had my paralegal search Middelton's records in Chicago: court records, newspaper clippings, bank records, an obit. Well, it confirms what you've been saying. Joseph Middelton was convicted of money laundering for a phony union fund and sent to prison in Joliet. They believed he'd squirreled away hundreds of thousands for himself. But he died in prison before any of it was found. Also, that your Iris was a somewhat influential writer, married to a career diplomat, Herbert Paulson. It's all true, darling. I'm sorry I doubted you. I'm sorry."

He paused, "You're onto something, not sure what, but your pieces are falling into place. Looks like it might amount to something," his voice drifting off.

After a long pause, she tested the waters, "So, now you believe me?"

"About Middelton? Yes. As for the rest?"

She mulled over his answer, trying to assess what's meant by "the rest."

"Well, there's only one way to find out."

"I know, and if that offer to join you in Montreal stands, I'm in."

"You are? Oh, thank you George, so much!"

"Can't make it more than a long day trip. I'll see what I can do to arrange a flight and contact the bank, let them know we're coming."

"I've Friday off," Carol crooned, "would that work?"

"Will let you know, love. I'll see. Gotta' go; see you tonight?"

"You better believe it, Bucko," Carol sparkled, suddenly filled with joy and playfulness, "I love you."

She placed the phone back in its cradle, filled to the brim with expectation, "It's going to happen, it's really going to happen!"

The merry-go-round started up again in her head, sounds of the calliope growing ever louder.

CHAPTER THIRTY TWO

*Service is the rent we pay for being. It is the very purpose if life, and not
something you do in your spare time.*
-Maria Edelman

George thought he'd taken care of everything.

He had contacted the central trust office at the Bank of Montreal, explaining that he represented a client with an interest in holdings in their bank's possession, under the name of Joseph Middelton, a United States citizen of Chicago. "That well could be," the officer responded, "our bank has a long history serving many Chicago clients, both individual and corporate, as far back as the nineteenth century."

George stated he needed to confirm that, in fact, there were holdings in the name of Middelton. "And," he added, "if so, I and my client, a close relative of the Middelton's, request an appointment to review the contents, as soon as is reasonable."

Within a day, he heard back from a senior trust officer who, in a somewhat surprised tone of voice said, "Yes, we do show a long-standing holding here for a Mister Middelton as you've described. One of our larger safety deposit boxes, secured by a combination code."

The man couldn't hear George's sudden exhale both in surprise and relief at the news.

"Yes, good," he nonchalantly stated, "I believe my client is currently in possession of the combination for the box."

"Very well," the officer replied, "rather odd though, seems this particular account is pre-paid, for a period of ninety-nine years.

150

Something we seldom see." He paused, then added, "may I inquire, as to the nature of your interest in this deposit box."

"As I told your associate, I am acting as a representative of the deceased and the estate," George declared, "also, my client assuredly is in possession of a number code, keyed to the deposit box. She would like to review the contents, to see if we can determine what properties may be deposited there."

"I see," the voice on the other end of the line said, "you say she, your client, has the combination code that opens this particular box? How was it she came about it Monsieur?"

"From other files of the estate," George answered. "The box is apparently the only estate property yet to be identified. And since my client has the combination, we feel it imperative to open it, if only to learn its contents."

"And you would take possession of the contents?" the officer questioned, his tone suddenly wary.

"No sir," George cautiously replied, "not until legal ownership is proven. We know better than that."

"I see, I see," the officer relieved. "When would you like to do this?"

"Soon as I can make arrangements with my client," George exhaled with a breath of relief, "I'll call you to confirm our plans. Your name, sir?"

"Décolleté, Henri Décolleté," he announced. "I look forward to meeting you and your client Monsieur, what is it, Mansbridge?"

"Yes," George offered. "I'll call you, hopefully later this week. Good bye."

"Bon jour," Décolleté responded, clicking off to end the call.

George leaned back in his chair, glad the conversation was over, "What am I doing?"

The next day, George called Harrison to see if Global could provide him access to a charter aircraft for a day, "Just a quick trip up to Montreal and back, shouldn't take but a few hours." Harrison called back, having arranged for a BeechJet 400 through Blue Sky Airways, a charter aircraft service.

"They'll take off from Logan," Harrison conveying the logistics, "and get you to Mirabel International, a private airstrip just outside the city. Flight time's just a little over an hour, each way. What's this about, anyway?"

George cleared his throat, "Just checking on a financial transaction at the Bank of Montreal. Soon as I set up the meeting I'll call you back to confirm the trip. Thanks. Gotta' dash," hanging up before a response could be given.

As he dialed the trust office of the bank, he thought, "Sweet Mother Mary, with any luck Carol's 'Middelton treasure hunt' will be resolved within a day."

He sighed, "Maybe that'll shut her up and I can get on with my life."

CHAPTER THIRTY THREE

None of them knew the color of the sky. Their eyes glanced level and were
fastened upon the waves that swept toward them.
-Stephen Crane

Carol shifted uneasily in the soft leather seat, eyes fixed on the clouds they were passing through, then breaking completely from their cover, suddenly basking in a sun-kissed reality that's been here all the time, just out of sight from the world below. She marveled at the metaphorical aptness of what she'd just experienced—a breakthrough, like an echo of her quest.

"How you doing?" George asked, placed his hand over hers, a reassuring smile brightening his face.

"Nervous, classic case of anticipatory anxiety: a fear of failure mixed with a slim estimated chance of success."

"Thank you for your professional assessment, doctor," he laughed. "But how are you?"

"Fine, George, fine. Just that, well, it's just, I feel like with this trip, I'm placing everything on one roll of the dice. If I hit it, wow! If not, I'm out of the game."

"You mean that? That this may end your pursuit, if it doesn't pan out?"

"I guess so," she hesitated, sensing the skepticism in his tone. "Let's just wait and see."

George removed his hand from hers and turned slightly to look out the window into the bright morning sky.

"The waiting," Carol murmured, more to herself than to George, "it's like standing in the eye of hurricane, knowing that something's coming, something big."

George's eyes snapped back to her, smiling, "like in West Side Story," he sang it in tune, "*something's coming, I don't know what it is, but it is,*" she joined him in singing the final phrase, "*gonna be great!*"

"How you folks doin' back there?" shouted the co-pilot, then without waiting for an answer, "we'll be leveling out now, so you can remove your seat belts if you want. Doesn't look too bumpy up ahead. We should be touching down in about forty-five."

George nodded his acknowledgement, placed his hand back upon Carol's, turning once again to look out the aircraft's window. Below them, under the cover of cloud was the area of pollution caused by the Global subsidiary that he was protecting, "Make that hiding," he corrected his thought, from the proper regulators.

"Some difference," he whispered under his breath, lightly biting his lower lip.

Carol, sensed George tensing, "Something wrong sweetheart?"

"No," shaking his head, "nothing. Nothing's wrong. Let's just cross our fingers in hope that whatever we find in the bank, settles the question of Iris Middelton once and for all."

"You know, if we do find something, anything that confirms what I've seen—do you know what that means?"

Before he could answer, "It means that past life regression has merit. That it's real. That it's a valid treatment. It's that important."

She paused, her words hanging in the air.

"A medical breakthrough" she beamed. "It's that significant."

George stared at her in silence, his mind forming the thought, "Wow, what implications would such a finding have on the legal system? This could turn jurisprudence up-side-down; guilt, innocence, property rights, inheritance law, all up for grabs."

His eyes clouded, the thought chilled him to the bone, "Maybe, in the short term, things looked unfair, but in the long term, over many lifetimes, what defines the meaning of justice?"

His inner voice screamed, "Shut this crap down, boy, shut it down!"

Before long, the aircraft was gliding back through the clouds until the winding waters of the Saint Lawrence River and the outskirts of Montreal came into view. The plane landed smoothly at the private Mirabel airstrip. Slowly coming to a complete stop, the aircraft's engines were turned off, the sound of silence a surprise. George and Carol unsnapped their seat belts.

Throughout the flight they had never taken them off.

CHAPTER THIRTY FOUR

At the deepest level, there is no giver, no gift, no recipient...only the
Universe rearranging itself.
-Henry David Thoreau

A short taxi ride brought George and Carol to the towering Bank of Montréal, a granite edifice befitting the royal French heritage. Upon crossing through the iron gated entrance, they were greeted by a middle-aged man wearing a conservatively tailored three-piece suit, grey with a subtle pattern of vertical stripes, slightly darker, perfectly appropriate for his profession.

"Bon Jour Monsieur Mansbridge, Mademoiselle," he greeted with a perfect French accent, "I am Henri Décolleté, with the Private Client International Trust Department, Banque de Montreal at your service. Welcome to our country."

Taking Décolleté's hand, George made it a point to squeeze it with a show of strength, not really knowing why.

"Nice to meet you, Monsieur," George answered, "this is Doctor Carol Klein, my client." Smiling with a little too much effort, Carol extended her hand which the bank representative lightly squeezed her fingers, bowing slightly from his upper body.

"Come now, would you care for some café?" he asked, extending the bank's international hospitality.

"No thanks," George quickly replied. "We've very little time today, Thanksgiving and all."

"Ah," Décolleté nodded, "yes, your Thanksgiving. You hold it a month after it should be, the Canadian way, no?"

George and Carol said nothing, staring blankly at the Frenchman, who continued, "But since you represent the deceased and have the combination. Then, let us be off to it."

"Si," George nodded. "Uh, oui, yes." Décolleté discreetly rolled his eyes.

Décolleté led them towards a small vault-like room, protected by a locked door of steel bars, in which safety deposit boxes of varying sizes lined two walls. A large velvet-covered shelf, divided into three cubicles filled the back of the vault room.

"This is a strange one," the French banker disclosed. "Pre-paid for a century, yet no one has inquired since the deposit nearly sixty years ago. Are you certain this is the one?"

"Yes, oui," George anxiously replied, nodding his head for emphasis.

"Yes, that one," Carol gasped.

Décolleté looked her in the eyes, "With your permission, due to the unusual nature of this deposit, I have been instructed to stand with you upon the opening to see that nothing is removed. *Je fais confiance que c'est acceptable?*"

"Uh," George mumbled. "Yes," Carol acquiesced. "Of course, fully acceptable. We just want to know what's being held here."

"Mae oui," Décolleté satisfied with the arrangement, "then, we shall begin."

He led them to an oversize deposit box on the floor level of the room, inserted a key and pulled open a door covering the box itself. On the front of the box was a round combination lock-face dial.

Décolleté pulled the box out from its compartment, lifted it to the velvet-covered shelf, bowed and stepped back, allowing Carol to approach the now freestanding box.

Carol's heartbeat increased rapidly as she placed her fingers on the dial that had not moved in six decades, testing it with a turn to the right, then to the left. Her mind was clouding, her face flushing with color.

"Carol?" George urged.

"I'm okay," she trembled. "Just, give me a minute." She bowed her head, saying something undecipherable under her breath, raised her eyes. Took a deep breath and began to turn the dial, first to the left, then to the right, as if by instinct. Sweat beads broke out on her forehead as she turned to each number in sequence; 5 Right, 29 left, 19 right, 7 left, 8 right, 20 left.

Carol squeezed her eyes shut tightly, opened them. Nothing had happened. She had felt no tumblers click. Nothing.

"Perhaps, Madam" Décolleté's voiced laced with skepticism, "your numbers? Incorrect?"

"No," Carol said with a note of desperation, "I'll try again. Please."

"Relax, Carol," George instructed. "Try again. It's all right."

Carol, felt the air became unbreathably thick with tension. She felt like time was standing still. She shook her head forcing her mind to focus.

"Think, Carol, think!" she commanded herself into concentration. She spun the antiquated dial all the way left, then all the way right, letting her fingertips get better acquainted with the grooves on the dial.

"Okay," she sighed with all her resolve, "this time, this is it!"

She turned the dial, ever so slowly to the left until hitting the number five. The dial stopped. "Did I just feel something?" she thought, "was it?"

With her free hand, she wiped her eyes, then, began turning the dial to the right, stopping at number twenty-nine. She felt nothing. Sweat beads formed again, bathing her forehead. "Come on," she urged, "come on!" She turned the dial to the left, back ten spaces, landing on number nineteen. Without hesitation, she turned the dial rightward to the number seven, then left, slowly, all the way back to the number eight.

Now, she had but one more number to reach. Every ounce of her attention peaked. Her breath shallow and fast like sucking for air in a vacuum, her eyes darted to George. He was standing stiffly, also holding his breath. She heard Décolleté clear his throat, a nervous rumble. She turned the dial again; to the right, to the number twenty.

She felt it, a click, a strong click.

The top of the box loosened. It lifted slightly. It had opened!

"Voila," announced Décolleté, a smile in his voice.

Carol's shoulders began shaking. It was open! Tears flooded from her eyes uncontrollably. George reached for her, pulling her in, holding her in a close hug, grinning at their host.

"This means a lot to her," George covering his tracks, "a whole lot."

Décolleté smiled, *"Évidemment,"* he agreed, grinning at the hugging couple, adding, "and now, to open the lid, no?"

Carol turned to face him, slipping out of George's arms, wiping her eyes and cheeks. She smiled at the banker, saying, "Merci, Monsieur. Oui."

Décolleté reached for the lid, lifted it gently, setting it upon the floor.

All three of them peered into the box.

George's piercing whistle hung in the air.

CHAPTER THIRTY FIVE

There is no security on this earth; there is only opportunity.
-Douglas MacArthur

They stared into the box in silence.

Bars of gold bullion, a half-dozen, took up half the box, the other half, a mixture of Treasury notes, stock certificates and bonds of the Chicago Mercantile Exchange. George lifted them up and out of their dormant resting place, having not seen the light of day for over sixty years. His first instinct was to thumb through them, quickly categorizing the contents and calculating their current market value. And then, he saw it. Stopping him cold. Atop the bullion lay a sealed envelope upon which, in cursive handwriting, was written:

DISTRIBUTION INSTRUCTIONS:
ALL ASSETS HEREIN ARE INTENDED FOR
MRS. IRIS MIDDELTON PAULSON ONLY.

Carol gasped, eyes widening as the words on the envelope soaked into her mind, "For Iris Middelton Paulson. It's true!"

She looked up at George, unable to speak, eyes pleading.

"Holy Mother," he croaked.

"It appears to be a small fortune," Décolleté's voice floated in the air like a vapor. "A gift from a very generous man."

George's eyes turned to the banker as he gathered his thoughts. The enormity of the contents had knocked the wind from his sails. He felt compelled to say something lawyerly, something profound.

But, he said nothing. His eyes returned to the revealed contents. He reached in, lifted the sealed envelope up and out of the box, higher, until he could view it against the light from an overhead lamp.

"There's a letter or something inside," he whispered.

Carol leaned in to see the outline against the lamplight.

"Should….," she gasped, "should we open it?"

"No," George gently cautioned, "best to wait."

He turned to Décolleté. "Monsieur?" he asked.

Décolleté nodded his agreement, "Oui," he replied, "you wanted to see what the box held, now you know. This is enough?"

Firmly, he exerted his position of power, "As you know, we cannot release anything without the proper authority, who in this case may be this Mademoiselle Paulson. You know of her?"

Carol stared at him, dumbstruck, eyes darting, unable to answer.

"Yes," George broke in, "we do." Carol's neck nearly snapped as she shot him a wide-eyed glance, one dripping with bewilderment.

"Well then," the banker continued, "perhaps you should inform her of this discovery, no?"

Thunderstruck, George stared back at Carol. "Yes. That's what we will do," placing the envelope back in the open box.

Punting under the weight of this proof, George blurted, "I've a request. I'll need to provide some evidence to support our claim that the contents of this box are exclusively intended for the benefit of Iris Paulson. I trust you understand."

George continued on despite the skeptical expression on Decollete's face, "Perhaps, a copy of this envelope and letter with a certificate of authenticity."

Decollete's expression softened knowing that the contents would continued to be safe in accordance with the bank's regulations.

"Given what is at stake here," George re-emphasized, "I don't think this is too much to ask. You agree?"

"I understand. This can be done," Décolleté concluded. "For now, I must return your finding to its pre-paid home and I will be glad to oblige your request. You may trust it will be secured well by the Banque de Montreal."

He lowered the lid, lifted the heavy box awkwardly, placing it back in its slot with George's assistance.

The men stepped back. "I will contact you within a day or two with your request satisfied. Please let me know if I may I be of further service," Décolleté said, offering his hand to George.

"Of course," George reciprocated, shaking the man's hand. "We will be in touch. And thank you again."

"Au revoir, monsieur, mademoiselle."

Within minutes, George and Carol walked down the granite steps of the towering building, wordless until they reached the street. George stopped, looked deep into Carol's eyes.

"Unbelievable," he whistled. "Unbefuckinglievable."

"What now?" her voice shaking, her eyes still moist and reddened.

George looked skyward, took a deep breath, exhaled, glanced back, "Right now?" he directed, "catch a cab."

Carol, still reeling, nodded in agreement to his logic.

George turned, waved his arm as a taxi approached, slowed and stopped.

"Bon jour," George tried his best to match the local dialect, fearing that, in fact, he was butchering it. "Le Mirabella? Aero-poor-o-tea-o?"

The cab driver grinned at him, "Nice try Mac," he laughed, "I'm from Brooklyn. Hop in."

The two of them spoke little during the short ride to the airport where the chartered Beech Jet awaited. George turned away from Carol to look out the cab's window. His mind was racing as he watched the cityscape flow past them. Carol stared straight ahead, every now and then looking down at her shoes.

As the airport neared, she turned to George, "I'm sorry."

He looked at her, "For what?"

"For," she stuttered, "I don't know. I've pulled you into this, and now…" she stifled a sob, "now, I don't know what to do."

He nodded in understanding. He was in complete agreement. He didn't understand either, but he wouldn't let on, "No sense both of us drowning."

The taxi pulled to a stop just as the sun drifted over the horizon.

As they strode towards the waiting airplane, the eerie glow of a late

October afternoon was just beginning to take dominion.

Once strapped into the BeechJet, Carol leaned back deep into her seat, stifling a sniffle. George placed his hand lightly over her forearm. Patted it reassuringly.

"Don't let all this upset you sweetheart, I just might know what we should do; aren't lawyers known for buying time and coming up with angles at the eleventh hour." He'd pulled legal magic out so many times before, that he couldn't imagine that this situation should be any different.

She looked into his eyes with hope, her eyes big as saucers.

"You do?"

"Maybe, give me time to think it through. You need to relax now. It'll be alright."

Carol leaned into George's shoulder, closed her eyes, whispered, "Okay darling, Thank you."

"Takin' off folks," the co-pilot hollered, "been cleared."

"Bon voyage," George shouted back as the jet engines' howl filled the cockpit. The plane roared down the runway, smoothly lifting, striking a sharp upward angle into the evening sky. Below, lights of the city were coming on, broken only by the blackness of the curving river bisecting the scene.

Within a minute after liftoff, Carol fell fast asleep, her head lolling falling onto George's shoulder. He looked down at her lovingly as she slept. "How vulnerable she looks," he thought.

As the plane leveled off and began to shoot through the night sky, George leaned into her, lightly brushed a lock of her hair away from her face. He kissed her hair, then whispered, "Sleep well, my darling."

"Dammit," he muttered, "you were right."

CHAPTER THIRTY SIX

*Someday after mastering winds, waves, tides and gravity, we shall harness
the energies of love. And then, for the second time in the history of the world,
man will discover fire.*
-Pierre Teilhard Chardir

When they arrived back in Boston, the last of the sun's light had fallen
behind the horizon, leaving only a remnant hue of gold in its wake
before nightfall was complete.

Words were unnecessary. They drove straight to Carol's apartment.
They were each other's foil for the day. The excitement of the events
fanned a white-hot spark of deep emotional desire born of a
conspiratorial bond. The flame aroused visceral yearnings that
demanded release of their most primal physical fulfillment as they
hungrily fell onto each other a top her feather bed, their intimate
bonding now deeper than ever before. Boundaries blurred, their
lovemaking both tender and intense, the perfect blending of give and
take, selfish and unselfish. How well they fit together was nothing less
than magical.

Carol reached the peak of her bloom in synchronicity with George,
sated and panting, they lie in each other's arms, legs intertwined, deep
breaths receding, neither able to speak. There was nothing to say that
hadn't been expressed through the language spoken by their bodies.

Making love with George left Carol feeling both transcendent and
airborne, syncopation with a fluid jolt. These moments defied the
expectations of ordinary life, astonishing peaks that left her

breathlessly triumphant, yes, and grateful.

The 'during' required vigor and concentration, an energetic meeting of two magnetic poles; first resisting, then in perfect unity, both seeking absolute equilibrium; a captivating tension of infinite power drawing the poles back to each other; sharing intimacies, visceral experiences that cannot be taught. Like a great opera that builds towards the climax of a fleeting final act with a transformative power, 'during' brings one to the pinnacle of awakened senses.

But, for Carol, 'afterward' was even better. She savored the warm honey-like glow that seemed to orbit her body, from the top of her head, down her spine, circling back up the mid-line of her torso and finally landing within its target—the center of her heart.

Yes, afterwards was definitely the best. Lying here in George's arms as he pulled the comforter around them, ever so tenderly, both now purring like contented kittens snuggling under her warm winter quilt.

George pulled his arm free and propped himself up slightly on an oversized down pillow. He bent his head, cooed into Carol's ear, "I love you."

"I love you, too." Carol reciprocated, her antenna up, searching for added reassurance.

Picking up her subtleties, with gimlet eyes George put his toe in the water, "So, what are you going to do?"

An electrifying shiver traveled down her spine responding to his tone. Although she couldn't identify it, she knew this familiar sensation, feeling on the brink of something significant but she couldn't put into words.

She looked at him with calm steadfastness, partly from her post-coition glow, partly from an irrefutable resolve, "I've no choice. I know what I know, George, my experiences, all the facts. I don't have a choice!" He frowned slightly, sharply aware of the intertwined, ever-tightening threads of their lives, swirling together.

"Know what you're doing? You're putting your career in jeopardy. And quite possibly mine."

The arrow of his retort pierced her heart, her afterglow evaporating into nothingness. Outside, the cold drizzling rain, dampening her cedar roof shingles, was the only sound in the room.

She uncoiled her legs from his, sat up, pulling the sheet over her breasts, "I know George, I know. It's just ... she buried her head in the sheet, "oh, God!"

An inner voice screamed, "I've got to! It's that simple. With what I know, I can't walk away!"

Losing it, she sobbed through, quaking shudders, "It's something I have to do." Her head raised, eyes redden, "I don't want this to be a risk for you George. It's my burden. My monkey, not yours," her voice trailed off, eyes filling with tears, "but ..."

George had been down this rabbit hole before. Like most members of his gender, he'd rather face a raging bull on steroids than a hysterical woman. He was well aware of Carol's retreat into the part of her mind that was her own secret hideaway, a no-man's land. She was barricaded and armed to the hilt. He knew there was little he could do to coax her out of her dark cave.

As a last resort, he'd always relied on his confident lawyer persona, past that, when all else failed, the magic words, "Carol, just know that I love you."

Instead of being the abracadabra he was hoping for, the words took a tailspin. He felt like an impotent magician with nothing to pull out of his hat.

"And, I love you. Of course I do. But, damn it all," her voice escalating to falsetto.

She lifted her head, faced him, eye rims red, "Didn't you say you might have a plan?"

"I said I'd have to think it over," he sputtered, a snared rabbit caught in a trap.

Carol stared at him, then slowly turned away, lifting the quilt from her bare body. She slipped out of bed, grabbed her robe, shrugging into it in one fluid motion.

She needed to create a distance between George's reason and her intuition. She walked to her vanity table with its familiar and welcoming chintz flowered skirt and winged mirrors. She sat down slowly, her back to George as she picked up her hairbrush and began stroking her hair, each stroke reinforcing her resolve. She set the brush down, turned around to George, "Don't you see? It's just like the Salem trials. Your point was they were punished simply for being out of step with the superstitions of their time. You said so yourself!"

George looked back at her, a blank look in his eyes. "Didn't she realize the difference between politics and real life?"

"It's the same damn thing with past lives today!" she insisted, her voice an octave higher than usual.

George leaned up on one elbow and locked eyes with Carol, feeling the contradictory aspects of his stance. "Okay. What would you like me to do?"

She leaned forward with renewed determination, her robe parting revealing the slopes of her breasts, "Maybe, at least do this. Go see Doctor Lee. Talk to him. He has case after case of past life regressions that only a handful of people know about. Maybe he can give you the evidence you're seeking," tears began streaming down her cheeks, "since, apparently I can't." Adjusting her robe, Carol turned back to stare into the mirror, pleading, "Would you do that for me?"

The silent abyss between them seemed unbridgeable.

"At least, you could do that," she heaved a sigh, stifling a sob.

"Naked is no state in which to negotiate," he muttered as he rolled out of bed. "Okay, if you think it'll do any good," stretching his languid limbs as he rose and walked to the adjoining bathroom, mumbling something about, "once and for all, goddammit."

He entered the bathroom, closed the door and stepped into the shower, rushing water suddenly the only sound in the room.

"Good God, why is it always this hard with him? Is love so easily broken?"

She stared straight ahead, the winged mirrors reflecting her image into infinity, much like the Great Hall of Mirrors in the Palace of Versailles. She froze for a moment, staring at the multiple images of herself, each smaller and farther away: Carol Klein, a continuum without end. Her eyes squeezed shut, forcing the thought, "shift gears, girl." She had to admit—she was pleased they were able to talk, to ask each other hard questions, even if the answers weren't pretty. More than anything, she loved George, but she also loved her career. She was putting both in jeopardy.

She was thoroughly conflicted, "If I do what I know is right with this Iris thing, why can't I still be the politician's good wife? Where's the balance? After all we both just want to be happy."

In her heart of hearts, she knew this was a futile argument. First and foremost, she was a scientist, trained to pursue facts and move knowledge forward. *Fait Accompli*. She wanted to leave her mark, a professional legacy in psychology, just as much as George wanted to leave his signature etched in politics.

"Madness!" screeched her inner voice, "you have blinders on." His reluctance spoke volumes; they were nowhere near being on the same page. Heavy hearted, she cringed at the tug-o'-war between her search for answers and keeping George from collateral harm.

Yet, he'd also seen the contents of the safety deposit box! He'd confirmed the existence of the information she'd learned during her regressions. All the evidence he needs, is there laid out on a silver platter. There's nothing else I can do.

Every fiber of her being wanted to scream, "If you loved me George, if you really loved me, you'd …," she stopped herself, the thought blasting, "don't go there. Don't *ever* go there."

She rose from the vanity, walked into the living room and plopped herself onto a couch, awaiting George's exit from the shower.

Within minutes he appeared, hair damp and fully dressed, mumbling an impotent excuse about, "Having an early campaign meeting in the morning." She recognized the impasse first. Tonight, there was no place else they could go. The conversation had come to an abrupt halt, the end of the road.

He quickly walked over to her, placed a perfunctory kiss on her hair, and weakly departed "Goodnight love, I'll call," and skulked out of the apartment. She heard the door open, a cold rush of night air chilling the already frosty room, then, closed. Shut.

The deafening silence of his absence left a hollow shadow in its wake.

CHAPTER THIRTY SEVEN

When you cannot find peace in yourself, it is useless to look for it elsewhere.
-La Rochefoucauld

Morning came much too soon and now fully awake, Carol agonized over last night's shake-up with George. Even though she'd convinced him to be her partner in crime in her clandestine errand, she'd yet to get his buy-in to her cause. "Okay," she thought, "although I was able to ask George for advice, it's probably too much to expect him to become my accomplice." She knew full well that the information gleaned in Montreal had pushed her deeper into her pursuit and further from George.

It was evident that they were on separate tracks, with too many blind twists and turns. She wrangled over what it would take to get George fully on board. Was it time for a new tack? "If I could get him to talk with Doctor Lee, maybe then, he'd see why this is so important."

Sighing, she buried the unpleasant ending of the evening. The Montreal trek swallowed up the day she ordinarily devoted to completing the loose ends of her practice, to say nothing of those pesky household chores and the hours required to transfer notes from her last week's client sessions and writing lesson plans for her students.

She now realized what it feels like to be living outside the margins. With that thought hanging, she dropped the subject from her focus.

The most important item on today's agenda was selecting the proper gift to bring to George's parent's home for Thanksgiving, an event she saw as a double celebration, dinner with the traditional festivities and perhaps, the 'official' announcement of their engagement to his family. The coming-out party to his clan.

She wasn't exactly a model match for the Mansbridge family album. "Oh well, I'm engaged to George, not his Mother and Father!" Still, she felt like a square peg trying to fit into a round hole.

Nevertheless, she wanted to make a positive impression on her fiancée's family. The pressure she felt had been growing and now was enormous. "What if … ?"

She spent much of Saturday afternoon hunting and gathering through the festively decorated shops in Cambridge. She enjoyed being out and about, galaxies away from the rigidity of academia and her profession. Such excursions brought out Carol's bohemian soul, allowing her to pursue her alter ego, seeking that lure of sensual potential that leads to exquisite adventures.

Carol found the Christmas displays adorning storefronts off-putting. "Couldn't wait until after Thanksgiving," she muttered. "First pumpkins and cornstalks, then turkeys and Pilgrims and now, Santa, reindeer and candy canes — already?"

Even so, she felt there was something distinctly warming in the displays, extracting memories of childhood, magical days, filled with wonder. She noted the general mood of joy in the faces of her fellow shoppers as piped-in holiday songs filled the aisles with good cheer.

Carol returned the smiles of others, while attempting to fight off the returning trauma of memories this season brought. It was a Thanksgiving weekend when her mother disappeared from her life forever. The scene rolled by bit by bit, in slow-motion, temporarily blinding all else from her view.

She was so young; so certain her mother would return home—any day now. Life as she had known it ceased. She slipped into a dark chamber of denial and Pollyanna fantasy, certain that her mother's return was imminent, she conjured up the warm feeling of her mother's caress, breathing in the fragrance that was distinctly hers. To this day, that loving scent was still with her, filling her senses on command. Living in her fantasy, she had been unable to eat or rise from bed for days on end.

In time, with the loving patience of her grandmother, she came to face life again on its own terms. Grammy did her best to fill her daughter's place in Carol's life, eventually pulling her out of her depression on the belief that, yes indeed, she would meet up with her mother again on some far-off day ahead. This was the belief that allowed Carol to return to life, more appreciative than ever, ready to embrace the love and trust that her grandmother offered so generously. Soon, buoyed by her mother's spirit, Carol was ready to enjoy the fruits of her childhood and teen years with an open heart.

Now, she'd noticed that since reading Doctor Lee's journals, the pain in her heart from her Mother's disappearance had softened considerably. She found much solace in his source material detailing where loved ones go after departing this world. His studies seemed to confirm that while our physical body is mortal, our real self, our soul is immortal. We rest in the transition we call death, but our existence is eternal.

While our five physical senses have inherent limitations, he'd shown how our sixth sense, our intuition, can pierce the veil separating the physical world from subtler dimensions; just like invisible radio signals, so too, does the human heart penetrate these subtle worlds.

The convergence of her inner thoughts collided with the swirling holiday ambiance all around allowing her to focus on the happiness and support her grandmother had provided and her own return to life's pleasures. She joyfully called to mind the happiness she now shared with George, including the depth of passion of the other night. "Just before, well,…. never mind."

She walked into the 'Wave o' the Sea' gift store, and after wandering through the aisles, she beamed at having found the perfect 'meeting-the-family' present, a lace tablecloth in a classic colonial pattern she hoped, an ideal middle-of-the-road gift.

With the brightly wrapped gift box in tow, she walked out of the store, encountering an elderly woman, bundled-up in a festive red scarf ringing a hand-held silver bell for the Salvation Army. Fumbling in her purse, she dropped a five-dollar bill into the canister.

"God bless you," the woman sang out, her words muffled by the thick red scarf covering her mouth. Carol nodded back with a genuine

171

warm smile in recognition of the woman's commitment to her cause, impressed at her dedication.

That's when the epiphany hit her, "There it is: the heroine's journey, a dedication to a cause so much bigger than oneself. Such an ordinary looking woman willing to stand in the cold and snow for the benefit of others. I wonder if she realizes the ripple effect of the many lives that will be changed by her virtue. Who knows why we are each are tapped for the task we are handed!" She walked away, eyes tearing up humbled to witness how the pieces of the vast mosaic fit together.

Later that evening, deepening clouds rolled in from the south, low-hanging, threatening rain mixed with snow. "'Tis the season," she chimed to herself.

As the darkness deepened, she realized she had not heard from George all day; not that that was unusual, him being wrapped up in the campaign and all. "Still, hadn't he said he'd call? Would have been nice," she sighed. "Oh, well." Humming to herself, she thought ahead to what Monday would bring: client notes updated, lesson plans complete. She so relished staying ahead of the curve.

She slept well, oblivious to the sound of thunder, distant and rolling, coming ever closer.

CHAPTER THIRTY EIGHT

The gem cannot be polished without friction, nor a man perfected without trials.
-Chinese proverb

George was surprised as he entered his office. There he found his father standing stiffly aside his desk, Uncle Nick and Harrison both seated in client chairs, all awaiting his entrance.

"Well," George said cautiously, "to what do I owe this honor gentlemen?"

The men tossed glances at each other. Harrison smirked slightly.

"It's you," his father's icy voice crackled, "that's what!"

George's face drooped, abruptly sensing an attack.

"While you've been flitting about the damn country, Global's been hit with charges by the feds," his father said sternly. "And you were missing in action."

"Sterling, actually," Harrison announced. "Some newsman broke the story right after we left."

"What?" George bleated in pitched voice, "didn't I tell them to ..."

"To what," Nick chimed in, "to take off for Canada when things get hot?"

George's mind whirled in confusion. He could almost feel the pinpricks of the glares the three men shot at him.

"What?" he stammered, "when did this ..."

"Last Friday, when you and your bimbo decided to fly off to Montreal while things are blowing up," Nick spewed, "on Global's ticket, no less!"

George felt his fists clench, "Now wait a minute," he spat seething, "you've no right to…"

"Back off, Nick," George's father interceded, "let's keep things civil," moving to an open client chair, turned to George in calm voice, "sit down, son. I agree you've got some explaining to do, but first we need to take care of our client. Harrison here has come up with a plan that may sound like overkill, but after the spot you've put us in, we've little choice but to act on it."

George fell into an adjacent chair, eyes steeled with a mixture of fear, rage and abject confusion.

"Jack," his father turned, "tell him our plan."

"Okay," Harrison cleared the croak in his throat, "here goes. Georgie, the problem is, well, two-fold. You were mentioned in the story that broke, and in the indictment, as a conspirator in the plot cover up of Sterling's on-going polluting."

"Horse shit," George felt the like he had just been sucker punched, his face reddening.

"Let me finish," Harrison continued. "Global needs you to clear your name as much as it does theirs. They realize that. Even though your little jaunt to Canada ploy kinda' pissed them off," he grinned it.

"What's that have to do with …," George sputtered.

"So they want you to be the face of their defense. You know, clear your own good name along with the good corporate citizens at Global."

"My name IS clear!" George bellowed, loud enough for it to reverberate around the room, "for God's sakes!"

"Not anymore," his father piped in. "You've been named, singled out as a conspirator with the intent to cover up and continue the practice of polluting. Breaking federal and state laws."

"But," George attempted to respond.

"No buts about it," his father replied angrily, his eyes turning to Harrison, "Jack, go on with the rest of it."

"Okay," Harrison continued, "here's the kicker, part two, with these charges hanging over you, your run for Congress is in the shitter. So you announce that you're suspending the campaign to clear your name and to bring the actual polluters to justice, denying any personal knowledge of the polluting whatsoever; assuring the media that no one at Global was involved."

George's emblazoned eyes flew to his father, "Suspend the campaign?" pain evident in is voice.

"The way we look at it," Nick underscored, "you throw yourself on the grenade. It goes off. You've smothered it and come back looking better than ever. Ready for a run next time around."

"What the fuck?" George gulped. "You've got this all planned? Just like that?"

"Cleared it with the boys at Global," Harrison's sly gap-toothed grin suddenly most irritating to George. "They like it. You do this, they guarantee you the congressional spot next time around."

George's head was spinning. None of this made sense. And it was coming way too fast.

"Wait one friggin minute," he spouted. "They're the law breakers, not me. Since when is it our job to bail them out?"

"George," his father calmly taking the helm, "our job is to bend the law to the benefit of our clients. It's that simple."

"We've already written your suspension speech," Nick added, "nice job, if I say so myself."

"Hold on," George shouted, eyes flashing with anger. "Just fucking hold on," he yelped, before catching a breath, his head turning to take in the entire scale of the scene.

"Let's recognize something here," he said. "They're the polluters here, filthy fucking polluters. And Monson's about as piss-poor stupid as they get. Don't you see that?"

"Right on target, my man," Harrison grinned ear-to-ear, "we blame it all on Monson and the dumbfucks at Sterling. Separate them from Global. Take the high road by throwing them under the bus."

"Jesus," George spewed, his head hurting, "Jesus H. Christ."

His head fell heavily into his hands as he slumped deep into the chair.

"Alright," his father announced," it's all set. Nick will release the story early on Thanksgiving day, when nobody watches news or reads newspapers, just parades, football and dog shows on TV; before planting themselves down before a baked turkey. News? They could care less."

George shifted uncomfortably in his chair, trying to get his arms around the skewed logic of his father's words.

"George, we want you to lay low for a few days, say until the Monday after the holiday. Then, you come out with your statement. We'll write it for you. All you need to do is be there and answer a few questions. Don't worry, we'll have them planted. Should be over in minutes. Understand?"

George nodded. "Yes," he understood, fully.

"Then, gentlemen," his father concluded, "let's get cracking."

"Wait," Nick interrupted, staring icily at George, "first, what's with you and that little jaunt to Montreal? Using Global's resources, on your own. What possible reason would you fly off to Canada?"

George lifted his head, sneered at Nick, "You wouldn't understand."

"Try me," Nick sniped.

"Really, Georgie," his father interrupted, "what was that all about?"

"Okay," George heaved leaning back in his chair. "I was probably out of line in using Global's entrée, but I wanted to get up and back as quickly as possible."

"But," his father persisted, "why Montreal."

George sighed, knowing his answer would come off as totally lame. "It's Carol," he said. "Something came up of importance to her. She had to get to Montreal and asked me to help, so I did."

"So important?" his father pressed, "that you commandeered a charter flight?"

"It had to do with her research," George stammered, a plea for understanding on his face. "Has to do with therapies she's working on, with her patients. And ..."

"Drop her George," Nick barked. "She's bringing you down. Dump her before it's too late."

George turned his head, scowled at Nick.

"That's it, gentlemen," his father summarized. "Let's move it along. We've lot's to do."

George, not moving from his chair, watched as the three men began filing out the door. His father looked back at George, "You be coming over for thanksgiving?"

"Yes, yes," George snapped, "I'll be with my fiancé."

His father glared, walked out, slamming the door behind him.

George sat there, alone with is thoughts. "Jesus H. Christ," he muttered.

His life had been hijacked.

CHAPTER THIRTY NINE

There are two ways of spreading the light: To be the candle or the mirror that reflects it.
-Edith Wharton

Monday morning found Carol at her Watson Hall office early, arriving even before Elaine, usually the first one in. Feeling quite chipper after a good night's rest, she turned on her computer, sat back in anticipation of it's awakening.

She found eighteen new e-mails, each demanding to be read. Discarding the ones she new to be spam, she opened Doctor Yarnell's from last Friday.

> *Doctor Klein, I will be referring yet another patient, Mrs. April Rawlings, to you for recommended hypnotherapy. Let's hope we can keep this puppy rolling. So far, results have been excellent, exceeding my expectations. Let's meet up after the holidays. I want to know more about you're therapy treatments. Best. D.Y., M.D.*

She smiled at the 'rolling puppy' reference, clicking her mouse to save the e-mail, then continued to scroll down the monitor screen.

She heard her office door opening. "Morning Elaine," she said, eyes still on her monitor.

"No doctor," Isobel Freeman's voice announced, "it's me."

"Morning Doctor," Carol replied, "be through here in a moment."

"No." Isobel emphatically repeated, "you're through now."

Carol froze at the icy tone of her voice, turning to face the woman who stood stiffly in the doorway. "What … ?"

"You are through," Isobel repeated. "You are hereby suspended until further notice."

Carol's head whipped around, "What? You're …"

"I told you explicitly not to be in contact with Phonyong Lee," she spat. "And I see by you e-mail log that you have chosen to disregarded my directive."

"But," Carol sputtered. "Oh, Isobel, you can't. I …"

"I told you to stop," Isobel barked. "And still you've chosen to collaborate with him."

"Let me explain," Carol began, "I …"

"Enough," Isobel spewed. "You've had adequate warning."

"But, the results! The therapies into my patient's past lives, they've all been working."

"I told you to find another answer for Alden's recovery."

"Not just with Susan, with others. I can show you the clinical results, I …"

"You will do as I say, doctor. This is my department and these are the rules. Take note, Doctor Klein, you are suspended from using these facilities for your therapies until you agree to operate only under the standard, existing protocols. Do you understand?"

Carol stood, unable to respond.

"Do you?" Isobel stood resolute, her neck muscles tightening.

"Yes, doctor, my clients? I have appointments set, follow-ups. How can I …"

"That's enough," The Dean bleated. "I will allow you to continue teaching through the end of the term, but you will not be allowed to provide therapy in this university clinic unless you explicitly follow standard procedures. Until then, I will reassign your caseload to a qualified therapist. Do you understand?"

She looked down at the carpet, eyes misting, "But if you'd only listen to me, see the evidence, you'd see just how mistaken …"

"That's enough," Isobel Freeman shrieked, "this conversation is over." She turned on her heels, marched out the door, passing Elaine who had just arrived at her desk. Wide-eyed, Elaine rose, walked into the office, stared at Carol, "Wow, what was that about?"

"I," Carol muttered, "I've been suspended. Sorta."

"What?" Elaine wincing as she said it, "that's crazy. You've patients scheduled."

"I know," Carol sighed. "What time is the first one?"

"Not until four." Elaine answered.

"Who is it?" Carol asked.

"Mister Drew," Elaine said, "just a follow-up. Should I call and cancel?"

"Maybe so. Yes, do that. Apologize for me." She emitted a deep breath, shaking her head in utter disbelief at what just transpired, part of her identity evaporating like a mirage. "Holy cow—suspended!"

"You alright?" Elaine asked trying to defuse the electrical charge in the room.

"Uh, I don't know yet," feeling like a sinkhole had just swallowed her up. "Just, I have a lot to sort out right now. Look, after you reach Mister Drew, why don't you take the day off. I've some stuff to take care of," she paused, "and, well, other things. Okay?"

"Sure," Elaine answered, conflicted whether to leave Carol, "if … you're sure?"

"I'm sure," Carol mustered a smile, "run along when you can, enjoy the day. I, I've got case files to…"

"Okay, if you're really sure."

Carol nodded her head side to side in utter disbelief in this dismal situation. She waved her hand, "Please, go."

Elaine turned, walked to the door, closing it as she left.

Carol walked back to her desk, sat heavily into her chair, shaking her head. Tears began forming in her eyes. Looking upward, her eyes boring through the room's ceiling, she cried aloud, "Must this be yet another one of them Mom, more disappointments?"

Her shoulders quaking, tears overflowed with the sound of a wail.

It was the shock waves of hurt cascading through her body.

She shuddered, "Oh, mother, you're so right. It's life, that's it: one more disappointment! One more bump in the road!"

The heroine's journey came to mind, "Dammit," she spat out, "you won't stop me!"

Determined, she steeled herself, "Okay, the only antidote to crisis is action." With her marching orders, she picked up the phone, dialed.

CHAPTER FORTY

Everything is energy and that's all there is to it. Match the frequency of the reality you want and you cannot help but get that reality. It can be no other way. This is not philosophy. This is physics.
-Albert Einstein

"Yes?" the first word from her mentor, a balm for her bruised ego.

"Doctor Lee. I've been suspended."

"Predictable," came the voice, "fear always precedes break-through. Poor Isobel, she's always needed strict evidence-based science too much to move forward. She's simply not ready for the broader view. Do not let her opinions override the facts."

His voice soothed her jagged nerves.

"To enter the scientific frontier you must study the anomalies, like spontaneous remissions. Follow the data, not the theories. Trust your experience. Pursue only what you observe. Remember my case number twelve, in volume seven? The multiple personalities models; wherein one sub-personality is insulin-dependent, then in the same body, the same mind appears an alternate personality with normal blood glucose levels. What inner wisdom of the body knows how to switch this autonomic function on and off? Can we duplicate this in the lab to end the scourge of diabetes?"

She loved Doctor Lee's ability to imagine life's unlimited possibilities.

"Question everything. Assume nothing. There is no boundary to knowledge. Use your imagination to open possibilities more important than Isobel's limited data-base. Remember—dysfunctional systems only replicate more dysfunctional systems."

She reeled, trying to keep up.

"You, Carol, are becoming an ambassador between the physical laws of science and the natural laws of the universe. Your mind has the power of insight to link both worlds. You have been tapped to resolve a mystery of human consciousness, to explore one of nature's most guarded secrets, the realms of her subtler inner workings, the reality of reincarnation."

She gasped into the phone.

"Soon, you will learn to translate spiritual laws into scientific principles enabling you to prove the truth of returning life. You will use your scientific methods to uncover the realities of reincarnation. Your means will be to plumb the depths of human consciousness, to dissect the consistency of our identity over the eons of time. To explore the awareness, the continuity of the 'I', our 'I-ness', as an energy that is neither created nor destroyed, only transformed, as an energetic life force, on and on."

Then, with no other indication, "Enough, goodbye."

Silence.

Though outwardly dazed, she was inwardly inspired. She picked up a pen and began writing. Her pen danced across the paper without stopping.

Did she hear him right? A scientific ambassador? What's that mean? She visualized the bleached bones of those who'd gone before and failed the test of courage, strewn at the entrance gate to intimidate the faint of heart. She laughed at her own fool hardy bravado, big words coming from a girl only equipped with a bow and arrow against a cannon. And at the same time, savoring the sweet possibility of a final victory; living a significant life.

She was shedding her old skin; sloughing off her outworn ideas. Somehow, in some way, there was a shift: intangible, amorphous, yet identifiable as a dawning of a new perception of herself, a reawakening to a part of herself—once forgotten and now remembered.

"This is the end of the beginning," she whispered aloud, closing her journal shut; now knowing exactly what she must do.

CHAPTER FORTY ONE

Two roads diverged in a wood, and I—
I took the one less traveled by,
And that has made all the difference.
-Robert Frost

By late afternoon, an eerie silence had overtaken Watson Hall. There would be no client appointments today, or for the next, or anytime in the foreseeable future. Dean Freeman had made that perfectly clear. Her signature on Carol's pink slip deemed that her actions constituted an "extreme departure from the University's standards of practice."

That being the current status of her situation, she sat quietly in her office, imaging what it must be like to be entombed. The Day of the Dead had come and gone. "Or had it?" she wondered, now that she'd accepted the notion that lives were ongoing, one to the next. "There's no tomb capable of confining a soul, just the physical body," recalling Doctor Lee's admonition.

Still, she was haunted by the reality of her suspension; being clearly unable to plead her case and get a fair hearing—that was the ultimate injustice.

"I will not just sit here and let Freeman control my career. Who says I need her consent, or anyone else's?" As shadows of the need for approval, for acceptance by others, welled up in her mind. She shut her eyes, forcing the shadows away, instead trying to focus on a moment of ultimate acceptance—the moment George slipped the diamond ring onto her finger. She made a silent vow refusing to cave in.

She pushed back from her chair, stood, and walked to the window, looking out over the quad, surprised at the scene: it had begun to snow. She grinned, noting how early in the season they'd been getting these gifts from Old Man Winter. The scene glistened like thousands of polished gems refracting light from an early evening rising moon. Frozen liquid, lighter-than-air flakes, wavered past her eyes, seeking a final resting place on the hallowed ground of the campus she still called her own.

Her cell phone chimed, her reverie was broken. She picked it up. Opened the cover, pleased at the name revealed, "Phonyong Lee, M.D."

She put it to her ear, "Doctor, I ..."

He jumped right in, "What is the name, your full name given when born?"

Overcome for a moment by the unexpectedness of the query, she paused, "Uh, Carol ... Ann ... Klein."

"Yes, yes," he said, "and your date of birth?"

"September 17, 1972, why...? " She'd gone through this exercise with Lee before about George's information.

She was confused. Where was he going with this irrelevant data?

"Doctor, I've got to tell you," she blurted, "George, he knows. He was with me, in Montreal. He saw everything. I told him all about Iris and the Paulsons. And the fortune Iris's father left her."

"Yes?" An inquiry.

"He knows all this, but he's still doesn't believe me. He won't let himself believe it. He's in denial." Silence from the other end of the phone.

"Doctor Lee?"

Still nothing.

"I thought" she sputtered, "I hoped, maybe if he talked with you ..."

"You wish him to see me? Or me to see him?"

"You, he's got to see you. Maybe if he does, he'll ..."

He said nothing for a moment, then, without emotion said, "He'll what?"

"Maybe believe me," she nearly cried it out.

Dead silence. The only sound she could hear was the faint tapping of his fingernails on a computer keyboard, followed by the hum of the laser printer spewing out paper in the background.

"Yes, of course," talking to himself, "it's obvious."

"I... what?"

"It makes sense, yet another of Nature's secret's revealed."

"Secrets revealed?"

"From the ancient science of numbers, mathematical psychology, a revelation of the soul's unfinished business from the last incarnation. The..."

"Wait," she pled, "I'm sorry, Doctor, you've lost me."

"Yes, of course. The Sixth Century B.C. mathematician Pythagoras, he gave us the theorem, with right triangles, the sum of the squares of two sides will equal the square of the hypotenuses."

"Yes, sorta," she scrambled her brain cells to remember.

"He was also a great mystic."

"I didn't know."

"He went on to reveal the science of names and numbers; numerology. He discovered the vibratory rates in nature; that all things vibrate at specific frequencies. Everyone has a name. Everyone has a birthday. These are symbols for personal discovery, empowerment through self-knowledge. The soul's history."

She had no idea what to say.

"It's a symbolic representation of the universe's inter-connectedness, a law of Nature designed around sets of numerical relationships. There are no differences between the representation of universal laws expressed in these equations or the qualities of individuals, described in your name."

"My, name?" she whimpered, lost in his labyrinth.

"Pythagoras believed that imbedded in the vibration of your name is your destiny; that the letters within one's birth name may be read as numerical symbols, responsible for the nine stages of human evolution. Here, you'll find past-life lessons not yet mastered. And the key to your current life path, the lessons we've come back to learn."

"Cycles? Name at birth?" she was underwater with his information.

"Your George...this life, a one life path and a nine maturity number, he is learning leadership, independence, to do great things for selfless reasons that will benefit the world. He must however, follow his own leaning, his path, not other's designs. He has a number two soul motivation. In his last life he was a public servant, very heart-centered. In this life, he's more mental, with a blocked heart channel."

She balked at this description of her fiancée.

"In this life, his challenge —he scatters energies. He must learn to use it more constructively, not frivolously, or else ..." he paused, "he has great potential, but he is ignoring his spiritual side, overly analytical."

"But ..."

"And you? A double six in your core numbers. You're here to serve humanity and you're not afraid to do the inner work. You're unusually creative. You love nature, but with a low number of ones, you lack self-confidence. It's holding you back."

"Tell me something I don't know," she thought laughing at his interpretations.

"You also show a serious nine challenge. One that shows you have a very important lesson to be learned, in this lifetime...you must master the ability to help others in need, give without expecting anything in return."

Her curiosity piqued, "My past life ... ?"

"Missing fours" he snapped, "you misused your independence and avoided the in-depth work that was required. You missed the finer points. So, you've taken on this life to work on the details, to finish the old business."

Swirling in a haze, "Doctor?"

"The science of Numerology reveals the complete portrait of who you are, your soul, the blueprint of your life path. The design of your life is seen through your unique numbers. It describes the meaning of your soul's journey."

"How?"

"When you live in harmony with your numbers, your life flows.

You fight against them, your life stagnates."

Baffled, she reverted to her previous agenda, "No, no. I've … look, you've got to meet with George. Only you can explain the importance of what we're doing with him."

Speaking to himself, "The missing piece, the mosaic is complete."

"Doctor Lee!" She whined in raised voice.

"Of course, tell him we shall meet Friday, the night after your culture's Thanksgivingss ritual. Tell him things will be clearer by then."

"What time?" Not taking any chances, nailing down the iron clad details.

"Six o'clock. We meet at the gates of the Old Granary Burial Grounds, after dark, as the moon rises. I shall instruct him from that classroom."

"The Old Granary? But … "

"He will be there, he has no other choice. Good night."

Just like that, the conversation ended, over and out, dead and gone. Kaput.

Stunned, she looked out the window. The snow was sticking, piling up in soft drifts.

She looked down at the phone in her hand,, scrolled down, highlighted his name, and began to text: *"G. imprt.do 4 me. met Lee. Call me.ILU.C."* And pressed send.

"OK." Immediately returned.

Knowing he was there, she dialed. He answered immediately, "What's up?"

She did her best to explain the circumstances, imploring him to agree to meet with Doctor Lee as prescribed, knowing full well how preposterous this whole cloak and dagger clandestine meeting sounded.

"You know it, don't you?" She asked.

"Of course I know Old Granary, final resting spot for Adams, Hancock, Franklin's parents, but at night? In the friggin' snow?"

"I'm sorry that's what he said," the firmness in her voice surprising herself.

"What's happened to my life?" He asked himself.

"What's it hurt? Just hear what he has to say, that's all I ask."

Drawing a deep breath, she paused before saying it, "George, you do this for me and I'll shut up about past lives forever. If you ask me too."

The gauntlet had been thrown. The reward stated.

George realized he had no better choice.

CHAPTER FORTY TWO

Never mistake knowledge for wisdom.
One helps you make a living, the other helps you make a life.
-Sandra Carey

Early afternoon on Thanksgiving day, Maggie carried George and Carol through the bucolic landscape at the city's edge, passing progressively more regal homes of the social elite's upper rung.

Carol studied the shape and texture of George's profile. She adored his dashing figure, somehow enhanced while behind the wheel of Maggie—his chiseled cheekbones, his sandy colored hair, tousled in perfect disarray.

She tried to fight off the tenseness of at last meeting her future family. The anticipation of finally facing her future in-laws was daunting. With swarms of butterflies dancing somersaults in her belly, she reached for her security blanket, placing her left hand on George's right thigh.

Reading her coded message, he momentarily took his eyes off the road, gave her a reassuring glance, eyes answering silently, "They'll love you, as much as I do…stop worrying."

His right hand lifted off the steering wheel, wrapped around her cold fingers on his leg.

His warmth and strength was the balm of reassurance she needed. The acrobatic butterflies settled down.

They turned off the country road onto a quarter-mile long gated driveway, Carol's excitement accelerated. She anticipated a grand home—she was not prepared for an estate. "Were this Great Britain," she thought, "there would be titles—Lord and Lady of the Manor." The butterflies began sprinting. "What if…STOP!"

George pulled Maggie into a curved driveway before the entrance to the palatial home, cutting the engine and stepping out with a flourish. "Come, future Missus Mansbridge Three, your audience awaits."

"Thanks a lot George, as if that helps."

At the front door, George and Carol were greeted by Celeste, the family's housekeeper for the past thirty-plus years.

"Afternoon, Mister Georgie," she smiled, shooting a brief nod to acknowledge Carol, eyes giving her an instant once-over. George placed an affectionate kiss on the elderly woman's cheek.

"She's family," he whispered to Carol, guiding her into the inner sanctum of the Mansbridge mansion. Even from the foyer, Carol was awestruck by the grandness of his family's home: black and white marbled floors, a second story crystal chandelier, ancestral portraits adorning gallery-sized walls of a circular staircase leading up to the second story.

Well aware of Carol's apprehension, George escorted her through the foyer into the adjoining formal living room. She didn't know where to look first, the exquisite architecture, the remarkable furnishings, alluring paintings, and the seasonal fresh floral bouquets brightening each room.

"Stop it," she thought, "the family's what's important today, nothing else matters."

From the foyer, she could hear the banter of holiday conversation, then, viewing a tableau of a blazing carved marble fireplace framing George's Mother and Father, Uncle Nick and Aunt-by-marriage Roslyn, sipping cocktails, nibbling on crostini with goat cheese and figs hors d'oeuvres, accompanied by oysters Rockefeller.

As they entered the room, heads turned, conversation stopped.

Ignoring Monday's face-off that had transpired at the office, George held Carol's elbow as they walked up to his parent's, "Mother, Father — the beautiful and talented Doctor Carol Klein, my fiancé," George announced it boldly.

Althea, the ever present social hostess, well-seasoned in high diplomacy as a veteran politician's wife, broke the silence, "Welcome Carol, extending her hand, we're so glad you could join us today," staging a warm smile as she scanned this intruder to her tightly controlled dominion.

Celeste appeared with a tray of fluted champagne glasses, each perfectly half-filled.

Suspended in this incredibly awkward moment for Carol, the others, all took their respective cues, raising glasses in a mock-toast to the young couple; Nicholas offering a neutral, "Happy Thanksgiving," the words echoed by all.

Celeste reappeared, as if on cue, ringing a Waterford crystal dinner bell heralding in the holiday feast.

As her guests moved towards the awaiting chairs, Althea, tugged at her husband's sleeve, "Come, help me in the kitchen a moment, dear."

The pair vanished through the adjacent hallway that lead to the butler's pantry. Out of earshot, Althea pivoted on her heels, locked eyes with her husband, "Did you know?" she whispered, "I believe she's, a, a J--?"

"Don't worry, dear, your son's campaign is temporally suspended. We won't need her anymore." Finishing the last of the fruited bubbly in his glass, adding as an after thought as he turned, "We'll let her keep the ring, you know, a consolation prize."

Althea smiled in visible relief. Her master plan for her son's future was only temporarily detoured. "We'll be back on track," were her closing thoughts as the aromas from the kitchen caught her attention. She had a Mansbridge's holiday production to oversee.

Re-entering the dining room, the patriarchs took their seats as end caps at the head of the table; Althea and Roslyn facing George and Carol from across the table, set beautifully: platinum rim Bernardaud china with navy accents, Baccarat crystal glasses, and Christofle sterling silver flatware. Carol was amused that she recognized these brands; she'd read too many bridal magazines with never-ending nuptial registry recommendations!

At the head of the table, George's father raised his wine glass for a formal blessing of the day, "We give thanks for all You provide. Bless us as we receive Your bounty. Bring peace to my family and friends and fill the lives of all with Thanksgiving, God Bless America. Amen."

"Amen," the choir echoed in measured response.

Celeste brought the first course of butternut squash soup with sage served from an heirloom soup tureen, warm hazelnut bread with honeyed butter having been previously placed on the individual bread plates.

Carol drank all this in, doing whatever she needed to navigate this uncomfortable social challenge. She wanted more than anything for today to be the dawn of her new beginning, to belong to a family, to hopefully, soon, start one of her own. Not yet knowing how to ingratiate herself to her new relations, she put on her psychologist's hat and tried to read the dynamics going on around the table, sort of like a group therapy session.

Roslyn looked up from her plate to her nephew, "I liked your Salem trial exoneration speech, Georgie, Congratulations." He nodded in appreciation as she continued, "So, I was wondering, if you were their attorney back then, how would you have defended them?"

George III in visible relief to be on neutral territory replied to his captive audience, "Basically there were one hundred mostly young women, teenagers, indicted for witchcraft. Those times, like today, remember Kent State? were filled with uncertainly, they were just playing around with petty fortune telling. That's what started the whole firestorm. This crazy, frenzied fear of Satan."

Carol saw an opportunity to chime in, "They were just the nonconformists of their day, no worse than dissidents to the conventional thinking, of those times, I mean..." Hearing the clumsiness in her delivery, she quickly followed it with a sheepish smile, as a counterpoint.

"Ah," said Althea, well schooled in forty years living with a lawyer, "evidentiary test, the so-called witches identified by the signs, you know—*preternatural excrescence*—if you had a mark on your body, like a mole, the 'sign of Satan,' pretty much sealed your fate."

"A foolish time," Nicholas piped in, "a foolish time. Then again, that's democracy in America for you, take a political question and turn it into a legal decision," he laughed.

George III, pulling on his scholarly motif piped into this now lively banter around the dinning room table, glad that it was rallying around a subject that was not personal. "Law's the scaffolding, a framework to make some sense out of our crazy world."

"And let's not forget, to enable privilege," Nick grinned it.

"Well, I suppose," George III countered, "it can move us forward or backwards, impeding progress, or not. Let's just hope it stays on the right track."

Celeste cleared the soup bowls and served the second course of salad that consisted of chicory and romaine greens, red fall pears fanned on the side finished with sprinkles of toasted pecans topped with a buttermilk black and red pepper dressing.

Carol was in awe at the epicurean details of this cuisine.

Rosalyn enjoying the family holiday repartee, jumped in, "Think about it, the law affects absolutely everything, from birth to death and the whole lot in-between, education, marriage, work, business, travel, citizenship…"

Interrupting his aunt, "The history of law in America is the history of our culture, the pulse of the people. Think of the law in critical periods of American history…freedom of speech, the press, religion…"

Emboldened, Carol jumped in with both feet, "Yes, but does culture dictate the law or does the law sculpt the culture?"

Silence. Several looked down at their plates or fluted glasses.

"Well, my dear," George III smiling a bit too hard, "let's hope they'll work together."

Carol turned to her fiancé, her mouth on the brink of words. But, as if on cue, Celeste appeared, wheeling platters of food set upon a pewter serving cart, a fortuitous break from the suddenly unwieldy discussion.

The third course was to be served family style as Celeste placed the platters in the center of the dining room table. There were serving dishes of polenta adorned with pumpkin seed pesto and pine nuts, followed by herbed mushrooms on top of black and white wild rice dressed with dried fruits, yams baked with walnut streusel drizzled on top, cranberry compote, herb popovers, and the crown jewel and guest of honor for the day was a maple-sugar brined turkey with brandied dried plum gravy.

"Yes," Carol unable to stop her mouth from running away continued their train of talk, "but which one forces the other? Can law be used to foster cultural growth?"

"Yes, Doctor, uh, Carol," Nick's voice suddenly an orator's baritone, "there are many constitutional epochs—take Dred Scot, 1857, leading to the emancipation of slaves—a legal precedent of monumental proportions, it set in motion reverberations leading to Johnson's Civil Rights act and even into today."

George's father, not to be topped by his accomplished brother, added his one-up-man-ship in retorting Carol's naiveté, "The Scopes trial, 1925, evolution versus religious belief. There are still pending arguments, unresolved differences between society's backgrounds, the current culture and religious beliefs, including science versus faith; take the global warming dispute, ivory tower pundits positing against prosaic small-town America. The jury is still out, the arguments continue."

Conversation soon became subdued in direct proportion to the consumption of the Thanksgiving dinner. Maybe it was the tryptophan in the turkey, but definitely a mellowing had occurred from the previously keyed-up energies.

Flowing with the banter around the table, adding to the competition among the hard-edged legal minds, the youngest Mansbridge added, "how about Brown vs. Board of Education—the most far reaching implications of the twentieth century—the heart of our American ideals, civil rights—separate education is not equal education."

To Carol, this dialogue seemed more like a quiz show of contestants pitting their knowledge against each other for a prize. Not wanting to be out of the game, unable to resist, she added, "And Roe vs. Wade? Woman's right to choose."

Roslyn responded softly, "Yes, dear, a landmark decision. Nearly as much impact as Margaret Sanger, and her band of suffragettes in the last century."

Carol visibly winced at the mention of Margaret Sanger and yet sensed an ally with Roslyn, smiled adding, "Wasn't the attorney who presented Roe vs. Wade to the Supreme Court a young woman, only in her twenties, when she was able to make such a huge difference?"

Spontaneous laughter spilled around the table, each in succession, Nick finally speaking it, "C'mon Georgie, let's hear you say it, 'making a difference'. The laughter increased, Carol winced, then began to laugh along with them, uncertainly.

Althea lifted her wine goblet, "To my Georgie boy, to your successful campaign, eventually." Her train was back on the right track and she would pull her little caboose into the station, no matter what it would take. After all she was the conductor with her hand firmly on the throttle.

And all drank to the declaration of the family's matriarch.

Without further adieu, Celeste announced, "Dessert, coffee and drinks will be served in the library." The rich aroma of cinnamon, nutmeg and warm pumpkin was beckoning.

"So," Althea began, "just what hospital are you working out of, doctor?"

CHERYL A. MALAKOFF & ROBERT A. CLAMPETT

CHAPTER FORTY THREE

Our own life is the instrument with which we experiment with truth.
-Thich Nhat Hanh

The quiet and solitude in Carol's apartment was a welcome sanctuary following 'The Thanksgiving Dinner' with the family.

George and Carol finally caught-up with each other commiserating over Monday's mind-numbing events, comparing notes and offering condolences, one to the other.

In truth, George was not surprised to learn of Carol's suspension. Yet, in no way would he let on that, truth be told, he felt she'd brought it on herself.

"Can they really do this?" she asked sitting on the edge of a two-person love seat sipping her Chardonnay, "I mean, if you wanted to stay in your congressional race?" Standing at the kitchen bar pouring a nightcap of brandy, George looked over at her, "Seems that way, doesn't it," his body language revealing a defeated surrender.

"It just doesn't seem fair."

"Funny," extracting brandy from the amber bottle, "in some ways, I'm relieved." He breathed in the wonderful tawny aroma of the liquor.

Carol smiled at him, peering over the rim of her wine glass mischievously, "Your heart really wasn't in it, was it?" He turned, replacing the top on the bottle. "Don't know," he said quietly, "maybe not. All I know is, it was expected of me. That Mansbridge thing."

The only replay was to smile back, reassuringly, hoping that it conveyed all she felt.

"Of course," he continued, "I'd like to serve in congress. Could do some good."

"I'm sure you could, except ..."

"Except what?" asking as he crossed the room, joined her on the love seat.

She took a sip of wine, lowered the glass, eyes boring into him, "Well, I mean, if your father, Nick and the rest, if they can take you out of the race now, what'll they do once you're in office?"

"Gimme a break," cutting her thought train off at the pass, "it's not like that, not at all. It's just, well, the Global thing would've made the campaign a lot tougher, you know?"

He took a hurried sip, deliberately averting her piercing eyes, "I mean, we've gotta' win it if were in it. And if it's in jeopardy, which it would have been, well, better out than in. Right?"

Carol nodded, weakly. Instinctively, as a response, George leaned back, lacing an arm across the back of the love seat above her shoulders, quickly changing the subject.

"And how about you? Your situation?"

She feigned a smile, hiding behind her own inner demons.

"Oh, I'd say almost the opposite from you."

He looked down at her, "Oh yeah? How's that?"

She leaned forward, cocked her head, smiling, "I'm in it to accomplish something and I'm not pulling out!"

Getting wind of her defiance, George held his ground, contemplating her message.

"Accomplish something? In what way?"

"Not sure yet, all I know is— I'm not going to let go."

"You're crazy," George countered, grinning self-consciously. He reached over and began tickling her ribs, making her buckle in a combination of annoyance and laughter.

"Quit it, I'll spill my wine." He stopped, the two of them laughing awkwardly, knowing the elephants in the room were beginning their own parade.

"Look," gesturing towards a window. "Here it comes." Outside heavy flakes of fresh snow cascaded down in a ballet without music, swirling past the window to fluff into a blanket on the ground. Carol nodded, taking a short sip of her wine before setting the glass down on a coffee table. "Beautiful," turning back to George, leaned in and kissed him on the lips, "Happy Thanksgiving, darling, we've a lot to be thankful for."

"Each other," wrapping her in his arms for a much deeper kiss, the union of souls.

"With gratitude," looking up at him placing soft lips on his cheek, an intimate moment of surrender and intimacy.

"We couldn't be more different, could we? You, raised in a bastion of power brokers who've long ago mapped out a life plan for you, and me, raised by a grandmother of modest means, to say the least; learning to scramble to survive, hoping that I'd amount to something."

George hesitated a moment, nodding in agreement. "Believe me, yours is the better avenue, mine's no bed of roses. Felt like a pressure cooker most of the time." His head went back, eyes closing for a moment, "A family of pythons, I used to think that as a kid. What's that joke? How do you get out of this chicken outfit?"

Carol grimaced, reaching her hand to cover George's.

"Come on now, you had a loving, large family around you all that time. You should feel fortunate. God, how many times I wished I'd had a full family."

George knew enough to remain silent, giving her time to reminisce.

Then, in a whispered voice, he summoned the courage, "You know, you've never told me, well, how did you lose your parents?"

Carol's eyes moistened. This was something she had kept to herself, bottled up within, her own nugget of precious, sacred knowledge. It was true, never had she shared this information with George. Of course he would want to know. And eventually she would share it with him, this the man with whom she would share the rest of her life. Could she say it now? Out loud?

Voice cracking, she began, "It, it was, a car accident—the day after Thanksgiving. There was a big snowstorm. Their car slid off the road into a riverbed. I don't have many details other than that, because Grammy wouldn't discuss them with me for years. She just kept telling me that my parents had gone somewhere, and that I'd see them again, some day, sometime."

She stammered the words, "Of course, they never came back. I, I pressed Grammy, 'Grammy, tell me the truth!' Finally she relented. She took me to the spot where they died, and to their gravesite. I'd never seen it! No one let me know, I still thought they'd be…," She began weeping openly.

George put his arms around her as she dabbed her eyes. "It's all right now, darling, I'm here for you," squeezing her ever tighter, "thank you for sharing it. Thank you."

"Oh, dear God," she breathed heavily.

"The day after Thanksgiving?" he stammered at the awareness, "that's tomorrow."

Carol wiped her eyes with the back of her hand, "tell me about it, I know, only too well. Friday." She looked up at George, "You're still meeting with Doctor Lee, tomorrow night?"

He looked at her without speaking, feeling trapped, "Of course, dear, of course I will."

He thought to himself, "After this how the hell could I not?"

Carol stood, wiping her eyes again, "I'll make us some tea," turning to walk into the kitchen.

George lifted his arm, looked at his watch. An hour had passed since Nick was supposed to release news of ending his candidacy to the news wire services and the Associated Press.

"It's done," he muttered to himself.

Carol returned with a tray, tea mugs and creamer.

As night came to an end, they fell into bed, wrapped in each other's arms.

George listened to Carol's regular breath of sleep as he lie awake, looking at the world outside through a window, directly into a landscape of disbelief.

The snow continued to fall, performing its silent ballet.

CHAPTER FORTY FOUR

Don't be afraid to take a big step if one is indicated. You can't cross a chasm in two small jumps.
-David Lloyd George.

George was first to rise in the morning. Donning a robe, he walked unsteadily into the bathroom, splashed water in his face, paused looked into the mirror, asking his reflection, "Who are you, really?"

He walked to the kitchen where he pushed a button on the coffee brewer, thankful he'd thought to grind the beans and set the machine up last night. He sauntered across the room, heading to the front door. He opened it. There was the thickened Boston Globe, stuffed with post Turkey Day sale ads and dozens of retail fliers, stretching its wrapper to the limit.

Within minutes, he had settled into a kitchen chair, coffee at hand, cautiously looking at the Globe's front page. He chuckled at the oversize photo showing children throwing snowballs filling the bulk of the page. "Run big pictures, go home early," he snickered at the insider mantra of the newsroom.

Spreading his arms, he turned the page. There it was page three, column six and seven, nearly four inches deep, headlined: "Mansbridge Campaign Ends In Controversy." Scowling, he began reading.

Boston—Facing recent charges of participation in a cover-up conspiracy, candidate George Mansbridge III announced Thursday the suspension of his campaign for the U.S. Congress.

In a prepared statement, Mansbridge said, "I am ending my campaign to devote my energies to clear my name and bring to justice those responsible for any and all violations of local, state or national environmental rules."

He denied involvement in a cover-up of environmental violations by Sterling Chemical, a New Hampshire-based company his law firm represents. Sterling is accused of multiple environmental violations, permitting the release of pollutants into Winnisquam Lake, the fourth largest in that state.

"I am obviously very concerned with this matter and will be working with the appropriate government agencies to determine the source of this release and to support the government's prosecution of those responsible," Mansbridge said. "In this process, I will be fully exonerated from any and all charges filed against me. The former congressional candidate said that halting his campaign at this time is in the best interests of his supporters and the citizens of Massachusetts.

A half-mile long spill of industrial material, caustic wastewater consisting of lye and floating petroleum coke, was reported last week by employees of the chemical firm, which has run afoul of rules protecting air and water in the past.

Mansbridge was not available for comment.

George folded the pages shut, throwing his head back in the chair, shutting his eyes tightly.

"So that's it," he muttered to himself, "they left Global Industries completely out of it."

He reached for his cup, took a long sip of the still-warm coffee, savoring its taste in his dry mouth. Rising from the chair, he set the newspaper down on the table. He walked, slowly, to the bathroom. He removed the robe, reached into the shower, turned on the hot water, then stepped into the awaiting cascade of water. Grabbing a fresh bar of soap, he began rubbing it forcefully over his nakedness, attempting to cleanse himself, thinking, "body, mind and soul."

When he emerged from the shower, patting himself dry with one of Carol's oversized, fluffy towels, he found Carol, at the kitchen table reading page three of the newspaper, half filled coffee cup in hand. She turned, looked up as he entered, "You saw this?"

He sadly nodded, "Yes."

Carol paused a long moment, unsure of what to say next. She folded the newspaper closed, cleared her throat. "You okay with it?" she asked.

He again signaled, "Yes."

Carol rose from her chair, walked to George, reached out, grasping his hands and pulling him close. "Oh sweetie," she whispered into his ear, "it must be so hard," squeezing him close.

George's arms reflexively circled her, returning the tight hug. "Yeah," he said. "It is. It really is."

Releasing him, Carol stepped back a pace, looked deeply into his eyes. "What are you going to do?" she asked, her own eyes moistening feeling deep compassion for his disappointments.

"Not sure," he said, his voice breaking up. Clearing his throat, "Got the press conference Monday. Till then, guess I'll just lay low. Right here, if that's okay?"

"Of course, darling," she answered.

She turned, walked to the refrigerator, opening the door. "Mushroom omelet okay?" she asked, turning her head to reassure at him, "or are you still stuffed from last night's bird?"

"Omelet's a go," he chirped relieved to put his mind on a more reasonable problem to solve.

"Now don't forget," she added, "Doctor Lee tonight."

He looked blankly at her for a moment.

"Serious?" he asked. "Still think I should go through with it? Laying low and all?"

She closed the fridge door, egg carton in her hand. "You promised! Might do you some good. Besides, who's going to see you in a cemetery at night? Now, sit down and read your paper. The kitchen staff's on duty if you want your eggs anytime today."

George shook his head, smugly. "Damn, woman," he joked, "stooping to bribery are we?"

They both laughed as George picked up the newspaper and returned to his chair.

"Guess I've gotta' do it," he thought to himself, "get it the hell over with."

CHAPTER FORTY FIVE

Sooner or later everyone of us breathes an atom that has been breathed before by anyone you can think of who lived before us–Michelangelo or George Washington or Moses.
-Jacob Bronowski

Evening was upon them before they knew it. The snow had stopped, but in the cold blue cast of twilight, its surface had hardened, turning to virtual-ice. Adding to the darkness, the sky had cleared, the blackness of a winter's sky punctuated by sparkling starlight and an early-rising full moon.

George arrived late by five minutes at the entrance gate, frozen snow sticking to the fur collar of his heavy overcoat, snow boots crunching deep into the ice-covered snow. The rising moon illuminated the scene before him, dozens of monuments and headstones, in stark relief against the white of piled snowdrifts beyond the gated metal entrance. His own shadow eerily visible against the snowy whiteness, the night air silent, traffic in the distance the only sound.

George heard a snow crunch.

"You see the tracks," said a voice from the darkness, "a doe, come to visit. The divine guide to destiny."

George's head whipped toward the voice, a shape in the shadow of the entrance wall.

"It is a good sign," the voice said, "a very good sign." The shape moved, a slight man covered in a long winter jacket, boots crunching the snow, closing in on George.

"Lee?" George pleaded, "Doctor Lee?"

"Master Mansbridge," Lee replied, "at last, we meet." He extended his bare hand. Reflexively, George reached, shook the hand, eyes fixed on the man's face.

Lee turned his head, gesturing towards the cemetery grounds. George followed his glance, seeing for the first time the hoof prints of a deer, deep holes in the snow, moving evenly into the distance. He looked back at Lee's face, imperturbable, nodding his head in encouragement.

"Yes," George said, his voice lower than usual, "we meet, Doctor."

Lee released George's gloved hand from his grasp, motioned towards the gate. "The wait is over. Come. We shall walk."

"Why here, now?" George protested.

"Soon, you shall see," Lee stoic, looking up into George's eyes. "It helps to be talking in the company of righteous people. This is hallowed ground. Being in the presence of these gravesites strengthens your connection with such exalted souls. You will need their support."

Lee turned and began walking towards the gate, normally closed this time of day but left open due to the severity of the snowfall. George hesitated a moment, then followed, his bulk dwarfing the Asian man treading before him. He quickly caught up with Lee, walking in stride beside him. Ahead lie a snowscape peppered with headstones of various shapes and sizes.

"Doctor Lee," George began, "I'm here because of Carol. Can you tell me what …"

Lee interrupted, "You and I have much of importance to discuss, and little time left."

George sputtered, "Yes, this is about Carol, right?"

"Even more so," Lee replied, "it's about you."

George stopped in his tracks, recoiling from the comment. Lee kept walking, up a slight hillock, footprints in the snow following behind. As if frozen, George stood, unmoving.

Coming to the top, Lee stopped, turned, watching George, now striding quickly to catch up. Soon he stood alongside Lee, breathing hard.

Lee's eyes slowly turned skyward. Intently watching the Asian man, George looked up into the starlit sky as well, the full moon filled the ethers with white light.

"The ancients called this wintry moon the Hungry Moon," Lee stated. "For man, a time to hunt. Or a time to perish."

George lowered his eyes, looked at Lee, his face suddenly stern.

"What did you mean by that?" he baulked, "it's about me?"

"Soon enough, you will see," Lee answered, astutely aware of George's agitation. "There is much at stake here."

"Much at stake?" George reacted frantically, "what? What's at stake?"

"It begins with Carol's legacy," Lee confirmed, "her gift of Iris."

"Gift?" George questioned, "you mean what she found in the safety deposit box? Did she tell you about that?"

"Of course," he replied, "I know it all. And it's falling into place, just as it should. Like I said, the wait is over."

CHAPTER FORTY SIX

Anything by itself, we find it hitched to everything else in the universe.
-John Muir

George took a step back, attempting to sort out Lee's obtuse words.

He shook his head, a scowl forming on his face as he challenged Lee, "She told you about the bonds and gold shares didn't she; worth millions? Is that what this is really all about, Doctor? For you to …"

"Not in the slightest," Lee countered. "We have more at stake here than your monetary concerns, much more."

George stared at Lee, more curious than ever.

"Listen to me!" Lee insisted, his voice a command. "Your Carol is on the verge of a critical scientific breakthrough. A reality that, once recognized, will change humanity's view of science, medicine, of spirituality, life and death, forever."

George leaned back slightly under the force of Lee's barrage.

"Professor Einstein showed us that time; past, present and future, is relative, interchangeable. He called it the 'optical illusion'. This is the simple truth, which your Carol has visited. Her ability to reach into the past has allowed her to alter the reality of the present."

George blinked. Bewildered.

"I have devoted my life to examining," Lee continued, "to probing this phenomena, studying the reality of reaching into the previous existences of hundreds of people. She too, has this ability, the talent to plumb the depths of one's psyche until the seeds of the past are called forward."

"But," George interrupted, "what does that …"

Ignoring the interruption, Lee went on, "in my studies, I have seen what can be achieved by reaching into the struggles endured in the past, by addressing the scars, by applying science to exorcize the current suffering."

Lee stopped to take a long breath. His voice now calm with a tone of reassurance, "You see, my new friend, I have the bounty of truth."

His face broke into a broad smile, visible in the moonlight, his voice at once firm and powerful, "Look at this way, your Carol is the subject. I am the object. And you, sir, you, are the predicate."

George stared at him in confused disbelief.

"Without you, we are a partial fragment, together, we make the complete statement."

Suddenly silent, Lee's eyes shined in the darkness, beams penetrating George's very being.

After a long moment, Lee repeated, "Thus, the wait is over."

George shook his head, "Doctor Lee, forgive me, but I have no freaking clue what you're talking about."

"Let me help," he volunteered. "Through this synchronicity of universal timing, the confluence of you, Carol and my work, we are in position to bring the issue of past lives to fruition. To illuminate for mankind the ability to recognize and finally accept this inescapable truth."

George, flustered, walked away from Lee, circled back, raising his open hands in an appeal, "What do I have to do with this?" he nearly screamed.

Lee stared at him defiantly, "Don't you see?" he softly disclosed the obvious, "you are the one to make the difference."

"Me?" George screeched an octave too high, "I don't see …"

"I have hundreds of cases documenting this inexorable reality," Lee answered, "more proof than you'll need to prepare your case in court."

George stiffened, mouth dropping open.

"This is the hunt you must pursue," Lee pushing his advantage. "Not to seek riches, but to validate this universal truth, where it matters most," Lee paused to take a breath, adding, "in your court of law."

George self-consciously crossed his arms, shielding himself from this onslaught. "Take this, what? Into a court of law? You out of your mind?"

"To gain the truth," Lee said in a monotone, "you must be the one to claim the bounty left rightfully to Miss Iris by her father. In your court of law, you will challenge the heirs of Iris for that which rightfully belongs to Iris, who now, is your Carol. Your case will be based upon sound evidence, from the medical, scientific, religious and spiritual disciplines. I will provide you with all you need. Then, my friend, you shall show the world the validity of reincarnation, and all its ramifications, to all mankind."

George's eyes grew larger.

"Each and every moment of life is new and rich with potential." Lee placed his bare hand on the headstone to his left. "Every thought we ever had is registered for eternity. In the end, each life is fully accounted for, there is no place to hide. Every one emanates a unique pattern of energy, a soul signature, that remains for all time. And for those, like myself and now Carol, who can read these permanent records, there can be no secrets. There is nowhere to hide from the truth. George, this is your time. Grab the opportunity. You can build the bridge that spans the laws of man to reach the laws of nature."

"What?" George squealed.

"You claim to want to make a difference? Make it one that matters."

Lee swiveled on his feet, looked out over the many headstones in the burial ground, raised an arm pointing towards them. "Here you see the truth," Lee pointed out, "yours, mine, everyone's."

Dropping his arm, he turned back to George. "What passes from essence to nature, we call birth. What passes from nature to essence, we call death. Your existence today?"

Lee stopped, as if waiting for an answer.

"Soon, it will be your past life."

George swallowed hard, saying nothing.

"Today," Lee whispered, "we call it dying. Tomorrow, with your help, we shall call it graduation."

Lee leaned closer to George for emphasis, saying, "that, my friend, is the difference."

CHAPTER FORTY SEVEN

We are not human beings having a spiritual experience.
We are spiritual beings having a human experience.
-Teilhard Chardin

When he walked through Carol's front door, George looked like he'd seen a ghost.

He looked at her, unmoving. Carol, sensing the worst, hesitated to speak.

Finally, he turned, shed his coat, slipping off his boots in the tiled entrance that served as a mudroom. He rubbed his hands together, "Brandy," gotta' be a brandy."

Carol nodded, sprang from her chair, walked into the kitchen to pour a snifter of Courvoisier, one for George, one for herself. She returned to find George seated, hunkered over, fighting off a chill. She handed the snifter to George who immediately sipped at the nectar as if it were Mother's milk.

Carol sat in a chair across from him, taking a slight sip herself. "Well?"

George looked up, his eyes over the lip of the snifter.

"He wants you to sue the Paulsons."

Carol nearly dropped her glass.

"He what?" A look of astonishment draped her face.

This man, your Doctor Lee, has a cockamamie idea that by suing the Paulsons' in the name of their dead mother, he thinks that's you by the way, that the overall issue of reincarnation would be brought into a court of law."

Carol's eyes widened, "Me? Sue the Paulsons?"

"Not for the money that's just to get in the game. What he really wants is to set a legal precedent that recognizes past lives, reincarnation as legitimate in the full legal sense both in law and medicine."

"Really," a smile forming on her face.

"Don't you see?" He's using you!"

Carol's eyes squinted, "How, I mean, how much?"

"Here's the deal, he's taking your circumstance; your belief that somehow you are, in fact, the deceased Iris Paulson. He wants to use you to prove past lives remain intact within people, people alive today and that episodes from them are traceable as incontestable facts."

He paused, looked into Carol's eyes, "He wants to make an example of you as a legal test case to prove his point."

"Could it work?"

"Fat chance. Every judge I know would throw it out of court as frivolous."

"You sure?"

"Damn sure," taking another sip of his brandy.

"And Doctor Lee, what'd you think?"

"Gotta' admit, he's an interesting guy. He thinks he has it all figured out," setting down his snifter, "except for the fact that it won't work."

Carol leaned back in her chair, a contemplative look on her face. "You know, I see his position. And forgive me, counselor, but it seems to me there just might be enough supporting evidence to make the case, even from my practice."

"Oh, come on! Not you too."

She exhaled, an exasperated sigh. A full minute passed before either said anything else.

George broke the silence. "He said he thought I could make a real difference, taking this on, and that he could supply all the evidentiary material needed to make the case." He drained the rest of his brandy, held out his snifter, "Any more where this came from?"

Carol half smiled, eyebrow raised, rose, took his glass, "One more, that's all," walked toward the kitchen. Looking back, "Do me a favor, at least look at his cases. I'll give you my cases. I mean, if there was any way, any way at all for this to happen, it could be, well, monumental."

He stared back at her, saying nothing.

"George, what if he's right?"

CHAPTER FORTY EIGHT

Growth is the only evidence of life.
-John Henry

Monday's press conference, held in a hotel meeting room, attracted nearly two dozen reporters, including political columnists, photographers, television cameramen and soundmen. Nick opened the conference by reading a prepared statement, handed out as a reprint, giving the reporters the easy-way-out they so enjoyed.

George was hustled to the stage for questioning after Nick had set the ground rules: questions must be submitted in writing in advance, then George will answer selected questions for ten minutes.

His senses were in a heightened state as he stepped to the podium, Nick sliding behind him, slightly to the side to strategically remain in range of a camera lens, eyes darting throughout the room, scanning the scene, his politically hardened face frozen in a frown.

Standing tall in the saddle, George took each question with serene focus, one at a time, handling them easily. Throughout the interview, he made it a point to smile into the cameras, exuding confidence in his ability to rebound and build off of his general likeability, "my strong suit," he thought, still focusing on his next election opportunity.

"As you can see, I have taken this action in order to prove my innocence and do the best for the people of the Commonwealth and its neighbor to the north. That said, I thank you all for your faith in me and for the difference for which I stand."

With that, he stepped back, the camera lights went dim and the dozen or so reporters closed their notebooks, grasped their statement reprints and, bumping into each other, exited the hotel meeting room. Two others approached George, notebooks still open, pens in hand. Nick stepped in, backing them off, "Gentlemen, this press conference is over."

George looked up, "Hey, it's alright, Nick. Hi, guys."

Nick sputtered. "George, not a good idea!"

The two reporters grinned at each other, knowing they were going to penetrate the human shield that was Nicholas Mansbridge, who stepped back a pace, standing at the ready.

"So George," one said, "what's been your role with Sterling Chemical? And for how long?"

"Our firm's been representing Sterling's parent firm, Global Industries, for some twenty years. I've seldom been required to step in on their behalf."

"How far back does your involvement with them, with Sterling, go?" asked the other reporter, baiting for the kill.

"No more than two months," George replied. "Like I said, I've not been involved, nor associated with Sterling and its management until just recently."

"In that time, were you not aware of their polluting practices, or their environmental violations."

"Of course not."

"But you say you have been involved with them for the past two months," pressed the other reporter.

"Yes," he stammered, "when asked, I would oversee some of their dealings, contracts and such. That's about it, nothing to do with their operations. Ever"

"Any chance you'll restart your campaign this time around?"

"You never know what lies ahead. I certainly didn't see this coming, these trumped-up charges."

"Gentlemen, that's enough," Nick interceded in a loud, commanding voice, "he has other appointments waiting, a full docket today."

"Thanks, George," mumbled one of the reporters, "good luck. One more thing, how can we reach you if we need to?"

"Well," he said, "I may be out of touch for awhile, as I look into where these charges came from and what they're all about. Meanwhile, try my office. I'll get your message through them."

Both reporters walked out the exit door. Nothing bagged today. But there will always be another day for the hunt.

Nick grasped George by an elbow, twisting him away from the departing men. "What the hell do you think you're doing? That was stupid! Have them call you at the office? You didn't have to answer them."

"Come on, Nick, I've known these guys for years."

"We went to great effort to keep your name and Global's miles apart from Sterling, and now you've got yourself joined with them at the damn hip. And, you jackass, you friggin' mentioned their tie to Global? That's what we're trying to conceal, you dipshit!"

"Geez, Nick," George pulled his arm loose from Nick's grip, "lighten up. No big deal."

"When the hell are you gonna' learn to do what I say?" Nick bellowed, "Now shape up before you're toast, mister big shot!"

George backed away, "What's with you, Nick?" he hollered back. "I don't need your paranoia right now!"

"Oh you don't, do you?" Nick hissed. "Global and I've just about had it up to here with your antics. You'd better shape up, or ..."

"Or what, you'll fire me?"

Nick's face reddened, cheeks puffing as he stared daggers at George.

"Don't rule it out, you're damaged goods. You're barely of any use to us now."

"Gonna' throw me under the bus, along with Monson?"

"Don't push me kid, don't you ever push me."

George turned on his heel, stomped away, leaving Nick alone on the stage.

CHAPTER FORTY NINE

*Remember the final measure of your life won't be how well you live, but
how well others lived because of you.*
-Bill Gates

That evening found George at Carol's once again, both on the love seat
watching the televised evening news of that day's press conference.

"That's not you," Carol whispered, "that's just not you."

"What?" George turned to look at her.

"So smarmy," she blinked, "you're not at all like that."

"Shhh," he hushed her for the TV reporter's closing comments.

*"So, the promising campaign for Congress of a member of one of
Boston's oldest families comes to a screeching halt over the holidays as
George Mansbridge the third seeks to clear his name of any
involvement in the cover-up of what is described as an ugly case of
environmental pollution. From the State House, this is Frank
Moran, Channel Seven News."*

George threw his head back into the cushion, eyes to the ceiling.

"Ugly case of pollution; could he have used any more damning
words?"

Carol's eyes stayed fixed on the screen as a local car dealer
commercial filled the screen.

The phone rang, insistently, three rings, then four, then five.
Silence. Neither of them wanting to engage with the outside world.

For the moment they were temporarily insulated.

"Should I check the message?" Carol asked.

"Might as well; didn't think anyone knew I was here."

She rose, lifted the phone and stood, listening for nearly a minute; her expression growing increasingly intense. George watched as she lowered the phone, looked at him.

"You should listen to this."

"Shit, now what?" He rose as she replayed the voicemail.

"It's Doctor Lee," handing him the phone.

He took it, put it to his ear.

"Carol," Lee's voice was clipped, "your George, he is in trouble. He is with those who would cannibalize him. The signs are blatant. He is being set up, for a fall. It is most important now, he must separate from them."

The voice cleared its throat, continued, "I see design in this disorder. By showing the world the truth of your past life, that will be his salvation. Nothing less. His success is in your hands. He is destined to make the difference by bringing the truth of our past into the future. Remember, Carol, you were born to build this bridge between these worlds."

Lee's voice stopped, replaced by the sound of papers rustling, then, "Carol, I'm sending you summaries of my research, for George to use in building his case and supporting papers from scientists, physicists, doctors, enlightened religious leaders; including addresses. He needs to read them. I will be here to instruct, if needed. But for now, it is vital for you to convince him of the importance. You are his muse. Together, like two halves of a whole, you are life movers. It is time for this truth to gain legal acceptance. He is the one to do it. The man I saw on television, that was not the true George Emerson Mansbridge, the third."

"Click," the message ended. George looked at Carol, deep concern spread over his face. He handed her the phone. She quickly pushed the button saving the message, staring back at him.

She placed the phone back on its holder.

"He knows my middle name," George muttered, wonderment in his voice.

CHAPTER FIFTY

If the door of perception were cleansed everything would appear to man as it is, infinite.
-William Blake

By week's end, Carol had received three large box-loads of material from Doctor Lee. Included were dozens of case histories from his own research, published works in scientific journals on esoteric findings of respected physicists, medical cases in which past life therapy had proven effective in eliminating patients' symptoms and articles on the history of reincarnation within a variety of beliefs penned by religious scholars of all stripes.

Carol spent several hours the first day the initial batch arrived, sorting and browsing through the documents, fascinated by the depth and breadth of the information. Realizing the fortuitous timing, as she now had these extra hours to devote to this task, thanks to having been relieved of her client caseload at the university.

"Thank goodness I still have my graduate classes," she thought, having been kept on the payroll and allowed to access the school's library and other university facilities. She was able to crosscheck the validity and background of the authors of these treatises sent by Doctor Lee. Not surprising, in every case finding verification of their authenticity.

"Ironic," she thought, "Isobel grounds me, giving me all the extra time I want to research what she swears is wrong, and I know is right."

The deeper she dove, the stronger her beliefs became.

"Now if I could just convince George."

Across town, George had returned to take up residence in his own condominium. He needed to be back on schedule in his office since there was still unfinished legal business that required attention. He ordered his assistant to examine environmental records of Sterling Chemical, along with their profit and loss statements for the past decade, while he began researching the relationship between Sterling Chemical and Global Industries.

By week's end, he had learned that Sterling's environmental shortcuts began within a year after its acquisition by Global and that since then, Sterling's work force dropped thirty percent, pollution control procedures had been compromised and the company's profits had begun to climb.

Ever since the transition of ownership, Chester Monson, son of the company's founder, had managed to remain president and served in that capacity for nineteen years prior to the takeover by Global and was allowed to remain in office. Stacks of correspondence revealed Monson had pleaded with Global for the return of veteran employees and reinstating the pollution control procedures, "Before we face a disaster that nobody wants to see."

In every instance, the record showed, Monson's pleas were either ignored or rejected.

Browsing through a pile of correspondence, George stumbled across the smoking gun he was searching for: a memorandum from a Global vice president to Monson.

" ... Not only are your continued rants about our current practices counter-productive, our technical team reports that you have been delinquent in activating our recommended pollutant-concealment procedures: increasing the amount of waste-water laced with our cocktail of masking chemicals. Mister Monson, you are hereby ordered to enable this procedure or face severe readjustment of your current responsibilities."

There it was. Chester Monson was not the villain here; it was Global, pure and simple.

George backed away from his desk, walked to stand before the wide expanse of his office window, Boston Commons to one side, Old North Church in the distance to the other.

Doctor Lee's words spoken at Old Granary came to mind: "This is the hunt you must pursue, to validate a universal truth, where it matters most, in your court of law."

He hit the intercom 'on' button, "Carolyn, get me Chester Monson, Sterling Chemical in Danbury, I think it is. New Hampshire. Thanks."

Ten minutes passed when Carolyn knocked on his door.

"Come in," looking up from his desk.

"Um, they said Mister Monson's no longer there."

"Not there? You mean he's out?"

"The way they said it, it's like he's no longer with the company."

George blinked, "Damn."

"Want me to try somewhere else?"

"No, no," his hand grasping his forehead, "that's alright, thanks."

"Doesn't look good, does it?"

"No," he looked up, "it doesn't."

"If there's anything I can do ... "

"No, no, I, I'll take care of it. Thanks. I'll buzz you if I need something."

She understood, turned, walked out the open door.

George hit his fist on the desk.

He sat for several minutes, eyes looking around the room, searching for he knew not what. He pushed his chair back forcefully, rose, walked purposefully out the door, up the hallway towards a bespectacled woman at a desk outside a closed-door office.

"He in?"

She nodded. He opened the door, in full stride walked in briskly. His father, seated at the end of a long mahogany table, looked up, his expression a question mark.

"Georgie?"

"Monson's gone. Why?"

His father rolled his shoulders, "How would I know?"

"There's something rotten in Denmark, and it looks like Global."

His father blanched, "Oh, it does, does it?"

"Look Dad, I've been looking over the records. It shows clearly that

Chester Monson did all he could to comply with whatever rules he had to, but he was stopped by guys upstairs at Global. They're the ones responsible, not Chester."

"And your point is?"

"Let's look at the facts, show the record. Put the blame where it belongs, and that's right on Global's shoulders."

"You're kidding, of course."

"No."

"Are you out of you mind?"

"Dammit, Dad, I'm in my right mind, maybe for the first time in quite awhile. I mean, what are we doing here? Just what are we doing?"

"Don't lose it now, boy. You're in enough of a hole as it is. Last thing you want to do now is go against the boys at Global."

"It's not fair."

"Fair?" his father laughed out loud, "fare is what you pay a cabbie."

"Oh, come on!" George shouted, his voice louder than it should be. "Don't we stand for anything? Are we decent attorneys, or just a bunch of whores?"

"Get a grip, sonny. You know as well as I do how it works. Don't get your panties in a bunch. Forget about Chester Monson and Global's involvement in this thing. We're doing our best to keep them out of it."

"So, Chester takes the fall and Global stays pristine and blameless."

"You might say," his father began turning away in his chair. "And you should learn from it. It's called taking one for the team."

George reeled, stared bullets at his father.

"If this is the way the team works, I just may want a trade."

Turning on his heel, he tread heavily out the door, closed it hard behind him.

Exasperated, he stomped back towards his office, face turning red as he heard Carolyn, "You have a call. Mister Monson, line four."

George stepped into his office, closing the door behind him. He picked up the phone, "Chet?"

"Hi George," Monson sounded chatty as usual, "glad I caught you. I heard you were trying to reach me."

"I was. They said, you're no longer there?"

"That's right," a distraught edge in his voice, "didn't take 'em long, did it."

"What happened?"

"Global. They just dropped in, told me I had 'till the end of the day; that was it. Orders from above. Just get the hell out."

"Shit. When?"

"Monday, about ten in the morning," his voice lowering, "forty-seven years with a company, founded by my father, and I'm out in a matter of hours."

"Uh, you, they offered you a buyout or something."

"Oh yeah, on condition I don't talk to anyone about the case."

"Sheeze," George blew out.

"Oh, there's more. They told me you're on the block. They want to blame the two of us for planning the whole thing. Our own little conspiracy they knew nothing about."

"What the fuck?"

"It's horseshit, of course. But that's what they're up to. That's why they want you out of the mix. Thought I owed you a heads-up."

"Wait a minute, isn't there a…"

"Watch your back, my friend," Monson interrupted, "these guys play hardball."

Glancing out his interior window, George saw Harrison in the hallway, chatting with Carolyn.

"Anything else?"

"Nope, just that they're not going to take this rap when they've got pigeons on the wire."

George saw Harrison's eyes dart towards him, piercing through the window.

"Thanks for the heads-up, Chet. Sorry you got shafted. You need anything, stay in touch, and best to Martha. Keep that chin up, buddy, okay?"

"Will do. Let me know if, uh, make that when—they drop the anvil on you."

"Thanks, I think. Take care."

He set down the phone, looked out the interior window. Harrison was out of sight.

He buzzed Carolyn, "Could you come in, please."

She opened his door. Took three steps in, "Yes?"

"Harrison, he here to see me?"

"No, at least he didn't say so. Might be with your father. Don't know for sure."

He blinked, eyes on the interior window, "Okay, that'll do. Thanks."

Carolyn walked out, turning, "Open or closed?"

"Closed," he turned, dropped in a heap into the leather cushions of his chair.

He stiffened at the loud buzz of the intercom.

"Here it comes!"

"George," his father's voice, "come in here please." It was a command.

George pushed the speak button, "Be right there."

Steeling himself, he knew what was coming.

Pushing up from his desk, he grabbed the manila envelope with the return address clearly embossed on the top left corner, Bank of Montreal. Without thinking, he stuffed the envelope into his jacket pocket, for some reason it just felt like it belonged there.

CHAPTER FIFTY ONE

If you cannot find the truth right where you are, where else do you expect to find it?
-Dogen

George entered his father's office. His father, Nick and Harrison were seated around the conference table, all eyes upon him. Flashing a reassuring smile, Harrison pulled out a chair for him. He acknowledged the gesture, sat down next to Harrison, facing his father and uncle.

"You heard about Monson." Nick began, his voice a low whisper.

George nodded, "Yeah, just now."

Nick flashed a glance at his brother, his eyes returning, steeled on George.

"He had to go, kid. Shows the regulators what we're willing to comply with …"

"Horseshit, Nick," George exploded, "what it shows is he's been made a scapegoat."

"So, that's how you see it?" his father barked. "A scapegoat?"

"Look," George said, "I've seen the records. Chet did all he could to keep the company clean. It was his father's baby, for God's sake. It was the bastards at Global, pushing for more profits that messed things up. He tried like hell to stop it."

"You think so." Nick said, a crooked smile curling his lip.

"Yes, I do."

"And what if you're right?"

George stared at Nick, unsure of what he wanted.

"Then what, kid?"

"We ought to put the blame where it is. Call out those who ..."

"So that's what you think? We're whistleblowers to our most important client."

"No, Just ..."

"What else would you call it?"

George blinked, looked at his father, then back at Nick.

"Nick, it's just, well, it's just that it doesn't seem right to put Monson in the dumper. Guess it bothers me more than it should."

"He's being well taken care of, believe me. You shouldn't worry about that."

"Long as he keeps his trap shut," George shot back.

"And he's perfectly willing to do just that," Nick smiled it.

George shuffled in his chair, face turning crimson.

"Damn it. It's just ..."

"Let it go," Harrison piped in, whispering. "It's a done deal."

"George," his father's tone reassuring, "you've had a hard couple of months. Why don't you take a few weeks off. Take a month if you want. We'll see to it your accounts are covered. What do you say?"

George's eyes narrowed. "So you're putting me out to pasture too. Just like Chet."

"No, no. Nothing of the sort. I just think it's in our best interest now for you to stay out of the limelight and get some rest. What do you think, Nick?"

"You're right. The kid needs to get his head together."

George looked down at his hands, rubbing them together tautly.

He looked back up, glaring at Nick, "In our best interest, eh? So, what you want me to do is get out of the way, right? Just get the hell out of the way."

"Don't look at it like that, son," his father said. "It's the best thing for everyone, you especially."

"And I suppose that means I'm not to say a word to the press about why the hell I'm not responding to the charges against me? You guys gonna' take care of that too?"

"Exactly," Nick said. "All you gotta' do is keep a low profile. We'll get you out of this clean as a whistle. Right, Jack?" Harrison nodded, "Not a worry. Pass a coupla' news cycles, we're back out of the woods."

George leaned forward, head in his hands, upper lip curled.

He dropped his hands, looked up. "Okay, let's be sure here. I stay out of the picture, take a month or so off, and you're satisfied. Right?"

Nick shared a glance with his brother. "Right. That's all we ask. And whatever else comes up, you've got to trust us that, in the end, everything will be back to normal."

"That what you're telling me, Nick? Trust us?"

"That's it. That's precisely what I'm saying."

"All right," George pushed his chair back, ceremoniously stood, peered over the table as a capstone atop their contract. "Gentlemen, you've got yourself a deal. George the third is out of here, on sabbatical, vacation, whatever the hell you want to call it."

The three men watched him warily, fidgeting in their seats.

"Anything else?" George asked.

"That's it," his father replied.

"You're certainly taking this well," Nick grinned.

"No," George leaned in, both hands splayed on the table, "you're certainly taking it well."

His father and Nick exchanged hurried glances as Harrison bent forward in his chair.

"After all, you've given me time to work on a project that's been percolating for a while."

They looked at him, curiosity on their faces.

"Something's come up?" his father asked, suspicion in his voice.

"Yep. Something I've been putting off too long. And now, I have you to thank you all, for allowing me to proceed."

"Anything we should know about?" his father asked.

"Probably, I'll let you know when the time's right. That it?"

Looking puzzled, his father motioned, "Yes."

George turned, bumping Harrison on his way, "Sorry, Jack." He said, with a snicker.

He walked down the hallway toward his office, his eyes wide, vision clear. He patted his jacket pocket feeling the envelope tucked inside.

He was smiling, ear-to-ear.

CHAPTER FIFTY TWO

The best doctor is one who can treat sickness before it occurs, instead of after it appears.
-The Yellow Emperor's Classic Internal Medicine

When sorted out, they realized their twin suspensions gave them more time to review the past life therapy summaries forwarded by Doctor Lee documenting case after case of patients having resolved conditions after recalling episodes from their previous lifetimes.

"Friggin' amazing," George whistled.

"That's exactly what I've seen from the regressions with my patients," Carol's spat out in frustration, "and Isobel made me stop!"

"Okay, professor, which came first, the scientific data or the clinical applications?"

"That's the tightrope between empirical science's question, 'why something should work,' and the clinical application, how does it actually works in the real world?"

"And the answer is …?"

"That's the edge of science. It's never linear. We really don't know what actually happens in healing. It's a complex puzzle, a work in progress. You'd be surprised how much is simply assumed; how little is objectively demonstrable."

George snickered, "So, let me see; nothing's static, it's all fluid? Even measuring something doesn't give the answer? Great! Carol, you work in a world that's the opposite of mine. The law is the law. It's black and white, right there for me to apply it for my clients. So, just how do you heal your patients?"

She tilted her head back, "I guide them to the place where they can do the work themselves. The body knows how to heal itself. I try to steer them back to their essential nature, where their functional wisdom resides. That's the nature of psychology, rediscovering the archival places that hold the answers."

He bent his head in a gesture of skepticism.

"Believe me," she continued, "deep down inside, we all have the tools to restore our own well being. Ultimately, all healing is self-healing, a skill most of us have forgotten. Me? I'm just the tour guide."

"Where do I sign up for the trip?" he laughed, tumbled onto her with unbridled affection.

"Honey, now's not the time," she chided, hesitatingly, not quite so sure herself.

"Okay, but I'll get you for this."

"You'd better, counselor," she purred, grasping his face tightly to her breasts, his kisses raining down over her sweatshirt-covered chest, moving down over her belly before sitting back up, grinning ear-to-ear, "rain check."

They went back to the mound of papers before them.

He craned his neck as Carol dissected the case studies, "See the pattern? Find the event from the past, then apply it to relieve the pain of the present. It's always the same."

By the end of an afternoon of immersion into the sea of Lee's verifiable results, George was becoming a convert under Carol's tutelage. Soon, they began diving into subjects more and more obscure, less tangible; each a challenge for them both.

"I'm having a tougher time with these physicists' papers than I had with your therapy cases," he said. "This whole space-time continuum thing: their belief that our view of the world is relative, and wholly personal. And that space and time cannot be separated. Blows me away!"

"Me too. These physicists have altered how the world is viewed through their far-reaching paradigms. They believe that the power of consciousness shapes the world. And that our mind–body connection fluidly interacts with an unlimited intelligent source. Some think we're nothing but a container of living matter, swimming in a sea of energy, creating the universe moment-by-moment. I'll bet no more than one per cent of the rest of the world knows what they're talking about."

George laughed, "Then I feel better, I guess."

CHAPTER FIFTY THREE

The most important thing is this: to be able at any moment to sacrifice what we are, for what we can become.
-Charles Du Bois

Two evenings a week, Tuesdays and Fridays, Doctor Lee joined the two of them, adding his medical expertise to interpret the role reincarnation had played in his documented cases, sometimes delving into tenets of ancient eastern philosophy to prepare the augugnmt for Iris's claim.

This evening, as the three of them were sitting cross-legged, on the carpet of Carol's apartment, Lee began the dissection between the differing beliefs of the East and the West.

"In eastern thought, the most important characteristic of reality is unity, the inter-relationship of all things, all events. It is a basic Oneness of Being. In many ways, this is the essence of all eastern faiths, Buddhism, Taoism and Hinduism. Your western view is mechanical, the eastern, organic, ever-changing. In this view, each and every particle, every action in the universe, it's all inter-connected."

"How do you mean, mechanical?" George lost in the clouds.

"It goes back to Descartes, his *cogito ergo sum*, 'I think, therefore I am.' It led western man to overstate the importance of his mind as the key to his identity, rather than just one part of the self, not the totality of the complete organism. The Frenchman's view celebrated the mental self to the exclusion of everything else, negating the soul's significance. Such an erroneous perspective is as limiting as it is distorted."

George nodded, his eyes glazing over.

"Do you not see the difference?" Lee asked.

"Sort of," he half-responded, "but, how does any of this apply to, what we're doing?"

"It is this: over time, with the advance of science, we have adopted an increasingly holistic view of the universe. With the discovery of molecules, atoms, and their component parts, starting in 1500 AD with the advent of the microscope, opened a world previously invisible, beyond our powers of observation. Of course, these elements were always there; we just couldn't see them. Now, they are all accepted. Well, today's physicists have gone beyond, locating even smaller elements. Waves become particles; particles become strings. It is now accepted that everything in our universe is, in fact, composed of energy and matter, ever changing, fluid—in other words, George, an evolving dance of nature and spirit; matter and energy all one and the same. There is no difference."

George shook his head back and forth, confused.

Lee stopped, inhaled. "Eastern mystics rely on direct insights into the essence of reality. Physicists rely upon observations of nature and experimentation. Are such techniques so different?"

"Throughout the twentieth century, the two systems have grown closer, nearly inseparable. Einstein's contribution on relativity moved the play eastward. Quantum mechanics moved it even further. Today's modern physics and the beliefs of Eastern mystics are nearly parallel."

He handed a bound notebook to Carol, "Read these treatises from some of the world's leading physicists, all of whom subscribe to the distinct feasibility of our reaching into previous existences through the relativity of time and space."

George stood, stretched his arms over his head, eyes squeezed shut.

"Sorry doctor," she snickered, "I'm afraid you've left George speechless."

George laughed, "Doctor, that's not easy to do, you amaze me."

"I do not mean to," Lee's words clipped, "my only goal is to assist you to be confident and competent in building your case, to fully comprehend the totality of material you have at your disposal."

"Then I believe it's time we begin focusing on the specifics of

Carol's immersion into Iris," George said. "I'll leave the science to the scientists. Since it's Iris I'm representing, I'd better get to know her better."

"Well stated counselor," Lee smiled, "you seem now to be prepared to meet her."

Carol slowly rose, looked pleadingly at Lee. "Are you sure? Is this a good idea?"

"Of course, there is no better way."

Rising, Lee turned to George. "You must remain silent throughout. I ask that you only observe. You shall see her reality for yourself."

George gulped, locked eyes with Carol, who looked back at him with reassurance.

His education in past life therapies was about to take a sharp turn.

CHAPTER FIFTY FOUR

The physical journey is to serve the soul journey.
-Doctor and Master Zhi Gang Sha

Lee motioned for Carol to be seated on the love seat. George watched as she settled in, pressing her back into the cushions. Feeling out of place, he walked toward the window, "Should I shut the blinds?" Lee shook his head. "No thanks, just relax and observe."

George hesitated, ambled to a chair across from Carol, "Am I in the way … ?"

"Not in the least, please, be seated."

Moving like a duck out of water, George sat down, not five feet from Carol. She winked at him, fully enjoying his awkwardness.

Lee stood before her, stared into her eyes for several seconds. She looked up, her eyes locked in on his. He spoke to George in low tones, "As you will see, Carol has a trained mind that allows her to slip into a meditative state very quickly. With little or no prodding, she is capable of placing herself into a hypnotic trance. All I need do is assist her in reaching deeply into her psyche, her subconscious. Once her rational mind is silenced, her intuitive self comes forward, heightening awareness. I will tap into her unconscious storehouse, seeking her intentional awareness of Iris. From there, it is up to her, as the transition will be completed."

She felt a warm glow in the validation of her mentor's comment.

George nodded, as if in understanding.

Lee turned to Carol, "Are you ready?" He asked, his voice as comforting as a hug.

"Yes," she sighed in a soft voice, her eyes closed.

Doctor Lee raised his right hand, tapped three fingertips several times at the center of her forehead. He pulled his hand back, directed in a near whisper, "You see the tunnel, follow it down, further still. Deeper. Good, now, just rest for a moment in this, the place, you find yourself. Just relax even more."

George fidgeted in his chair, eyes widening.

"Iris?" Lee targeting in, "tell me," testing his subject, "would you be willing to meet my friend here, George?"

"Certainly," her voice now ragged and an octave lower than Carol's.

She turned her head, closed eyes tracking his voice.

"George, say hello," Lee prompted.

"Hello," George muttered, staring at his fiancé, his world turning upside down.

"Nice to meet you, George, have we met before? "

George looked at Lee in near panic, unsure of what to do next.

"George is down from Boston," Lee interjected, "he's a friend of mine and he's here with us today to ask you some questions, Iris. Is that okay with you?"

"Well then, yes, I guess it'll be just fine."

Lee's eyes prodded George to begin.

"Uh," George stepping out on the ledge, "Iris?" unsure of just how to begin this process. His own voice a surprise to himself, "Iris, please, can you tell me more about your locket, the one your father gave you?"

"Well," she began, an air of gaiety in her voice. "It was one of the happiest day's of my life."

"Yes?" Lee coached, "tell us more."

George looked at Lee, confused, fidgeting uncomfortably in his chair, eyes widening.

"It was the Investiture Ball in the spring of 1929, for all the new appointees in the diplomatic corps. We were all dressed for the occasion. Herbert looked so dashing in his black tails and white tie; such a handsome man. My red satin gown had a flounce train that swished as I moved. My whole family was there to celebrate my husband's appointment. It was such an honor. Life felt so saturated with unlimited hope for all our futures that night. My sister Anna, oh, she was so elegant in her royal blue rhinestone gown. When she danced, the dress sparkled like hundreds of tiny stars. And my older sister, Ethel, in her layers of green chiffon, so beautiful, like a mist of swirling clouds. Oh, and my brother Louis was there, too, looked like a big penguin in his tux!" Laughter peeled as she relived this vivid experience.

Lee nudged George, encouraging him to direct his questions to get the specific answers he was seeking. "Uh," George stammered, "Iris, the locket?"

"Oh, yes, sorry. I was just so enjoying the sights, being with my family and all," her voice drifting.

"Please, continue."

"While Herbert was occupied with his colleagues, Joseph my father, twirled me onto the dance floor. I wish I had known it was to be our last dance together...forever," her voice once again trailing into silence.

"...And?"

"Well, right in the middle of the dance, the orchestra in full swing, Dad, waltzes me over to the outdoor terrace. What a breathtaking sight. Washington D.C. all lit up. So awe inspiring, everywhere I looked it was history!"

Doctor Lee, jumped in sensing George's unfamiliarity in the timing of this territory, "Iris, what happened next?"

"Well, Dad was quite serious and tense, there was so much going on, he was rushed, there seemed to be an urgency. He reached into his jacket pocket and pulled out this gold chain with a heart. He opened it up and showed me the inscriptions of my son's birthday's. He told me to put their pictures inside when I was ready, he'd 'run out of time.' Then, he slipped it around my neck with the instructions, 'that whenever I was ready it would....' her voice broke. She began to sigh deeply, tears streaming down her cheeks, lips quivering.

Lee took the helm. "Good, that's enough for today, thank you Iris, you did well, very well." Lee leaned forward, tapped the side of Carol's right temple with his fingertips three times, then three again, saying,

"Carol, you can come back now. You did a wonderful job. You will remember nothing of this visit. It was all for the benefit of George."

He leaned back, clapped his hands together loudly. Carol's body jerked. Her eyes flew open. She looked at Lee, then at George, still wiping her wet eyes.

"What was ... ?" she trailed. "Did I miss ... ?"

"No," Lee reassured, "your Iris just met George."

George's head was spinning, where to start?

"Carol," he stammered, "did you, do you, I mean ..."

"Don't worry," she cooed, "it's alright. It's what happens in therapy all the time. You see? Like I've been telling you, we can reach past lives from the depths of our own consciousness."

George looked at her, mystified, itching to find a place where he could put this in his world. He rose, walked to the window, looked back, "I, I don't know what to say."

"What you should be saying," Lee began in a stone cold sober tone, "is that you now know how best to demonstrate the existence of your client in your case."

George looked back at him, frozen, "You mean, do this, on the stand, in the witness chair, in court?"

"If you so choose," Lee continued, turning to face him, "counselor, the case is yours. The most I can do is provide you with rock solid evidence."

George walked back to a chair across the room, he needed some space, sat heavily, eyes locked on Lee's, "Holy, Holy Shit."

"You've seen the quality of the evidence," Lee recounted, "the results of my work, the works of top scientists, religious leaders. You've seen Carol's cases. You know how strongly she feels about them and the testimony from physicians whose patients she's treated successfully through regression. You've seen the letter and the gifts left by her father, naming Iris and only Iris as the legal recipient."

Lee paused, reflecting the astonishment on George's face, "And now, my friend, you have seen Iris for yourself. What more could you want?"

George shook his head, desperate to get back on solid footing, "A cocktail."

Lee and Carol looked at him incredulously.

"No, just kidding, I see your point. Holy Cow. Wow. Double Wow!"

He rose slowly from the chair, stretched his back, exhaled a long breath, "Whew. 'Dead woman sues her elderly children'. We're going to raise a lot of eyebrows once word gets out on this filing." Mobilizing his instincts and gearing up his initial strategy, he blurted, "So, we'd better plan to get ahead of the curve."

"What do you mean?" Carol questioned.

"Publicity, an organized PR effort, news releases, features, interviews, the whole enchilada, 'cause we're gonna' need it."

Lee looked at him in curiosity, "How is this done?"

"I'll take care of it," George asserted. "I've some PR folks, some flacks who owe me more than a few favors. And believe me, getting advance tips on a law suit filed by a dead person, they're gonna' love it!"

He stood, walked over to Carol, took her hands in his, "Sweetie, it's gonna' be one hell of a ride."

She looked up at him, uncertain of this on-coming whirlwind ahead of them, "What of your father? Will he …"

"Don't worry, I'll handle Dad," For the first time in ages, George could feel a genuine smile emerge. "They want me on suspension? Time I see what I can do on my own."

"But, your position at the firm?" She worried for him.

"There's ways. Not to worry. There's ways."

"You need an office?" Lee offered. "You can work out of mine?"

"Thanks, Doc, no thanks. I'll set something up. Not to worry, people. Let's get cracking."

Within a fortnight, George would file a complaint in the name of his new client known as Iris Middelton Paulson, claiming rightful ownership of a recently discovered and heretofore unknown fortune.

The U.S. District Court in the vicinage of Boston had never before seen an action like this one. George started ticking off the names of sitting civil judges wondering who would be assigned. He only hoped that it'll be one who's aspiring political career hadn't been derailed by his family's overzealous ambitions.

CHAPTER FIFTY FIVE

There is one thing stronger than all the armies of the world, and that is an
idea whose time has come.
-Victor Hugo

George joined his father at a window-side table at Number 9 Waterfront, a high-end restaurant overlooking Boston Harbor. Outside, frozen snow covered the wharf railings like frosting, while piles of snow blanketed several moored boats—a peaceful winter scene worthy of a postcard.

"Right on time," his father greeted, an uneasy expression on his face.

George nodded, pulled out a chair, sat across from the man. They had not met nor spoken since George had taken his hiatus from the law firm.

"Good to see you, son," his father reaching out across the table to shake his protégées hand, "you look well."

"Thanks. As do you."

"Enjoying your vacation?"

George grimaced, "That what you call it?"

"That's what it is, isn't it?" turning his eyes to pick up the luncheon menu. He handed one to George, who said nothing as he reached for the offering.

Both men opened their menus and read in silence, conversation having come to a halt.

"Anything new with Sterling?" George broke the peace, eyes still on the menu.

"Coming along, coming along."

His father set down his menu, looked at George.

"In fact, just last week, two supervisors admitted to instigating the dumping."

George leaned back in his chair, shoulders slumping, "How ..."

"In order to speed up delivery, a shortcut. For bonuses and all."

"They admitted this? On their own?"

His father leaned back in his chair, set down his menu, satisfaction written all over his face, "They testified you had nothing to do with it. Monson was the only one who knew. Puts you in the clear, clean as a whistle."

George looked quizzically at his father, set down his menu.

"That easy, huh?"

His father guffawed. "Yup, that easy. You ready to order?"

George hesitated, wanting to get up and walk away, but reconsidered, "Sure, let's order. Then, I've got something for you."

A waitress arrived at their table, pad and pen in hand. George senior, used to taking charge in such situations, spouted, "We'll both have the Codfish filets as an entrée with a shared appetizer of steamed clams."

"Uh," interjected his son, "sorry Dad, not today." He turned to the waitress, "I'll have the lobster salad."

The waitress picked up the repartee between the men. A busboy appeared behind her, set down a small wicker basket, brimming with streaming fresh-baked rolls.

"Something to drink?" the waitress added.

Both men shook their heads, no thanks. "Alright then," she said. "Be right back with the appetizer." She turned, walked away, leaving them alone.

"Dad," George said, "I won't be back for awhile."

"What's that?" his father asked, intent on opening a warm sourdough roll.

"I said, I won't be back. Not till I finish a new case."

His father stared at him, blankly. George stared back, waiting for a reply.

"A case? This the one you said was coming up?"

"Yes," George leaned back, a stoic expression crossing his face, "that's the one."

"And?" his father's voice lilting, creases deepening on his forehead.

"It's pro bono," he announced.

"Pro bono? On your own?"

"Yes sir. It's something, a cause of sorts, I've, well, come to believe in enough to take it pro bono."

His father looked at him warily, unsure of what to say.

"It's not right for the firm." George added, "This one's mine to ride, win or lose."

Flush-faced, his father blurted, "What the hell you talking about?"

"Something I've come to care deeply about. Something, well, something I feel, I've got to do."

George paused, looked down at his hands, looked up, steely-eyed at this father, "And Dad, this case will do more to elevate my profile than any of your paid-off Sterling stooges."

George's father slid back in his chair, his face reddening.

"Look," George explaining, his tone mellowed, "it's a lot like what I did to exonerate those Salem innocents at the State House, and the witch trials."

"Good God, son, not another powdered wig fiasco," his father moaned, a torn roll in his hand.

George laughed, shook his head side to side.

"No, Dad, that's one thing you don't have to worry about."

"Well, what do I have to worry about it? What is it?"

"Nothing, so long as I keep this as my own and not involve the firm."

"Why the difference?"

"Let's just say, it wouldn't be good for you, or the firm, to bring it inside the practice."

"It?" his father asked, "what the hell is this … it?"

George leaned forward, took a deep breath, "It has to do with changing the legal definition and medical interpretation of death and the legitimacy of certain legal rights."

"Certain legal rights?" his father screeched. "What in God's name …"

The waitress approached, a bowl of steaming clams for them to share. She set it down between them, chirping, "Bon appetit."

The two men looked at each other, stalemate expressions on their faces.

George's head dropped, "Look, you've gotta' trust me on this. I wish I could tell you more, but I can't just yet. It's better if you don't know all the details. Just know that I wouldn't touch it if I didn't have more than enough evidence to make a solid case."

His father looked away, reached for his napkin, tucked it into his shirt collar, covering his tie.

"I've leased this small office, just outside Cambridge. Things are coming together. Once it gets rolling, I mean, this could be something big. Really big."

His father shook his head back and forth, "George, who the hell do you think you are, the prodigal son?" Quickly returning his attention to the bowl of clams.

"What if I am?"

His father snapped his eyes back, leering menacingly at George.

"You're a Mansbridge! You can't just walk out and start your own thing. Anything you do reflects on our name, on the firm. You know that!"

"I'm sorry. But listen, it's, just, of course, I know I'm a Mansbridge. But, I'll cast this as something totally apart from the firm. I'm making a point of that. I can do it."

"You still haven't said what's this *it*, that's so damn compelling?"

George took a long breath. "Dad, I love you, very much.…and, well, I've got to be unleashed, free, to pursue my own dream, my way, to be true. I can't fake it anymore."

His father frowned, nodded, reached for the clam bowl.

"I'm prepared to give one hundred percent to this case. And I've got to tell you, it's probably going to be the biggest risk of my life. I don't know how it'll turn out. I just know I've got to give it my all. Do or die!"

His father's arm stopped, hung in mid-air, "Stop. This sounds a little too melodramatic for a court case! Do or die? For God's sake, boy."

George acknowledged his father's comment, "I've got what I need to try the case, scientific evidence, legal precedent." He paused, added, "Dad, I'm about to blow a hole in our country's entire legal system."

"Sweet Jesus," his father placed the bowl between them, "this is what I get when I leave you alone for a couple of weeks?"

"I know, it sounds cryptic and radical, but, a man's gotta be, what a man's got to do."

A quizzical look replaced the frown on his father's face.

George noticed the change in expression, "This case….?" His father asked, "why so much mystery? In God's name, for what?"

George nodded knowing he'd have to tell his father something plausible.

"For rights to an inheritance, one specifically designated for, well, for the person who, apparently hasn't been fully acknowledged by the legal system, yet."

His father blinked, mouth agape. "Son, to what? Your being very evasive. Please just don't make a complete fool of yourself!"

"Believe me. I've got expert witnesses, all the chops I'll need."

"So," his father said almost in a whisper, "this is about….?" His father leaned, reached for another helping of clams.

"Property rights, Dad, Yes. And …"

"Take some clams, son."

"Just know that no matter what, I'm going to do my best."

"I never doubted that part son. Just, take some clams."

Then, a long blank silence between them. Knowing full well that his father's sudden quiet was neither a sign of acceptance nor even a truce, George leaned forward, spread his napkin over his lap and reached for a spoonful of clams.

His father had beaten him to it.

Reaching for a plate, George complied, lifting a couple of clams from the bowl.

"Let me explain it this way," he filled in a few blank spaces.

Over the next half-hour, George laid out in the most cryptic way that he could without tipping his hand this, out-of-the-box, proceeding. He explained his litigation strategy, his supporting details and his list of potential witnesses. His father listened in silence, largely diverted by his plate of clams, occasionally nodding, either in understanding or impatience. George was unable to detect which one it was.

At the end of lunch, his father leaned back, wiped his mouth with his napkin and said his first words in more than thirty minutes, "Georgie, let me say this. It better be good, because you've just put your future here in jeopardy. And, oh, you're buying."

This bout was just beginning.

CHAPTER FIFTY SIX

The mark of your ignorance is the depth of your belief in injustice and tragedy.
-Richard Bach

Only time would tell.

They knew they had only one chance to set a legal precedent for their radical idea. While they knew much was riding on their efforts, Carol and George each harbored private doubts that they could pull it off.

"Lot done today," George heaved, his eyes blurred from reading documents. Legal pads filled with notes skewed across his desk and spilled down on the floor.

Lee nodded, "...and yet a long way to go."

George was being pulled along like a reluctant puppy, a trail of doubts littering his path.

"Lee, you said you'd provide me all the evidence I need; so far, I ain't totally gettin' it."

"Patience," Lee assured him, "the totality of cases, mine and Carol's, combined with the findings from preeminent scientists and the veritable religions of the world, soon will erase your doubts."

"It's not my doubts, it's the doubts of the judge I worry about. You realize we're up against centuries of doubt and dogma when it comes to reincarnation. What we've gotta' do is find ways to convince the hard-core non-believers."

Lee smiled at him, "And you are just the one to do it."

Carol emerged from the kitchen carrying a tray of thick sandwiches on rustic country bread accompanied by large piping hot mugs of tomato bisque soup and some lemon frosted cookies for dessert.

She was the first to break the barrier of introspection. "How goes it?"

"Progress is in sight," Lee said.

"Got a ways to go," George jumped in, remnants of his sandwich entrenched on his lower lip, "just 'cause we buy into it doesn't mean anyone else will."

Carol nodded, "Our argument's got to be solid enough to convince people like Isobel, and believe me, that doesn't seem likely."

Lee smiled, "Our friend is a good measure, as we're asking her to throw off her wardrobe of beliefs for an entirely new design," noting Isobel's slavishness to fashion.

George ventured, "You worked with her, for awhile."

"Yes, for several years. Of course, that was before she disappeared into administration."

Carol laughed loudly, causing both men to stare at her in surprise.

"Was that when you began your research, into past lives?" George asked.

Carol shot a sideways glance at George, a taken-by-surprise look written all over her face at this, an obvious question she had failed to ask.

"Somewhat. But in many ways, it was well before that," Lee stretched his legs in a unhurried manner with an 'I-was-wondering-when-you'd-get-around-to-that,' grin.

"I had three events in the summer of eighty-four when I was an intern at Mercy Hospital as a primary care physician and part time finishing a research grant with my senior colleague, Matthew Goslin, a great mentor, a genius researcher and a good friend. Tragically, on the morning of June twenty-second, he had a fatal brain aneurysm.

He paused, looked out in the distance, "That summer, I was house-sitting on the north end of town."

He looked up, eyes a deep pool, "Two days after Matthew's death, precisely at two-AM, the intercom system in the house began bellowing loud static, so loud it jarred me out of bed. I flew downstairs to the kitchen, to the master intercom console. It was off, yet the static continued, went on for hours. Next morning, I called the homeowners and told them what had happened. They said it hadn't happened before."

He looked both of them in the eyes, "I dismissed it as a surge of electricity phenomena. But I had this strange feeling that it was something more, it made me think of Matthew."

George shrugged, "So? Static noise? What's that got to …?"

Lee ignored the question, "Weeks later, the end of July, I was on hospital rounds; one of my patients, Pamela Phillips, was in the final stage of congestive heart failure. I knew from her vital signs and the amount of pain meds she was on, that she might not make it through the night. She reached out her frail hand, asked if she 'could see me again.' I said, "of course.""

He shook his head, "Pamela died in her sleep, about six hours later. I knew her end-of-life was expected. One week later, to the day, well after midnight, I was having a restless sleep, then, between sleep and wakefulness, I became aware of a presence. I opened my eyes, and there, standing at the foot of my bed, was a young-looking Pamela."

George squinted, questions piling up.

"She wore blue pants, a white sweater. Remember, I had only seen Pamela in hospital gowns, yet here she was, standing strong, dressed, glowing, the picture of health."

Carol glanced at George, noted the strain on his face.

Lee's eyes moistened, "She just stood there, without words; but I heard her voice in my mind, 'Thank you, doctor. Thank you for all you've done. Now, I'm happy and healthy again.' As I was grew more awake, she just, vanished. I had no reference points for this. I spent many days reliving this reel in my mind. Had I made this up as a means to justify death? As a scientist, I tried to make sense out of it."

Wanting more, Carol asked, "And?"

"Then, late August, same summer, my cousin, Wan-Li, daughter of my beloved Aunt Tai-Shu, was getting married. The wedding was traditional Chinese, tea ceremonies and all. The bride was dressed in a ceremonial red silk embroidered gown. It was a picture-perfect day."

He paused, reliving the moment, "The very next morning, five-AM, I got a phone call from the new bride, crying, "mother is dead.""

He wiped away a tear, "My favorite aunt, a massive heart attack, just hours after the wedding. She was only sixty-six years old."

Lee's voice trailed off, his gaze on his two listeners, "Next night, sound asleep, then suddenly awakened, although, as I remember it, my eyes were closed, but I saw everything as clearly as I'm looking at you. There she was, my aunt Tai-Shu, as a young woman with long black hair and porcelain skin. She came to me, hugged me close, her skin was cool to the touch, but there was warmth radiating from her body. Then she spoke, "Phonyong, the doctors were wrong, I was asleep, but now I'm awake.""

Carol's head shook back and forth, her eyes widening.

"Then," Lee added, "she told me of her present experience; that the unconditional love she longed for on my side, was all there was on her side. She said all her faults, her shames, they were no longer relevant, and that our concept of death as finality—it's erroneous, that we're misreading mortality from our side of the veil."

Silence draped the room.

"She said she felt more alive, more complete, than anything she'd experienced on Earth; that over there, profound truths were visible; that the deepest levels of knowledge and understanding were seen clearly as part of each soul's journey toward the Source."

George dropped his head; no idea what those last words meant.

"As you can imagine," Lee said, "I was entranced and took it all in. Auntie said that, unlike life in a physical body, there was a clarity as to how everything fit together. That there was a precise plan unfolding and that we were all playing out an integral part of this big mosaic. For a brief moment, I was awash with her state of awareness, it felt like; pure bliss, indescribable peace, wholeness. I actually felt everything Tai-Shu was sharing. It was as if I was piggy-backing on her awareness."

Lee whistled, remembering the moment.

"She said things like, 'Earth is not our real home. It's simply a temporary schooling in which we learn to master the laws of creation. And as we master these laws, we grow more advance abilities...skills like the ability to heal others. Expanding our soul powers is how we advance our assignments. It's all about service, that's the key, everything we do ultimately must benefit others. Our gifts and talents are to serve and accomplish this one goal. That's the purpose of life in a physical body, to serve."

Lee's face broke out in a wide grin, "She said 'think of a body as a self-repairing space suit for the soul, designed to survive in Earth's atmosphere."

George glanced at Carol, grinned.

"I sensed her time with me was waning." Lee's eyes closed, recounting the last precious moments. "She stressed, with an urgency, that each of our actions determines the course of our life; that we possess the power to alter our destiny at any time. Then, I shall never forget her final words,'Phonyong, remember this, love is supreme, it is the One Reality'."

In the silence, the words echoed for several seconds.

"Quite the odyssey, Lee," George said, his voice cracking a bit.

"That summer was my introduction to the afterlife and beyond. I'd had three callings. What was I going to do with them, ignore the evidence? Three people I had cared deeply about—each made an extraordinary effort to show me the way. It was up to me to make this elusive obvious more visible to others. That's when I began to explore reports of life after death, life before life, using the tool of regression into the body's storehouse. The evidence I found was too compelling to deny."

He sighed, "and that my friends was the end of my former medical career. I studied everything written on the subject from ancient scrolls through modern neuroscience, until I could study no more. That's when I began my services at your university," he nodded towards Carol, "only to find that my explorations into what mattered most were unappreciated."

George leaned forward, reached for the last lemon cookie.

Lee leaned forward, swept his hands across the now empty cookie plate, "Note the lesson, George," his eyes narrowed, "once emptied, this plate no longer serves a purpose; it is no longer needed. It must be put away."

He grinned it, "So too for the body, once our tasks here are completed, they have no use."

George nodded as if a bobblehead.

CHAPTER FIFTY SEVEN

In nothing do men approach so nearly to the gods as in doing good to men.
-Cicero

George stood, walked into the kitchen, plate in hand.

"Done," he chimed from the other room, then walked back, empty-handed.

"More?" He asked.

"Yes. You have to realize who's driving the bus," Lee called out.

"Bus?"

"Driving?" Carol chirped.

"In the words of the great Buddha, 'We are what we think.' All that we are arises with our thoughts. With our thoughts, we make the world." Lee stated.

"You will find that each one of our lives is intertwined with the quality known as virtue. It's the Buddhist's karma, the Christian's deed, the Taoist's Te, Hebrew's gilgul: different words for the same thing. It is simply the process of cause and effect that choreographs every aspect of our life."

"You saying karma, it defines our lives? George groaned. "But, how?"

"Cast off your old assumptions as to how the world is organized," Lee instructed. "You can't understand reincarnation without the concept of karma. They're the flipsides of the same coin."

Settling in, George and Carol nodded tentatively.

"You see, karma operates on a very simple universal mathematical system. Think of it as a cosmic bank. When we make deposits, like acts of kindness, compassionate service, loving gestures, generosity, forgiveness, then, what comes back to us are in-kind withdrawals. We are repaid with good health, financial abundance, loving relationships, blessing and seeming miracles."

Lee paused, watching as the eyes of both listeners blinked.

"Conversely, when we make poor-choice deposits, like deliberate harm, greed, lying, cheating, stealing, jealousy, anger; what is returned are lessons; opportunities for correction. Both provide lessons to be learned and mastered."

Carol chimed, "Lessons?"

"Yes. They can be in many forms: broken relationships, illnesses, financial stress. When any area of your life becomes thwarted, the reason is karmic blockage. Your choice is to learn your lessons now, or learn them later. There are no other options."

Carol slumped her head back into the couch cushion looking up at the ceiling blankly, "So, this throws out my Ph.D. in psychology. If karma is the single cause, the root of our successes and seeds of failures in this life, and in future ones...then...," her voice trailed off reviewing the carnage of her education.

"Doctor, you mean my clients emotional conditions, relationship challenges, mental states originate in their own karmic cause and effect ...?"

"Yes. Karma is the directive under which the Universe operates. It's the law of reciprocity. If you plant tomatoes, you can't expect radishes. Your life is the harvest of what you've planted. Get the picture? Both good and bad deposits have the same purpose: to direct our soul's journey. Every word you say, every action you take, every thought you think is like dropping a pebble in a pond, each has a ripple effect that reverberates back to us. It's the law of energy, no more, no less; not good, not bad, just what it is."

George was visibly unnerved, "What about effects that seem that have no apparent cause; like random events, winning the lottery, car accidents, things that come out of the blue."

"Yes, that seems tricky. It's because of the construct called time. What seems like a lag between cause and effect; events that appear disconnected, are not at all. Every deposit, good or bad, will result in a like return. You've simply forgotten what you have already planted. What you've set in motion. Everything counts. Your future is either collecting the dividends on your good investments or paying the penalties you owe. Nothing flies under the Universe's radar; it has a meticulous accounting system that never fails. We get exactly what we deserve; we've earned it all!"

George moaned, "I'm doomed."

"You're in good company, kiddo," Carol whimpered, "we're all in the same boat."

"Don't waste your time analyzing what you've done in the past. Keep your eye on the end game; get free by paying off your karmic debts. It's a simple solution. Everyone comes to the point in their journey when they no longer want anymore lessons; the moment one realizes suffering no longer is an acceptable way of life. Suffering is like pinching yourself. It hurts. But you fail to notice that you are the one inflicting the pain on yourself."

Lee stopped to let this idea sink in. Carol and George exchanged nervous glances.

"Look, when you begin to understand that you're the one causing your life's circumstances, not outside influences, then the whole game changes. You become more aware of what you say, no more lying, complaining, or judgments. You avoid negative thinking such as anger, greed, jealousy. And you monitor your actions; putting a stop to taking advantage of others. You make life right with right actions. Think of it as in the Greek archery term, sin, meaning 'missing the mark'—make a course correction, take aim and try again."

George's reprisal, "I feel screwed, glued and tattooed."

"Once you get the rules of the game, and you know what's going on, you can form a good game plan. You exercise the power of choice. You don't get sucked into life's seductive illusions. Remember, karma is a debt that requires repayment."

Swirling through George's overtaxed mind were thoughts of walking on hot coals or becoming a monk.

"You have free will, to choose." Lee said in a monotone, "virtue."

"Virtue?" George visibly relieved, feeling like he'd struck a match in a dark cave, "as in doing the right thing?"

"As you understand the Laws of Nature, it's like obeying road signs by driving on the right side of the highway, you get to where you're going with less aggravation. There are no short cuts. Do good, you get blessings, do harm, then you get an opportunity for correction. It's designed as the fastest route to your freedom, though not necessarily, the easiest path. Time is a relative idea; whether it's tomorrow or a million lifetimes from now, the goal is assured. It's not *if* we get free, but *when*. That's your free will... how many times your lessons are repeated or how quickly you accelerate your liberation. You choose. The lessons are choreographed to quicken your journey. Even when they're not what you want. They are always exactly what you need, to correct your mis-takes. You get to re-write your history everyday. No matter who you are, president or pedophile, multimillionaire or murderer—we're all on the same journey. Make the most of every opportunity. Pay attention. Learn quickly."

Having exceeded his audience's satiation point, Lee closed the evening, "The first sign that you're on the right path is when you cross an invisible inner line from seeing the world from 'what's in it for me' to 'how can I serve it'. You'll notice that your body becomes calmer, and your restless, noisy mind chatter quiets. Once you accept that karma is the core-organizing principle of all, then you'll know how and why to live your life."

"No longer a mystery, you're driving the bus."

CHERYL A. MALAKOFF & ROBERT A. CLAMPETT

CHAPTER FIFTY EIGHT

What is essential is invisible to the eye.
-Antoine De Saint-Exapery

The initial filing of Paulson versus Paulson in the Massachusetts' District Court went unnoticed, until Michael Flannery, a popular Boston Globe columnist and longtime acquaintance of the Mansbridge family, devoted half a column to it.

Thumbing through the newspaper while George filled the coffee maker with fresh ground beans, Carol found the item at the top of its designated spot, front page, local section, columns one and two. The words jumped out at her like a panther.

Dead Woman Suing?
At first look, a suit claiming ownership of riches heretofore unclaimed by one party over another, Paulson v. Paulson, may not seem newsworthy. Except that in this case, the claimant has been dead for over thirty years. But wait, there's more. The claimant, the deceased Iris Middelton Paulson, bases her claim against her own children, William and Ethan Paulson of New York City, on the twin beliefs that (1) she is specified as the one and only recipient by the donor, her long deceased father, and (2) she exists today in the form of a yet unnamed woman, who's full identity will be revealed at the trial.
Shades of Bridey Murphy.
What's more, the filing, posted last week, was made by disgraced

former congressional candidate George Mansbridge III, who ended his campaign only months ago following charges of his involvement in a conspiracy to conceal environmental pollution by a chemical firm in New Hampshire.

Put it all together, you've got—well, this is going to be good, yet one more among the many bizarre cases paraded within the commonwealth.

So far, no trial date has been set. Not to worry, I'll keep you posted.

You bet I will.

Carol caught her breath, "This is what you call getting out in front? Bridey Murphy?"

"Relax." He sighed, "now it's been said, it'll be long forgotten by trial. Did you notice? You oughta' thank me for keeping your name out of it."

"So far," she added.

"What am I going to do when it does come out?" Carol frowned.

"Hey," he smiled, "this whole thing is your idea. You ride it or you don't."

Carol put her palms to her eyes, "I know, I know, just, I guess I hadn't prepared for being under the magnifying glass."

"Magnifying glass?" George chuckled, "lady, this case is going to viewed with a microscope before it's over. But, that was the idea, wasn't it?"

"Yes, yes, I know."

She wiped her eyes, crossed her arms. "Okay," shifting gears, "what's next?"

"Well," he said, "we await a response from the Paulson boys, through their attorney. Then a pre-trial scheduling conference."

"Their response," she queried, "what do you expect?"

George couldn't hold back, peeled with laughter, "Expect? All hell to break loose."

CHAPTER FIFTY NINE

My life is my message.
-Mahatma Gandhi

"C'mon in, gentlemen," said the ruddy complexioned, balding Sidney Green, partner in an out-of-the-way Queens, New York based legal firm of Straub, Mickleson and Green.

The Paulson brothers, both slightly bent-over, walked into the small two-room office, with chairs scrunched together before a somewhat dusty desk. Stopping, they waited for instructions. "Sorry for the looks of this place, we've been trying to fix this dump up, know what I mean?" Green chuckled, dusting off a chair, "Sit, sit down, please."

The brothers looked at each other as the squat man plopped into a faded leatherette chair behind his desk, both bumping their chairs together awkwardly before slipping into them.

"Gentlemen, any trouble getting here?"

"No," replied Will, "like you said, a straight shot off the 'L' line subway. No problem at all."

"Coffee?" Green offered.

Ethan looked at Will and answered for both. "No thanks."

"No problem, no problem, and remind me again, who referred you?" Green rambled, reaching for a thin folder before him.

Ethan stammered, "Uh, well we..... you see Henry Straub Sr., was an old friend of the family when they lived in Forest Hills and well, we haven't needed a lawyer in decades and just didn't know who ..." his thoughts trailing off.

"Gotcha'," Green interrupted, quickly opening the folder, "I can hardly believe what I'm reading here."

The brothers glanced at each other, unsure of his comment.

He looked up, eyes furrowing, "You know this is frivolous, don't you?"

"Frankly, Mister Green," Will said, "we don't know what to think."

"How can this be?" Ethan piped in, "a law suit by our mother?"

"It's nuts," Green said, "just nuts. Have you guys found how much we're talking about here?"

"No sir," Will said, "but according to the complaint we received, it looks like millions."

Ethan nodded, "Honestly, we were left enough to maintain our lifestyle but really don't have the cash funds to pay out sizable legal fees, which I am sure this will cost."

Green was stunned, never before had the possibility of such a haul cross his desk. He did the math. Quickly. Green came back with confidence, "Don't worry. I'll take this on a contingency basis. I'll do all the work and pay all of the expenses. And when we succeed, and hear me out, not if, but when we succeed and you collect the money, then, I'll receive a percentage of the recovery, say twenty percent, which is less than I usually charge. What do you say?" Green held his breath.

Ethan nodded his head in agreement with Will following suit.

"Great I'll draw up the retainer papers and have them to your place this afternoon," Green broadly smiled. "In the meantime, let's make this matter our top priority. I'll want all of your mother's estate papers, like birth and death certificates. I am going to win this one big, for you boys. I want you both to rest assured, this claim is so out there, you've got nothing to worry about."

"But, how can ... ? " Will persisted, "how can someone represent our mother? When she's dead and gone?"

"They can't," Green stated, leaning back in his chair, placing a hand on his ample abdomen, "that's the key. Gentlemen, this is a slam-dunk. You, both of you, are the rightful heirs to anything held in the Paulson estate, clear and simple. You've got documents showing your mother left it all to you. Everything. I don't know where they're coming from."

"Mister Green," Ethan asked, "why do you think, well, how is it they think that it's not ours?"

"That," he answered, "my friend, is for us to find out. What I love about this, besides that it's a slam-dunk, is that it's filed by one of those high-falutin' Boston bozos who think they know everything. Well, we'll show them a thing or two about good old New Yorkers, eh?"

Both brothers cringed as Green's boisterous laugh cackled throughout the cramped office space, echoing off the walls not unlike that of a murder of crows.

CHAPTER SIXTY

Whatever you can do or dream you can, begin it. Boldness has genius, magic
and power in it. Begin it now.
-Goethe

What began as a trickle soon became a stream, then a river. Within a
month, a flood of news coverage burgeoned from the pages of
newspapers throughout the nation, detailing what had become known
as, "The Trial of Two Lives."

The oddity of a deceased mother filing a claim against her own
children soon captured the imagination, not only of the public but also
the street-hardened veterans of the news business themselves.

Flannery's initial commentary on the case in the Boston Globe was
followed by a flurry of news reports seeking to describe details of what
seemed a newsworthy oddity within the legal system. Associated Press
coverage landed on the pages of newspapers across the nation. All at
once, phones were ringing off the hook as reporters sought interviews
with George, allowing him to control the message to the public.

With the trial scheduled six months following the filing, George
had plenty of time to conduct a directed campaign of publicity on the
case.

Careful to protect the identity of Carol Klein as the mysterious
claimant from public disclosure, he insisted his client was Iris Paulson,
herself in a reincarnated form. Reporter attempts to scour the court
filings turned up little, George having carefully worded his complaint
with no identifying information leading back to Carol. However, as

the complaint clearly stated that the value of the property sought to be claimed was valued in the many millions of dollars. George essentially bought himself a media frenzy pandering to a lottery fantasizing audience.

George being media savvy, played his hand well using this platform to drill down on the more substantive details.

"We have provided you with the relevant points of this case," was his standard answer, "let me suggest that, as the trial unfolds, you will see that our claim is based on solid scientific grounds, backed by clear historic precedent. What may seem unusual to you now, will soon prove to be indisputable fact."

His first appearance on television was CNN's Barry Wheeling show, where George easily fended off an array of generalized queries, often more amusing than substantive, by the erstwhile host of the show.

His appearance on the widely acclaimed Jocelyn Lancer's show, syndicated nationally from a studio in Chicago, was notable for his host's agreement and enthusiastic support of his position, stating her own long-standing belief in life after death. "What you're dealing with," she said, "is that you're delving into a subject people consider taboo. Hands off. And it disturbs them. Of course, they're wrong. And from where I sit, I see where your case is a step forward, by at least bringing to light a subject too many have chosen to ignore."

A completely different tack was taken by William O'Leary, on his Fox News show, 'The O'Leary Report', on which George faced antagonism and a barrage of pointed questions attacking his sincerity, if not his sanity.

"You really know what you're doing here Counselor," O'Leary prodded, "you're creating a smokescreen that could mess up all sorts of things; from defining inheritances to belief in religion. Can't we just accept death as the final bow it is? Can't we just die and be over with?"

"That's what we're planning to show doubters like you and others, after all, wouldn't you agree that the world is full of the 'invisible obvious' that very few care to observe? Why don't we just let the court decide on the first hand evidence?"

George shifted in his chair, "It's a mistake to put the cart before the horse. Let's see the facts, analyze the data before jumping to conclusions. We can't just twist our so-called facts to suit only your worldview. Shouldn't we at least consider the scientific proof —not guessing, that we've lived before; then take a good hard look at the possibilities reincarnation offers us? Why shut our eyes? Don't just guess—learn and know!"

"Just what kind of scam is this?" O'Leary challenged, hot around the collar.

"You characterize this case as a scam?" George fired back, "just because it challenges today's conventional beliefs? Because it makes you accept a truth beyond your limited understanding? Is that it?"

"When I see a scam, sir, I call it a scam."

"Well," George smiled, warmly, turning to face the camera, "did you know that Charlie Chaplin once entered a 'Charlie Chaplin Look Alike' contest? When the judging came in, he finished third."

"What's that got to do ..." O'Leary blurted.

"Sometimes our eyesight fools us," George smiled. "Here's hoping this case will improve yours."

CHERYL A. MALAKOFF & ROBERT A. CLAMPETT

CHAPTER SIXTY ONE

To improve the golden moment of opportunity,
and catch the good that is within our reach,
is the great art of life.
-William James

It was following the item in 'The Nation' section of TIME Magazine that the flood of mail into George's office became overwhelming. Scores of letters arrived each day, each begging to be opened, screaming with equal amounts of vitriol and praise for George, a man now seen as a national advocate for the cause of life after death.

Dozens of letter writers shared stories of near-death experiences that had given them a brief look into what proved to be a common thread in the process of dying. In letter after letter, they wrote that as they approached death, their consciousness would rise above their departed body, which they could view clearly from above, then to be pulled through an embracing tunnel-like enclosure towards an all-consuming bright light, followed by deep feelings of well being. "I felt a peace unlike anything before," wrote several respondents.

"If it weren't for the concern of my family, I would not have chosen to return," noted several others. Many stated they believed their experience was a sign that life beyond this one was a certainty, just in some another form, and now they had no fear of death.

Others, many others, expressed absolute outrage, accusing George and his so-claimed deceased client of outright blasphemy. Several cited scriptures claiming religious commandments of the holy church were being violated. Others accused him of leading a Communist plot to destroy America.

But none sent a chill through him like the terse message on official letterhead from the American Bar Association, Commonwealth of Massachusetts chapter:

In our judgment, your actions constitute serious violations of your professional responsibilities and as such threaten your current standing and licensure status. We as the governing body have a fiduciary responsibility to oversee and protect the quality of law practiced in the State of Massachusetts. We find you currently in critical violation of the following three ethical areas of the rules of professional conduct.

1. Meritorious claims: you are pursuing claims that are frivolous as having no basis in fact. The premise of your claim violates the 'good faith argument' for extension or change in the existing law.

2. Conflict of Interest: There is evidence to support a serious violation of your having a conflict of interest with your client and that as such, would compromise your legal responsibilities for providing diligent representation.

3. Trial publicity. Your extrajudicial public statements may have substantially and materially prejudiced these upcoming adjudicative proceeding on your claim and exceed the boundaries as to acceptable comments on pending litigation.

Exercising our disciplinary authority and having jurisdiction as to your breach of accepted ethics expected from a licensed attorney in the Commonwealth of Massachusetts, you are hereby placed on notice that your conduct is being reviewed and may result in the filing of formal ethical charges carrying disciplinary sanction ranging from suspension to disbarment. You will be notified as to the ethics charges that may be lodged and any change to your status as a member in good standing with the bar.

In summary: We consider your current course of litigation to be in violation of your ethical obligations which jeopardize your status to continue to practice law. Your actions and professional choices threaten the very stability of our legal system by seeking to usurp established precedential law governing contracts, property rights and inheritance rights. The potential impact on our legal system is unprecedented and in our opinion, unwarranted and reckless. Be guided accordingly.

Setting down the letter, shaken he picked up the phone, dialed the number of Doctor Lee.

"Doctor," he blurted, "I'm not sure I can do this."

"What's happened?" Lee asked.

"I've just received a serious warning that my actions in this case may cost me my career as an attorney. The state bar is threatening me with disbarment! My God, me, a Mansbridge, disbarred? There goes my life, right out the window. And for what? This insane long shot?"

"George, when the universe throws you a curve ball, it wants to move you in a different direction. One door closes, another one opens. Realize there is a perfect plan, for you, for Carol, for everyone—and it's unfolding now in a flawless way. Finish up this most important case and have faith that the universe will guide you to where it wants you to be next. Quiet your mind, be receptive, then you will know what's next. Besides, what are you worried about? Haven't we all just followed the bread crumbs anyway?"

Lee paused, adding in his most soothing tone, "Remember, you said you wish to make a difference? This is it."

Nodding in utter disbelief of his colliding worlds, George set down the phone without answering.

The very next day, George received three letters threatening bodily harm. He decided it wise to seek police protection from the Boston Police Department, wherein his connections as a still-active attorney paid off handsomely.

"You sure stirred up a fuss," said Detective Charles Blake, a veteran officer taken off his duties on minor crimes to head a three-officer surveillance team to provide 24-hour security for the suddenly embattled attorney.

"Yeah," George said, "more than you know. Maybe I've bit off a bite a bit more than I could chew."

"Never heard it quite like that," Blake smiled, "then again, all you damn lawyers talk funny."

George laughed, nodding in agreement. "We get tongue-tied more than you know. That's how we learn to fake it."

Blake chuckled, shook his head, "Least this duty's less a bitch than them at down in Southie at Holy Cross diocese. This whole sex abuse thing, man, priests diddlin' little boys? It's gonna' blow things sky high."

George looked at him, a puzzled gaze on his face. "You think so?" he asked. "This really big?"

"You oughta' see the protestors they're getting'. People get pissed, think their kids are bein' molested, 'specially by priests. Bunch'a damn perverts."

George stared at Blake, "Wow. I read about some of this, but, really? It's that bad?"

"Yeah." Blake spat it out, "really bad."

CHAPTER SIXTY TWO

Do not wait for the last judgment, it takes place everyday.
-Albert Camus

Charges of long-standing abuse and cover-up had rocked the Boston diocese within recent months, much to the concern of Cardinal Francis Long. Pressure was mounting daily as alleged victims of the assaults, many from the Boston diocese, came forward with claims against the Mother Church. To make matters even worse for the Church, there was a recent release of redacted records detailing years of cover-ups and moving offending priests from church to church where they continued their abuse, along with a league of attorneys seeking to collect millions in damages.

"From the time we were little, we learned you never wanted to be alone in a room with a priest," stated one claimant in his filing. "In my neighborhood, abuse was rampant. A friend of mine committed suicide because of it. I prayed, 'in the Holy Mother's name,' make it stop."

As publicity of George's case hit the Boston newspapers, a young vicariate of the diocese's north region, during a morning visit to Sacred Heart Church in nearby Lynn, read a follow-up article on the upcoming case with interest.

"Blasphemous bastards," he spouted. "They spit in the eye of the Lord." That afternoon, he contacted his superior by telephone with his concern.

"We must do something," he said. "This reincarnation thing, it's an affront to the church, to the holy word." Finding agreement on the other end of the phone line, he was assured that the issue would be presented before the diocese.

One month had passed before the item was brought before the Boston Archdiocese, discussed at length in a council of Auxiliary Bishops. There, the issue was thrashed out on its potential influence on the church and its followers. Would such attention being paid to reincarnation have a negative effect on the holy church? What becomes of our scriptural messages, resurrection or of the carrot of heaven or hell?

The council decided to bring the issue directly before the Cardinal Long.

"Your holiness," began a prelate, "the council sees this development as a clear threat to the teachings of our Savior and the Holy Church. Should people begin to even consider it, they need not fear purgatory, and that they well may come back for another life on Earth, our teachings may be severely undermined."

The Cardinal stared at the prelate for a full minute, saying nothing, stroking his beard. His hand dropped, his head bowed, "Glory be to God," he murmured, "He has answered our call."

"What better way," he reasoned, "to divert the media's attention from these abuse stories, keep it out of public view, than to re-direct their attention to this, our crusade to fight an affront against God's teaching? This gift from the Lord places the Church where it should be, on the side of good, on a large stage, with a cast that is loud and large."

The prelate stared at the Cardinal, a confused look on his face.

"Yes, my son," Cardinal Long said, "we shall organize protests to this heresy. Oh yes, loud and large shall they be. We shall bring in people of all faiths. We must do this, in the name of Our Holy Mother, our Lord. Come. Pray with me."

With that, the Cardinal and the prelate lowered their heads, the Cardinal spoke, in measured tones: "Our Sanctus Matris, beatus nos ut nos es humilis hac, vestri donum. In vestri nomen, iam nos may purgo vestri nomen quod nostri ex ugliness of today's headlines. Nunc they ero vestri. Ave Caltha. Amen."

The English translation from Latin soon was inscribed in the large Book of Prayers he maintained in his private office.

"Our Holy Mother, bless us as we are humbled by this, your gift. In your name, now we may cleanse your name and ours from the ugliness of today's headlines. Soon, they will be yours. Ave Maria. Amen."

Soon, his flock would be carrying signs in protest of a blasphemy. Praise be to God.

His prayers had been answered.

CHAPTER SIXTY THREE

All ideas which have far-reaching consequences are usually simple.
-Leo Tolstoy

Dawn had not yet risen as purple and coral streaks emerged across the horizon. For most, it was an unholy hour to be at the Philadelphia television station. But here he was, Doctor Phonyong Lee, about to perform his least favorite role—yet a part he knew only he must play. George's public-relations firm said that getting him booked on the nationally syndicated 'Best of Beth Show' was a coup, adding both credence and reach to their cause.

Seated across from Beth Gordon under banks of too-bright lights, Lee noticed her startling eyes, obviously an asset to her television career. Her signature style of placing expert guests on the hot seat had been kind to her ratings.

"Welcome, Doctor Lee," she said, flashing her practiced smile towards the camera.

"Thank you; an auspicious opportunity."

"I'm glad to have you. Doctor, you claim to be an expert on past lives and reincarnation."

"Yes, so I am told."

"Let's just jump right into the deep end. You're involved in the upcoming trial of a woman you say died some decades ago, but is claiming a very substantial inheritance as that reincarnated person today. Do I have that right?"

"Basically, yes. This woman you refer to is the same as she was before she passed beyond the veil years ago. Today she is beginning again to finish a task from her previous life."

"And why do you believe this?"

"As a scientist I am convinced by the irrefutable facts of reincarnation."

"Wait, back up a moment, you said … to finish a task?"

"Each life has a mission, a purpose. Sometimes, we fail to complete it. We run out of time, our life ends too soon. We come back again, to accomplish the goal. That's what this trial is setting out to prove, the continuity of our soul's journey."

"Speaking of facts, my staff found some data that shows an estimated eighty million Americans believe in reincarnation, but cannot recall anything from their so-called previous lives. Why would people believe in something they can't remember? Why don't we have better recall?"

"Well Beth, there are many theories. For example, there may be a biological basis. Medical science has identified the chemical compound oxytocin, which is secreted into the womb during pregnancy and also is found in the brain of those suffering amnesia. And, we have strong psychological evidence for childhood suppression in adulthood as a defense mechanism to filter out painful memories. It may be the same sort of suppression that allows us to forget having died from a trauma or some horrible disease. Forgetting saves us from needless suffering and frees us to live for our future."

Lee paused, noting Beth nodding in understanding. "But remember, there is no more important life than the one you're living now. So why focus on errors from the before? The mind may not have the recall, but our hearts know it. It's an intuitive connection to our essential nature, the soul."

"But," she interrupted, "what makes you so sure that we've lived before?"

"First of all, Beth, can you even remember what you did a year ago? Five years ago? Just because you don't have recall of every specific event, does not mean that they didn't occur. Memory is very selective. Think of it this way; every night, while you sleep, you're experiencing a mini-death. In your dreams, you could be anyone, anywhere, doing anything, at any time. You follow?"

Beth squinted, "I guess you could …"

"Then, in the morning, you awake, and you're back in this life, here and now, like you were before sleep, picking up right where you left off, right?"

Beth nodded.

"What you've experienced," Lee beamed a broad smile, "is a mini-reincarnation. Does that seem so far-fetched to you?"

Beth parted her lips, saying nothing.

"All of us will die someday. It's foolish to fear this fact; a complete waste of time. Beth, I assume you look forward after a long day to let your body go to sleep. It's the same with death. It's a state of rest, for rejuvenation from this temporary state we call life."

Beth nodded.

"So," Lee grinned it, "so, laugh, my friend, laugh at the illusion of death. It is no more than a passageway, a gate through which we pass in order to rest. Until once again, we return."

Beth uttered her own nervous laugh.

"Okay, okay" shaking her head, "you mentioned soul...what you mean by that?"

"By soul, I mean your one true, immortal nature. Your essential soul is sheathed temporarily in your body, which is no more than a vehicle to carry you on your soul's journey. Just as we cast off worn-out garments and take on new, so the soul sheds worn-out bodies and takes up the new."

"Is that the journey you say your soul, your spirit I believe you said, is on?"

"Yes. It's wherever you are, right now. Now is your most important time; every situation, circumstance and relationship is an opportunity for growth. This, your latest incarnation, is the sum total of everything you've ever done in the past. The twists and turns in your life today are the results of our actions in the past."

Catching the wrap-up cue for this segment of her program from the producer, Beth rushed her question, "Doctor Lee, what evidence have you to make me believe I've had earlier lifetimes?"

"Miss Gordon, we have been able to reach into past life experiences for centuries. Only during the last five hundred years have science and spirit had a painful divorce. We are spirit, living a human experience, in a scientific world. It is time for science and spirit to reconcile. My hope is that the upcoming trial will answer your question," noting that her hair stayed in place as her head shook.

"Doctor," she smiled, "you've written that we travel in our lives with others from earlier times. Can you tell me, have we met before?"

"It is for both of us to answer."

She settled back in her chair, smiled, "Well, nice to see you again." Laughter erupted among those on the set.

Raising her voice, "One last question, if, as you say, this belief has been around for centuries, why is there such continued controversy over reincarnation?"

"Over the years, society has constructed a wall blocking recognition of the importance of past life influences to maintain order over those in charge of the here and now. This is especially true in Western religions and politics, both of which are top-down structures. Fortunately, truth is not decided by a show of hands. May I now ask you a question?"

"Miss Gordon, if you knew how many lives you've lived in and died with; what would you do differently to change your current life?"

"You mean if I knew I'd had many past lives? Not really sure. Guess I'd be ahead of the game, if I knew what to look out for, what to do better. Wow! That's quite a question you've painted there. I guess I'd be somewhat relieved; things would have a lot more clarity. Some questions of 'why' would fall away. Guess I'd just know more and relax, not worry so much."

He smiled, now the interviewer, "And …?"

"I suppose," she mused, "things would make a lot more sense, based on what I've learned before. If I remembered, that's the kicker; what would I remember?"

"Follow the cues, the coincidences, synchronicities. Align with your inner guidance. Your soul will lead you. Listen to your heart. Let your life flow unobstructed. Do not just live in your head. Follow your soul's wisdom. That is what must be learned."

Catching her 'cut-cue' from the side, Beth reached out to shake Lee's hand, "We've run out of time. Thank you Doctor Phonyong Lee. Good luck in your trial, I'm sure we'll all be watching. Will you come back someday?"

He wondered if she recognized the significance of her own words.

CHAPTER SIXTY FOUR

What we are today comes from our thought of yesterday, and our present thoughts build our life tomorrow: our life is the creation of our mind.
-Buddha

Autumn had turned into winter. Winter had moved into spring.

And as this late afternoon rolled into evening, Bostonians settled into homes, apartments, bars, gyms and other venues, many watching a familiar local TV anchor delivering the six o'clock news in his overly theatrical voice.

"And in Boston, the long-awaited Tale of Two Lives Trial, set to begin tomorrow, will pit a woman, rumored to be a psychology professor at a Boston-area university, who claims a substantial inheritance based on her previous life, against the now-elderly sons of the very woman she claims to be. Protesters have begun lining up at the courthouse, where we find our Alicia Rhodes, Alicia?"

Framed against the backdrop of marble courthouse steps, Alicia Rhodes holds her gaze at the camera, fingers pressed into an earpiece to hear over the crowd lining both sides of the street.

"What do they want, the protestors?" asked Walter from the network anchor desk.

"They're objecting to the whole concept of reincarnation, Walter, as you can see."

She pivoted on her heel, glanced over her shoulder at the myriad of loud boisterous protesters waving their signs, following her cue, the cameraman panned the sea of shouting protesters, sign boards bobbing up and down into the sea of humanity.

" My afterlife's in heaven"
"John 3:16"
"Reincarnation is Satan's Tool"
"Allahu Akbar"
"Jesus is the Answer!"

"The lines certainly have been drawn. Protesters, many representing churches, synagogues, even some area mosques, are in force. This case has struck a nerve around the nation, some are here from as far away as California, Washington state and Alaska, all gathered to protest what they call the blasphemous nature of this case. I've been able to catch up with a few. Here's what they're saying."

In a quick cut, Alicia is seen standing before a three-deep crowd, she holds a microphone pointed towards a balding, bespectacled priest sporting a white collar.

"This as an affront to our faith and the word of God," he said. "Letting this dispute go forward only enhances those who doubt our teachings and believe in reincarnation. We can't have this."

"And now that it's about to start?" Alicia asked.

"We ask people of all faiths to pray for a speedy end, one with a verdict that decries such falsehood, once and for all."

"Just what do you expect from tomorrow's proceedings?"

"I expect the word of God to be heard. Hallelujah"

"So there it is," Alicia said, her face a close-up in the television screen. "Many here see this trial as an attempt to subvert the teachings of their religion, their most closely held beliefs. They feel deeply about it."

From behind, a graying African-American woman in a heavy overcoat leaned in towards Alicia, shouting, "This'all bull crap." she blurted. "Who's she think she is, this professa' lady?"

Following her instincts, Alicia quickly moved the microphone towards the woman. "You think she's wrong to do this."

"Yo, she's wrong. My Jamaal, shot dead by a gunman las' year, in Bal'more?" she screamed, "Killed da'id! That ain't right! Tell you this!

My man, right now? He's waitin' fo' me in Heaven. Evil'z dude'z shoot him? Burn in Hell. And ain't no professa' lady go'n tell me different."

A quick cut brought the scene back to Alicia standing before the courthouse steps, a sheet of paper in her hand.

"Walter, I've just been handed a statement issued by the Boston Area Council of Churches, representing, it says on their letterhead, nearly one thousand churches, mosques and synagogues. It says, and I'm reading directly from it, 'we are united in objecting to the this, and any other notion that embraces reincarnation. The church states that life is a one-time gift from God on this earth, with an eternity in heaven as the reward for those ascribing to the tenets of our faith'."

Slightly hunching over, she read further, lips moving in silence, then looked back up directly into the camera. "At the heart of this legal controversy, Walter, is whether a person may claim property awarded in what they allege was their previous life. And, as you can tell, critics are lining up, declaring that the impact of this decision could alter much more than our understanding of property rights, but would also impact our legal system, religion and how we define life and death."

She stopped for a split second, inhaling a quick breath, head shaking slightly, having been cued through her ear piece to wrap it up, signed off with her moniker, "This is a trial that could last days, weeks or, some say, only a few minutes. Reporting from the Massachusetts Superior Court, Alicia Rhodes, Boston."

CHAPTER SIXTY FIVE

The only good is knowledge and the only evil is ignorance.
-Socrates

This day awakened like any other.

The sun rose, poking through the overnight haze of the city; people stirred, slowly climbed out of the comfort of their dreams, washed the sleep from their eyes enough to brew coffee, select their uniform of the day, grab a quick breakfast and stumble too-soon out of their homes, at last on their way, wherever that way was and going about their stated business, oblivious of happenings outside their private circle of awareness.

Just like any other day.

But unlike others, this one held the promise of something different. One of potential importance. Like most days of marked significance, the ones that revise the understanding of ourselves, all too often are grasped only in increments, over a long period of time.

But now, this day, the day of Carol Klein's trial, at last, was here.

She had been preparing to take on this moment for months, prepping with George and Doctor Lee over and over on the myriad of endless details. She believed she was more than ready, and that the case George had constructed, replete with distinguished expert witnesses and reams of supporting data, was both thorough and compelling.

That's why it came as such a surprise, that once she entered the courtroom, all prior confidence evaporated. The majesty and solemnity of the courtroom weighed on her with an emotional impact beyond what she had ever expected. This room, these walls, somehow reflecting the echoes of ghosts from cases past, overwhelmed her. Suddenly, she realized just how ill-prepared she was with what was about to come.

Escorted to the plaintiff's table, she was seated, right alongside George who smiled up at her reassuringly. This pebble of assurance was crushed by the boulder of these walls, the overflow gallery behind her, and the polished cherry wood judge's bench towering above.

Carol slowly turned her eyes to her right, across the aisle, to the other table. There they were. A cold sweat engulfed her. She tried to gauge the stares, like bullets, she was receiving from the two elderly Paulson brothers, seated a mere few yards away at the defendant's table, just like hers, with their attorney. A sense of overwhelming guilt twisted her gut. Could she dare to imagine what was in their minds, behind those piercing stares? What must they be thinking? Of course, that she had betrayed them. That she is the most loathsome person on the face of the earth.

Their eyes flashed raw vehemence: "How could you? We allowed you into our home. We shared with confidence, our cherished memories of our own dearly departed mother's life. For what? To end up here, in a courtroom, forced to fight you for something that's clearly ours? And what gall you have, claiming to be, my, our reincarnated mother? Could there be any assault more scurrilous, more immoral, than that? Just what kind of egregious scam artist are you?"

How she wished, she could talk to them, explain the importance, the significance of, what, why she must do this! This assignment, this, this, what is it? A task to be finished, the one I've been tapped for! She certainly didn't ask for it. "No," she thought, "can't you see? I'm really, I'm, a good person!"

Her thoughts soon were drowned out by a louder voice, resonating from the base of her alter ego, "Miss Klein, what right did you have to drag them into this, your own, personal primal quest? What kind of person does such a thing? Shame! Shame on you!"

Any remaining confidence, that was so prominent earlier in the day, continued to dissolve further into a puddle of mush. All composure gone, she wished only that it didn't show; she was a wreck, tossed on the shore of her despair. Now, it was too late. She was too far into it to consider these questions. There was no way to turn back, no choice but to lean into the storm whatever today was going to deliver; whatever the outcome, win or lose.

Although in truth, she had no clue what winning or losing actually meant. Her only realization was that today, she had a part in writing history.

Scattered throughout the courtroom Carol saw a handful of familiar faces; George's intern Becky, Doctor Lee, her assistant Elaine, Isobel Freeman, a few other fellow department members, Doctor Yarnell, even the banker from Montreal, "What was his name? Décolleté, Henri Décolleté." Then, she noticed some of her clients, Susan Alden, her young French guillotine patient, Jonas Tomlinson, among them. Although she was glad to see them, she hoped these proceedings wouldn't detract from their clinical progress and make a mockery of their experience.

And sitting in the first row directly behind her, she felt the piercing eyes of George's father and his uncle Nicholas boring into the back of her head. Did they also believe that she'd tainted their reputations as well? It tormented her to think of the compromising position she'd put all of them in.

Even with George seated next to her, she felt adrift on a raft in a raging sea.

Reading the body cues of the court clerk, a balding man in a blue uniform, Carol saw he was signaling the court transcriber, a young woman, in the front of the courtroom. She gestured back at him, fingers perched over her keyboard, ready to go.

The tension in the room was palpable; it could be cut with a knife. The checkered flag was about to drop.

CHAPTER SIXTY SIX

There are only two ways to live your life. One is as though nothing is a miracle. The other is as though everything is a miracle.
-Albert Einstein

The clerk announced in a deep baritone voice, "All rise, the Honorable Judge Charles Carleton presiding."

Judge Charles Carleton, a robed man of medium stature and thinning gray hair, bifocals resting on the bridge of his nose, strode to his oversized black leather chair. Clearing his throat, he grabbed a large wooden gavel, looked up at the overflow gathering, banged the gavel a little too loudly, then in a commanding voice called out, "This court is now in session."

Carol could hardly breathe. She wanted to be hyper-alert, absorbing every word that would be spoken today. She wanted to soak it all up, every bit of it. This was no dress rehearsal; this was real life, her ever-so-real life. And apparently, that's exactly what was on the line.

All eyes were on Judge Charles Carleton as he began setting into motion the proceedings of the day. "Counsel, your appearances for the record please."

George stood tall and proud, "George Mansbridge, III on behalf of the plaintiff, Carol Klein formerly known as Iris Middelton Paulson."

Following the courtroom practice, "Sidney Green, for the defendants, William Paulson and Ethan Paulson, the rightful heirs of their mother's property."

"Appearances only, no argument yet, please," Judge Carlson glared at Green. "This court is being asked to resolve a civil dispute over inherited property, between the legally recognized offspring of the deceased, Iris Middelton Paulson, who are her sons and legal heirs, defendants, William and Ethan Paulson, and the plaintiff, Carol Klein, nee Iris Middelton Paulson, who claims an identity for whom that property was specifically intended and bequeathed."

The silence in the room was deafening, both in disbelief that the idea of this trial had gone this far and the mind-boggling implications of how this, or any other court, would navigate these uncharted waters.

Following the time-honored set of rules, Judge Carleton locked eyes with Attorney George Mansbridge, saying, "Counselor, you may proceed with your opening statement."

George rose up from his chair, stood stiffly, then began to stride towards the Judge's bench, his mouth opening, about to speak.

Before George could utter a word, Sidney Green, the Paulson's attorney, shot up from his chair, loudly asserted, "Your Honor, I call for an immediate dismissal of this proceeding on the grounds this claim is frivolous and without merit," adding a visual exclamation mark by nodding to his clients, affirming his claim to reason.

"Counselor," Judge Carleton said, staring daggers at Sidney Green for this untimely interruption, "your time for filing a motion to dismiss prior to trial passed months ago. I set this deadline in the pre-trial order which you obviously did not follow. We will proceed with opening arguments. Motion denied."

Sidney Green sat back down unaffected and wearing a Cheshire smile knowing he had the full weight of the law on his side, silently planning an early celebration luncheon with his clients. Sensing the forthcoming slam-dunk, he couldn't wait to get back to the firm to gloat of his victory over a Boston bigwig in a high profile, albeit way-too-easy, court case.

"Thank you Your Honor," George huffed, his eyes burning into the back of Sidney Green's skull, "regardless of the callous affront to this court's proceedings, and the premature actions of my impatient colleague, I intend to show the court that my client, Doctor Carol Klein, a respected scientist and licensed psychologist, is, in fact, the sole individual for whom this property in dispute was, and is, intended."

Modeling after his Salem exoneration presentation before the Massachusetts Assembly, George confidently strode forward to the lectern near his opponent's table, from where he could squarely face Sidney Green and his elderly clients, while addressing the Judge. "Your Honor, we will show that Iris Middelton Paulson is named as the only, the rightful, recipient of the specific properties in dispute, which are in fact intended as a gift, for her and for her only, as designated by her father, her own flesh and blood."

George placed his hands on the table and leaned towards the trio, inches from their faces, "The evidence will also show, beyond any reasonable doubt, that my client, Doctor Carol Klein, who sits in that chair today, is in fact the reincarnation of, Iris Middelton Paulson and as such, should be determined by Your Honor, to be the rightful owner of the property at issue. This said property was set aside for her alone at the Bank of Montreal in a safe deposit box by her father, Joseph Middelton some seventy years ago."

Gaining confidence, George continued, "The evidence is irrefutable. Carol Klein, through medically accepted practices of hypnosis, regressed to her prior self as Iris Middelton Paulson. The information about her previous identity led to her sons, still living in the same Park Avenue apartment. Furthermore, additional information directed her to discover the specific safety deposit box at the Bank of Montreal that had been sealed for seven decades."

"The odds of guessing a six number combination code to a unknown safe deposit box sealed away in the vaults of a Montreal bank are unfathomable." Pausing to catch his breath, George continued, "Yet we know that Doctor Klein opened that box with the exact and specific code only discovered through her regression. The only explanation for the impossible is what is in fact, a reality— Carol Klein is the reincarnation of Iris Middelton Paulson."

George paused to give the Judge and all in the courtroom a moment to grasp the significance of his case. "Accepting this as true, Your Honor, Doctor Carol Klein, formerly known as Iris Middelton Paulson, is the rightful heir, the rightful owner, the only one entitled to take sole and exclusive possession of the contents of the safety deposit box."

Turning to look Judge Carlson in the eye, "Your Honor, we all know that this case is different and challenges our core beliefs and the laws as they stand, but Your Honor also knows that the evidence must be applied to the laws. Your Honor has faced difficult choices before and is known to be just. All we ask is that you apply the same even handed justice you are known for in your tenure on the bench to this case, hear the evidence, and make a reasoned decision on the evidence. I trust you will make the right decision. Thank you." George, sensing his ownership of the courtroom, returned to his seat at counsel table.

Judge Carlson did not like being baited and knew that had just happened. Like it or not he had to respect Mansbridge's opening remarks and recognized he was in this case to the end. "Defense counsel, your opening please."

Sidney Green slowly rose out of his chair. "Your Honor, I will keep this brief and to the point. The law is the law. William and Ethan Paulson are the rightful heirs at law to their mother's estate. All of it, without exception. Plaintiff's claims are nothing but slight of hand and hokey theories about reincarnation which have no place in this court and certainly under no circumstances warrant ignoring time honored precedent and laws which govern the rights of inheritance. That property belongs to my clients. That is the only decision Your Honor can make in this case. Regardless of what the plaintiff intends to 'prove' in this Court, that money is Ethan and William's. That's all." With his declaration of truth stated, Green sat down.

Judge Carlton scanned the courtroom with furled brow and obvious tension around his pursed lips, and emphatically announced, "Chambers gentleman!"

The courtroom went from reverent silence to an unraveled rumble of a crowd speculating, "Was it, is it over, just like that? Could this case, one that caused all this media disruption, could it really be over so soon?"

The three men walked inside the Judge's chamber, the walls filled with the codified rulings of western civilization, leather-bound, embossed volumes of legal precedent, including those they stood on today.

Carleton lowered himself into his desk chair, George Mansbridge and Sidney Green stood at attention awaiting a signal from their presiding judge.

"Mansbridge!" Carleton bellowed, lifting his glasses from his head, "Your actions border on bullying and I won't have that in my courtroom. Understand?"

"Yes, Your Honor," George answered, rather meekly, well aware of his transgression, goaded by his opponent's premature action. "It won't happen again."

Setting his glasses down on his desk. "And her existence in her body? Is that your argument? In my courtroom?"

"Your Honor, the fact is that my entire case is contingent on recognition of the phenomenon of reincarnation. At least as a concept. We have witnesses, respectable experts, whose testimony supports that argument. Impeccable witnesses. At least let me present them to the court."

"Looks like you've got a circus on your hands, Your Honor," Green smirked.

Dismissing the self serving comment, Judge Carleton squinted at George, raising a hand to his face, rubbed his closed eyes for several seconds, "How far you planning on taking this?"

"Only as far as necessary to prove our case, Your Honor."

George paused noting the tentative acceptance, continued, "I know what we're doing here is unusual. But that shouldn't obviate our case. I've a duty to present my client's case as best I can. And present my witnesses, who deserve to be heard. Please, Your Honor. Give us that chance for a fair unbiased hearing in the face of the law."

Judge Carleton's eyes widened and said directly to George, "All right. But, Mister Mansbridge, one false step, just one, and your through. Understand?"

Interlacing his fingers together until his knuckles began to turn pale, Judge Carleton picked up his glasses, returned them to the bridge of his nose, "Both of you. I insist that you conduct yourselves in an impeccably professional manner. Do I make myself clear? Okay counselors, let's go back."

Judge Carleton rose, his robes swirling behind him, walked out the door of his chambers.

Both men waited for him to pass, then jockeyed for position, each diving for the hole-shot, first one out the door.

CHAPTER SIXTY SEVEN

The mystical is not how the world is, but that it is.
-Ludwig Wittgenstein

Carol was dying to know what had transpired in chambers, but George had turned his back to her arranging a set of papers before him. She was about to speak, when Judge Carleton's gavel signaled the court to order.

"Please continue, Counselor," nodding towards George.

"Your Honor, before we proceed with our first witness, I wish offer responding remarks to the accusations of defense counsel about our case having no merit. We will present evidence, and testimony from impeccable witnesses, validating our position. This evidence, drawn from the disciplines of science, modern medicine and long-standing beliefs of religions throughout the world, will provide the foundation for our stance, which, admittedly, is intrinsically tied and contingent upon, acceptance of the phenomenon commonly referred to as reincarnation, the doctrine that asserts the continuating journey of one's soul."

A cascade of groans rumbled through the courtroom; shouts denouncing George's rhetoric.

"Order," Carleton shouted. "There will be no such outbursts, or the court shall be cleared."

"Thank you, Your Honor. It comes as no surprise that our position should evoke such responses, such as the one that just occurred. However, let us not allow the restrictions of current thinking and superstitions obscure the facts of this case."

Pivoting on his heels, George turned, gestured towards Carol, "This evidence, and our position, will lead the court to one, and only one, conclusion. That Doctor Carol Klein is, in full fact, the embodiment of, and the same as, the one and only rightful claimant to the disputed property, Iris Middelton Paulson."

Catcalls from various corners of the courtroom shattered the silence.

Judge Carleton slammed his gavel, glared out at the gallery in an attempt to regain control over the spontaneous outbursts. "Order! I said no more of that!"

Quickly turning to George, "Be careful, Counselor!"

George nodded, acknowledging the request, recognizing the thin ice he was skating on. "We are fully aware, Your Honor, of the unusual nature of our claim and start with the preliminaries."

Turning to face the gallery, Mansbridge found the banker from Montreal in the third row. "Monsieur Henri Décolleté, will you please take the witness stand. The distinguished banker took his seat next to the Judge and was sworn in by the court clerk.

"Monsieur Décolleté, I show you the document that I have marked as exhibit one. Do you recognize this Certification of Authenticity as signed by you and notarized by your bank's lawyers?"

"I do," he replied, "this Certification was prepared, at your request, attesting to the circumstances under which Mademoiselle Klein opened the safety deposit box in our vault last year and to the instructions provided to the bank by Joseph Middelton, that the contents were intended solely and exclusively for his daughter, Iris Middelton Paulson."

"And can you please tell the Court, how the safety deposit box was opened by Doctor Klein?"

Monsieur Décolleté exhaled under the weight of his explanation, "The safety deposit box had been pre-paid for ninety-nine years, and according to the bank's meticulously kept records, the only time this box was ever accessed and opened since it was set up by Joseph Middelton, was by Carol Klein having entered the six digits in the correct order."

Shifting uncomfortably he continued, "The only way to open this safety deposit box was by a six number code. The bank had no key nor the numeric code to open the box. Only the holder of the code could ever have accessed and opened it. Upon opening the box, its contents were inventoried, including a letter from Mister Middelton."

"And do you have that letter with you?" George asked.

Slowly, Monsieur Décolleté reached into his breast pocket of his jacket and like a magician pulling a rabbit out of the hat, presented the ancient yellowing letter and handed it to George.

George took the letter, raising it high in the air so that it was visible to the back row of the courtroom.

"Your Honor," he said, turning back to face Judge Carleton, "I introduce into evidence this letter, written by Joseph Middelton, in his own handwriting, bequeathing this gift solely to his beloved daughter Iris Middelton Paulson, and thereby, this day, to my client, Doctor Carol Klein."

He handed the document to the clerk, who in turn passed it up to Judge Carleton who speed-read the brief note, turned it over and back, set it down on his bench top, hesitated, "Evidence is entered into record."

With an inaudible sigh of relief, George marked a plus on his invisible scorecard, he had successfully established through the proper chain of custody the very foundation for the right to bring this suit. "Thank you Your Honor. That's all for now."

He walked back to his chair, flashing a sideward glance toward his father and uncle, then sat heavily alongside Carol, a grin of contentment on his face.

A muffled buzz rose throughout the room.

Carleton turned his gaze to Sidney Green, "Counselor?"

Sidney Green rose from his chair, walked directly to the Judge's bench, two documents clutched in his hand.

"Your Honor, I present herewith to the court, two documents, one, a copy of the signed, dated and notarized death certificate of Iris Middelton Paulson; the other, a copy of her Last Will and Testament, signed, dated and notarized, naming as sole heirs to all properties in her possession, to her only offspring, my clients, Ethan and William

Paulson."

A low buzz returned to the courtroom as he handed them to the clerk, who in turn presented them to the Judge Carleton. He looked at both documents, for some length of time, finally handing them back to the clerk.

"Defendant's evidence admitted to the record," he said, looking back at Counselor Green.

"Clearly," Green offered, "these documents must be honored by the court."

He paused to leverage his next comment. "Unless, that is, you buy into the cockamamie fairy tale concocted by my colleague's slightly deranged client."

Laughter broke out from the upper gallery as George Mansbridge began to rise from his chair.

"Enough name-calling counselor," Judge Carleton admonished.

George sat back down, a scowl on his face.

"I request this proceeding be adjudicated in favor of my clients," Green continued in a more respectful tone, mindful of the Judge's admonishment. "As nothing besides these documents need be provided to this court, at this, or any other time, as no other proof is necessary, or required by law. These documents establish my clients are the rightful heirs of Iris Middelton Paulson. I submit that it matters not how the property was located in the Montreal bank. The point is the property was located. In fact, Your Honor, the plaintiff has just established that the contents of that box were intended solely for Iris Middelton Paulson who is no doubt deceased and this property belongs to her sons."

Judge Carleton leaned back in his chair, his head nodding up and down while he appeared to be sizing up the stature of Sidney Green, whose chest oddly puffed out before him.

"Request denied." His bark drawing a slight gasp from the gallery.

Sidney, smelling blood in the water, continued. "In that case your honor, as there is no merit to this claim, I call for the immediate dismissal of these proceedings and the awarding of all found properties to my clients, Ethan and William Paulson."

Hearing an audible clamor in the courtroom, Green took it as affirmation from all intelligent beings of his position; adding up the new-found money in his pocket, smiling at his clients.

"Motion denied," Carlson bellowed. Green's neck nearly snapped, jerking to stare back at the Judge. A thunder of mumbles erupted, causing Carleton to bang his gavel, yet again.

"Have you anything further to offer?"

"No, nothing else, I mean, yes, that's right, no." Green returned to his seat a bit nervous. He had not prepared for this case to go past this point.

A few snickers rode across the courtroom.

"Then please, be seated," Carleton first turned to Monsieur Décolleté, " thank you sir, you are dismissed."

"Now, let's move on, Counselor, your witness, if you would?"

George rose, slowly, looked up at the bench, then back, as if gauging the gallery.

"I call as my first witness, the renowned scientist, Doctor Theodore Hunt."

CHAPTER SIXTY EIGHT

With all your science can you tell how it is, and whence it is, that light comes into the soul?
-Thoreau

As he rose from the gallery all eyes fell on the portly Doctor Hunt.

In his early seventies, dressed in a corduroy sport coat with leather elbow patches, he walked slowly with a slight limp, a clerk guiding him to stand before the witness chair.

A buzz circled the gallery as this man, well-known as recent winner of a MacArthur Award, stood at attention before the witness chair.

"So help me, God," he said.

"You may be seated," directed the clerk.

Taking his seat in the witness chair, he adjusted himself into this unfamiliar venue as George approached.

"Please give the court your full name." George said, his voice dripping with confidence.

"Theodore Lawrence Hunt. Doctor Theodore Lawrence Hunt."

"Doctor Hunt, please state for the court your professional standing."

"I am Professor Emeritus, and Chairman of the Institute for Advanced Scientific Study, at Princeton University."

"Your specialty?"

"I specialize in the study of molecular physics, with an emphasis on quantum theory as it relates to the holographic residence of human consciousness."

"Could you tell us about your work?"

"Yes, I oversee a wide range of projects, exploring the interaction of quantum fields and living systems. This discipline includes the exploration of particle physics dealing with the fundamental units of matter and energy as the interface to the dimensions of human consciousness."

Taking a momentary pause, he added, "We look at the universe as a whole, our quest is seeking a unified theory to the ultimate nature of physical reality. I have authored numerous articles which have been published documenting my findings and those of other esteemed scientists in my field."

George nodded, walked back to his table, scooped up several inches of folders, retraced his steps to the court clerk.

"I submit, as evidence, twenty-five peer-reviewed scientific papers written by Doctor Hunt and others that offer irrefutable evidence verifying the quantum mechanical model of human consciousness. These studies bring together quantum physics, super string theory and human energy fields. All of which are imperative and relevant to my case."

Sidney Green bolted to his feet, "Your Honor! I object to the introduction of these papers as they have no bearing!"

"Sit down, Mister Green," Judge Carleton barked, "this submission of evidence will be permitted." Judge Carlton stared at the stack of articles, knowing he would have to do his best to plow through them later that evening.

Green stared at the Judge, unmoving.

"Sit down, now," Carleton ordered.

Green hesitantly sat, a grin aimed at his clients indicating he was still in control.

"Counselor, continue."

"Doctor Hunt, could you explain to the court the role of science in our society?"

"The aim of science is to discover the hidden determinants that unify all life; to examine, describe and explain the world in which we live," adding, "while we're fairly good at describing, explaining is another matter entirely."

"Please, go on."

"Since the adoption of relativity theory and quantum mechanics, we are able to describe the sub-atomic forces of the universe, such as magnetism, electricity, and gravity. However, the challenge is, we can't fully explain them."

Listening intently, Carol took in the whole scene at once: the courtroom artist completing a sketch of Sidney Green objecting, Judge Carleton shifting in his chair, George trailblazing virgin territory, Theodore Hunt on the stand.

"You see," Hunt continued, "today's physicists no longer accept the limits of the four dimensions of height, width, depth and time. We now have convincing evidence of other hidden dimensions, embodied in the world of the super string theory. Here, quantum mechanics and the theory of relativity come together, which has altered the old model of space, time and gravity."

He paused, letting that thought sink in. "Super string theory indicates there must be at least eleven other dimensions, most curled up, beyond our current ability to observe them. It shows that matter is composed of minuscule, filament-like strings of vibrating energy. And at different vibrations, these strings produce a multitude of different types of particles. At one oscillation you get an electron, at another, a quark, still further a proton or a graviton. It really gets far out in terms of describing the nature of duality, almost bordering on the esoteric."

"Esoteric?"

"Yes," continued Theodore Hunt, "you'll find similarities between the views of many of today's physicists with those held by the ancient mystics. In fact, you'll find there's as much truth to ancient mystic's conclusions as our scientific deductions. More and more of the mystical esoteric beliefs are being confirmed through scientific experimentations."

Hunt titled his head, glanced towards Judge Carleton, "That was the subject of my MacArthur Award, the connection between modern physics and metaphysical traditions."

Carleton nodded, waiting for more.

Hunt cleared his throat, "It's all the same. The ancient mystics sought to know Nature, to know their place in the cosmos. To understand reality through contemplation or other means, including psychotropic drugs, or meditation revelations. Many religions, including Christianity, are explained through revelations. Likewise, physicists use our methods of experimentation to test and explain natural phenomena. So, whether it's finding the sub-atomic levels of particle physics or a deep state of meditation, all separation disappears. It's all one. There is this interdependent unified relationship with everything. This is the central theme of the mystical experience of Reality, the web of nonlinear interrelation of every part affecting the whole. Scientists have demonstrated the same conclusions; that all matter exists within this quantum field and is in constant inseparable communication with all things."

"Any other conclusions?"

"The mystics believed there is but one ultimate Reality. One that is alive, dynamic and in constant motion and growth. And that everything is simply seen as different forms of the One."

"And physicists reconcile these beliefs?"

"Yes. Physicists see the cosmos as the same web of interrelationships at the subatomic level where nothing can be isolated, only interconnected. At the quantum level there are no independent smallest units, no basic building blocks, only an elaborate web of vibrating relationships within the Universe. The conclusion is that at the formative level, there is unity where energy forces and matter appear as merging into, transforming and re-emerging back and forth, one into the another."

"And all this means?"

"Simply that energy and matter, are both the same, only in separate forms. Matter itself is pure energy that is ever-changing. Therefore, neither energy, nor matter, can be created, or destroyed. Only transformed, one to the other."

"So," George pounced, "matter can become energy and energy can become matter?"

"Yes, correct. There is no end," stated Hunt.

"Your Honor! Where's he's going with this?" Green interrupted, rising tentatively.

Carleton pointed at George, "Get to the point, Counselor."

"Yes, Your Honor,"

"Sit down Mister Green," Carleton snapped, "you'll have your turn soon enough."

"Continue, Counselor."

"Yes, Your Honor. One last question. Doctor Hunt, as a physicist do you validate the scientific possibility of reincarnation, one life, moving on to the next?"

"Most assuredly. Let me put it this way: since matter and energy can neither be created nor be destroyed, each can only be transformed from one to the other, and since the human spirit at its core is but one aspect of universal energy, and given that all time, past, present and future, are equally contiguous; then, I must say 'yes'. That the phenomenon of reincarnation, as the continuity of consciousness, is indeed, quite logical."

Catching his breath, "Scientifically, there is a reasoned possibility, even a probability, that human spirit may be reformed from one time, to another. The only logical conclusion is that matter is information, information is consciousness, and spirit can change from energy back into matter."

"Doctor Hunt, you are saying?"

"I am saying, that from a purely rational perspective, reincarnation, as the result of energy, matter and consciousness merging is not only possible, but very, very likely."

A sudden outburst of shouts and groans silenced Hunt, who grimaced at the response from the gallery.

"Where is your common sense?" someone shouted.

Smiling Hunt raised his voice, "As Doctor Einstein said, common sense is that body of knowledge best forgotten, once past adolescence."

Groans and catcalls from the audience increased.

"Order! Quiet or I'll clear the courtroom!"

Doctor Hunt's head turned and looked directly at Judge Carleton as he explained, "Most assuredly, resulting events from our past can profoundly alter our present. I believe as a scientist, that if we were to embrace the research of the continuity of consciousness as reincarnation on par with the same focus and resources of scientific experimentation and statistical methodology we use in the research of hard sciences like physics, then the credibility and potential would move out of the realm of metaphysics and into the realm of scientific fact."

George sensing patience running thin, summarized, "Thank you Doctor, no more questions."

Carol focused her attention again on the courtroom artist that had just completed a picture of Judge Carleton with his gavel raised.

George walked back to the chair beside Carol, glancing at his father and uncle seated in the first row. His father nodded, a grin on his face. His uncle avoided eye contact, staring straight ahead, his jaw firmly set.

"Counselor," said the Judge looking at Sidney Green, "your witness."

"Thank you, Your Honor." Green jumped up and confidently approached the witness stand, "Doctor Hunt, how is a rubber band and a snake alike?"

George shot out of his seat hawking, "Objection, Your Honor, relevance?"

"Mister Mansbridge," Carlton huffed, "let's afford Mister Green the same professional latitude. Over ruled, continue."

"Thank you Your Honor," Green continued, ignoring George. "Doctor Hunt, if you would, please answer the question."

"Well, they both can stretch and then recoil back to their original shape."

"Thank you Doctor Hunt," Green smirked. "That's the right answer. Now, Doctor Hunt, answer this question, how is a Last Will and Testament like quantum physicist?"

"Uh, well... I don't really know." Hunt taken off guard stammered.

"Again, perfect answer," interrupted Green. "Nothing! What about physics and probate? Property rights? Case law?"

"Objection. Badgering the witness," George howled.

"Sit Mansbridge." Carlton commanded.

"Where are you going with this, Mister Green?"

"I'll wrap up with this witness in a moment Judge." Green turned to face-off with Hunt, "Nothing from nothing is nothing, no matter how small the quantum matter is dissected. Although, I will give you that your testimony was educational, even though you have wasted the court's time. Doctor Hunt just one more question, what makes science work up in the stratosphere of your ivory tower?"

"It's based on systems, order, and principles that are abided by collectively to understand the information that builds the bedrock of scientific laws."

"Ah," Green gloated, "yes Doctor, we do the same down here on earth with our legal system with similar guidelines and rules, all for the purpose of defining and regulating justice, equality and fairness for all." Green rose, looked down at his notes for effect, "No further questions for this witness Your Honor, as his views have no relevance to our contention and does nothing to discredit our claim. Our evidence, as submitted, specifies that both of my clients are their mother's rightful heirs." Taking as long a pause as permissible he ended with the declaration of his unwavering position.

"Oh, sorry, yes one more moment Your Honor."

Carlton nodded.

"Thank you for your expert testimony Doctor Hunt." Green dipped his hand into his jacket pocket and plunked a fist sized tan rubber band onto the witness box. "Doctor Hunt, I just wanted to leave you with this souvenir from today's proceedings, maybe you will be able to stretch this around something you need to hold together."

He marched back to his chair in triumph, Green sat down heavily, emphasizing his position.

"Very well," Carleton turned, rolling his eyes, "you may step down. Thank you doctor."

Sitting at his table, George reached for a yellow legal pad, scribbled out in bold letters, *Hang in there, kid.*

CHAPTER SIXTY NINE

My religion consists of a humble admiration of the illimitable superior spirit who reveals himself in the slight details we are able to perceive with our frail and feeble mind.
-Albert Einstein

"There's the bell," George murmured to Carol, "round one, a win on points, round two, comin' up!" He stood, called out in raised voice, "Your Honor, we call upon the esteemed historical theologian, Doctor Dean Maxwell, to approach the witness stand."

An man in his sixties walked purposefully to the stand. Facing the gallery, he caressed the Bible as the clerk swore him in.

"Doctor, give the court your name and title please," asked George.

Sitting with perfect posture in the witness chair. "Doctor Dean Maxwell. I am Director of the Institute of Comparative Religions, Taos, New Mexico and Professor Emeritus of the Divinity School, University of Chicago. Also, I serve as a director on the Ontario Millennial Project for Religious Tolerance."

"Tell the court, Doctor, your area of specialty, please."

"I have made it my life's work to study the history of religions to find how these beliefs influenced their culture."

"Your Honor," shouted Green, " I fail to see..."

"Chambers, gentlemen," Judge Carleton declared, rising from the bench.

The words sent shivers down George's spine, reminiscent of having been called into the headmaster's office at prep school.

Sidney and George trailed in the dust wake of the Judge's invisible footprints. When they arrived in chambers, the Judge was pacing back and forth, obviously angered. Red-faced, he stood toe-to-toe with George, "What is this?"

"Your Honor, it is imperative to my case to furnish solid, empirical evidence proving the continuity of consciousness. Maxwell's testimony will validate my client's claim to reincarnation. There is no better advocate anywhere than Doctor Maxwell. He's a treasure trove. I need him to make my case."

"Treasure trove?" smirked Green, "you, sir, are reaching."

"Your Honor, I told you upfront that my entire case depends upon an understanding, and acceptance of reincarnation. That's what this witness provides. You must hear him out."

Carleton scoffed, "Counselor, this is my courtroom, not a classroom. Drop the lectures and move on. Wrap up this witness, or I will entertain a request for dismissal."

"Thank you, Your Honor," Green chimed in sensing with relief a turn of events in his favor.

"You may have your witness Mansbridge. Just be careful, very, very careful," The Judge warned.

George blinked, nodded subserviently. "Yes, Your Honor, I understand. I'll do my best."

"It best be better than that," opening his chamber's door. Robe trailing, he walked back to his bench, two attorneys, like ducklings, followed behind.

Carleton resumed his place at his bench, looked out over the gallery, "Counselor, you may proceed."

Refocused, George wasted no time, "Once again, Doctor, would you please elaborate on your specialty?"

"I have made the history of religious practices and their effect on cultural traditions my life's work."

"And just how has religious belief affected cultures?"

"From the earliest days, religious belief was needed by man to explain the unexplainable: mysteries like birth and death; as well as plagues, earthquakes, floods, droughts, volcanic outpourings: calamities beyond man's control. They needed to know why? This resulted in a series of myths, stories and legends that leaned heavily towards beliefs of the influencing factor in the unseen supreme powers; thus—religion; from the Latin *religio*—to tie fast."

"And you have published in this field?"

"Yes, extensively. My best known works include the books titled: 'Why Religion Matters' and 'A Brief History Of Religion In Society.' Both were on the New York Times book list for some months. I have also published numerous articles and have spoken on this topic around the world."

What are the similarities among these religious beliefs that recognize reincarnation?"

"Your Honor, he's leading the witness," Green barked without rising.

"Sustained," Carleton said, "rephrase."

"Doctor, can you tell us whether there are any similarities between the major religions of the world?"

"The five major religions of the world; Buddhism, Christianity, Hinduism, Judaism and Islam all share in common eight foundational principles, belief in a Universal God, responsibility for one's actions, love, peace, forgiveness, spiritual values, the golden rule and immortality of the soul."

"Anything else?

"Yes. Additionally, each celebrate the same four elemental beliefs, with their own refinements."

"And, what are these beliefs are?"

All people have the basics in common; the experience of bodily birth and physical death. The great world religions seek to find meaning and purpose in these observable facts through common beliefs: The first, bedrock belief is in a Supreme Divine Presence. Second, an interconnected link between all of creation and the Creator. Third, that all paths seek the ultimate conclusion, a reconciliation between the limitations of physical life with spiritual existence. And fourth, that there is a Divine Plan with the ultimate goal a reconnection to the Eternal."

George nodded for Hunt to continue.

"There are other similarities with the postulates of four. Foundational to many religions.

"For instance?"

"In Christianity we have the four cardinal virtues of prudence, justice, temperance, and fortitude. In Hinduism, it's the four virtues of non-violence, truth, purity and self-control. Buddhists honor four noble truths, four mental principles, four bases of success, four divine states of mind and four virtues of social welfare. Sioux Indians recognized four virtues of bravery, fortitude, generosity and wisdom. Even Plato offered his own foursome: wisdom, courage, self-control and justice. Take all these words, the concepts are the same. The codes of morality and faith, from one religion and belief structures to the other."

"Fascinating," the words slipped form Carleton's lips.

Maxwell smiled at Carleton's comment, "You might note the root of these construct of virtues reflect the natural segments of our planet: four corners of the Earth, four seasons, four phases of the moon, four directions of east, west, north, south, and four basic elements of water, earth, fire and wind. It shows how closely religions have been tied to the natural world."

"Doctor, based on your research, when did belief in life after death, the continuity of consciousness known as reincarnation, begin?"

"From the beginning of time, when the questions of death, the end of physical life, emerged. Why are we here? What is the meaning of life? What happens after the body dies?"

Maxwell paused, letting the words settle in the minds of the gallery.

"Evidence of a belief in a life beyond goes back to a finding in what now is Turkey, where an unearthed graveyard used by the Neanderthals, more than one hundred thousand years ago, was discovered. A study of fossils confirmed that they had buried flowers and other items alongside the departed, indicating a belief in some form of an afterlife."

"You say an afterlife. Like, what?"

"That's hard to say. Gravesites from all over the earth, including the great pyramids show tangible evidence of belief that, after our mortal death, we survive in some form or another."

"Could this be survival in, say, a heaven or hell?"

"Zarathustra, an Iranian prophet, who lived approximately fifteen hundred years before the birth of Christ, was the first to conceive the concepts of heaven and hell."

"What did he mean by these terms?"

"For those whose life was moral, he envisioned a eternity of bliss; for those who weren't, an eternity of misery. This put responsibility for the outcome squarely on the shoulders of the individual. Live a good life, be rewarded; choose evil, you pay. His vision evolved to where the good, the worthy, were able to return to earth in a new form, as a person with a new identity. Of course, different approaches evolved. Whether yours required several gods, one god or no god at all, the reward of an afterlife would depend upon how well one prepared through good works, honorable living, bravery, sacrifice, obedience, and whatever else were determined to be the constituents of the culture."

Maxwell paused, took a deep breath, "Belief that man could return to earth in his worldly state was part of all early religions, worldwide, for some forty thousand years. At various points in history, the western, Abrahamic religions of Islam, Judaism and Christianity, turned to strictly linear paths, while the eastern beliefs of Buddhism and Hinduism retained a cyclical view of life and rebirth; one in which one could return to earth, again and again, usually in order to perfect him or herself."

"Are there other historical precedents? "

"Yes. When Moses was given the ten commandment at Mount Sinai, he was also given the esoteric teachings of the Kabbalah, which was passed on only as an oral tradition until the middle ages when it was finally committed to parchment. These teaching embrace reincarnation in great depth. The Hebrew word for reincarnation is 'gilgul' which means the 'revolution of souls'."

"Christianity also?"

"Yes, Reincarnation was well embedded into Christian culture, completely taken for granted, during the life and times of Jesus. In fact, the first father of the very early Church, Origen, who lived A.D. 185-254, developed a theology based on Jesus' teachings as an ardent supporter of both pre-existence and reincarnation; as was Clement of Alexandria and Saint Jerome. Origen stated in *De Principiis*: "The soul had neither beginning nor end...[They] come into this world strengthened by the victories or weakened by the defeat of their previous lives."

A low rumble from the gallery made Maxwell pause for an instant.

"Additionally with the discovery of the Dead Sea Scrolls, from the Christian Gnostics in 1945, which was written barely one hundred years after Jesus lived, were teachings that Jesus spoke frequently of reincarnation and of final salvation."

George squarely faced Maxwell, "So then, you're saying that belief in reincarnation has been accepted, in many religions, for thousands of years?"

"Let me show you."

George turned to his right, "Bailiff, the easel please."

The bailiff shuffled an easel with charts covered by wrapping paper to the front of the bench. Slowly he raised the cover from Chart One with a bolded heading: "Religions With Belief In Reincarnation."

"Thank you," George chirped, "Doctor?"

Maxwell shifted in his chair, "It's been a belief in every culture, on every continent, in every century, for at least forty thousand years that we can document. As you can see from this chart, worldwide there are more people that embrace the belief in reincarnation than do not. When that many people, the world over, share a similar belief, isn't it irrational to discount it?"

```
                            Chart #1
        Religion's that include a belief system in Reincarnation:
Bon                                                     100,000
Buddhism                                            360,000,000
Cho Dai                                               6,000,000
Chinese Religion                                    394,000,000
Druze                                                   500,000
Eckankar                                                500,000
Hare Krishna                                          1,000,000
Hinduism                                            900,000,000
Jainism                                               4,000,000
Judaism                                              14,000,000
New Age                                              25,000,000
Scientology                                           1,000,000
Sikhism                                              23,000,000
Wicca                                                 3,000,000


Additional  belief  systems  contained  in  indigenous  cultures
including Australia, Pacific Islanders, Native Americans, and cultural
tribes in Africa, and South America which have not yet been counted.
   Gross approximation of individuals whose belief systems include
reincarnation is over three billion people, which is approximately half
of the world's current population.
```

Green began rising, Carleton glared him down, "Sit down, Counselor!"

"Please go to the next chart. As you can see in the each of the five major religions, Christianity, Buddhism, Islam, Judaism, Hinduism, each one has made the universal soul, one that lasts through eternity, a pillar of their belief."

"Bailiff?" George prodded. The bailiff moved quickly to remove the first chart, revealing the next.

Maxwell waited a long moment, allowing the words on the chart to be read and digested.

Chart #2

Reincarnation Beliefs Eastern and Western Wisdom

New Testament: Thou art not yet fifty years old, and hast thou seen Abraham?' Jesus said unto them, Verily, verily, I say unto you, Before Abraham was, I am. – *Bible: John (8:58)*

The Kabbalah: The souls must reenter the absolute from where they have emerged. They must develop all the perfections; the germ of which is planted in them; and if they have not fulfilled this condition during one life; they must commence another... until they have acquired the condition that fits them for reunion with God.- *Kabbalah (Zohar)*

Hinduism: A man acts according to the desires to which he clings. After death he goes to the next world bearing in his mind the subtle impressions of his deeds; and, after reaping there the harvest of those deeds, he returns again to this world of action. Thus he who has desire continues subject to rebirth. He who lacks discrimination, whose mind is unsteady and whose heart is impure, never reaches the goal, but is born again and again. But he who has discrimination, whose mind is steady and whose heart is pure, reaches the goal and, having reached it, is born no more.- **Upanishads**

Buddhism: Samsara—the Wheel of Existence, literally, the 'Perpetual Wandering'—is the name by which is designated the sea of life ever restlessly heaving up and down, the symbol of this continuous process of ever again and again being born, growing old, suffering, and dying. (It) is constantly changing from moment to moment, (as lives) follow continuously one upon the other through inconceivable periods of time. Of this Samsara, a single lifetime constitutes only a vanishingly tiny fraction.- *Gautama Buddha*

The Quran: God generates beings, and sends them back over and over again, till they return to Him.- *Quran*

"As you see, Hindus and Buddhists believe that what we call our reality, is an illusion. Buddhists honor impermanence, the transitory nature of all existence. They see the body as a mirage; that it is our souls that continue on a path through time, until they become perfected. This also is what Hindus mean when they say, that 'deep within one life, abides another'. And what Judaism is saying, 'he restored my soul'. All of these are just another way of saying, in the Christian precept, 'that the dead will be raised, to live again'."

"Your Honor," bellowed Sidney Green, "this line of questioning is improper. It has no relevance here in this court of law."

Carleton leaned towards Maxwell, "State your point."

George jumped in, "Doctor, cut to the chase. Tell the court why you believe the religions of the world accept reincarnation as a reality."

"Bailiff, one more time please, chart number three. Thank you."

The bailiff removed the second chart, revealing the third.

```
                          Chart #3


          The Golden Rule — ethics of reciprocity &
              Law of Karma — cause and effect.


Buddhism: Hurt not others what you would not like yourself.
    Then there will be no resentment against you, either in
    the family or in the state. Analects 12:2
Christianity: Do unto others as you would have them do unto
    you. Matthew 7:1
Confucianism: Do not do to others, what you would not like
    yourself.
Hinduism: This is the sum of duty; do naught onto others
    what you would not have them do unto you. Mahabharata
    5,1517
Islam: No one of you is a believer until he desires for his
    brother that which he desires for himself. Sunnah
Judaism: What is hateful to you do not do to your
    fellowman. This is the entire Law; all the rest is
    commentary. Talmud, Shabbat 3id
Taoism: Regard your neighbor's gain as your gain, and your
    neighbor's loss as your own loss.Tai Shang Kan Yin P"ien
Zoroastrianism: That nature alone is good which refrains
    from doing another whatsoever is not good for itself.
    Dadisten-1-dink, 94,5
```

"At the heart of every culture is the impersonal law of justice as the golden rule. Think about it in this light, if each life was just a one shot deal, then it's pretty unfair. It's very hard to make any kind of sense out of all the obvious inequities. Life would just be one big roll of the cosmic dice; not very fair. The Golden Rule, however, evens the playing field. Our progress is either delayed by our wrong actions or advanced by our good endeavors. Exerting our free will is no excuse relative to 'ignorance of the law'. Without the principle of reincarnation, the gross inequities and apparent rampant injustices might lead us to erroneously conclude that the Universe is unjust."

Letting it soak in, George probed, "Doctor, could you elaborate?"

"The belief is that you get back in exact measure what you do to others. No more. No less. The doctrine of reincarnation set forth in the Hindu scriptures states that man's fall from grace forces us to return to earth, again and again, until one is perfected through karma, to return to the home of the Divine. The same tenants grew into Buddhism in the sixth century. The Buddha's teaching shared the secrets to salvation through successive cycles of reincarnations."

George broke up Maxwell's discourse, "You're saying?"

"It's the same across the board. Several Hebrew and Christian scriptures affirm reincarnation, the Bible, the Christian Gnostic gospels, the Hebrew Bible, the Torah, the Dead Sea Scrolls, the Kabbalah, the Zohar and the Apocrypha."

George interrupted, "And, Christianity?"

"Yes, there are many references. One, when Jesus identifies Elijah as the previous incarnation of John the Baptist in Matthew 11:13.14: 'and if ye will receive it, this is Elias, which was for to come'. There is Reference to both spiritual and physical rebirth in (1 Corinthian. 15:51) 'Listen, I tell you a mystery. We will not all sleep, but we will all be changed'. Again in, Psalm 51:5, 'Surely I was sinful at birth, sinful from the time my mother conceived me'. Without the concept of reincarnation, this Bible verse of sin before birth is meaningless and understandable only if sin had been committed in a previous life. And of course, in Revelation three-twelve speaks to it, 'he that overcometh will I make a pillar in the temple of my God, and he shall go out no more.'

Sidney Green leapt to his feet, "Oh, come on!"

"Sit," Judge Carleton ordered, turned back to the witness, "Go on, please."

"So, Doctor, you say reincarnation is a belief of Christianity?"

"Yes, from the beginning, until it was condemned by the Roman Church and declared heresy at the Fifth Ecumenical in Five fifty-three A.D. It was a tenet of Christian belief until Constantine disposed of it to strengthen his control over the populace of believers."

"Your Honor! I move to strike this entire line of questioning. There is no relevance here," Green shouted, eyes squeezed tightly shut.

"That's all from this witness, Your Honor," George said, a smile on his lips, "thank you, doctor."

Carleton turned to Green's table, "Denied. As the finder of fact, I will assign it the weight I deem appropriate Counselor, your witness."

"Nothing, Your Honor," Green's voice a near-whisper. "Nothing relevant. Wait. Yes," leaping to his feet and bellowing from his table, "Doctor, you claim to be an expert in religions?"

"Yes. It is my specialty, if that's what you're asking."

"And you? What religion do you profess to believe in?"

"I take the wisdom from a variety of faiths, but personally, I am a member of the Unitarian Universalist Church of America."

"And his Uni-Uni whatever, does it accept this preposterous reincarnation nonsense to be true?"

"My church neither supports nor denies it. It recognizes it as one way of thinking."

"So. This malarkey your spouting isn't even supported by your own church. It really is just your own personal belief."

"Objection," George rose."

"Overruled." Carleton said, his voice tiring from it all, "the rules governing expert testimony are clear. The personal opinions of an expert are irrelevant. Only what is generally accepted in the expert's particular field are admissible. Knowing the line here is relevant and important." Turning to the witness on the stand, Judge Carlton asked, "can you clarify for me, where that line lies?"

"If I may," Maxwell asked, "my testimony today is nothing more than a recitation of well-documented historic and cultural records, fully accepted by the majority of the faith and values community. And nothing less."

"Now that that's settled," Judge Carlton turned to Green, "anything further?"

"That's all, Your Honor." Green responded, turning his back on the witness in a dismissive gesture.

"Any redirect?" Judge asked Mansbridge. "No thank you. This witness has made his point clear enough."

"You may step down now," Carleton addressed Maxwell, who stood to his full height, walked away aware of the conflicted glances following him to his seat in the gallery.

Looking back to George's table, Carleton asked, "Counselor, your final witness for the day?"

"Thank you Judge," George said, still standing, "I call on Doctor David Yarnell, M.D."

CHAPTER SEVENTY

We make a living by what we get, but we make a life by what we give.
-Winston Churchill

George waited for his witness to be sworn in and assume his seat.

"Welcome, Doctor. Please give the court your name and title."

"Yes," he stuttered, shifting in discomfort, "my name is David Yarnell. I'm a physician at Boston General and have been practicing medicine since 1984. My area of expertise is orthopedics, specializing in chronic pain management."

"Chronic? You mean on-going pain?"

"Yes, on-going, often to the point of debilitating."

"So, how do you manage debilitating pain?"

"Each case is different. Sometimes, physical therapy or corticosteroids are the answer. But in severe cases, opiates, electrical nerve stimulation; even local anesthetics and nerve blocks are necessary. Often, I design a regimen of medication management, including injections, physical therapy, and cognitive–behavioral therapy techniques, among others."

"Are their dangers with chronic pain going untreated?"

"Yes. Patients with chronic pain often become depressed, physically inactive, sleep deprived and, far too often, they become chemically dependent, addicted to their pain medications."

"And, if these steps don't work?"

"Then worst case, if needed, surgery; with one exception. I've found that hypnotherapy often can be successful in mitigating pain in certain patients."

"Why do you think it, hypnotherapy, works, when other methods have failed," George asked.

"Well, I'm not an expert in the field, but it seems to me clinically that by reaching the subconscious mind of the patient, the therapist can uncover the possible underlying causes of the symptoms in some cases."

"Objection, this witness admits he's not an expert in this field," Green spat out, "he can't be allowed to testify on hypnotherapy."

"I concur. Limit your questioning to the area of your witness's expertise, Counselor," Carlton directed.

George nodded, knowing he would have to go through the backdoor to get to the front entrance, "Please tell the court how it was that you referred your patients to Doctor Carol Klein for hypnotherapy treatment?"

"Yes, I was referred to her through a colleague. Doctor Klein has excellent credentials as a psychotherapist and is well trained in the art and delivery of hypnosis treatments."

"So then, as a treating physician you have prescribed hypnosis as an acceptable medical protocol?"

"Yes. Hypnosis often proves effective when other methods fall short, particularly in difficult cases."

"Difficult cases?"

"Cases in which standard protocols fail to adequately relieve a patient's underlying condition."

"In your view, how effective has Doctor Klein's work been for your patients."

"Extremely successful. She's been able to bring marked, quantifiable relief to a number of my patients."

"And are you currently still referring patients to Doctor Klein?"

"No, I've been unable to since she was suspended from the practice of psychotherapy by the Dean of Behavioral Medicine at the University."

"What have you done since?"

"Since then, I've been referring my patients through the department head for cases where I believe hypnotherapy treatment is advisable."

"And how's that been going?"

"Not as well. The patients I've referred have not benefited as much as those treated by Doctor Klein."

"What do you conclude from this?"

"Based on the results I have seen as the treating physician, whatever treatments Doctor Klein provided apparently worked significantly better than the those given by other psychotherapists."

A buzz vibrated throughout the courtroom.

George raised his voice over the buzz, "Doctor, are you aware of the technique Doctor Klein was using, which based on your observations produced better results?"

"Yes. She was using regression, regressive hypnotherapy. Bringing her patient's consciousness back in time."

"Are you aware of how far back in time she was going?"

"Not specifically for each patient. However, what I do know is that however far back she took them, it worked. My patients came back with markedly reduced pain following her treatments."

"Are you aware as to whether or not she may have taken your patients back into a previous existence? Past lives?"

"Leading the witness," Green shouted, not moving a muscle.

"Sustained," Carleton said, "rephrase."

"Doctor, when you read Doctor Klein's treatment summaries, and examined your patients and saw for yourself the results of her therapy, what did you conclude?"

"That something remarkable had occurred."

"And that might be?"

"I considered that maybe, she might have regressed my patients back into a time past their childhood, to resolve some underlying trauma, maybe a psychological blockage, from possibly an earlier existence."

"You mean, from an earlier lifetime?"

Yarnell paused, assessing the question, "Well yes, in fact that is what I considered. As I said, after she left, nothing's worked as well or has had the enduring results I saw following her treatments. So, yes. I had to consider it. As a doctor working through differential diagnostics, there is a process of elimination in which I rule in or rule out conditions and their causes. Here, I worked through all the possibilities for my patients unusual improvements and while I could not validate it with medical certainty, it clearly fell in the realm of medical probability."

A muffled groan rolled through the courtroom.

"Doctor, you say you could not validate that her therapies reached into past lives, with medical certainty, but at the same time, you say her success rate has been higher than other psychotherapeutic interventions?"

"Yes. That I can say with medical certainty which is what supports my opinion that there must be another aspect of Dr. Klein's treatment that is producing unprecedented results"

"And after having been suspended, was she no longer available for your patients?"

"That's right."

"On what grounds was she suspended? For being too effective?"

"Speculation!" Green shouted. "This is a most improper line of questioning!"

"I will rephrase. Doctor, do you have an opinion as a treating physician, as to how new modalities of treatments are received or recognized in your field?"

Yarnell's eyes brightened, "I know what you're asking and yes, I thought the same thing. I can give you my professional opinion on the challenges that treatments like those provided by Doctor Klein might face."

"Please do."

"It has to do with attachments to professional egos. And the big money that the business of medicine generates."

"Please elaborate, if you will Doctor."

"Those of us in medicine are so invested in what we're used to: what we've always done, that, you know, we've put in so much time and money into our education that it's hard to move on from such an enormous outlay. Compare this expenditure and personal sacrifice to these, new therapies, especially low tech ones like acupuncture and hypnotherapy, whether they work or not, are shunned by the medical community because they just don't generate the return on investment that more technical treatments offer."

"Is that it, just a hesitancy to ..."

"And that's just a part of it. Beyond that, there's the money, enormous investments that are made, the pressure to secure research grants. Competition's fierce. Between the mid-eighties to this year, medical research spending ballooned from one billion to over twenty-three billion dollars annually."

He paused as George nodded, stroked his chin.

"You see what the business of medicine is up against? Research translates into funding to develop new medical protocols. It's the money that makes medicine move. Add to that the pressure from hospitals, insurance companies, pharmaceutical houses. Everyone's after their piece of the action."

"I see," George said, "so, how does this affect the acceptance of Doctor Klein's work with your patients?"

Yarnell's face reddened, "That's just it. Low-tech treatments, like hypnosis may be effective, but they're not particularly lucrative. With hypnotic regressions, where's the money? It's a hands-on, low-tech treatment that is labor intensive and requires a highly trained specialist. Not very mass-produceable, let's say like dispensing a new drug. So, it may be highly effective, but overall, not very financially lucrative."

"So, you're saying that, how did you phrase it, 'low-tech treatments,' even if they prove effective, are shunned due to a lack of financial return?"

Nodding as his upper lip curled downward, "Yes. 'Conflicts of interest' is a frequently discussed problem within the health care community. There are rarely simple answers to such complex issues."

"To your knowledge, is past life regression therapy a reimbursable code under current medical insurance plans?"

"No, I do not believe so, today."

"So, in order to be sure that this Court understands your testimony correctly, would it be correct to say that it is your opinion as a treating pain specialist that past life therapy appears to have a high efficacy rate in comparison to other similar treatments for your patients. Yet, it is not recognized as a legitimate treatment by either the profession or the insurance industry?"

"Yes, that is correct."

"Anything else you'd like to add, Doctor?"

Taking a deep inhale, Yarnell pondered his answer, "We always face the problem of finding what's in the best interests of our patients. We want badly to translate the latest research findings into clinical practice. Unfortunately, too often clinical practice is years behind scientific research."

"Why is that?"

"Again, mostly financial. Change is costly. There's too much invested in the old schools of practice. It comes down to institutional guidelines. I know of many medications being prescribed today whose effectiveness is negligible. Not very acceptable in terms of patient care. And ..."

"Your Honor?" Green called out.

Before allowing the objection, George cut it off, "Thank you, Doctor that's all."

"Yes. Mister Green? Your questions for this witness will have to wait until tomorrow," Carleton declared.

"Oh yes, Your Honor," answered Green.

"You may step down, Doctor. And thank you for your testimony."

Carleton picked up his gavel, "This court is adjourned until ten o'clock tomorrow morning." The sound of his gavel's bang echoed like a gunshot.

"All rise," shouted the court clerk, his voice muffled by the sound of a sudden cacophony arising throughout the gallery.

"What a load of ..." someone shouted over the buzz.

The crowd dispersed quickly, many pulling cell phones from their pockets as they emerged outside the building. Within minutes word of the proceedings spread throughout the city, the nation and the world.

CHAPTER SEVENTY ONE

Trials are but lessons that you failed to learn presented once again, so where you made a faulty choice before you can now make a better one, and thus escape all pain that what you chose before has brought to you.
-Course in Miracles

Within minutes, Cardinal Long received the call. He listened intently, uttering not a word, nodding his head sporadically.

"So be it," he said, ending the call.

Slumping in his overstuffed chair, he inhaled deeply, exhaled a long, slow breath.

"So be it."

Looking up he called an aide, "Brother Jenkins, I must write a cable to the Vatican. It must go out immediately, do you understand?"

"Yes, Your Eminence," the aide nodded, "I am at your disposal."

Cardinal Long turned to his notepad, grasped a pen, he began to write, drawing on his best Latin, with a follow-up translation into English.

Your Holiness

Tentatio has exorsus. Ut vereor, is has adverto ultum interventus intentio, nonnullus of is contrarius ut optimus interests quod sensa Nostri Sanctus Catholic quod Apostolic Templum. EGO vadum geminus nostrum protestor incursus praevenio ullus porro detrimentum. EGO precor Nostrum Senior coincidentally, in suus sapientia smites is turpis uredo per reddo a denique verdict in nostrum ventus. EGO vadum servo vestri edoctus.

Senior exsisto vobis.
  Vestri obedienter vernula
  Cardinal Suffragium Long

  Your Holiness
  The trial has begun. As feared, it has attracted much media attention, some of it contrary to the best interests and teachings of Our One Holy Catholic and Apostolic Church. I shall double our protest efforts to forestall any further damage. I pray Our Lord, in His wisdom, smites this ugly blight by rendering a final verdict in our favor. I shall keep you informed. The Lord be with you.
  Your obedient servant,
  Cardinal Francis Long

Confident that his note would be received with gratitude, and coincidentally would elevate his own standing within the Holy Church hierarchy, "Not that that matters," he thought to himself, a satisfied smile of on his lips, the Cardinal called in his aide.

Just as the Cardinal had predicted, newspaper and television reports that evening focused on the most sensational elements of the trial, enhancing the statements of Doctors Hunt and Maxwell.

> *Boston—Extraordinary testimony filled a courtroom here today, as the first phase of what has become known as 'The Trial of Two Lives,' came to a close.*
>
> *The trial, in which a Boston college professor and practicing psychologist, has claimed to be the reincarnation of a woman who she asserts is the rightful recipient of a vast amount of money.*
>
> *Dramatic testimony by a Nobel Prize nominee scientist and a well-known authority on religious history gave supporting evidence for the existence of reincarnation.*
>
> *Nobelist nominee Theodore Hunt rocked the courtroom saying, 'from a purely scientific perspective, that reincarnation, from one person into another is not only possible, but likely,' while author Dean Maxwell stated reincarnation has been a belief in religions the world over for centuries, with the Christian church disclaiming*

it in the sixth century,'to ensure its control over the populace of believers.'

Final witness for the day was a local physician, Doctor David Yarnell, who stated that a handful of his patients have been dramatically helped through regression therapy administered by Doctor Klein, stating, 'she might have regressed into a time beyond their childhood, to experience some trauma, back in, an earlier existence.'

The trial resumes tomorrow in the court of Judge Charles Carleton.

Response from the Pontiff was received overnight. The Cardinal had it read to him, in English translation, over his telephone:

Cardinal Long,

Your recent cable is distressing. That such a blasphemous public hearing be permitted is beyond understanding. You must fulfill your vows and find a way to subvert this, a true threat, to our One Church. This is yours to fulfill.

As you may know, there is still a serious downward trend of true believers we must stop this bleeding of faith from the Holy Church. Any event, such as your trial, which threatens to further diminish our ranks must be purged.

Go With God. Archbishop Donatelli

That morning, more than one thousand believers of the One Holy and Apostolic Catholic Church hit the streets of Boston in organized protest of a threat, one suddenly perceived and roundly feared.

CHAPTER SEVENTY TWO

The greatest discovery of our generation is that human beings can alter their attitudes of mind. As you think, so shall you be.
-William James

Day two, the courtroom seemed somehow more crowded than the capacity crowd of yesterday. George had reassured Carol that, "So far, so good." The trial was going well. He'd even heard from his father, who's 'attaboy' came in the form of a, "nice goin' kid."

Initial news reports seemed to be favoring his witnesses. Even the Globe's curmudgeonly columnist Michael Flannery seemed leaning towards Carol's corner, having written:

"Could it be, that right here in the Bay State, the man who engineered final exoneration of the Salem trial victims now is about to knock the dust off reincarnation as an entity who's time has come? So far, George Mansbridge III has showcased some pretty powerful arguments in defense of his client, and not incidentally, his fiancée, Carol Klein, Ph.D."

As she walked into the courtroom, Carol felt all eyes upon her, sensing the sneers and mumbled epithets that greeted her. "Am I really up for this?" she pounded herself, worrying, "is this what 'going well' feels like?"

She noticed all the players shuffling into position as the gallery filled in behind her. Court clerk, Bailiff, transcriber, courtroom artist, Sidney Green and …her heart hurt whenever she looked over to see the two Paulson brothers. How she wished she had been allowed to, somehow, to tell them what this is really all about, that their own mother, the Iris she had visited and embodied, would explain it all to them; that what she's trying to do is bring a powerful truth, one that can be proven, to the forefront. To finish the task. If only....

George joined her at the table, quickly sitting and placing his palm over the back of her hand, squeezing it tenderly. Their eyes met, neither said a word. There was nothing more to be said.

"All rise," the announcement shattered her reverie. "Judge Charles Carleton presiding."

People scuffled to stand as the be-robed Judge entered his courtroom. "His arena, his ring, his world," she thought to herself, comforted by the knowledge that, so far, he had allowed their witnesses to express themselves, despite the onslaught of objections against them.

Carleton took his place in the tall chair, towering over the bench. He slammed his gavel down hard, one time, then once more.

"Order," he boomed. "Order. Be seated. I shall tolerate no outbursts, of any kind, or the courtroom will be cleared. This court is now in session."

He placed his glasses low on his nose, looked down at a sheet of paper, looked up, his eyes peering over the lenses, looking at George, "Counselor?"

"Your Honor," he said glowingly, "with the court's permission, I should like to recall Doctor David Yarnell, back to the witness stand."

"So ordered. Doctor Yarnell, please take the stand."

Having previously been sworn in, David Yarnell immediately took his seat, looking far more comfortable than he had the previous day.

"Good morning, Doctor," George smiled, "a few brief questions for clarification, if you will."

"Certainly."

"Yesterday you indicated that the regressive therapies administered by my client, Doctor Klein, clearly proved more effective than subsequent attempts by others, is that correct?"

"Yes. The clinical evidence supports that conclusion."

"To what would you attribute this?"

"Well, I couldn't say for sure, but it likely boils down to differences in skill, training and possibly procedures."

"Assuming the levels of skill and training are roughly the same, could you elaborate on the differences in procedures?"

Doctor Yarnell shifted in his chair, crossing one leg over the other.

"Of course, I can't really say, but I was given to believe that Doctor Klein's procedures did differ, to the extent that she was suspended for employing them."

"And do you know how her procedures differed, from those that came later?"

"Not exactly but I can offer you my opinions based on my contacts with Doctor Klein and assessment of my patients. The situation at hand is really not that different from a common dilemma in physical medicine." With no interruption, Doctor Yarnell continued to explain, "Two Doctors will give the same medication to two different patients with the same diagnosis. One patient thrives; the other deteriorates. One size does not fit all. The human condition is so complex there is no one simple solution. For instance there are many Jungian analysts, but there was only one Doctor Carl Jung. Can you tell me the difference between the original and the subsequent trained models? The same, but very different."

"Thank you for putting this in context, but Doctor, could you tell me what you thought might be the difference here?"

"Speculation," Green shouted.

"Sustained," Carleton replied. "Rephrase."

"Doctor, you were aware that the procedure employed by Doctor Klein was regressive therapy through hypnosis, were you not?"

"Objection," Green shouted, "leading."

"I'll allow it," Carleton said, "please, answer the question."

"Yes. While I'm not allowed to really go into detail, HIPPA laws and all, I do know that hypnosis can be used to trigger a regressive response, at times, yes."

"Are you aware of any restrictions on just how far back regressions may go?"

David Yarnell blinked at the question, "Uh, no. Not really, not at all."

"There are no restrictions, are there doctor?"

"Objection," Green shouted, jumping to his feet. "Your Honor, he..."

"Objection sustained. Be careful, Counselor."

George smiled reassuringly, "Does your profession believe that if one procedure is more effective than others, whether or not it's considered standard medical practice, if it works, if it solves the problem, if it proves to be an efficient form of healing, shouldn't it be employed? For the benefit of the patient?"

Yarnell smiled, "Yes. If it works, yes."

"Doctor, a follow up question from your testimony yesterday." George strolled over to his prosecution table and lifted up a yellow legal pad, "you indicated that after many other standard medical interventions at your disposal with the first patient you sent to Doctor Klein for treatment that her 'regressive hypnosis therapy' was successful and subsequently eliminated the pain in, let's call your patient 'Miss X'. Is that a fair summary?"

"Yes, after over a year of standard pain management therapies with 'Miss X', it was Doctor Klein's treatment that had the most substantial results."

"I see. And had you not referred 'Miss X' to Doctor Klein, what would the course of treatment likely had been in your professional opinion?"

"Probably, given the progression of the continuing debilitating condition; increased pain medications, which as you know have inherent potential long term side effects, not the least of which is addiction. I'd say the possibility of surgery, which I'd already discussed with the patient."

"The cost of surgery, hospitalization and physical therapy as well as additional medications, doctor?"

"Potentially, it could run as high as hundreds of thousands of dollars long term."

"And in your opinion, the success rate of this surgical protocol for 'Miss X,' long term?"

"No guarantees."

"And the cost or shall I say investment of Doctor Klein's therapeutic protocol?"

"Considerably less, I suppose."

"So, you're saying, that not only were her treatments more clinically effective than the current alternatives, they also provided an excellent result on a modest investment of both time and money?"

"Absolutely. When you look at the cost of health care today."

George turned, faced the gallery, in a loud voice, "So it is your opinion and conclusions that not only are Doctor Klein's treatments apparently more effective, they also are less costly than other conventional means."

"Yes. That is true."

"I thank the court for allowing this testimony, George added, "Doctor, that's all I have for you. Thank you for your cooperation."

Judge Carleton turned to Sidney Green, "Counselor? Have you any questions of this witness, now?"

Green sat unmoving for several seconds, head down, looked up, "Yes, Your Honor, I do." Rising from his chair, he patted Ethan Paulson on the shoulder as he walked past, stopping a few feet in front of the doctor in the witness chair, a notepad in his hand.

"You say you're a medical doctor?"

"Yes."

"With a specialty in, what is it, pain management?"

"That is correct."

"And what do you usually prescribe to your patients?"

"We, in this field use a wide variety of medications, from acetaminophens to opiates such as Morphine, sometimes in combination, in order to achieve the best results."

"You ever prescribe medical marijuana?"

Yarnell blinked at the question, "Well, yes, I have, when a particular patient finds relief from ..."

Green interrupted, "Wacky Weed? Hoochie?"

"Now see hear," Yarnell pleaded, "it's a proven medical fact that ..."

"So you dope them up, then you ship them off to a shrink's hypnosis shop?"

"Objection," George bellowed, "he's insulting and badgering the witness."

Yarnell's mouth gaped, saying nothing.

"Sustained. If you have a question, Counselor, ask it."

"Yes, Your Honor."

Green pivoted, walked in a small circle, returned to face David Yarnell.

"Doctor, what is it, Yarnell? Yes. You say your patients came back from Doctor Klein's treatments suddenly, miraculously cured."

"No, I did not say that. What I said is that I saw marked improvements in their conditions."

"Let me see," Green looked down at the note in his hand, "you said, something to the effect, that if something worked, you're all for it? Is that correct."

"Yes, I mean, if it helps the patient become free of chronic pain."

"So, if I had a sore hand, and, to end the pain, you'd be okay with cutting it off: a therapeutic amputation, since, in your view, it would cure my problem?"

"Come on, that's not fair, and not what I have advocated for, here or in my practice." David Yarnell shot back.

"Your Honor," George shouted.

"Counselor, I warned you."

"Your Honor, you asked me to ask a question, and I did."

"Make it one that's relevant or sit back down, sir."

"Okay. Doctor, do you know exactly what procedures Miss Klein used in working with your clients?"

"Well, I've read the reports and..."

"So, you don't really know if she employed, what does she call it, past life therapy?"

"No, I do not." Yarnell had to admit. "As I said before, after full evaluation, that is a medical possibility that I have considered."

"Okay Doctor, a possibility right? That's all just a possibility. Anything is possible right? Let's take a different tack." Green pulled a file folder off the defense's table. "Doctor Yarnell, describe for the court the progression of death."

"Uh, well, there are many causes of death such as disease, malnutrition, trauma, of course, suicides and accidents are factors as well, but about nine out of ten Americans die due to senescence."

"Senescence?"

"Yes, commonly known as biological aging."

"And Doctor, please describe for the court the process of dying?"

"Relevance?" George questioned from his seat.

"Counselor?" Carlton asked.

"Establishing my prima facie case of entitlement to the inheritance, Your Honor."

"Continue, Mister Green." Carlton heaved a sigh.

"Well, the process of dying goes through several stages that are predictable. Usually the lungs begin to fill with fluid, which in turn substantially weakens the heart's ability to function, thus the blood supply to the whole body becomes compromised. Additionally there is a subsequent shrinkage of the kidneys resulting in the body's toxins becoming unable to be eliminated."

"I see." Green nodded. "Would you agree, that a working definition of death is when all biological functions cease to sustain life? That there are no more vital signs; no pulse, brain waves, heart beat?"

"Okay, that's a good enough definition." Yarnell acquiesced.

"Doctor Yarnell," Green pulled several papers from his folder, "would you examine for the court these documents?"

"Yes, this is the Death Certificate for Iris Middelton Paulson."

"And cause of death, Doctor?"

"Congestive heart failure."

"Is there anything unusual, inconsistent or suspicious about this or any of these documents associated with Misses Paulson's death, including the autopsy report?"

"No, they all appear to be in order and meeting the medical standards."

"Do you believe that Iris Middelton Paulson is dead, Doctor Yarnell?"

"Uh, yes given these documents, cause of death and this death certificate from the Coroner's office from the State of New York with all the accommodating stamps and records. Then, yes, I would absolutely conclude that Iris Paulson is deceased."

"Thank you Doctor. And just to clarify for the record, legally defined by this death certificate issued by Doctor Leonard Raff, Iris Paulson's death has constituted her loss of personhood under our current legal definition. In other words, due to her death, she no longer exists as a person." Green with a look in his eye of having swallowed the canary added, "That's all Your Honor, I got what I wanted from this witness."

Judge Carleton leaned forward, "Let me remind you both, that any more inappropriate questions will not be tolerated from here on. Understand?"

"Yes, Your Honor," both attorneys responded in unison, forming a brief chorus of litigational harmony.

Along with the court reporter, the courthouse artist was recording today's biography, employing the Chinese axiom: 'One picture is worth a thousand words.' Sketching quickly, he added final touches of Sidney Green and David Yarnell locked on a stare-down, both man's eyes electric with challenge.

"Counselor?" Carleton said, looking at George, "Your next?"

"Your Honor, I call upon as my next witness, Doctor Phyllis Buchanan."

CHAPTER SEVENTY THREE

Humankind has not woven the web of life.
We are but one thread within it.
Whatever we do to the web, we do to ourselves.
All things are bound together. All things connect.
-Chief Sealth

A silence came over the gallery at the appearance of a tall, strikingly beautiful woman, fashionably dressed with close-cropped blonde hair. Smiling, she approached the stand, placed her finely manicured hand on the Bible, as the Bailiff read the oath, to which she replied in a silky voice, "Yes sir, I certainly do."

Seated, she turned to acknowledge Judge Carleton, then adjusted herself in the chair, crossing her long legs and turning to face George.

"Doctor Buchanan, could you please give the court your full name and title?"

"Yes. I am Phyllis Doris Buchanan, Executive Director of the National Organization for the Advancement of Patients' Rights."

"Would you tell us about your organization?"

"Yes," she shifted slightly in the chair, "based in Indianapolis, we are a two million member organization run by a Board of Directors of leading officials in the health care, legal and social welfare industries. Our mission is to advocate for fairness and responsibility in the medical and health care fields, for the benefit of patients nationwide. We were chartered in 1968 and have been growing ever since."

"And, just what services does your organization provide?"

"As I said, we advocate for improved care for all patients. This includes working legislatively where needed; lobbying for enhanced government oversight, and most specifically, in providing assistance and guidance to patients who report mis-handlings of all types from their medical experience."

"Such as?"

"Among our most pro-active programs is a set of guidelines on how to negotiate settlements for medical negligence with the loss officers of hospitals who are responsible for medical errors and injured patients under their care."

"Really? And does this happen often?"

"Much more frequently than the public knows; whether from misdiagnosis, improper medicating or simply violation of treatment protocols by attending physicians or the nursing staff."

"And, you are a Doctor?"

"Yes. But not in medicine. My Doctorate is in Economics. My role in the organization is overall management. I oversee a staff of some three hundred employees in offices around the country."

"I see. Doctor, are you familiar with the term, 'Death by Medicine'?"

"Yes."

"Please tell the court what that commonly refers to."

"Death that is caused as a direct result of medical care. It is referred to as iatrogenic deaths."

"Iatrogenic death. As a result of ... "

"Yes," she interrupted, "according to authoritative peer review medical journals as well as current government statistics, medical care in America causes an alarming amount of unintended harm which often leads to catastrophic injury or death."

Waves of murmurs signed throughout gallery.

Flashing a smile, she continued, "You want numbers? According to the latest reports, last year, well over two million patients in US hospitals suffered adverse drug reactions. Unnecessary antibiotic treatment numbered over twenty million, needless surgical procedures performed were estimated to be seven and one half million. Project that out over the next decade some two hundred seventy million people in the United States will undergo medical treatment that is unnecessary."

Gasps reverberated from the courtroom walls.

"However," she continued, "the most striking statistic: last year, the total number of patient deaths directly attributed to conventional medicine—almost eight hundred thousand deaths."

"Just in the last year?" George reeled.

"Yes. you can look it up."

A mild snicker roiled through the gallery.

"In fact, according to the record, today's medical system is now considered one of the leading causes of injury and death in the United States."

The silence was deafening.

Her silky voice turned to steel, "This is why our organization was formed. To protect the interest of patients by mitigating this horrifying record of incompetence, mis-management, neglect and abuse in medical care level."

"In your view," George offered, "what are the net result to the public, the patient consumer population?"

"Today, what we have within medicine and health care is a failed system. It is failing its patients, failing its providers, failing the public at large. And, all that with a price tag of almost three hundred billion dollars last year alone. And, within this population of patients, eight million of them, over the next ten years could become an iatrogenic death statistic. Thus, the Patients Bill of Rights was drafted along the lines of our charter."

"You cite statistics claiming that last year alone, eight-hundred thousand died as a result of medical care mismanagement, et cetera. That's a pretty hefty number."

"Yes, it certainly is. Let's look at it this way. That number, eight hundred thousand, divided by three hundred sixty five days, gives you a death count of more than two thousand each and every day."

A muffled groan from the gallery caused her to pause.

"Here's another way we look at it," she beamed knowing she was center stage. "Take that daily number of two thousand. Each day. Now, think of a jet liner, seating maybe five hundred passengers. So, let's say four jumbo jets, carrying four to five hundred passengers each, fell out from the sky, crashed and burned, everyday, for a whole year due to pilot error. Do you believe that some regulatory agency, like the FAA, to say nothing of Congress, might ensue to find out why the planes were falling out of the sky?"

Green bolted up from his chair, shouted, "Relevance? Your Honor, this is a property rights case! We're not putting the American Medical Association on trial!"

Carleton, with notable reluctance, he ruled, "I'll allow it, for now, small window here counselor, small window."

"Thank you, Your Honor."

"Your Honor," she retorted, "it is important to demonstrate the contrast between what we accept and what we don't. These numbers reveal that the patient's bill of rights is at stake here. We have an out-of-control medical system that is causing great harm to many Americans through greed, stubbornness and sheer ignorance, while suppressing effective treatments such as low-cost, non-invasive alternatives therapies that may help mitigate the underlying causes of a patient's condition."

"And, Doctor Buchanan, how does your organization propose we correct this situation?"

"First, we must recognize that the current medical model of symptom reduction and management is unacceptable. Medicine must starting moving toward preventative measures first. We believe existing medical standards are not comprehensive enough to understand the full complexities of human beings; that a new paradigm is needed, one in which we include for consideration the research that supports among others, the possibility, including past life regressions as yet another diagnostic option and treatment choice."

"How can this be done?"

"Instead of treating the physical symptoms in disease management first in non-emergency cases, we should focus on bridging the underlying emotional and maybe even the spiritual issues as the first level of wellness care and work backwards from there, into progressively more invasive, treatments that potentially could be harmful."

George let out a deep sigh, "So, in summary, from the point of view of you and your two million members, perhaps the consideration of past life therapy is a viable and valuable form of treatment with a minimal downside."

"Yes. I agree whole-heartedly. Unlike the adverse effects of many toxic drug interactions. Our latest survey reports that up to one half of all Americans are at risk with potentially bad consequences."

"No more questions, Your Honor. Thank you doctor, your testimony has been a most illuminating."

George walked back to his chair, a swagger evident in his demeanor. He quickly glanced into the gallery, eyes catching his father's, who sat wide eyed and stone faced.

"Mister Green?" Carleton said, "Your witness."

Sidney Green rose slowly walked to the stand, eye-balling the witness up and down.

"Miss Buchanan, that is Miss, is it not?"

"Well, actually I prefer Doctor."

"Since you've never married, I'm sure you do. Tell me, living in Indianapolis, how does dressing like a Park Avenue model go over?"

"Excuse me?"

"Your Honor," George jumped up.

"No more of that, counselor," Carleton spat.

"Okay. Tell me, what kind of salary do you command?"

"Relevance," George stood. "C'mon."

"Fair line of inquiry. Goes to potential bias and motivation of this witness, Your Honor. Does she believe what she is actually saying or is it all about the money?"

"It's appropriate, I will allow it," Carleton ruled.

"Sorry, Your Honor. Let me ask the witness, is fund raising a part of her job?"

"Yes, a critical part of my responsibility is the growth of the organization. I raise the majority of donations for our organization and I'm paid a small percentage of funds raised."

"To say nothing of the growth of your personal portfolio," Green snickered. "One more question. Miss Buchanan, you say your doctorate is in economics?"

"Yes."

"Now, economics is all about money, right? You know all about money don't you? Isn't your testimony here today going to be exploited to solicit even more members for your organization? And won't you stand to make more money, yourself personally, based on the increased membership? Don't bother answering, Doctor, we all know the answer."

As George began to rise, Green turned away, spouted, "No more from this witness Your Honor. We've heard enough."

George hoped that the weight of Dr. Buchanan's testimony was not completely undermined by Green's effective cross. Must keep moving forward. As George leaned back in his chair, he felt the full weight of his next witness to potentially upend the foundations of case law.

CHAPTER SEVENTY FOUR

Human reason can always find the 'pros and cons' for good and bad actions
alike; it is inherently disloyal. Discrimination acknowledges only one
polestar criterion: the soul.
-Paramahansa Yogananda

The gallery went silent as Phonyong Lee slipped into the aisle, walked briskly to the front of the courtroom. Placing his right hand on the closed Bible swearing to tell the truth, the whole truth and nothing but the truth, he answers, "So help me Gods."

The court clerk shrugged in acceptance.

Seated, Lee bowed his head, acknowledging the be-robed judge sitting on high above. Lee smiled, knowing that he alone understood the precarious decision that would be weighing down upon the Honorable Charles Carleton.

George began, "Please state your full name for the court."

"My birth name is Li Tse Phon Yang. My American name is Phonyong Lee. Doctor Lee."

"Please tell the court what qualifies you as an expert witness here today."

"I have been licensed as a doctor of medicine for thirty-two years, adding a doctorate in clinical psychology eighteen years ago. Early in my career I served as research director for the Santa Barbara Center of Consciousness. I also held the chair as Associate Dean of Behavioral Medicine both at the Jakarta Institute in Indonesia and most recently here at Tufts University. I have been named a Fellow of the London

Psychiatric Société."

"And, today?"

"Today, I am in private practice with an expertise in alternative and complementary medicine, specializing in the research of hypnotic regressions. I also am the Editor of The Journal of Scientific Frontiers, a quarterly publication."

George nodded, "Are these journal's peer reviewed? Meaning recognized in your field of medicine as sufficiently reliable so as to be considered authoritative?"

"There are a small but growing number of professionals from different disciplines in both medicine and science who have been advocating alternative healing therapies, that examine and verify the evidence in past life regression's effect on specific medical conditions."

Lee paused, then continued, "There is an editorial board with members from leading universities and research facilities from around the world who review all the studies prior to being considered for publication, making sure that they adhere to the most rigorous established principles and practices before ever being approved for submission So, yes, it is peer reviewed and recognized as authoritative in the field."

George pivoted, "Your Honor, I submit as evidence twenty-four editions of The Journal of Scientific Frontiers, documenting more than two hundred published cases of past life regressive therapeutic procedures covering a period of seven years, with the full results verified and confirmed by qualified licensed peers."

"Object Your Honor," Green shouted, "relevance."

"Overruled. Evidence admitted! Continue." Judge Carlson looked at the stack of Journals perched on the ledge and wondered when he would find the time to review them before the end of this trial.

"Doctor, could you describe for the court the evolution of your medical specialty?"

"I became disenfranchised with the orthodox theories of human behavior because they did not comprehensively decipher the complete human experience. This is when my medical research shifted. I began to use the diagnostic and treatment aspects of regressive hypnosis as a therapeutic tool. This experience led me to observe that, in the majority of my patients, factors such as personality, motivation, desires were more than a by-product of our genetic inheritance or environmental experiences."

"Could you elaborate?"

"Yes. For the past thirteen years, I have administered hypnotic regressions to hundreds of patients, most for healing of emotional trauma and physical ailments: many for relief of long-standing pain. During this time, I observed that when my patients experienced events back beyond their childhood, back to what I have substantiated as previous existences, there was a healing effect following past life therapy."

"You mean, past lives"

"Yes. That was what I observed."

A muffled buzz rolled through the gallery.

"Doctor, this past life therapy; in your own words, how does it work?"

"Through hypnosis, the mind is free from the constraints of the present self awareness. Once regressed, patients are able to recall events from a previous existence that have direct bearing on their current conditions."

"Your Honor," Green erupted, "how long are you going to ..."

"Move it along Counselor," Carleton barked.

"Yes, Your Honor, Doctor, please."

"As both a medical doctor and a clinical psychologist, I have been trained to draw on both the physical and psychological aspects of the human make up. I saw that once a patient, deeply regressed, revisited a past life event in need of resolution, and confronted it—the result remarkably would relieve their emotional and physical pain."

Carleton let out a long sigh.

"And, what did this indicate to you?" George prodded.

"As the result of meticulously collecting this data and classifying the evidence in these cases, I concluded that their problems, both medical and psychological, were caused by some unresolved, residual issues from a trauma endured in an earlier life."

"C'mon," Green spouted. A growling buzz throughout the gallery followed his outburst.

Carleton slammed his gavel, "Order! Counselor, continue."

"Thank you Your Honor. Doctor, in your words, how do you explain the root cause of your observations? Why does it seem to work?"

"There is a science for understanding the soul and its journey though many lifetimes. The application of this science results in the expansion of our consciousness; the true purpose of reincarnation. Just as we've decoded the human DNA genomes and can pinpoint the chromosomal malfunctions that cause metabolic disorders on a biological level, so too, are we now mapping the karmic-genetic code at the soul level that demarks the underlying reasons that determine all of life's conditions."

Lee paused, took a sip of water. Leaned back in the chair, cleared his throat.

"Go on," George prodded.

"As an analogy, the soul is like the electricity in a light bulb. The glass bulb only functions when electricity flows through it, otherwise it's just a piece of useless glass. You see, our bodies are the vehicles through which the soul's travel on their evolutionary journey. Karma is the universal law of cause and effect that enables the soul to learn life lessons, that allow it to complete its journey. The whole purpose of life is to support the soul's growth to realize its true nature. Reincarnation is necessary to allow the soul to fulfill its purpose."

"And, this 'soul journey' revelation is true in the case of Doctor Klein?"

"Leading," shouted Green.

"I'll let it stand," Carleton said.

"Doctor?" George prodded.

"In Doctor Klein's case, yes. But since the resolution has yet to occur, this case study is not among those I consider fully verified. Not up to this point. Although we have corroborated the connection with Iris Middelton Paulson."

"And Doctor, just what is the unresolved issue facing Doctor Klein?"

"In this case it is her soul that is seeking to complete a specific mission, a task unfinished from before."

"Her soul?"

"The one soul that continued from Iris Middelton Paulson and now to Carol Klein."

Incredulous sounds rippled through the courtroom.

"And how does this impact her case?"

"Iris's soul traveled a journey with a calling, a passionate mission. And now, like in a relay race, Doctor Klein, as the next reincarnation of the same soul, has been asked to pickup the baton and move it towards the finish line."

"Asked? Who asked Carol Klein to do this?"

"Only one, the soul who's last incarnation was Iris."

The crowd uttered a collective gasp.

"Doctor, how was it you came into contact with Doctor Klein?"

"She came to me, seeking answers. In her practice, she'd also observed the healing power of past lives with her clients. When she was discouraged from exploring this phenomenon by her supervisor, she came to me seeking help. I saw that she would greatly benefit from a direct personal regressive experience, her own. Remaining ignorant of our true natures is our greatest affliction."

"So, you regressed her? And what did you find?"

You could hear a pin drop in the courtroom. Lee's answer could be the missing link upon which the entire case pivoted.

"I found that she had reached her previous existence, Iris Middelton Paulson."

Judge Carleton was forced to bang his gavel nearly a dozen times, shouting for order as a cacophony of groans, hoots and unintelligible mumbles exploded throughout the courtroom, drowning out for a moment the anguished cry of Sidney Green, calling out objections.

"One more outburst and this courtroom will be cleared," Carleton rasped. "Objection overruled. Now, move along."

George nodded for Doctor Lee to continue.

"Doctor Klein's recall was profound, and occurred easily, she reached her most recent existence as Iris Paulson almost immediately."

"How do you explain this occurrence?"

"It appears her soul's need to find resolution was compellingly strong."

"And, what would be that need, for resolution, exactly?"

"I believe it is to complete a task that her soul felt very important to finish, in one lifetime or the next."

"And you base your belief on?"

"On the evidence, and the very specific details Doctor Klein was given while regressed."

"Tell us, if you can, just what details she obtained."

"They were remarkable. She had clear recall of living her life in New York, of her home, her children, her husband. That's what led her to visit the apartment in Manhattan; to meet up with the two men, Iris's two sons. William and Ethan Paulson. And to verify that which Iris had shown her truly did exist. In every detail."

Lee paused, smiled warmly, nodded to the two elderly men seated stoically alongside Sidney Green.

"Go on," George urged.

"Also, Iris's father. Doctor Klein was shown a personal note from Joseph Middelton, one for his daughter's eyes only. That's what led her to Montreal, to confirm what she had been told."

"And what was in that note?"

"That there was a sizable inheritance, left solely to Iris Paulson; for her to continue her life's work."

"Doctor, when you look at each of these incidences, all taken together, what do you conclude?"

"Together, they all intended to lead her to a place, well, to exactly where we are now."

George nodded, looked at his shoes, then back up, at Lee, "How do you mean, this place, where we are now?"

Lee leaned forward, pursed his lips, "What I believe it to be?"

"Yes, please."

"I believe the soul that reincarnated as Iris Paulson and is continuing the journey through Carol Klein wanted to bring the issue of past lives into a public forum, to disseminate information regarding the truth that a human being has both a physical life and soul journey. I believe her soul knew it is time, now, for society to accept that our past lives are a reality, and should be recognized spiritually, medically and legally."

A stifled murmur rolled through the gallery as Judge Carleton, mouth gaping, raised his gavel then slowly set it back down.

"And the reason for this," George pushed on.

"The roots from our past and the seeds of our future reside in our present life. As I previously stated, reincarnation is the workhorse. It's a means to an end—the fulfillment of a soul's purpose in life. We take incarnations to continue our succession of lives to improve and ultimately graduate from the repetitious cycles of rebirths."

Waves of spontaneous commentary from the gallery washed over the proceeding. Carleton banged his gavel, dimming the chatter.

"Doctor Lee, how well accepted is your documented research in the medical community?"

"Scarcely acknowledged."

"Why is that doctor?"

"Culturally, we are in denial of our most fundamental truth, just like the resistance of other medical breakthroughs, such as in the sixteenth century; the use of the microscope, when the cell theory of life and the germ theory of disease was revealed. So too, with the discovery of x-rays in the nineteenth century to see the workings that were previously invisible. Now, in the twenty-first century, the theory of reincarnation will be heralded as a significant scientific breakthrough, mapping the karmic-genetic blueprint design of human life. Herein lies the new medical revolution of the future."

"Why would it be important to accept the reality of reincarnation now?"

"To answer your question is very simple. If there were but one life to live then what, in heavens name, what would be the point of self improvement, helping others or making any effort beyond the limited hedonistic whims of selfish satisfactions. If there were but one life it appears to make a serious mockery of religious convictions. It would seem to be a very unjust universe where some are born strong and others weak. There has to be a greater law that governs a more just system that accounts for all the infinite variations of human differences. The succession of many lives is for the purpose of progressively overcoming our imperfections and self imposed limitations to attain our inherent perfection."

"No more questions, Your Honor," George said, stepping back, a broad smile on his face.

A breeze burst seemed to wash the air in the courtroom as George sauntered back to his chair besides Carol, who sat, frozen, expression one of awe and disbelief, her fate had been cast. She was past the point of no return.

CHAPTER SEVENTY FIVE

We are potentially all things; our personality is what we are able to realize of the infinite wealth which our Divine-Human nature contains hidden in its depths.
-William Ralph Inge

Carleton sat stone-faced, mulling this run-away train; nodded towards Sidney Green, "Counselor, your witness."

"Oh, yes. Thank you, Your Honor." He walked hurriedly to the witness's chair. Leaning into Lee's face, he scoffed, then in raised voice, "So, the great Doctor Lee. I ask you, sir, what does any of this have to do with my client's property rights?"

Lee grinned. "Sir, if I may, what greater property is there, than your soul's future?"

Green leaned back, eyes fixed on Lee's.

"Okay, Doctor. Besides hypnotizing people, telling them they have past lives, what else do you do?"

"I take exception to your mischaracterization of my work, sir." Dr. Lee knew that maintaining his calm would diffuse Green's baseless accusations. "My work is devoted to healing, research and teaching."

"So, you probably make a pretty penny, hawking this so-called journal of yours?"

Having seen Green's cut-throat play on personal financial gain with the last witness, Doctor Lee was relieved to have the opportunity to head that one off at the pass. "On the contrary, I established a blind trust with a modest endowment funded by a research grant which subsidizes the costs of the Journal while removing myself from any personal financial ties in order to maintain its professional neutrality."

"Don't you think you're way out-of-bounds, over the edge in your profession?"

"Badgering," George called out.

"Take it down, Counselor," Carleton cautioned .

Lee stared down Green, "Sidney, psychology is the study of human behavior. It has gone through several major schools of thought; psychoanalytic, cognitive-behavioral and now past life therapy, mapping the soul's journey. And no, I am not alone in this pursuit. I am joined in this work by Carl Jung, Edgar Casey, Woolger, Wambaugh, Fiore, Stevenson, Weiss. I trust you are familiar with the work of these great minds?"

"Jung, I've heard of him, but none of the others." Sydney confessed.

"Sir, your admitted ignorance of these intellectual pioneers is most unfortunate. Their work has inspired such institutions at Stanford and Princeton to establish departments researching the seemingly unlimited potential of human consciousness, in this life and beyond. No doubt you recognize the significance of Ivy League support of this research."

George was admiring the very honest and subtle way that Doctor Lee was taking control over his own cross-exam.

Green, knowing he was losing ground, went on the attack. "Okay, isn't it true you were fired from your last position at the University? And that the board deemed your research as lacking scientific rigors; that your evidence was inconclusive; that the results were in direct conflict with the scientific principles and that there is no acceptable theory of reincarnation."

"At the time of my research, those observations were assumed. And as a result, yes, I was relieved of my duties. As it turned out, the dismissal allowed me to pursue my quest for the truth, to scientifically prove the continuity of consciousness. Truly, a blessing in disguise."

"The truth?" Green spouted, "the truth is you and your unsound ideas don't work. It's a sham and you know it."

Lee stared at Green, silently shaking his head as though he was dealing with a petulant child.

"Doctor, would you agree that in our culture, the end of life is considered a conclusion, a finishing point? And that whatever possessions of the decedent are remaining are given to their family, their heirs. True?"

Lee shrugged his left shoulder, conceding the obvious. "Yes, that is the way it has been done."

"So, let's say at the end of my life, I'd make sure that anything that had been important to me was either distributed to my heirs or donated to charity. Whichever way, my possessions are disposed of at the completion of my life in accordance with my wishes. The slate is thus wiped clean, right?"

Lee nodded, "You might say that, we do forget what was; who we were, like the disposal of our possessions; our old identity."

Ignoring Lee's response, "So, Doctor would you agree then, as Iris Paulson's old identity is complete; that the inheritance from Ethan and William Paulson's mother, bequeathed from their Grandfather Joseph Middelton in unequivocally their rightful inheritance?"

"Ah, I see, but....."

George bolted out of his seat, "Objection! Calls for a legal conclusion. This witness cannot render an interpretation on the law."

"It's on the line. Overruled. I want to hear his answer." The Judge looked down at Doctor Lee.

"If one were to look at things on a singular plane, that would be an easy question to answer. But in truth, are we not to give full effect to the wishes of Joseph Middelton? Was it not his intent to bequeath the contents of the safety deposit box only to Iris, his daughter. Is not Iris, his daughter, right here? In the body of Carol Klein? Using your construct, Mister Green, the contents of that box should go to its rightful heir who is Iris, now known as Carol Klein."

"That is preposterous!" Green lunged back. "There is an entire body of case law that governs inheritance rights that you are proposing we toss right out the window based on your faulty scientific evidence. This is nothing more than a transparent sham of bilking two elderly gentleman out of their lawful and rightful inheritance. That, doctor, will never happen. The established laws of the land will prevail and justice will be served."

Lee, smiled, "Counselor, is there a question, or are you lecturing me? Assuming the former, let me respond in kind. Our science is based on what we try to understand, what we study and what we can deduce from those efforts. Science is a fluid and ever-evolving field as it must be and upon which all of our great discoveries and accomplishments have been based upon. What you refer to as established law, is only based on what you and others happen to agree upon in a given set of circumstances. If those circumstances should change, should not the law evolve as well?" He paused, "Mister Green, which sounds most like the truth to you?"

Realizing that Doctor Lee had turned the tables completely, Green regrouped and proceeded in a more direct manner, "Doctor Lee, are you familiar with the term 'agnotologn'?"

"Yes, of course, it's was coined in the nineteenth century as a branch of philosophy by James Frederick Ferrieer. It is the study of ignorance."

"Yes," Green went on, "but more specifically, culturally induced ignorance, such as seeding doubt in the mind's of the public for the purpose of manipulation; intentionally perpetrating misleading information for personal gain."

"Yes, that is always possible in the hands of those with little conscience or ignorance of consequences, these unscrupulous actions could transpire out of neglect, secrecy, or even more maliciously, out of selective suppression of information."

Green seized the opening, "Doctor Lee, aren't you exploiting the public's collective fear of death? Tainting your testimony with misleading information about death being uncertain? Aren't you just as guilty of perpetrating inaccurate information by establishing a controversy without hard scientific evidence? You sir, are guilty of wholesale fabrication of the worst kind! No more than a sleight-of-hand magician, only you use words as your method of deceit. Aren't you actively aiding and abetting the erosion of truth? Think of the multitudes of good innocent people of America, and around the world, you're giving them false hopes, fabricated information, fictitious beliefs about their departed loved ones. Shame on you, Doctor Lee, a conjurer of smoke and mirrors, not unlike the séances of the early twentieth century. You dishonor your title, Doctor. To what lengths will you go to deceive the world for your own gain! There is a fortune at stake here. And it rightfully belongs to the designated heirs, the children of the departed Iris Middelton Paulson."

Murmurs resonated from the courthouse gallery as Green strategically turned his back on Phonyong Lee. Then whipping around, pointed his finger at the witness clamoring, "Doctor Lee, I am here to prove that you have usurped the power of this court for your personal benefit and that your righteous airs are dangerously close to ..."

"Your Honor," bellowed George jumping out of his seat. "Objection! This is so out of bounds, please."

"Sustained," Carlton ordered, "get to your point now, Counselor."

"With pleasure, Green smugly grinned. "Doctor Lee, you took an oath earlier swearing to tell the truth, the whole truth and nothing but the truth, is that correct?"

"Yes, I understand the far reaching consequences of deceit on so many levels. That is why I answer to a much higher standard of truth and superior set of laws than the ones you hold so dear."

Ignoring Lee, Green continued, "Do you realize that by swearing this oath and falsifying information in this court proceeding you could influence the outcome of this case?"

"Yes, your premise is correct, if I did not tell the truth."

"Perjury, Doctor Lee is a very serious offense. So serious in fact that it constitutes a miscarriage of justice and is considered a felony that carries up to five years in prison."

"Threatening the witness, Your Honor," George bellowed, defending his key witness.

Seeing George rise up out of his chair Judge Carlton ordered, "Get to your point now Mister Green."

"The truth and nothing but the truth, Doctor Lee, I contend that you were the mastermind, chief steward, architect and organizer that initiated this treasure hunt for the reprehensible self-serving purpose of not only stealing the rightful inheritance of these elderly brothers but robbing millions of innocent people of their sacred beliefs in the dignity of death."

Dead silence pervaded every corner of the courtroom.

Drawing breath, Green leaned in to the witness box, "Phonyong Lee do you deny that you initiated, methodically schemed and choreographed the collaboration with psychologist Doctor Carol Klein and attorney George Mansbridge to serve as the pawns on your game board for the purpose of your personal gain and private agenda?"

George leaped from is chair, screaming, "Your Honor........."

The courtroom gallery erupted in a cacophony like the Tower of Babel, as Judge Carlton slammed down his gavel, "This court will adjourn until 2 PM."

Even though no one was really listening over the loud clamor, Sidney Green concluded for his own satisfaction, "No more questions, Your Honor. He's said enough," as walked back to the table with a Cheshire cat's grin ear to ear.

As the courtroom crowd thinned, George slumped heavily back to his chair with an audible moan. His house of cards unraveling, tumbling in a free fall with no net.

CHAPTER SEVENTY SIX

The true meaning of life is that it stops.
-Franz Kafka

Avoiding a crush of reporters, George swept Phonyong Lee and Carol out of the courtroom and secreted them in a vacant attorney's conference room.

Carol noticed George, obviously upset, was perspiring.

"Better sit down," he sputtered. "We've a real problem on our hands."

Lee smiled, slowly lowered himself into a polished mahogany chair, sat straight-backed, watching George, an expectant look on his face.

"You seem upset," Lee offered.

"Hell, yes," George spouted. "Green's just about buried us out there. Posing you as the larcenous mastermind of a plot that includes all of us? He's just about kicked the shit out of us."

"But, well it's not true, is it?" Carol nearly wept, crumbling down into her chair.

"I could not lie," Lee said, "how it is characterized is not for Mister Green to determine."

"What counts is Judge Carleton. How he characterizes it. Jesus. I've got to come up with something."

"Let the power of the truth be our strength," Lee said, "lean on the certainty of the facts."

"Look, if the Judge thinks you lied, committed perjury you could go to fucking prison, I could be disbarred and Carol, well, she could be indicted for conspiracy and stripped of her license. That's what," George's face reddening, head down as he paced back and forth, "Jesus!"

Carol was speechless. George looked up, stopped in front of Lee, "I advise us to withdraw our claim and let the chips fall where they may. By dismissing this suit now, I may be able to head off the worst of these consequences. It's probably our best shot."

Lee stared back with a stoic calm, "No. That must not be done. We must continue. I insist."

"Even with the jeopardy we're in? You out of your mind?"

"No, my friend. I know what we must do. And I know, so do you."

George stared back, his eyes widening.

"And what, in God's name, may that be?"

"It is that which you have already seen. Let that reclaim our objective."

"What are you talking about?" George asked, desperate to find a way out.

"Let us be the ones to show the world the timelessness of our cause. It is the only way."

"You mean," George gasped, his words trailing off.

Lee nodded reassuringly, a knowing they both understood, added, "show them our crown jewel of evidence."

Shaking his head, George grimaced, looked at Carol, head bowed, sobbing, hands covering her eyes.

"Look, you two," George said, "you guys stay here. You can't be seen; not until we resume. I've a call to make. I'll be right back, okay?"

They both nodded.

Slowly cracking the door to see if the coast was clear, George scooted out of the room and through the door of the clerk's office. Finding it empty, he grabbed a telephone, quickly dialed the number, leaned back against the desk, in wait.

"Father," he said, "it's me. You see what happened in there?"

Hearing the raspy voice in answer, George cried, "I know, I know. I was blind-sided. Doesn't help to yell! Look, I need some advice, here. From what's just happened, what do you think I should do?"

His shoulder's slumped as he listened for what seemed like forever.

"You really think so," he said. "That bad."

Pulling the phone away from his ear, he waited for the rant to end.

"Okay. Thanks. Guess I'll have to. Thanks."

He set the phone back down.

Now, he had to tell Carol and Lee that it was really over.

CHAPTER SEVENTY SEVEN

Do not follow where the pathway may lead.
Go instead where there is no path and leave a trail.
-Ralph Waldo Emerson

George heard their laughter as he approached the door.

Walking in, he stopped, disbelieving his eyes as Carol and Lee were grinning ear to ear.

"What's so funny?" he asked, incredulously.

"Excuse us," Lee implored, "I was sharing with Carol that children are often frightened by the dark but men must not be fearful of the light; obviously the answer to our dilemma. What you heard as laughter was the sound of reprieve."

"What are you talking about, the answer?"

"You see my friend, once again, the universe has left us breadcrumbs to follow. We have been shown the way."

"Sheesh, now I'm starting to feel like Green, with this malarkey." Towering over the two seated before him, George let them have it: "We're through. Washed up. I'm going to volunteer to take a dismissal, before things get any worse."

Lee and Carol glanced at each other, in surprise and dismay.

"George," Carol said, "wait until you hear what Lee has to say, will you, hon?"

Reeling, George barked it, "Didn't you hear me, we're through!"

"Please," Lee urged, "sit and listen to what I have to say."

George scowled, unsure what to do, finally dropped into a chair, eyes hard on Lee, "Shoot."

Lee smiled, spoke slowly in his most reassuring voice, "This is the way. First, you call me back onto the stand. I have more to say. And I'll be saying it directly to the Judge. You see, he is an aged man, contemplating his own mortality. He is ripe for our message. He does not know it, but I do. I will assuage him, erasing all the uncertainties of his mind and in his heart."

George blinked, saying nothing.

"Of course," Lee continued, "that will not do it alone. We will then need to follow up with our most convincing, our most compelling evidence of all; in order to show the court, not just tell it."

George grimaced, "And just what is that, our most convincing, compelling?"

"In your heart, you know what it is," Lee grinned it, reaching over, patted George's leg. "I will help you make the impossible easy."

George stared at Lee, mute for a full five seconds, then whispered it, "Iris."

CHAPTER SEVENTY EIGHT

He who assists someone up the hill cannot but get to the top himself.
-Chinese Proverb

George stood, "Your Honor, may I re-direct the last witness?"

The Judge reluctantly nodded his assent.

George rose, slowly walked to the stand. "Doctor Lee, please tell the court how all this, your theories, your observations, your research, applies specifically to this case; to Doctor Klein, to the deceased Iris Middelton Paulson, her father and now her two sons."

"Specifically? Doctor Klein realized through her regression that, in fact, she was the embodiment of Iris Middelton Paulson's soul. Everything she has observed to date has proven to be accurate and true. Without question, she is the heir of her father's will and the current incarnated soul of the two brothers' mother."

As a buzz rose through the gallery, Carleton, in frustration, interrupted, "Can't the witness please explain, so we're able to understand how we've gotten here?"

"Gladly, Your Honor. In all the sciences, including medicine, our ability to know truth, amongst other factors, is limited by our senses."

Grabbing the steering wheel back, George directed Doctor Lee to take this testimony straight home. Make the point, open the door, "Could you give us an example?"

"Of course, take sunlight. What we see now actually was emitted eight minutes ago; starlight from the Milky Way? It glowed thousands of years ago. Many of the stars we see today, they no longer exist; yet the light continues. From our view, the sun and the moon appear to be the same size. But now, obviously, we know the sun is vastly larger. What we see is not always true."

George nodded, "Your point?"

"The point is, by expanding our awareness and information, scientific understanding is revised. We no longer take what we see only at face value. Our universe is far too complex. Take something as simple as water. We now know it's two parts hydrogen, one part oxygen, H-two-O, whether solid ice, liquid or vapor, as steam, it's always the same; unchanged, in all its forms."

He paused, inhaled deeply, "So, too, with the 'Self': that which makes up who we are. We have learned, through our studies into past life therapies, that the Self also remains the same, unchanged through many lifetimes. While moving from one existence to the next, our self-identity does not change. Think of it as a wave that comes out of the sea, it arises, crests and falls back into the ocean, only to be reformed into yet another wave."

A murmur rolled through the gallery. Carleton rapped the gavel, one time.

George stood steadfast against Carleton's impatience with Lee's explanation, "So, you're saying our souls continue intact, from one life to the next?"

"Yes, definitely. Think of it in these terms: You're in Boston, planning a trip to Los Angeles. You jump into your blue Chevy, diving west. Then, somewhere outside Davenport, Iowa say, the car stalls, unable to go any farther. You find its parts have worn out and you can't replace them. So you acquire another car, this time maybe a red Honda. And you're on your way again in order to complete your journey."

Lee paused, noting the gallery, some nodding in understanding, others staring wide-eyed. "Well, it's the same with the human soul, migrating from one body to the next. So the journey may continue, until the goal is reached."

"So, you're saying that, in your professional opinion Doctor, my client Carol Klein, is in fact, the soul that was the previous incarnation of Iris Middelton Paulson."

"Yes. Undoubtedly."

A communal groan filed the hall.

"Doctor, I must ask you. How does this work? What process is …"

"Yes. You must ask."

Lee cleared his throat, "It's not unlike the process of human conception; millions of sperm swim furiously toward their singular goal—fertilizing the female ovum, to unite the DNA code that begins a human life. So too, at the moment of conception, a spark signals the formation of a new body, a vehicle for the soul, as a precious opportunity for a human incarnation. And just like only one sperm will tenaciously make it through to fertilize the egg, so too, just one soul will victoriously meet the perfect criterion of its karmic curriculum. The soul seeks a specific karmic-genetic code that will enhance its evolution."

"A karmic-genetic code?"

"Yes. It is karmic-genetic coding that carries one's unique character traits and delineates our circumstances. Karma, from the Sanskrit root Kri, for action. The Universe operates on an unremitting chain reaction, based on the tension between cause and effect; wherein a good cause yields a good effect; a flawed cause, a negative. Physicists have shown us that energy is never lost, only transformed. So too, are we reciprocally affected by our actions and thoughts. Thus, your life reflects your karma. It is what you have already set in motion as past choices, like a boomerang. And it is always subject to change; by exercising free will; there is no fate, you design your destiny."

"Where's he going, Your Honor?" Green pounded his table.

"Wrap it up, Counselor," Carleton growing weary with this witness.

George raised his voice, "So, doctor, you have testified the soul of Iris Paulson is continuing its journey, in fact, with my client. Is that correct?"

"Yes. That is correct, entirely."

"My question, then. In your professional opinion, Doctor, along with claiming her soul, does my client qualify for all rights due her, as the living embodiment of Iris Middelton Paulson?"

"Yes. It is a given."

"There is no question?"

"None. Past lives should not be the question, they should be the answer."

"Doctor. Even after her death, you say her soul has transmigrated into the body of my client."

Lee nodded, smiling, "Yes. Death is that part of life that gives us the opportunity to move on. Over time, death has always been feared because its impact has been beyond our understanding. But now, with the verified results of our research, we know what lies beyond that which we call death. And that, sir, is the opportunity to begin again with a clean slate. Death is nothing more, or less, than an advancement. Actually, in its own way, a death certificate is the a diploma. Death? We should call it graduation."

"Good God," Green was heard to mutter, a bit too loudly. As waves of noise and, boisterous commentary from the courtroom gallery threatened to interrupt the court's proceedings.

George gulped a sigh of relief having finished this marathon. "Thank you Doctor. No more questions, Your Honor."

The Judge nodded to Lee, "Thank you Doctor. You may step down."

Lee bowed his head, "With gratitude, Your Honorable."

Carleton couldn't hold back a grin as he turned to George, "Counselor?"

It was now do or die, George's next utterance was his Waterloo. Everything around him was in slow motion knowing what he was about to spit out was career suicide. In a raised voice, he dove into the deepest part of the pool, "Your Honor, I call as my final witness, Missus Iris Middelton Paulson."

Bedlam erupted in the courtroom as every member of the audience had a passionate opinion on this incredulous, impossible, outrageous assertion.

Sidney Green gyrated loudly in front of the Judge's bench, "Objection!"

Ethan's head dropped to the tabletop. Will wrapped his arms around his brother's shoulders; both men trembling.

Carleton cracked his gavel down loudly, shouted, "Order!" Rising, he directed the bailiff to clear the court. Only those standing close could hear, "We will recess until nine a.m., tomorrow morning. Court adjourned. Counselors, chambers, now!"

The trio faced each other once in the Judge's chamber room; Sidney, red in the face, George, head bent down, sensing what was coming.

"Mansbridge! My court is not a circus!" Carleton barked.

"Your Honor. There is no better way to demonstrate the validity of my case."

"You intend to pull this off? How?" Carleton turned his back, slipped out of his robe.

"By putting my client under hypnosis. To demonstrate the soul's memory from one incarnation to the next, remains intact; to show the continuance of consciousness, from one life to the next, as demonstrable and valid."

Carleton whipped back around to face George, cheeks glowing crimson.

"Your Honor, this is the only viable option for a fair hearing. There's always been a first time for case precedent to establish new legal ground. The law is always evolving; this is no different. This is an important test case. I'm begging the court for some leeway."

"Mansbridge ..."

George gasped, "Judge, we've gotten this far, Please, just let me finish."

"Talk about a circus," Sidney blurted, "Your Honor, Carol Klein and this, this Phony—young quack, they probably have some snake-oil act all rehearsed."

"Your Honor, can you think of a better way to settle this once and for all?" George pleaded, a look of desperation on his face.

The air had been sucked out of the room, before the Judge replied, "I may regret this. But here's the deal. George, you may place your client, Doctor Klein on the stand. But, I will not allow Doctor Lee to be the one to hypnotize her."

With that declaration, he turned, stared into space, "Find someone else. I don't care who it is. Anyone but this Lee fellow, or forget it."

Throwing a self-serving life ring to a colleague, Sidney uttered, "You know Mansbridge, this stunt'll put a stake right through your reputation."

A deadening silence filled the room, broken only by the Judge, "Here's what I expect from now on. Mansbridge, you keep your questions on the mark, or else. Sidney, I'll set the court's precedents, as I see fit. Questions?"

Sidney stepped up, his face inches from Carleton's, "Your Honor, enough's enough. None of the evidence presented so far is relevant, and you know it. I've submitted all the legal documents needed to prove my client's claims. It's an open and shut case."

"Like I said, I'll make these determinations, Counselor," Carleton stared him down.

Green paused, "So, you want I should call for a mistrial?"

"Now see here," George jumped in, "you haven't heard our entire case yet."

Judge Carleton put an end to it, "Okay. Tomorrow, George, keep your eye on the ball or Mister Green here gets his dismissal. And that's final. Good evening gentlemen."

Green turned on his heels and stormed out of the Judge's chambers muttering, "What a friggin' shock, their mother on the stand! Geez!"

George walked into the hallway that led to the courtroom, closing the Judge's office door behind him. Green stood, waiting for him.

"Mansbridge," he said, "look, I don't know why the fuck you're doing this. You know you can't win. And, damn it, why tarnish your career now? You go through with this, you're about to embarrass yourself and the entire field of case law! Don't you see it? You're committing professional suicide!"

"Thanks. I appreciate your concern, Sid. I really do. But, at this point, I see no turning back."

"Why not just concede? Drop your claim. You might salvage some respect doing that."

"Sorry, no can do. Let's let it play out. I think you'll be surprised."

"It's your funeral, George. It's your funeral," turning he walked away, heading into the courtroom to assuage his clients.

George stood there, frozen in time. Everything was eerily silent in comparison to the ruckus of just a few moments ago. It felt like he was standing on a precipice and saw history march before him. Only now he had to lead the parade.

CHAPTER SEVENTY NINE

The purpose of life is a life of purpose.
-Robert Byrne

For the first time, a sickening sense of fear gripped Carol and was burrowing in.

News from the car radio added to her dread, "A most unusual development today in the Boston Trial of Two Lives, as a dead woman, Iris Middelton Paulson, who died decades ago will be called upon to testify as a witness, in this ensuing inheritance battle worth millions. Hundreds, if not thousands, are expected here to witness this historic, if out-of-this-world event. Protestors, many carrying signs with religious references, have already lined up behind barricades at the entrance of the courthouse. A heavy police presence is expected. This is Joel Wolf, WBZ, news radio, Boston."

"I'm scared," she whispered. George kept his eyes on the now-familiar route to the courthouse.

"Don't be sweetheart. I've taken all the precautions we need. We're well prepared and the tides in our favor, so far."

"So far? That's not it," tears forming in her eyes. "Don't you see? I have no control, none, over anything! I'll be under! I don't know what I might say!"

Ahead, they saw thickening crowds amassing behind the barricades in front of the Court steps.

"You might want to duck down," George cautioned, his voice a cold monotone.

"Oh shit," she moaned, sliding down low to the car seat.

Passing the throng, George pulled into an assigned underground parking slot, alongside a Boston police car. Turning off the engine, George saw two uniformed officers step from the car, motion for both to open their doors.

"Morning, folks," one said, "how you doing?"

Carol looked up, open-mouthed, nodded, eyes glistening.

"Don't worry Ma'am. We'll walk you in. Best of luck today."

Stepping into the cold air, George and Carol, flanked by the officers, began the long, somber walk over the concrete chill of the parking garage floor, slipping into the side entrance of the courthouse. Neither said a word.

. . .

As she entered the already crowded courtroom, a buzz roiled through the gallery; the words repeating in her head, "Iris Middelton Paulson, who died decades ago."

"All rise," the bailiff's shout sent a chill through her body. "The Honorable Judge Charles Carleton presiding."

As the Judge entered, Carol could not help but compare his black robe with that of an executioner.

"Be seated," Carleton ordered, settling into his chair on high. He shifted some papers on his bench, lifted his gavel, banged it three times, loudly. "This court is now in session."

Turning to George, he chimed, "Counselor, as we discussed with you and counsel for the defendants, we shall proceed with your wishes by employing a neutral, but qualified, professional to conduct the requested hypnotic regression. Have you selected such a person?"

"Yes, Your Honor, we have. I have issued a subpoena requesting Doctor Isobel Freeman, a licensed psychotherapist to conduct the hypnotic regression I have called for."

"Doctor Freeman, please approach the bench," Carleton commanded.

All eyes in the courtroom scanned the crowd, finally spotting a woman rise to her feet, sporting an all-black, fitted business suit.

Sliding to her row's exit, she walked stiffly down the aisle to approach the judicial bench; for her the equivalent of walking the plank, having been ordered against her will to abet this fiasco.

"State your name and title please," George asked.

"My name is Isobel Teresa Freeman. I am Dean of the Department of Behavioral Medicine at Tufts University."

"Thank you, Doctor." George smiled, "Your Honor, may we proceed?"

"First, Your Honor," Isobel interrupted, "let me ask: may I refuse to do this, as it clearly violates my professional ethics?"

"I appreciate your ethical concerns," Carleton intoned, "but you do have the necessary skill and experience to proceed?"

"Yes, Your Honor, but ..."

"Come now, doctor. This court requests your expertise. You have been placed under subpoena. As such you will proceed, or be held in contempt of court. Understood?"

Nodding, she stiffly stepped back from the Judge's bench, "Yes sir," eyes shooting darts at George and Carol.

"Your Honor," George announced, "I call Carol Ann Klein, to the stand, a.k.a. Iris Middelton Paulson."

Carleton stifled the buzz with one slam of his gavel. "Get on with it."

The bailiff, a confused expression on his face, instructed Carol to put her hand on the Bible, "Do you intend to tell the truth, the whole truth and nothing but the truth, so help you God."

"I do," she mumbled, "er, we do."

A silence chilled the gallery, dumbstruck.

Once in the witness stand, Carol was confused by the mix of feelings coursing through her body; trembling with foreboding, while her mind felt uncharacteristically calm and in control.

George smiled at Carol, "Just relax. We will call forth Iris Paulson with the aid of your colleague, someone with whom you are familiar, Doctor Freeman."

Carol nodded, overwhelmed by the irony of the situation.

"Doctor Freeman," Judge Carleton advised, "this court has authorized a list of questions—submitted and approved by both counsels, from William and Ethan Paulson, descendents of the deceased. These questions were prepared in my chambers this morning and are in this sealed envelope. I have taken these precautions to avoid any inference that this witness knows the questions and has been prepped to answer them. They are to be asked of this witness, while she is under hypnosis."

He paused, removed his glasses, wiped them, ruminating on what he was about to say.

Looking back up, glasses back in place, "I instruct you, Doctor Freeman, to proceed to place this witness into a hypnotic state and to cross-examine her with this list of questions in accordance with the standard procedures of your professional practice."

Having no choice, Isobel stoically accepted the envelope from the Judge and consented to proceed, "Yes, Your Honor."

The bailiff handed her a packet of papers. Isobel's shoulders slumped as she turned toward Carol, her mind flashing back to her former close relationship with her young colleague.

Breaking the seal of the envelope, she studied the list of questions before she looked up at Carleton, "I must have complete silence. No noise at all. None!"

"Then you shall have it, so ordered. There will be no outbursts. Silence in the court."

A low murmur ensued as people shuffled in their seats, anxious for what may lie ahead.

Isobel tugged at her suit jacket hem, positioned herself squarely in front of Carol, feeling like a surgeon holding a scalpel, knowing it would cut twice, going in and coming out.

Their eye contact was searing.

If eyes are the window of the soul, then the former colleagues were in deep communication; the elder saying, "I do not approve, but have no choice;" the younger responding, "trust, old friend, trust."

Isobel began the countdown to launch this event into history. Her good name and professional reputation would be collateral damage in this court of public opinion. "However this turns out, my life will be forever altered," knowing this reluctant cog in the wheel of evolution could not be stopped.

Isobel took a last long deep sigh of resignation.

"Carol," Isobel began, "please, find a point to focus your eyes on. Concentrate on that spot, Now more intently. Bring your inner attention to your breathing, light breaths, now lighter. Your eyes heavy. Drowsy. Good. Let your eyes close. See the screen behind your eyelids. Each time you breath in you will go deeper and deeper, counting down; going deeper still: three—you are very relaxed. Still deeper. Two—focus on your breath. Arrive at the perfect level of intent. One— you are there."

Carol leaned back, eyes closed, having crossed the line into full surrender.

"Good." Isobel noted her patient's arrival into a deep hypnotic state. Respiration rate was markedly slowed, eye movement in a resting phase, peripheral muscles relaxed.

"Are you ready?"

Isobel looked down at the list, her hand trembling.

"Hello, are you here?"

"Yes," in a quavering voice of an older woman, "I'm right here."

"Who? Who's here?"

"Me, Iris. Iris Paulson."

A muffled murmur from the gallery emerged out of the tomb-like silence of the courtroom. Isobel eyes snapped up, imploring enforcement of the order for silence.

Carleton put his finger to his lips and in a stage-like whisper, "Hush!"

Isobel continued, "Your full name?"

"Iris Middelton Paulson."

Will slapped his head and Ethan's body jerked at the familiar sound of their Mother's voice, now emanating from Carol's lips.

"I'd like you to tell me a little bit about yourself."

Head nodding, "Yes?"

"Where were you born?"

"Evanston, Illinois, outside Chicago."

"How long did you live there?"

"Until I was six, when my father moved us to Chicago. Soon after that, my mother died. Then, it was just my father and me."

"Tell me the names of the schools you attended."

"Oh dear, so long ago," grinning. "Northpark Elementary, first grade through fifth. Then, it was Nichols Middle School, on Greenleaf. High School was Evanston Township, back in Evanston, on Dodge Street. Funny nickname: the WildKits. My dad sent me there. I think he had to pull some strings to get me in. For college? My freshman year was in Evanston at Northwestern. It's a good journalism school. I learned a lot there, but then, I transferred to the University of Chicago for the next three years, I wanted to study fine arts and they had a better program. After that, I went to NYU, for graduate work in composition."

"And then, after graduation?"

"I got a job writing at the Chicago New Bureau, covering all types of stories."

"And how did that go?"

"Very well. I met a lot of people and gained some valuable experience. Sherwood Anderson sort of took me under his wing; helped me a lot. Of course, he was leagues ahead of me as a novelist and a meticulous writer. Have you read him?"

"Why, no, now that you mention it." Isobel looked down at the notes, coughed.

"You okay?" Iris asked.

"Yes, yes, thank you. Now," she looked back at George at the plaintiff's table, nodded to him. "I'm going to ask that you answer questions from a friend of mine. His name is George. It's perfectly safe. Would that be all right?"

George rose, walked up to Isobel who handed him the list.

"No. I mean, I'm not sure, I …."

Isobel faced the gallery, called out, "Doctor Lee. Could you help me out here," asking help from a colleague with whom she had not spoken in years.

Phonyong Lee nodded, rose, walked through the gallery, back to the witness box.

"Your Honor," blurted Sidney Green, "I..."

Isobel pivoted, a scowl on her face, fingers to her lips, "Quiet!"

Fluidly, Doctor Lee placed two fingers on Carol's right temple for several seconds and tapped lightly. He then stepped back, nodded to Isobel and whispered into her ear, "It was time, my friend, just the right time," turning, walked back to his seat.

Suddenly, Carol's eyes blinked, opened wide. She looked around the room in confusion, turning to stare into Isobel's eyes, a look of bewilderment on her face.

"What's ..." her voice trailed off.

"It's alright, you're safe. Now, if you're ready, here's George," Isobel winced, stepped aside.

"Yes. I guess so," her voice a whisper, "hello, George?"

"Nice to see you, Iris. Do you know me?"

Carol shook her head, "No. Sorry, not that I remember."

Carleton interrupted, directing Carol, "The witness will..."

Isobel immediately raised her finger to her lips, "Shh!"

The Judge cringed, lip-synched the words, "I'm sorry. Go on."

"Go on," George thought to himself. "It's now or never."

CHAPTER EIGHTY

After your death you will be what you were before your birth.
-Arthur Schopenhauer

George hesitated, realizing that these next few minutes would make or break the case. He was in way too deep to consider the implications either way. No longer did it matter.

His heart bled as he looked up, smiled into the eyes of the woman he loved, but who now quite possibly was someone else, someone he didn't even know.

"Missus Paulson," voice croaking, "I'd like to ask you a few more questions about your life. May I?"

"Of course."

"Is your maiden name Iris Margaret Middelton?"

"Yes."

You say you were raised in the Chicago area and eventually moved to New York City."

"Yes."

"Can you give me the address of your last home there?"

"I remember it well. It was 257 Park Avenue, a beautiful Victorian apartment, on the fourth floor. It had such lovely big windows, overlooking the park, very stately. I resided there with my husband and two sons."

"Could you give me their names?"

"Certainly. My husband's Herbert Paulson. He was in the diplomatic corps. He traveled a lot, mostly overseas. My sons are

William Robert and Ethan James. Ethan, my oldest, he was the artist in the family and William, very athletic. I called him Will. Both were very good boys, but a bit too competitive with each other. You know, being so close in age and all? They tussled a lot, but boys will be boys."

A brief murmur rolled through the gallery. From the corner of his eye, George saw Sidney writing on a yellow pad, no doubt updating his counter attack.

"And their birth years?"

"Ethan, nineteen-nineteen. Will, the next, nineteen-twenty."

Ethan and Will stared intently at this woman, unable to reconcile the facts with the face.

"Do you remember if they had any nicknames?"

"Nicknames? It's been so long. But yes, Ethan, he's my Sunshine."

Ethan slumped in his chair, as if hit by a body blow. Green leaned, whispered into Ethan's ear, something that appeared to assuage his anguish. "You see," the witness added, "there was a solar eclipse the day he was born. So, he became my sunshine. His friends called him Tanny, short for Ethan. But to me, it meant my Sunshine. William? He's is my Billy boy, like in the song. But, he's always preferred Will."

Mouth agape, Ethan looked pleadingly at his brother; both now shaking their heads in unified disbelief.

"What more could you tell me about them?"

"Let's see. Like I said, Ethan was the artist. He took to drawing at an nearly age, drawing cartoons, like comic strip characters. He loved the Katzenjammer Kids in the paper. He became quite good at sketching, eventually getting into charcoal and oil painting. He had a great eye. That's why he became an architect."

"Your other son?"

"He was a bundle. Always getting into things. Like I said, athletic. He'd try anything. He broke his wrist skating when he was nine. Couldn't keep him off the ice in winter. Then, of course, A few ribs playing sports in high school; football you know. He had to try it. Eventually he turned to basketball, much safer, and did very well. Of course, a few sprained ankles. But he enjoyed it all. Finally he settled down, joined the army, then went into government service, like his father, only he choose engineering after college at Michigan State."

Will's mouth gaped, shaking his head.

"Any pets you remember?" asked George.

"Oh dear. Let me think. For awhile, we did have a cat. Shadow. Yes, Shadow. Herbert didn't like pets, he had so many allergies and could be most irritable. Shadow was the only pet he ever allowed us to have."

"Male cat or female cat?"

"A female, I had to even the odds in the house with so many men around," she giggled. "We had her spayed as a kitten. She only lived about seven years. The boys loved that cat and missed her terribly. It's good for the boys, having a pet. Don't you think?"

"Iris," George whispered, "do you know that Ethan and Will are both here, right now, in this room, with you?"

Her body jerked as she leaned forward to scan the gallery, eyes suddenly widening having come to rest on the defense table. She let out a squeal with delight, then caught her breath, "My boys!" She cried out and began to rise from her chair. George, placing a hand on her arm, holding her back.

"Not yet, please. They're here to see if you remember their birthdays."

Bending over the witness box rail, still looking at her two boys, "Of course, Ethan's is in May, on the twenty-ninth. Will's is in the summer, July eighth. Mothers don't forget."

Slumping in their chairs, Ethan and Will glanced at each other, incredulous; their eyes, minds and hearts, all at once, flooded with emotion.

George turned the page on his list, only three more areas from the past remained: each critical issues testing knowledge of memories only she could have known, thus cementing the validity of her claim as the embodied Iris Middelton Paulson.

"What first brought you to New York?"

"Oh my. I was in my early-twenties, a young girl, really. My father's friend, the novelist Sherwood Anderson, recommended me for a job as a copy editor and sometime writer for a progressive newspaper, The Masses. They teamed me with some of the most brilliant activists and writers in America, Jack London, the Eastman's, Jack Reed, Margaret Sanger and more."

"Do you remember where it was you first met these people?"

"Yes. In the home of Emma Goldman, just before she left the country."

"And how long did you work for The Masses?"

"Only about a year. We were charged with conspiracy for opposing the draft of young Americans into the first World War and shut down by the federal government. So that's when I started writing freelance for other progressives, like Mother Earth, The Nation, McCall's, Pageant, Colliers."

She paused momentarily, recounting, then continued, "Several newspapers too. Some syndicates. I composed music also. But that came later."

"Is that how you met your husband?"

"No. It's funny, actually. I was attending an anti-war rally in the Village that he was sent by his agency to check out us rebel rousers. He was supposed to be infiltrating, but I called him out right away. He looked ever so straight. But, we hit it off and within six months we were married. Less than a year later, Ethan was born."

"So, after you were married, you stayed in New York?"

"No. We moved back to Chicago for a few years. Herbert spent a lot of time overseas, so we had to hunker down in the Midwest for awhile which was really nice to be near my Dad and for the boys to have their grandfather. Then, after Herbert had a few promotions, we moved back to Manhattan."

"Is that when you continued writing?"

"For awhile. I became a voice for social justice and raising awareness about sensitive issues. Herbert feared my columns would hurt his career; 'way too progressive,' he said. He even called them socialist, which maybe they were, somewhat. But, if you knew the temper of the country at that time, we became a warlike nation, almost overnight."

"So, what then?"

"Then I began composing music, so I could continue my work more surreptitiously. I felt my compositions would live on as a lasting inspiration, long after I was gone."

"As to your music compositions, were any of them recorded?"

"Not many. Mostly, I wrote for myself. But there was one."

"And what was the title of that?"

"Prelude, it was by far, my favorite."

"Prelude? Any significance to that title?"

"Yes, it was my message, written in the language of music. You see, each melody communicates much more than words can express. Music talks to the heart, which unifies, bypassing the mind that often misunderstands and separates us from our true spirit."

"How so?"

"It's a work for piano and orchestra. It features a recurring refrain, starting with single notes, then building into a near crescendo, but ending in a somewhat discordant minor chord. Minor chords are powerful; they create a sense of anticipation; that something is somehow incomplete. Then, it returns to the single note beginning, and on again, to yet another minor chord ending, and again. It's a musical affirmation that Creation is a continuous process, one that begins again, with no final end; just the continuance of life beyond what is called death."

"So," George reaching for clarification, "you're saying ..."

"That our current life should be looked at as one step leading to the next, a prelude."

"You believe that?"

"Thoroughly, completely; from the depth of my soul to the marrow of my bones, because it's real. Regardless of other people's opinions, when you know something is true, it cannot be made untrue. And ever-lasting life, I know, is true."

George nodded, strolled back to his table, picked up a sheet of paper set it down, walked back to face the witness.

"Now two more questions, Iris, could you describe for the court your a favorite memento?"

Iris's fingers reached for the base of her neck, "Yes, my gold locket."

"What made this locket so special?"

Iris closed her eyes, tears trickling down her checks, "It was a gift from my father with my boy's birthday's inscribed inside. It was at

Herbert's Investiture Ball in the spring of 1929. I didn't know it then, but it was the last time we'd all be together."

"What happened then?"

Dad's life unraveled when the stock market crashed a few months later. He was indicted on fraud charges and went to prison, I believed he was covering up for others."

"And the locket?"

"It was his way of validating my life's calling. He understood me, my quest. It was his unwavering support that got me through all of Herbert's rejections and ridicule. Even when I gave up all hope, there was always the locket."

"Please, one last question." Drawing in his deepest breath, "Missus Paulson, do you recall the bedtime song you sang to your children?"

"Oh, yes, I wrote it just for them," a smile shining from her eyes.

"Could you sing it for us now?" An audible quiver in his voice, "or at least, try?"

Pursing her lips, "Like I said, my own words. Like this." she turned, faced Ethan and William in their seats at the table and in the softest melodic a'cappella voice, she sang the words from long ago;

"Twinkle, twinkle, both my boys,
How I wonder who you are.
Up above the world so high,
like two diamonds in the sky."

Singing a lullaby to her boys, smiling with tender memories, she hummed to herself for a few private moments, eyes closed, savoring the sweetness of a mother's love. Then with a long sigh, cherishing this personal reminiscence, opened her eyes, continued singing,

"When the daytime sun is gone,
When she nothing shines upon.
Then you show your face bright lights.
Twinkle, twinkle all the night,

Billy Boy and Sunshine bright,
Now it's time to say goodnight."

Putting fingers to her lips, she threw a kiss to the two men, as if once again kissing them goodnight.

Ethan leapt up, "How can this be? How can she do this?" William grabbed his brother's arm, pulled him back to his seat, holding him tight for both their sakes.

Carleton had raised his gavel, stopped mid-air, raised his other hand placing his fingers to his lips directed an inaudibe"hush" at the defense table.

An eerie silence pervaded throughout the gallery.

"Missus Paulson, thank you for your testimony, no more questions."

George walked back to his table, notes in hand. The pang in his heart was the awareness of the empty chair next to his. He awaited the return of his Carol, missing her now more than ever.

Looking up, he caught the courtroom artist's pencil sketch—two elderly men gawking at Carol; her smiling back at them: a single snapshot that described more than words could ever explain.

Judge Carleton motioned silently to Sidney Green, "Proceed."

Adrenaline pumping, Sidney rose, planning to cut this witness to shreds.

CHAPTER EIGHTY ONE

Death is, to us here, the most terrible word we know. But when we have tasted its reality, it will mean to us birth, deliverance, a new creation of ourselves.
– George Merriman

Sidney Green had been waiting for this moment; savoring his chance to pull the mask right off Carol Klein's face; revealing to the court and the world the depth of the fraud she's attempting to perpetrate. He saw himself in the role of a hero, saving civilization from this seedy deception.

He approached the witness chair as Isobel Freeman rose, faced the witness. "Now, I'd like you to answer a few questions from another gentleman. His name is Sidney, Sidney Green."

She smiled at him, "Hello, Sidney," her tone milky warm.

Isobel sat back down as Green took center stage, turned to the witness, "Ma'am," hesitating, not sure how else to address her, "did you not intend to leave your estate to your children, William and Ethan Paulson?"

"Not intend?"

"I mean, did you decide to not grant your estate to your sons?"

"Of course not."

"And would that not include the monies left you from your father?"

"Yes. With some of it used for me to continue my work."

"And what work," he scoffed, "might that be?"

"My writings. To challenge the ignorance; to speak out for what's

374

right."

"And your idea of, what's right?"

"To help people realize that we're all connected; that our fear of death is pointless; that our anxiety is no more than a reflection of being held accountable for our actions."

"You say, you're not afraid of death?"

"Sidney, look at death as receiving a final report card on the way we've lived our lives. It gives us an opportunity to review our past choices and make better ones next time."

"Uh, okay. The money. What about your father's money?"

"Oh dear, I don't remember, I believe, it got left behind."

"Do you object to your sons having it now?"

"Oh Sidney, the money is of so little importance. Don't you understand?"

"Understand what?"

"That there are far greater treasures that supersede this money you are so concerned about. It's so trivial in comparison."

"Comparison to what?"

"Compassion, understanding, love, forgiveness. We must learn to end our negativity and to seek more balance. To open our hearts and live in harmony together. What's it worth to you to live in a peaceful heart, a quiet mind, Sidney? What would you pay for that?"

"Okay. So, you say you don't mind the funds being granted to your sons, is that right?"

"Yes, but just one last consideration, Sidney, about the intention of this money. It was to continue my work."

Green nodded, already tasting the sweet victory ahead. "What is that?"

"To write about the purpose of life—which is to learn the lessons of love; it's the only source of true happiness and dissolves all our barriers. Its power awakens us to our true selves and restores our wholeness. Love nurtures, forgives, and uplifts, expanding the positive and dissolves the negative. Few have learned to love unconditionally without needing something back in return. No one can master love in only one lifetime, that's why we reincarnate: to develop a deeper embodiment of being love without limits."

Sidney ignoring her explanation, pressed on, "Again. You have no objections to your sons receiving the inheritance left you by your father?"

Tears welled up in Iris's eyes casting a forlorn far-away look at the elderly men intently staring back at her. "No. Not now. Now that my work is complete."

"Complete?" Green's face gnarled in a question mark, "uh, then, you say, it's theirs to keep?"

Iris tilted her head up and stared at the ceiling as if remembering something long forgotten.

"Ah, Sidney, I, I meant to change my will. I ran out of time. I wanted to leave some monies to the causes I'd spent my life supporting. They were important to me."

Green grimaced at the mention of this curveball, "Causes, what causes?"

"That's what the money was for; to expand the understanding of our inter-connectedness to the universe, and of course, to continue research on the nature of the soul's journey after death. There were three worthy groups I hoped that my endowment would help."

Green quickly calculated the odds of her causes still being viable after all these years; slim to none.

"The first was introduced to me at The Masses when I met Upton Sinclair. He was a member of The American Society for Psychical Research at Cambridge University, researching the nature of human consciousness and exploring unexplained phenomena."

Never having heard of this group, Sidney dismissed it. "And the others?"

"It was also at The Masses that I met, Margaret Sanger. Her efforts to legalize woman's reproduction rights were heroic. She fought for woman's equal status.....and well you see why it's so important to support her organization; the American Birth Control League."

Smirking, Green asked, "And the last one?"

"The Hospital of Enlightenment, founded by Edgar Cayce. He was called the sleeping prophet for giving readings that healed thousands of hopelessly ill people while in a hypnotic trance. His work included research into reincarnation. I met Mister Cayce through my father's business client who was his benefactor. He had many famous followers."

"And they would be?"

"Woodrow Wilson, Thomas Edison, Irving Berlin, George Gershwin, to name a few."

Green cut her off, "You say you meant to? There's scant legal chance that your will can be amended now."

"Objection, Your Honor. Counsel does not determine that." George mouthed, respecting the court order for silence.

"Sustained." Carlton said in hushed tones.

Green huffed, "Thank you, Ma'am. That will be all."

"Thank you, Sidney. Without you, I couldn't have finished my work, I can't thank you enough."

Green stood stiffly, unable to speak. Carleton whispered, "Counselor?"

Sidney stumbled out of his daze, "No. No more questions, Your Honor. Nothing."

Iris continued smiling in the witness chair as Sidney turned his back to her and stumbled back to his defense table, mumbling something only he heard inside his head.

"Goodbye Sidney," she chirped, "nice meeting you."

"If there are no more questions or this witness," Carleton said softly, "I ask that she be, uh, revived out of her trance. Doctor Freeman, will you please, whatever it is you do?"

Isobel rose, walked to Carol, a glimmer of nostalgia in her eye, began in a soft modulated voice, "Iris, Please close your eyes. Good, now. I'm going to count up from one to five. When we reach five, you will be awake, refreshed and fully conscious. Are you ready?"

Iris nodded as she folded her hands on her lap and drew in a sigh of relief, preparing herself for the transition.

"One, a deep inhale, good; two, an even bigger breath in— hold for a moment, release. Good, now you are becoming more awake; three, you are more aware, even more than before; four, more refreshed. Feel it, five, you are completely awake, aware, alert, re-energized."

Carol's eyes flashed opened. She looked around the room, a puzzled look on her face.

"Isobel, I mean, Doctor?"

CHAPTER EIGHT TWO

We don't receive wisdom; we must discover it for ourselves after a journey
that no one can take for us or spare us.
– Marcel Proust

"Kinda' like the start of the marathon," Alicia Rhodes thought, watching the crowd running down the courtroom steps, "except looks like they're running away from something rather than towards it."

She glanced at her watch, noting that she had a good eight minutes before her report on the events from today's proceedings. She sauntered over to her crew's van in search of a hot cup of coffee. Just one of the occupational hazards of being a recognizable news star: spending so much time out in the cold, freezing fingers and toes, yet appearing unfazed in spite of the elements. "The fine line between reporter and actress," she mused.

"Alicia," shouted Tom Richardson, a camera slung over his shoulder, "gonna' set up over here," pointing to the southwest corner of the courthouse.

"Whatever you say Tommy," taking a sip of rancid coffee as she reviewed her notes.

Tom secured the lighting tripod as Alicia approached, "Tell me girl, what do you think of all this hoopla?"

"It plays well, you know, good drama."

"You don't think there's anything to it, this whole past life thing?"

"Don't know, seems to me they're trying to spin straw into gold. It's just not going to happen."

"Okay," Tom looked at his wrist, "get ready we're going live in one minute twenty-three."

Instinctively, she walked to a point centered by the light. She'd worked with Tom many years, their syncopation was nearly flawless. She shifted gears, found her professional persona. They locked eyes, he began his familiar cue; "Three, two, one..."

"Testimony in the Tale of Two Lives trial came to an end today," she delivered it with intensity, "with the appearance on the stand of Doctor Carol Klein, a Tufts University psychologist who claims to possess the identity of Iris Middelton Paulson, a Chicago born activist who died in nineteen-fifty-six. In a most unusual move, Judge Charles Carleton allowed Klein to be hypnotized, then questioned while under hypnosis. Doctor Klein answered a number of identity-specific questions that, it appears, only Iris Paulson could have known." Alicia momentarily paused, "Judge Charles Carleton will render his verdict tomorrow afternoon. Scott?"

"You say the witness was questioned while under hypnosis?" ABC News anchor Scott Valentine stated in his patented flat delivery, "That is highly unusual."

"Unheard of, really, Scott. But for this case, the bench felt testimony under hypnosis was the best, maybe the only way to determine the facts."

"And how'd that go?" Valentine asked. "Can you summarize some of the highlights?"

"The highlight came when she sang a bedtime lullaby, that she claimed she'd composed and sung to her children as their mother. The Paulson brothers, Ethan and Will, both in their eighties, appeared visibly shaken when she sang it aloud in open court. Apparently, from the Paulson's reaction, it was precisely what she said it was."

"That's pretty amazing. What's your take on it all?"

She hesitated, not expecting to be called upon for her own editorial opinion, "It seems to me that either she was well-rehearsed, or her claim to be Missus Paulson just might have merit. Judge Charles Carleton is expected to announce his verdict tomorrow."

"So, we'll find out tomorrow. Nice work Alicia."

Microphone held low, "From Boston, Alicia Rhodes. ABC news."

CHAPTER EIGHTY THREE

Success is not measured by what you accomplish, but by the opposition you have encountered, and the courage with which you have maintained the struggle against overwhelming odds.
—Orison Swett Marden

Heaving a sigh, Judge Carleton turned off the television.

"Thanks a lot, ABC," he said aloud, "sheesh!"

Turning back to his laptop, head swaying side to side, a flood of images filled his mind: eminent experts offering scientific support for the plaintiff's position, the doctor raving over Klein's successes with his patients, Doctor Lee, with his blockbuster research results, the stately blonde mesmerizing the gallery, the sorrowful expressions on the faces of the two defendants, then, that absolutely surreal sight of Klein somehow slipping into the identity of, "Dare he say it, the deceased Iris?"

His weary fingers pressed the laptop keys for the last shreds of confirming evidence he wished were not there. But there it was: the woman's three charities still exist, all providing legitimate services in their respective fields, including Sanger's group, now known as Planned Parenthood.

His eyes traveled to the stacks of submitted evidence before him, the roar in his head rivaled Niagara. Eyes shut, he saw himself stuffed in a barrel, plunging over the falls, thinking, "And now I'm to rule on a case that could crucify me as the Judge who blew up the entire American legal system!"

Restless, he rose, walked to a cabinet, opened a door and grasped a vintage bottle of Cyrus Noble bourbon, already opened. He poured the coppery liquid over three ice cubes in a tumbler while pondering his dilemma. "On one hand, a simple case of property rights replete with a last will, a death certificate—bingo, that's it! On the other, a letter showing clear intent that restricts the inheritance specifically for the Iris woman. Except she's dead, or not? Am I to rule on an entirely new definition of death, with all the snarled implications that'll entail. But what if …?"

He stopped, now treading on very dangerous thin ice, but couldn't stop the cascade of free-falling thoughts, "What if reincarnation hadn't been edited from the bible, as Maxwell stated? Would it meet the test of a priori? Would our view of life and death be redefined? And the evidence of life carry-overs shown by Doctor Lee, with medical results from deep regressions? Then again, all that testimony of experts supporting Mansbridge's client; it's all in the record! And, most of all …!"

He couldn't conclude the linchpin thought. Not now.

"Damn, what am I going to do with this?" he moaned. "Why did I have to be the one to draw the short straw of this blasted case?" Yet, there was no stopping this headlong crash, one that could smash his career into smithereens on the rocks awaiting him in court tomorrow picturing the brass ring of honorable retirement so close, reeling now out of reach.

Lifting the glass, he suckled the manna of the burning liquid from his cherished tumbler, clinking the ice as he sipped.

"Damn, double damn," he muttered under his breath, thinking, "shoot. Am I limited to adjudicate this one only on the laws of man? Wouldn't that ignore much of the evidence presented from the greater laws of this universe?"

He'd always believed his role was to see that justice prevailed above all else. "How else," he thought, "do we preserve the sanctity of our system? This case re-shuffles the deck. How do I adjudge the validity of these testimonies?"

He was running out of time and saw no viable alternatives. He would have to be the one to make the decision; one indelible ruling, his verdict would stand for all to critique. A bust of Socrates on his desk caught his eye. Swallowing he asked aloud, "Well, my sage friend, what say you?" The words hung in the air, like heavy drapery.

Thinking back to the testimony of physicist Maxwell, he asked aloud, "With all the unknowns, shouldn't our ever-evolving legal system be willing to accept at least some of the intangibles?"

He slumped deep into the leathery cushions of his chair. Reached for the bourbon, poured a double, not bothering with ice this round, "Why dilute the effect," watching the amber bourbon cascade down the sides of his glass. The clock was running.

"Hours from now," he muttered, "come hell or high water and in this case, quite apropos," letting the liquid melt the barriers of conflict.

Above all else, he'd admired the immaculate purity, the intellectual propriety that once defined the long-standing legal system. What this case offered was just the opposite: muddled issues, unclear boundaries and worst of all—no legal precedent to guide his verdict, absolutely none. If only he could have recused himself from the case at the start. "Too late," he mouthed, "that ship sailed, long ago."

Eyes shutting, he once again scanned the memory of the trial in his mind's eye, re-visiting in utter disbelief the sight of Iris Middelton emerging through the Klein woman on the witness stand. "What was I thinking? Allowing her on the stand like that, testimony from a dead person? If anything, I should have ordered her demonstration in chambers, behind closed doors. Was I hypnotized, along with Klein?"

He knew, down deep, that one fact no longer could be ignored. Along with the maybes, the what-ifs, there was one concrete piece of knowledge that could not to be overlooked: that without Klein's discovery of the missing inheritance, there would be no case. Yet, no one but Iris, long deceased, knew of its existence. "How did she do it?" he muttered, "that's the single piece of prima facie evidence that led to there even being a trial."

He took one long sip from the tumbler, looked at the ceiling, blurted in a loud voice, "For God's sake, unless Klein accessed Iris's memory, there's no case at all! None!" This piece of evidence rocked his foundation to the core.

He shuddered, downed the burning alcohol in a series of gulps hoping to shut out the building avalanche of dread. Despite the ethical tempest in his overflowing teapot, the alcohol elapsed his mental exhaustion as he fell briefly into the temporary relief of sleep, suspending the agony of his decision-making process.

Drifting off into a short fitful sleep, hoping subconsciously to glimpse something, anything that might help him connect the elusive dots, "Connect," he mouthed, "yes, connect, dots…"

He saw himself rising, orbiting above the Earth, much like an astronaut.

The sense of gravitational freedom was exhilarating, beyond description. Awestruck by the breath-taking Technicolor beauty of mother earth below, hanging without a thread, suspended in the vastness of endless black velvet space.

Suddenly, without rhyme or reason, his awareness shifted. He stood at a door, slightly ajar. He hesitated, pushed it open, walked through it. At once, the door slammed shut, locked behind him. There would be no going back. He stared into the darkness, an unfamiliar terrain with a faint pinprick of light, off in a far distance; the darkness clinging to his skin like damp, oversized hands. He pushed on, farther into the alien darkness, toward the distant light.

The farther into the dank darkness he went, the more foreboding he felt. There was no noise, no sounds, no references points, no help. He was frightened, more than he could ever remember. His voice had no power to shout out. His heart was racing, pounding out through his chest. Sweat poured down into his eyes, blurring his vision. Disoriented, he began running, running. Now panting, panicked.

Then, there it was, the source of light coming from behind a door. He pushed with all his might, it opened. All at once, the crack of light became a torrent of blazing radiance. He'd arrived on the other side.

Catching his breath, he relished the relief of his escape from the darkness. His dreaming eyes having adjusted, he saw a table, on which two objects were placed. One, a Caduceus, the staff of Hermes with two serpents entwined around a rod topped by a pair of wings, the symbol of modern medicine and the icon of eternal life, the reconciliation of man's spiritual life and physical life united. Alongside the Caduceus, a statue of Justicia, Lady Justice, her left hand holding scales that weigh the human heart, as she measures the strength of each case before the law. Clutched in her right hand was a double edged sword, welding the power of reason to execute justice. Her eyes are blindfolded against all prejudice, embodying wisdom and foresight before both divine and natural law.

Tentatively, he reached out with his right hand to grasp the Caduceus. His instinct burned with desire to weigh the evidence of eternal life as a legal doctrine. Much heavier than it looked, the sheer weight of the staff made his arm tremble. "How can this be?" his dream mind asked. With all his might he lifted it as high as he could and began to place it upon the scales of Lady Justice. He had to know, would they, could the scales balance? So, so heavy, so …

Abruptly, he was jarred awake, ripped away from his dream. Blinking, he scanned his surroundings, the stack of evidence, the judicial trappings, familiarity with these, his chambers.

He felt a calm wave of resolve. He now knew the solution, the one and only one with which he could live. He reached for his laptop and began to write the words that would seal his fate and the destiny of this case.

CHAPTER EIGHTY FOUR

Nature gave us one tongue and two ears so we could hear twice as much as we speak.
– Epictetus

The sense of anticipation was electric, a low buzzing sound filling the packed courtroom as the key players took their respective seats, eyes fixed on the empty judge's bench rising before them as if a monolith.

The bailiff stood, faced the gallery as the buzz slowly subsided, announcing in a loud voice, "All rise! The Honorable Charles Carleton, presiding."

Looking slightly bedraggled, the Judge entered from behind his chamber's door, robes flowing as he walked, unsteadily, reading glasses in his right hand, wrinkled papers in his left, to take the controls of this, his courtroom.

A study in tension, he stopped, awkwardly slid into his chair. Once seated, he leaned back, looked wistfully over the entire room, taking in the walls, the faces of his now-packed gallery and, at last, the expectant faces of those seated at the tables just before him. Slowly, he lifted his gavel, let it hang in the air a moment, banged it down with authority.

"Order!" he bellowed. "This court is now in session."

Before long, you could have heard a pin drop, no sound could be heard, not even the stirring of the air. Judge Charles Carleton raised his eyes, scanned the entire courtroom deliberately, as if he were taking a headcount of his courthouse. Pausing several seconds, he leaned forward, adjusted his glasses back atop his nose, grimaced at the wrinkled notes before him. At last, he looked up, removed his glasses, clearing his throat he took one long breath, exhaled.

"Throughout the ages," he stated, "artists of all stripes have argued whether art is created by bringing light into darkness, or created by bringing darkness into light."

He paused again, allowing his message to be absorbed.

"Today, we are faced with no less of a conundrum; and one every bit as imperative. For today, this court has the burden of balancing a weight, one for which it was never designed, nor intended, to measure."

Letting that preamble settle, he lifted the papers in his clenched hand, "Today, we are being asked whether or not property, in this case, property valued as much as seventeen million dollars and various personal effects, specified for ownership in one lifetime, shall be carried over to one in a following lifetime. And whether, as a legal precedent, reincarnation shall be recognized as a legitimate phase of the human life cycle."

Like a mirage appearing on the horizon of a scorched desert, the courtroom became alive, buzzing like a hive of bees, the gallery reacting to his words. Carleton lowered the papers in exchange for his gavel, took a long, leering look at the gallery, no further action required. Like a wave crashing onto the shore, conversation ceased in the courtroom. Setting down his gavel, he resumed staring at the cloaked decree to which only he had privileged access.

"This court has heard extraordinary evidence, both complex and compelling, some of which blurs the boundaries between what we know of science, religion, medicine and the law. Having heard evidence from qualified experts in these fields, and having received supportive materials and case studies, this Court accepts and fully admits all testimony, valid as presented."

The weight of the air became palpable.

Showing the strain of the last several days, he replaced his glasses back on to the security of his nose, began reading directly from his paper, "As to the question of whether testimony, from Doctor Carol Klein a.k.a. Iris Middelton Paulson, is to be an acceptable consideration in a court of law, this Court finds such testimony both acceptable and admissible."

Carlton raised his voice. "What this court had to balance, what was disclosed was neither usual or ordinary: the one unmistakable fact that—without the explicit testimony provided by the specific self-knowledge of the memories of the witness, Iris Middelton Paulson, the prima facie evidence, the very existence of the properties in dispute, would not, and could not, have been brought before this, or any other bench."

Pausing a moment, "I repeat, without the knowledge presented by this witness there would be no case."

Like a rogue wave, the buzz arose to a towering height, then ebbed just as rapidly in anticipation of the Judge's next declaration.

George grabbed Carol's hand, squeezed hard. If the case ended right here, right now, it would be a triumph, a victory beyond measure. She lifted the pen lying atop the yellow pad, scribbled, "Is it possible?" He jotted back a heart-shaped scribble with a smiling happy face.

An elongated pause allowed the observation to fully sink in.

"Where, and when, Iris Middelton Paulson leaves off, and Doctor Carol Klein begins, is at the root of this proceeding. The matters of what, how, or why, while presented in this courtroom, are deemed to be of little to no merit on this case at this time."

Sidney Green, confident in the legal process, touched the hands of both Ethan and William, assuring them he felt they were very close to scoring their goal.

Carleton knew this was about to become a turning point in history. The significance of the next several moments would be the banner, or the cross, he would have to bear the rest of this natural life. Yet, at this juncture there was no fork in the road, there was no alternative path. It was either going to be forwards or backwards. There was no other choice, but to continue.

"That being said," turning his papers face down, "this court is not here to place a verdict on the validity of reincarnation, or on any other commitments from previous lives. Rather, it is to uphold the laws of the Commonwealth of Massachusetts and the Constitution of the United States. Of course, there is a gold standard in case law regarding distribution of assets from one person to another. And that standard requires that we, within the law, observe the wishes of the donor, particularly when such wishes are codified in writing."

He slowly turned his head upward, looking high into the upper reaches of the courtroom, "In this case, the wishes of the donor is evident. Thus, I am required, by God, by the law, to grant the contested assets under dispute," pausing for an excruciating several seconds, "to Iris Middelton Paulson, as directed, without doubt, by her father."

A cacophony of sound, from gasps to shouts, erupted.

Looking down, sternly facing the gallery, Carlton pounded his gavel repeatedly, shouting, "Order. Order in the Court."

Raising his voice, "That being said, order! The court also recognizes that opposing counsel has submitted and attested to documents certifying the death of Iris Middelton Paulson, and the deceased's notarized Last Will and Testament, assigning all her properties designated for the named heirs, William Paulson, and Ethan Paulson."

Sidney, William, and Ethan clasped hands in anticipation, "Therefore," the Judge looked over the gallery, removing his reading glasses, "I rule that, as a valid inheritance, following the tenants of the Last Will and Testament of Iris Middelton Paulson, all found property, herein disputed, be awarded to the legitimate heirs, Ethan and William Paulson."

For several seconds, a frostlike silence coated the courtroom, now filled with facial expressions of confusion and disbelief. Then, as if choreographed, a flurry of sound and activity ensued; reporters flew from their seats and made their way to the aisles, raced to the courtroom doors, anxious to be the first to file.

Sidney Green leapt up, pumping his fist in the air as the two brothers embraced tearfully.

Carleton forcefully banged his gavel, "Order! Order, I am not yet finished!"

The buzz began to subside, only a few close enough hearing Carleton's final lament, "I shudder at the Pandora's box that has been opened here today. Someday, somewhere, a greater court than this will determine the full landscape of this, an entirely new legal frontier."

Setting down his glasses and leaning his upper torso over towards the front of his elevated bench, he raised his gavel to the height of his shoulder and as it came down on the block, his last words of the day where, "And with that, this court is adjourned."

CHAPTER EIGHTY FIVE

There is no path to truth. Truth must be discovered, but there is no formula for its discovery...You must set out on the uncharted sea, and the uncharted sea is yourself.
– Krishnamurti

Charles Carleton lowered his gaze to his trial notes, shaking his head side to side. "It is done," he muttered, fondling the papers before him.

Slowly rising from his chair, he paused before making his final descent down the three stairs from his bench to the courthouse floor. Turning, he looked out over the emptying courtroom one last time, fearing his decree would echo through the judicial community for decades to come. "Maybe this should be the last time I ascend these steps," he pondered, "from here on, perhaps there'll be a higher law in play."

He walked to his chambers, questioning the entire experience, very much alone. Entering the safe harbor of his private sanctuary, eyes moistening, he closed the door, silently.

George sat still, as if frozen, muttered, "What just happened?"

As a small crowd gathered behind the plaintiff's table, George turned to Carol, pulled her into his arms, hugging her tightly, "Guess we lost," he smiled into her ear, "or not."

He marveled at the thought: "A double ruling: one in our favor, the next against."

His mind flashed; just the few scant months ago, none of these events and most of these players were nowhere to be found on his game board. Yet, now he couldn't imagine going back to his previous set of beliefs and goals.

A milestone had been crossed, the existence of past lives validated; a new map of the future now charted. He didn't know where the endpoint would be, he just knew he had to keep going, hoping the signposts would reveal themselves at the right time.

Carol kissed his cheek, "Congratulations on losing our case, Counselor," she laughed out loud. "Bravo!"

"Thanks to Carleton," he whispered into her hair, "the man went to bat for us, above and beyond the call of duty. He must have believed in you and our case."

"That's all that counts," she squealed. Doctor Lee joined them, wrapping his arms around the shoulders of the couple, sporting a grin from ear to ear.

"A victory in a loss," he said, "it is music to my soul."

George released Carol from his embrace, turning to shake Lee's hand; hugged him instead, his voice cracking, "Thank you for, everything, Doctor. We've done it, haven't we?"

"Yes, I believe we have taken the first step. There will be many more. But the first, always the most difficult."

Lee clasped George's two hands in his, pressing them all into the center of his chest, to his heart. It seemed impossible to tell where the defining lines of one set of fingers began and the other ones ended. Lee then pushed the intertwined hands to the center-point of George's chest, nodding in respectful acknowledgement, "You made the invisible visible and impossible possible." Smiling, George nodded back, his eyes suddenly damp.

Stepping back a pace, Lee bowed from his waist. George reciprocated, bowed, somehow acknowledging a new understanding—a synergy of sorts, that 'the sum of the parts was greater than the whole' and that more was to be done.

Carol wiped her eyes, glancing over to the table where Ethan and William sat alone, talking quietly to each other, Will wiping his eyes.

Noting that Sidney Green had stepped away to organize the paper work with the court clerk, she walked, ever so slowly, directly to their table. They looked up, their faces depicting surprise, confusion and a look of near-total disorientation.

She smiled warmly, "Congratulations, I'm so glad you won."

They stared at her, eyes red and still moist. Rising from their seats, speechless, they stared at her as if she were a museum piece. Ethan teetered back a bit, stabilizing his emotional as well as physical stance.

Carol extended her hand, repeated, "I'm happy for you both."

William hesitated, then reached out and grasped Carol's hand, stifling a knot in his throat, held back a sob, his face expressing ten thousand questions. He blurted, "Her song, the lullaby? How? It's been seventy years. No one ... I mean, no one but us ever heard it."

"No one," Will added, "but you...?" The question hung in the air like a heavy cloud.

Carol reached out and with arms wide open like butterfly wings, embraced both men and drew them close. "I know," she whispered, "I know."

Ethan pulled back abruptly, "But, how did you know, I mean, all the words? All of it?"

"I told you. It's all true, that's how I knew," she paused, "I was there."

"I hope you can see how this is for us," Will said. "True, then ...?"

She nodded reassuringly, "Yes. It is. I know it's hard for you to see, but please, try to believe me. Our souls carry our experiences, our memories, from one life to the next. I was just able to improve my remembering. I was there, with you both."

Will stepped back, his hand reaching into an inside breast pocket of his sport jacket. He withdrew an envelope, held it out to Carol.

"If it's true, then," he stuttered, "there's, this letter," he said, "it's not meant for us. Then, well, perhaps then, you should have it."

He handed the envelope to Carol.

Her eyes locked with Will's. Suddenly, both sensed it, a bond, reflecting emotions of deep familiarity. Deeply moved, she stood, frozen, unable to receive the offering.

Reaching out his hand, eyes darting to his brother, Will urged her on, "Please, it's alright. We've talked it over, this is ... it's for you. With all we've seen," his voice crackled, "it was meant only for our mother."

Tears welled up in her eyes. She took possession of the envelope, stared at the addressee: "Iris Middelton," written in cursive. For a moment, she could not breathe. Both men smiled at each other, then at her, their message, a gift of reassurance.

"Please, read it when you choose. Really it's just for you," Ethan said as Will chimed in, "Then, there's so much to talk about. Would you? Do you think, … maybe, could we get together, again? You owe us at least that much, don't you think?"

"Oh, yes, of course. I'd like that, very much!"

A tear began rolling down Will's lined face, "Good. We'll be in touch. And, thank you."

She hugged the letter to her bosom, "Yes, please know that I …" Stuttering, she blurted it out, "I love you! I love you both, very much!"

Nodding, if as on cue, both men sat back down.

Turning, she walked away, eyes blurring with tears. She wandered back to her chair, the envelope clutched in her hand. She sat down, wiped her eyes with a handkerchief, held the envelope before her for several seconds, unmoving.

She glanced back at the two brothers, now in deep conversation, Will's arm wrapped around Ethan's shoulders. As if sensing her plight, Will smiled at her, nodded his head, "Go ahead, it's alright."

Fingers quivering, she carefully separated the envelope's flap, whose glue had long since dried and cracked after it's long slumber in the Montréal bank vault. The crease on the opening flap crackled as it was raised.

Inside, a neatly folded onionskin notepaper, cradled. She ever-so-slowly pulled the fragile, dated paper from its shell, unfolded it with loving care.

Hands shaking and holding back tears, Carol blinked, then read:

To my dearest daughter Iris,
This gift, I leave to you. I know you will use it well.
It is your destiny, my dearest daughter, to fulfill your dream.
No matter how long it may take. For time, I have learned, is a charade, one from which we escaped, now and then. On the day you receive this note, let it be, for you, and the world around you, a new beginning.
Let the past be what it has always been. A mere prelude—to the

symphony ahead.
With unending love, for all time,
Your Dad

She caught her breath, looked up as George and his uncle Nicholas approached. She folded the note, placed it back in the envelope, feeling protective of its contents.

"I'll admit it Georgie," Nicholas was saying, a bit too loudly, pretty damn impressive. Gettin' old Carleton to do your heavy lifting. But now, you know that you can just kiss your campaign goodbye."

George shrugged his shoulders, beaming a smile, "Sorry Nick. Guess I'll have to make a different kind of difference."

"Smart guy, huh," Nicholas jeered, "if I was your old man, you'd be out of the firm right now, partner or no partner. You've just blown it, kid." He turned on his heel, and before stomping away toward the courtroom exit handed George a folded note, "Here! Your dad wasn't able to stay. He had a meeting that couldn't be missed."

George tore open the note; "Well done, son, I'm proud of you. Dad."

George bit his lower lip. He had arrived, "Finally, enough," he exhaled.

"What was that?" Carol asked, still clutching the envelope.

"Just Nick spouting off. No worries. Right now, we've some celebrating to do."

Carol, George and Phonyong Lee lingered together in the courtroom for several more minutes, capturing the moment, until they were among the last people to leave the courthouse.

They stopped under the portico between the stone pillars to take in the new felt freshness in the air, reporters huddling in clusters conducting interviews with Sidney Green, Theodore Hunt, and Dean Maxwell, all getting their last licks in for the evening news.

Carol could only imagine tomorrow morning's news show lineup. These new 'science celebrities' would be the hot ticket for the week, until the next news cycle sensation would usurp their position for the insatiable appetite of a hungry audience.

Lee turned to both Carol and George stating, "Congratulations, we have taken a great step forward. As I told you, George, that night in the snow, you, we all have come to made a difference."

George replied, "Have we?"

"Soon enough," Lee said, "we shall see. Soon enough."

Then he turned, quickly vanishing into the crowd.

CHAPTER EIGHTY SIX

Souls never die, but always on quitting one abode pass to another. All things change, nothing perishes. The soul passes hither and thither, occupying now this body, now that... As a wax is stamped with certain figures, then melted, then stamped anew with others, yet it is always the same wax. So, the Soul being always the same, yet wears at different times different forms.
– Pythagoras

Spring, 2002. Once again, autumn had turned into winter; winter into spring; the promise of yet another beginning; a reminder that the present lasts but a fleeting millisecond between what is past and what will be the future.

All that had been dormant in winter now emerged with a voracious energy, obeying the warming sun. The smell of fresh green grass, the exploding colors of spring flowers mirrored the sounds and sights of birds, bees and butterflies; new life bursting forward.

So much had happened in the year gone by since the trial had ended.

Commentators of all stripes debated the now infamous Judge Carleton's decision, the man retiring from the bench under pressure. Doctor Lee's research had expanded, now underwritten by a generous grant from the Paulson brothers, whose newly formed Iris Middelton Paulson Foundation also funded other organizations favored by their mother.

Carol and George had become instant, if briefly noted, celebrities, with a book of their journey underway. Carol had left her university position and George had resigned his partnership with the firm, both now dedicated to pursuing new frontiers.

The bright lights of media intrusion into their lives had dimmed, ever since the tragic September 11 attack on the Twin Towers and elsewhere last year, altering the nation's consciousness and moving the trial away from the glare of the media news cycle.

And William Paulson, age 81, had only recently, passed on.

Speckles of quartz embedded in the granite headstone sparkled like diamonds, reflecting the light of the high noon sun. The headstone read:

William Robert Paulson
Born July 8, 1920
Died April 4, 2002
On His Continuing Journey

Holding a bouquet of purple irises and white roses, Ethan, flanked by George and Carol, stood graveside with a handful of people, heads bowed, as Phonyong Lee officiated William's memorial service.

"Great mystery of eternal life," Lee began, "here and beyond, we acknowledge the sweet synergy of energy and motion within which we are adrift."

Lifted his head, he looked up at freshly leafed tree branches, rustling in the wind, "We come here today, to celebrate the life and times of William Paulson, during this, his latest stay, a prelude for the next, as he now enters into a fresh form of a new beginning."

Ethan exhaled loudly, nodding his agreement.

"Spirit to spirit, it ever goes. Life to life; ever to begin anew as the glory of the never ending Source Itself. Life, too sacred to ever end. Thus, the secret; the secret of which few speak. We feel the presence, vaster than vast, subtler than subtle, nearer than breath, closer than a heartbeat."

Pausing, his eyes surveyed the setting, "As we know, everything on this physical level of existence is temporary. In death, we lose only that which is material. What we keep from our worldly experience is the love we've cultivated. Death cannot end loving relationships. Invariably, we shall meet again."

He smiled at the headstone, "Today, we glory in the long journey that William has enjoyed and fully expressed. We gaze into the future, wishing him well for this, his coming voyage into the ever flowing tide of earthly energy and eternal majesty."

He bowed deeply from his waist, hands together as in prayer, concluded with an ancient request; "From the unreal, guide us to the real, from untruth, lead us to truth, from darkness, lead us to the light and from the illusion of death, lead us to the Oneness of immortality. Bon voyage, William, mon ami. With gratitude and appreciation for your love and light."

Ethan placed the bouquet of white roses in front of the headstone, mourning the loss of the beloved brother he'd traveled with on his own journey. He bent down, said more to himself than the gathering, "Amen, my brother, dear, little, brother." Sobbing freely, he ended, "A-a-men."

He straightened, took several steps to the right and placed the deep purple irises on the headstone adjacent to William's that read:

Iris Middelton Paulson

"He's yours now, Mom," he whispered, "yours, I ..." his voice trailing, belying the internal schism within, catching himself mid-sentence.

Still staring at the marble headstone marking his mother's grave, he reached over, grabbing Carol's hand squeezed it tightly. Shaking his head, silently questioning, "Which reality was truth: the grave, or Carol's hand— Mom?" The starburst echoed through his fractured heart. The bedrock of his world had been inexorably shaken; today's events would do little to provide any resolution.

Trying to muffle his sobbing, his tears flowed freely, without restraint. Carol swiveled her body slightly, embraced Ethan, holding him tightly, whispered into his ear, "We'll all miss him. But, it's okay. It's all okay."

Ethan nodded, feeling a knot in his throat, obstructing the flow of words. Releasing Carol's hand, took a newly pressed white handkerchief from his coat pocket, wiped his eyes exhaling softly, "I know."

Carol stood, doing her best to comfort Ethan as Lee and George slipped past them, walking away, heading up the knoll. Glancing back at William's headstone, Lee turned to George, "There is time. There always is time."

George nodded. He heard Carol encouraging Ethan, "Come now. Let's go."

Slowly lifting his head, Ethan looked up towards the heavens, turned, lightly placed a kiss on Carol's cheek, "Okay." Together, they both walked over to join Lee and George on the rise of the knoll.

Ethan gathered himself, extended his hand to both Lee and George. "I," stifling sniffles, "I am so grateful."

"Rather," Lee said, "it is we who are grateful. You and your brother have given much."

George wiped a tear from the side of his eye, "It was rough, but now…"

Ethan nodded, "I know. The comfort you've given me, it's a help, a big help."

"Thank you," Lee nodded, "you're too kind; and your charitable gift? It's extremely appreciated, and much too generous."

Ethan shook his head, "No. What use have I for that much money? Let it be your endowment. Your research? That's exactly what she'd support. Mother would have wanted it that way."

Lee bowed slightly, palms together, "With deepest gratitude."

Ethan locked eye contact with Carol, smiled, "Besides. I want to do right by my mother before she decides to beat the tar out of me."

All four laughed at Ethan's welcome, and unexpected, levity.

Turning, they began walking towards the entrance of the cemetery in silence, absorbing the eminence of the sacred setting, each lost in their own inner dialogue around the meaning of the day.

Carol's thoughts triggered a sensitivity to her own loss, turning to Lee, she stopped, "Doctor, do you think, in your view, will I see my mother again? I miss her so. I had so little time with her, and dad."

Lee stopped, turned, with an uncharacteristic act of affection, touching Carol's cheek, "Never can you lose that which has touched your heart. Those we've loved become part of us forever."

He leaned down, picked up a delicate buttercup from the grass, handed it to her, "Life, Carol, as you've experienced, is eternal. The love we feel in our hearts is immortal. Death merely completes one physical lifetime. The ties that bind never end. See your mother's love in the sunshine that warms you. See your father's spirit in the smallest of everyday joys. Horizons, Carol, are defined only by our limited point of view. What looks like an ending is actually a beginning. On one side of the veil, what is seen as a loss, is on the other side, a coming home, a celebration. Which is more real?"

The walkway from the knoll leading to the cemetery's entrance gates was bursting with a multitude of spring flowers, rhythmically dancing to the songs they heard in the wind.

Carol and Lee caught up with George and Ethan, who was taking a last moment to drink in a memory of his brother, "Funny how it's taken us all these decades to realize how life works. It's comforting, knowing death is but a small bridge, that there's nothing to fear."

Lee cupped Ethan's elbow with his hand, "It is, and every bridge goes both ways."

"Now you're getting ahead of me," Ethan chuckled, "I'm just getting used to the overall idea, okay? Gimme some space, here."

They all laughed, a further bond together.

Near the end of the path, they passed a group of people, standing before a new gravesite as the service was concluding, including a young mother cradling her newborn baby who was wrapped in a pale yellow blanket sleeping quietly in her arms.

They all stopped in respect while the final words were being spoken.

The pastor stating, "Ashes to ashes. Dust to dust. Oh Lord, we ask for your peace. Praise the Almighty."

Ethan looked directly at the young mother and infant stirring in her arms saying, "A new life. Just beginning."

Lee acknowledged Ethan's observation as he placed his hand on his friend's shoulder and said, "You see the miracle. You have learned."

Carol started to tear lightly and said, "So precious."

"The beginning. And the return," offered Lee.

The infant squirmed, causing her mother to readjust her position higher onto her shoulder. The baby's eyes locked onto Carol's gaze. A timeless enigmatic expression seemed to radiate from her little face, as if reaching out to connect with Carol.

In a soundless whisper, Carol gasped, feeling an immediate inkling, like a remembered echo, she smiled back at the child.

Her mind teeming with memories, she looked away.

As they began walking, Carol squinted at Lee, "Do you think, someday, I will be able to see the return of my Grandmother, as well?"

He smiled warmly, "Maybe you just did."

She looked skyward, her eyes glimpsing a branch of budding maple leaves, waving, as if at her.

EPILOGUE

All you need is love.
– John Lennon

Facing the couple standing before him, Doctor Phonyong Lee beamed with pride, "The beauty of love is that it exists everywhere, in everything, for all eternity."

The three of them stood together amid the dunes of the cape at the all but deserted beach of Herring Cove. Only the seagulls remained as sentinel witnesses.

The day's last ribbon of light, now stretching from the distant golden orb, lay out a carpet of sparkling diamonds that lapped nearer to their bare feet. They marveled at the special glow that arrives only in late September, like no other time of the year, the sun cleaving to the last edges of the fading warmth of summer, finally reaching this special day, joined by a crisp salty breeze skimming off the grey Atlantic waters.

This was the first September in her lifetime that she was not back at school. That bridge had been burned, torched by a flame only now could she admire in its far-reaching grandeur. This is not how she planned it, but here she was with the two most precious people in her world. She loved them both, but for different reasons. One had opened her soul. The other had melted her heart.

He who had melted her heart stood beside her now, dressed in rolled up khakis and a navy polo shirt, more suited to clam digging than to taking a lifelong vow. He held her trembling hand in his, strong and sure of the promise they were making to each other.

Equally underdressed for the occasion, she stood in a short white linen dress, a crown of white gardenias encircling her head marking this—most special occasion led by the only man who could perform this, her next rite-of-passage.

"Without love," Lee spoke, "life is no life at all. Deeper than the ocean, enduring for all time, calm, pure, flowing through you as it becomes all of you. Love is what fills you, more than anything in the universe. From love we come, from love we grow and it is back to love, that we shall return. To all our ancestors, to the Great Spirit, the Divine Presence in all, sanctify this union of hearts and souls. Before the One, with joy and blessings, as the unity of your two spirits, to join as one."

The wind carried his words out over the breaking waves.

Lee nodded to George, who turned to face Carol. Only he could offer this sacred promise.

"I love you, Carol Ann Klein, with all my heart. I vow to be an honest and faithful husband to you all the days of my life. Come with me on this wondrous journey, my darling, the best is yet to come."

Smiling from the sheer joy of looking into her eyes, he slipped the simple gold band onto her left hand, "With this ring as a symbol of my love, end without end, let our two hearts bond together, as one."

She beamed, "George Mansbridge, the Third, yes. I will come with you on this, our lifelong journey. I marry you today for who you have been, who you are today and most of all, who we are to become together." She slid the matching gold band onto George's ring finger.

Lee bowed to the couple in approval, adding, "In the beginning there was only love and love divided itself into two, let your first kiss be the reunification of this one love as a living bond. Two people, one shared life. With the power vested in me by the Commonwealth of Massachusetts, and the Universe, I now pronounce you, Carol Klein and George Mansbridge the Third, husband and wife."

George swooped Carol up into his arms with a deep adoring kiss, bonding their love.

Taking handfuls of rose petals, red and white, from his jacket pockets, Lee showered the newlyweds with the fragrant petals of the heavens, anointing them with blessings of love, eternity and protection. "Congratulations, may your lives together be blessed and long."

He popped the cork from the bottle of Dom Perignon filling three fluted glasses. He raised his glass, giving the newly married their first toast, "To your spirit, power and passion, may they burn bight and illuminate all hearts that cross your path."

A wicker picnic basket was laid out on a beach blanket as the wedding banquet. Lee opening it's top, pulling out a small, white frosted wedding cake. He handed a wide blade knife to Carol, who, with George's hands entwined, cut slices for the three of them.

Lee beamed at them, "Well done you two, it was always meant to be. What's next?"

George and Carol looked at each other, knowing they could never go back to their old lives, that their next steps, while a blank canvas, would be inexorably intertwined.

"Some traveling," Carol smiled, "perhaps Europe, South America. Before settling down."

Looking out at the western sky, where sun and sea and sky converged, George added, "After that, we'll just follow the sun," nodding towards the sliver of fire dipping slowly into the horizon.

"West." Lee affirmed, feeling the cool offshore spray shift direction as the hairs on the back of his neck stood at attention.

"California," Carol echoed. "George has a Harvard buddy in Laguna Beach; might as well check it out," she paused, "really, there's nothing left for us here, in Boston."

Lee acknowledged their unspoken dilemma. "Yes, your tenure here is complete. You've fulfilled what was to be accomplished."

Wiping white cake crumbs from his lower lip, he added, "You're ready to hear another melody. This time, you'll write your own song."

Carol smiled at the reference.

Over the roar of the cresting waves, she couldn't have heard what was to come.

ABOUT THE AUTHORS AND THEIR JOURNEY WITH PRELUDE

Cheryl Malakoff, Ph.D.

The day I completed my Ph.D. in psychology was the most conflicted day of my life. While my mind had been crammed with theories, my heart cried out for wisdom. I wanted to be a healer, not a repository of ideas about the human psyche.

My education was like reading about 'love'—the physiology, chemistry, biology, and brain waves were all very interesting, but paled by comparison to the actual experience of 'falling in love'. Until you can embody the true meaning of love, as personal knowledge, you have no way to convey that understanding to others. This formidable challenge was my professional dilemma.

I had studied the models and methods of the great psychologists like Carl Jung and Eric Erickson, but this did not make me one of them. These great healers embodied attributes and abilities that enabled them to convey deeper truths. Healers can only convey what they embody. I knew this to be an immutable truth.

My heart relentlessly gnawed at my soul and thrusted me forward.

In abject despair, I cried out to the Universe, not as a beggar, but rather as the rightful child demanding my lawful inheritance of wisdom. My quest for the secrets of the human condition would not be quenched by anything less than the ultimate truth.

Shortly after this heartfelt demand, a life altering event occurred. I awoke on a leisurely Saturday morning and in a flash, a shift in conscious perception occurred, as if my inner vision had fully opened. I cannot say whether what occurred next was a brief moment or an extended period of time. All accounting was eclipsed by the direct experience. I 'saw' the entire story of *Prelude*, frame by frame, page by page. The story was told to me in vivid, exquisite detail. It was an indescribable experience to see the characters—George, Carol, Iris, Doctor Lee—and hear their stories, revealing all the details of their compelling journey in its entirety. The story was vividly alive. I was mesmerized and awestruck. When the story was complete, I heard an inner voice say, '*not now*'.

Not now! My unbridled enthusiasm wanted to shout this story from the rooftops. However, I felt so humble and privileged to be witness to this account that I obediently honored the source that had shared this story with me. The question I asked year in and year out for decades was, "why would you give me this narrative and have me just be its guardian?"

Year after year I wondered why I had been chosen to be the keeper of this saga and why it was to be sequestered for a quarter of a century.

It was only in the 20-20 vision of hindsight that I came to understand the twenty-five year gap. This story was both the answer to my quest and a gift beyond measure for my personal transformation.

I was in search of the truth to understand the root cause of human suffering and the source of happiness. Initially, as a young and inexperienced doctor, I was like a ship adrift on an uncharted sea. Why were so many people suffering and challenged in every aspect of life? I knew that until I could comprehend the core organizing principles of life, I would be unable to answer this question. Without the correct answers, I'd be unable to be of any guidance to help my clients and students. I had seen so many short-term cures that didn't last. My gold standard was endurance—the healings had to stand the test of time.

Meanwhile, throughout all the intervening years *Prelude* reverberated through my heart and soul. It was given to me for a specific reason. It was my teacher. I had to learn the lessons that were *Prelude's* underpinnings—disseminating the higher truths of life through a story that shatters the myth of death.

The old cliché of, 'be careful what you ask for,' was never truer than in my sincere, though naiveté request. My personal development unfolded through the fires of purification and spiritual testing. It was as if the Universe replied, "Okay, you want to be a healer, here's the curriculum. Let's see if you have what it takes to master the lessons."

Consequently, as a psychologist in private practice and as teacher, I've specialized in the science of transformation and the art of healing—dedicated to the restoration of soul, mind, body health by activating our inherent core–level abilities.

I've also had the privilege to be a co-founder of KnoU Profiles—a powerful tool for self-discovery with the goal to empower individuals through self-knowledge. It is only through greater self-awareness that we gain the ability to more fully manifest our true potential and embrace our real purpose in life. To learn more, please visit

www.KnoUProfiles.com

If you would like to see a free video from the author, leave an e-mail address for future announcements, learn more about the author's Soul Mind Body Healing Services or to contact the author please visit:

www.ReadPrelude.com

OTHER BOOKS BY THE AUTHOR:

Opening The Mind And Igniting The Heart.

10 Winning Strategies for Loving, Successful Relationships.

Prelude—The Screenplay, co-authored with Robert Clampett.

Robert Clampett

My journey with Doctor Malakoff, Cheryl that is, began with a phone call from a dear friend and colleague asking if I might be available to assist a locally based psychologist in writing a book. Having recently been relieved of duties as Editor of a national magazine and just wrapping up a collaborated screenplay with a Hollywood writer, I welcomed the opportunity. Little did I know what lay in store.

After a pleasant interview session with Cheryl and her husband in her elegant Woodinville, Washington home, I felt I'd done pretty good job of selling my skills, having presented copies of two of my previous books and about a dozen magazine articles; only to learn later that the primary reason for my being selected was based more on my numerology chart than my credentials.

The first step for my research required attending Cheryl's two-weekend-long seminars to experience first-hand the mechanics of the self-improvement course she taught, titled "The Transformation Lessons," a somatic and spiritual-based regimen designed to provide embodiment of body-mind-soul balance. This seemed a bit of a stretch to me, having been a trained skeptic; as are most journalists.

One month later, I found myself employing the Lesson's techniques on a regular basis with positive results. She and I would meet weekly for two-hour interview sessions, each conducted and tape-recorded for accuracy. During each visit, she would graciously provide snacks, ranging from sushi to chocolate-covered Biscotti. What's not to like?

Over the months that followed, the task of tracing her life's journey leading to the Transformation Lessons proved more difficult than either of us realized at the start. Problems of intellectual property rights were raised, stalling the project as we were nearing completion. Long story short, we mutually ended the endeavor.

Several months after quitting the Lessons project, Cheryl called, inviting my wife and me to dinner at an upscale Kirkland restaurant. At the meal's end, she asked if I would be interested in working with her again, this time a collaborative screenplay based on a story she claimed she was "given" many years earlier. Over the next hour, she laid out the elements of what was to become "Prelude"—a story I found to powerful to refuse.

The screenplay took years to complete. When finished, we shopped it around, gaining the interest of a reader at William Morris Agency in Los Angeles. While he liked the story, he advised us that it would be unlikely to gain financing required for a film, suggesting we consider recasting it as a book.

After several months of teeth-gnashing, we agreed that the story must be told, and if it required our tearing it apart and re-writing it as a full-fledged novel, so be it. The effort was immense, requiring years to complete. However, by turning it into a novel, we were free to add new elements, which have greatly enhanced the story. From Cheryl's perspective, the Universe had a reason for the delays we had encountered; waiting for the right time for the tale to be told.

Over these years working with Cheryl, I have evolved on a personal level to totally embrace the concept of one's soul journey from one life to the next. I now see the wisdom in the tenets of reincarnation that mirror science's First Law of Thermodynamics, which states that energy can neither be created nor destroyed, only transformed. While the body breaks down, the energy of the soul must live on; a belief I found most comforting when my wife Julie Lynn Valentine left her body at the young age of 54. As I see it today, she did not just die, she graduated; with honors, I may add.

So, as you can see dear readers, I have gained immeasurably from my journey in producing the book you now hold in your hand, thanks to the patience, the persistence and the vision of my co-author Cheryl Malakoff, Ph.D. Hope you enjoyed the read and received the comfort it has give me.

OTHER BOOKS BY THE AUTHOR

Prelude—the Screenplay

Other Women—the Screenplay

The Motorcycle Handbook (Fawcett Gold Metal)

The Moped Book (Simon & Schuster Pocket Books)

Everyone Plays: The Story of AYSO

Multiple Short stories

Articles (Saturday Evening Post, Essence, Playgirl, Sports Digest, Tennis Illustrated, Popular Mechanics, Pro Football West, and Multiple In-Flight magazines)

Editor: Costco Connection; Vacationer; Pasadena Business

ACKNOWLEDGEMENTS

Many times a day I realize how much my own outer and inner life is built upon the labors of my fellow men, both living and dead, and how earnestly I must exert myself in order to give in return as much as I have received.
–Albert Einstein

Cheryl Malakoff

First and foremost, with deepest gratitude to 'my friends in high places', who entrusted me with this task long before I was competent to complete the assignment. Countless bow downs for the privilege and honor to steward this project.

To my beloved Guru, the sentinel of my soul's journey, Paramahansa Yogananda, who's love found me again.

The most precious endowment of this lifetime has been the extraordinary enlightened masters that have quickened my evolution. To my beloved Dr. and Master Zhi Gang Sha and Dr. and Master Hai. The only way I can ever repay even just a fraction of your generosity and love is to serve, serve, and serve more, all the days of my life.

To all the other exceptional healers, teachers and friends, too numerous to list, who have so significantly contributed to my growth and development. And, especially to Robert Raleigh and The Transformation Lessons, thank you for everything you taught me.

To my dearly loved mother Pearl, who just a few months before her graduation into the soul world read *Prelude*, twice. Her enthusiasm and passion for the story will forever be amongst my greatest acknowledgements. My father Stanley's boundless encouragement and support are precious treasures. To my cherished brother Lance and adored sister Beth, both fellow spiritual warriors who have 'gone the distance' and 'done the work.' And to the radiant soul's of David, Andrew, Isabel and Elizah, who light up countless hearts.

In Divine friendship to Richie Goldman, thank you for the privilege of going with you on your soul's journey. To Jay Goldinger, who's embodiment of unconditional compassion and selfless service has illuminated 'the path' to countless souls. And who stewarded Prelude, the screenplay to the William Morris Agency, deepest gratitude.

To all my students, I am eternally grateful for teaching me about the many faces of love.

To Larry, my beloved husband, who's disciplined journey to Self Realization and sincere desire to contribute to serve humanity is a daily inspiration. Thank you for your enduring love and support; they were the essential spirit that unified this project.

To Bob Clampett—words can never adequately express my heartfelt appreciation and gratitude for your great instinct and skill in transforming this dream into *Prelude*.

And to our publisher Reagan Rothe and the team at Black Rose Writing, thank you, thank you, thank you. And especially to Dave King, who's stellar artistic creativity and loving, patient support has contributed beyond measure.

Robert Clampett

As with anything significant in life, there are many people to thank; whether for assistance, actual support or pure encouragement. I begin with Chris Barnett, my longtime Cancer-pal and cohort who was solely responsible for connecting me with my co-author Dr. Cheryl Malakoff.

To my partner in life and beyond, Julie Lynn Valentine, who's patience and love will inspire me always as she begins her next journey.

Special thanks to longtime friends, mentors and editors Al Drew, Richard & Patti Pietschmann, David & Cheri Frei; Gaylen Brule, April Rhodes James, Tom Shess, John Johns, Michael Nortness, Cliff & Nancy Hollenbeck, Fern & Ken Valentine, Helen Gurley Brown, Art Garcia, Barbara Creaturo, Julie Nixon Eisenhower, Jane Offers, Harry Miller, Michele Monograin-Uplinger and, of course, my children JoEllen O'Reilly, Robin Ludlam and Scott Clampett—who always have been there for me. A shout-out to writers Dennis O'Reilly and Will Ludlam, as well as my ultra-talented grandchildren: Ethan, Tatum & Eliza Ludlam and Maddie & Declan O'Reilly.

And I cannot share enough of my gratitude for the friendship, patience, perseverance and vision of my co-author Dr. Cheryl Malakoff; along with the support she and I received from her husband, Larry. Thanks a bunch, you two.

FURTHER READING AND ADDITIONAL RESOURCES

The ideas touched upon in *Prelude* are diverse and thought-provoking. Here are some resource suggestions that may be helpful in providing additional information on this important subject.

FURTHER READING

Eadie, Betty. *Embraced By The Light*. Gold Leaf Press, Carson City, N.V., 1992.
—The incredible account of one woman's near-death experience.

Esquivel, Laura. *Laws of Love*. Crown Publishers, New York, 1996.
—A novel that traces humanity's reincarnation journey.

Haich, Elizabeth. *Initiation*. Seed Center, Redway, California, 1974.
—A woman's journey of spiritual growth and recollections of past lives.

Dr. and Master Zhi Gang Sha. *The Power Of Soul.* Heaven's Library Publication, 2009.
—The way to heal, rejuvenate, transform and enlighten all life.

Dr. and Master Zhi Gang Sha. *Divine Transformation.* Heaven's Library Publication, 2010.
—The Divine way to self-clear karma, to transform your health, relationships, finances and more.

Marshall, George N. *Challenge of a Liberal Faith.* Pyramid Books. 1970.
—The definitive, dynamic story of Unitarian Universalism.

Paramahansa Yogananda. *Autobiography of a Yogi.* Self Realization Fellowship. Los Angeles, California. 1946.
—An absorbing story of the search for the truth that unifies the great religions of East and West. Selected as one of the 100 best spiritual books of the century.

Paramahansa Yogananda. *Man's Eternal Quest.* Self Realization Fellowship. Los Angeles, California. 1976.
—An anthology of lectures and teachings illuminating our relationship with the Infinite.

Tolle, Eckhart. *A New Earth.* Penguin Group. New York. 2005.
—A transformational book that guides the awakening to the life you are meant to live.

Weiss, Brian L., M.D. *Many Lives, Many Masters.* New York: Simon & Schuster, 1988.
—A true story of a psychiatrist and patient exploring past life therapy.

ADDITIONAL RESOURCES

KnoU Profiles – www.KnoUProfiles.com. This fascinating and informative site contains a video by the author that reveals the secrets for attaining more love, joy and success in your life, as well as personality style profiles that are extremely insightful and life-inspiring. These reports can help you to better understand your strengths, weaknesses, deep inner needs and emotions in this life time, which are directly influenced by your past life experiences.

Self Realization Fellowship – www.yogananda-srf.org. Founded in 1925 by Paramahansa Yogananda, SRF is devoted to healing of the body, mind and soul.

Soul Healing Institute – www.drsha.com. Offers holistic, spiritual and self-help training, with a mission to transform consciousness in order to create love, peace and harmony for humanity and Mother Earth.

Prelude – www.ReadPrelude.com. Content includes blog by the authors, additional resources, author contact information and e-mail sign-up for future communications.

Purchase other Black Rose Writing titles at <u>www.blackrosewriting.com/books</u>
and use promo code PRINT to receive a 20% discount.

CPSIA information can be obtained
at www.ICGtesting.com
Printed in the USA
FSOW03n1403010415
6090FS

9 781612 964973